# EMBER
# QUEEN

# EMBER QUEEN

LAURA SEBASTIAN

DELACORTE PRESS

Text copyright © 2020 by Laura Sebastian
Jacket art copyright © 2020 by Billelis
Map illustrations copyright © 2018, 2019, 2020 by Isaac Stewart

All rights reserved. Published in the United States by Delacorte Press, an imprint of Random House Children's Books, a division of Penguin Random House LLC, New York.

Delacorte Press is a registered trademark and the colophon is a trademark of Penguin Random House LLC.

Visit us on the Web! GetUnderlined.com

Educators and librarians, for a variety of teaching tools, visit us at RHTeachersLibrarians.com

*Library of Congress Cataloging-in-Publication Data*
Names: Sebastian, Laura, author.
Title: Ember queen / Laura Sebastian.
Description: First edition. | New York : Delacorte Press, [2020] | Series: [Ash Princess ; 3] | Audience: Ages 12 & Up. | Audience: Grades 7–9. | Summary: "With Astrea under the rule of a new leader, Theo returns to fight for her land and her people. But her enemies are more powerful than ever before and, if she is to win once and for all, she must risk everything and everyone if she is to reclaim her throne."—Provided by publisher.
Identifiers: LCCN 2019040009 | ISBN 978-1-5247-6714-3 (hardcover) | ISBN 978-1-5247-6715-0 (library binding) | ISBN 978-1-5247-6716-7 (ebook) | ISBN 978-0-593-17545-3 (int. tr. pbk.)
Subjects: CYAC: Kings, queens, rulers, etc.—Fiction. | Courts and courtiers—Fiction. | Adventure and adventurers—Fiction. | Fantasy.
Classification: LCC PZ7.1.S33693 Emb 2020 | DDC [Fic]—dc23

The text of this book is set in 11.6-point Sabon.
Interior design by Stephanie Moss.

Printed in the United States of America
10 9 8 7 6 5 4 3 2 1
First Edition

FOR ALL THE GIRLS
*who never felt strong enough*
*to be the heroine of their story.*
*You are.*

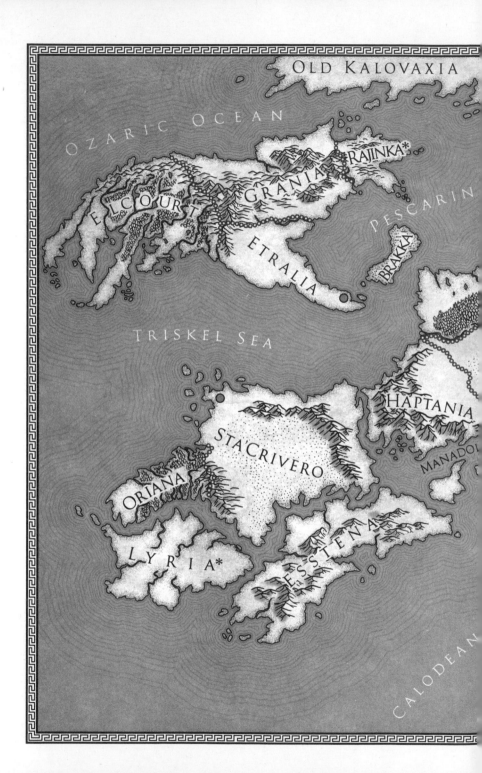

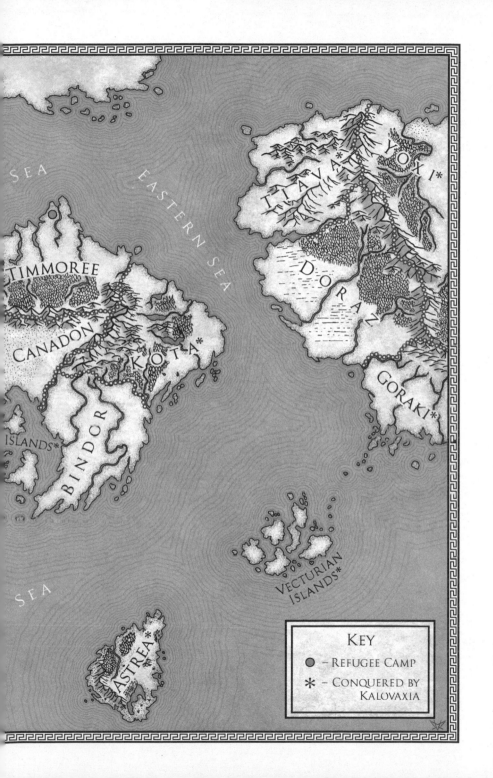

SEA

EASTERN SEA

ILAVA* YOXI*

DORAN

TIMMOREE

CANADON

KOTA*

GORAKI*

ISLANDS*

BINDOR

VECTURIAN
ISLANDS*

SEA

ASTREA*

KEY

● – REFUGEE CAMP

✳ – CONQUERED BY
KALOVAXIA

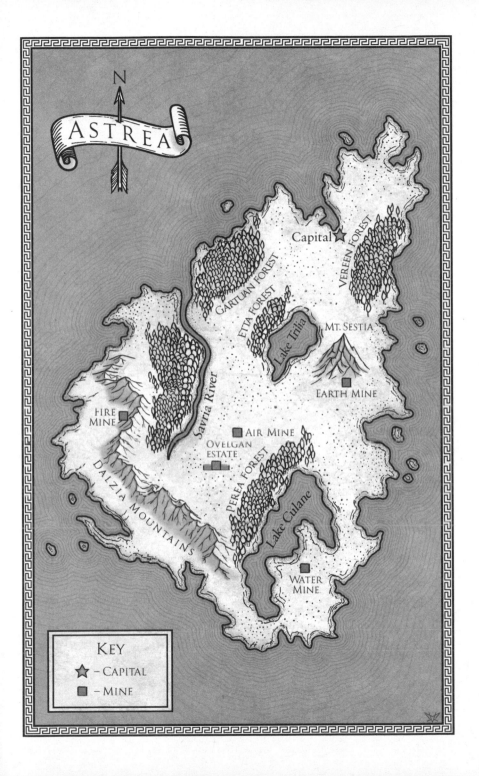

# PROLOGUE

I SPENT MUCH OF MY FIRST six years afraid of my mother's
throne the way most children are afraid of monsters lurking
under their beds. It was a terrifying thing to behold: tall and
shadowy black, sharp-edged, carved to look like dark flames.
I remember the bone-deep certainty that touching it would
burn.

Every day, I would see my mother sit upon that throne,
and I believed that it held her there, its obsidian fingers dig
ging into her skin. I watched it transform her into someone
else, someone I didn't recognize. Gone was the woman at
the center of my world, the soft-spoken mother who would
kiss my forehead and hold me on her lap, who would sing me
to sleep every night. In the throne, a stranger took over her
body—her voice boomed, her back was ramrod straight. She
spoke carefully and authoritatively without a hint of a smile
in her voice. When the throne finally released her, she was
exhausted.

Now that I'm older, I know that the throne wasn't a monster in the way I believed. I know that it didn't have a physical
hold on my mother. I know that when she sat on that throne,

she was still herself. But I also understand that in some way, I was right. She was never quite the same person on that throne that she was off it.

Usually, my mother belonged only to me; when she sat on that throne, she belonged to everyone.

# RECKONING

———•———

THE SUN IS BLINDING WHEN I step out of the mouth of the cave on weak legs. I lift a heavy, aching arm to shield my eyes, but the effort of even that small gesture makes the world around me spin. My knees buckle and the ground comes up to meet me, hard and sharp with rocks. It hurts, but oh, it feels so good to lie down, to have fresh air in my lungs, to have *light,* even if it is too much all at once.

My throat is so dry, it hurts to even breathe. There is caked blood on my fingers, on my arms, in my hair. Distantly I realize that it's mine, but I can't say where it came from. My memories are a desert—I remember stepping into the cave, remember hearing my friends' voices begging me to come back. And then . . . nothing.

"Theo," a voice calls, familiar but so far away. A thousand footsteps beat against the ground, each one making my head throb. I flinch away from the sound, curling tighter into myself.

Hands touch my skin—my wrists, the pulse point behind my ear. They are so cold, they raise goose bumps on my skin.

"Is she . . . ," a voice says. Blaise. I try to say his name, but nothing comes out.

"She's alive, but her pulse is faint and her skin is hot," another voice says. Heron. "We have to get her inside."

Arms scoop me up and carry me—Heron's, I think. Again, I try to speak, but I can't make so much as a sound.

"Art, your cloak," Heron says, his chest rumbling against my cheek with each word. "Cover her head with it. Her eyes are oversensitive."

"Yes, I remember," Art says. Fabric rustles and her cloak falls over my eyes, wrapping my world in darkness once more.

I let myself fall into it now. My friends have me, and so I am safe.


The next time I open my eyes, I'm on a cot inside a tent, the bright sun filtered through thick white cotton so that it is bearable. The pounding in my head is still there, but it's dull and faraway now. My throat is no longer dry and raw, and if I focus, I have a hazy memory of Artemisia pouring water into my open mouth. The pillow beneath my head is still damp from where she missed.

Now, though, I'm alone.

I force myself to sit up even though it intensifies the pain echoing through my every nerve. The Kalovaxians will return sooner or later, and who knows how long Cress will keep Søren alive? There is so much to be done and not nearly enough time to do it.

Placing my bare feet on the dirt floor, I push myself to stand. As I do, the tent flap pulls open and Heron steps inside, ducking his tall frame in order to fit through the small opening. When he sees me awake and standing, he falters, blinking a few times to ensure he isn't imagining me.

"Theo," he says slowly, testing out the sound of my name.

"How long has it been?" I ask him quietly. "Since I entered the mine?"

Heron surveys me for a moment. "Two weeks," he says.

The words knock me backward, and I sit down on the cot again. "Two weeks," I echo. "It felt like hours, maybe days."

Heron doesn't look surprised by that. Why would he? He's gone through the same thing.

"Do you remember sleeping?" he asks me. "Eating? Drinking? You must have, at some point, or you would be in much worse shape."

I shake my head, trying to grasp what I do remember, but very little of it solidifies enough for me to hold on to. Scraps of details, ghosts that could not have been real, fire flooding my veins. But nothing more than that.

"You should have left me," I tell him. "Two weeks . . . Cress's army could be back any day now, and Søren   "

"Is alive, according to reports," Heron interrupts. "And the Kalovaxians have received no orders to return here."

I stare at him. "How can you possibly know that?" I ask.

He lifts a shoulder in a lopsided shrug. "Spies," he says, as if the answer should be obvious.

"We don't have spies," I say slowly.

"We *didn't* have spies. But we got word that the new Theyn was at his country home, two days' ride from here. We were able to turn several of his slaves before they returned to the capital. We just received our first missive. The Theyn hasn't ordered troops back yet. Besides, the vast majority of the army has left. It's only Blaise, Artemisia, Erik, Dragonsbane, and me, plus a group of those still recovering from the battle. But even they'll be going to safety with Dragonsbane in a day or two."

I barely hear him, still trying to wrap my mind around the idea of spies. All I can think of is Elpis, of what happened the last time I made a spy of someone.

"I didn't approve the use of spies," I tell him.

"You'd walked into the mine the day before the plan was hatched," Heron says, his voice level. "You weren't around to approve much of anything, and there was no time to wait for you to come back. If you came back at all."

A retort dies in my throat, and I swallow it. "If they die—"

"It will have been a necessary risk," Heron says. "They knew as much when they volunteered. Besides, the Kaiserin is not as paranoid as the Kaiser, from what we've heard. She thinks you're dead, she thinks we aren't a threat, she has Søren. She thinks she's won, and so she's getting sloppy."

*The Kaiserin.* Will there ever come a day when I hear that title and think first of Cress and not Kaiserin Anke?

"You said the army had left," I say. "Where to?"

Heron lets out a long exhale. "You missed quite a lot of squabbling while you were gone—I almost envy you. The Vecturian chief sent his daughter Maile to assist us, along with his troops. With Søren gone, she and Erik have the most battle experience, but they don't agree on anything. Erik wants to march straight to the capital to take the city and rescue Søren."

"That's foolish," I say, shaking my head. "It's exactly what they'll expect, and even if it weren't, we don't have the numbers for that kind of siege."

"That's exactly what Maile said," Heron says, shaking his head. "She said we should continue to the Earth Mine."

"But we can't do that without marching past the most populous cities, without even the cover of forests or mountains," I say. "It'll be impossible to avoid detection, and then Cress will have an army waiting to greet us at the Earth Mine."

"Which is exactly what Erik said," Heron says. "See, you're all caught up."

"So who won?" I ask.

"No one," Heron says. "It was decided that we should send the troops to the cities along the Savria River. None of them is heavily populated, but we'll be able to contain the Kalovaxians, free their slaves, add to our numbers, and collect weapons and food as well. And most importantly, our troops aren't just waiting here like sitting ducks."

"Like we are, you mean," I say, rubbing my temples. The headache blossoming has nothing to do with the mine this time. "And now I'm here to break the tie, I suppose."

"Later," he says. "Once you can actually walk on your own."

"I'm fine," I tell him, more forcefully than necessary.

Heron watches me warily. He opens his mouth, but closes it again quickly, shaking his head.

"If there's something you want to ask me about the mines, I don't remember anything," I tell him. "The last thing I remember is going in—after that, it's a blur."

"You will remember, in time," he says. "For better or worse. But I know I never want to speak of my experience. I assumed you would feel the same way."

I swallow, pushing the thought aside. A problem for another day—and I have too many problems before me as it is. "But something is on your mind," I say to Heron. "What is it?"

He weighs the question in his mind for an instant. "Did it work?" he asks.

For a second, I don't know what he means, but I suddenly remember—the reason I went into the mines in the first place, the weak power I had over fire before, the side effect from Cress's poison. I went into the mine to claim my power, in hopes that I will have enough to stand against Cress when the time comes.

Did it work? There is only one way to find out.

I hold my left palm up and summon fire. Even before I uncurl my fingers, I feel heat thrumming beneath them, stronger than I've ever felt it before. It comes easily when I summon it, like it's a part of me, always lurking just below the surface. It burns brighter, feels hotter, but it's more than that. To show him, I toss it into the air, hold it there, suspended but still alive, still bright. Heron's eyes grow wide, but he says nothing as I lift my hand and flex it. The ball of fire mimics me, becoming a hand of its own. When I move my fingers, it matches each movement. I make a fist, and it does that as well.

"Theo," he says, his voice a hoarse whisper. "I saw the extent of Ampelio's power when he trained me. He couldn't do that."

I swallow and take hold of the flame again, smothering it in my grip and turning it to ash in my hand.

"If you don't mind, Heron," I say, my gaze fixed on the

dark pigment that smears over my skin just as the ash crown had, "is Mina still here? She's—"

"The healer," he supplies, nodding. "Yes, she's still here. She's been helping with the wounded. I'll find her."

When he's gone, I dust ash from my hands and let it settle into the dirt floor.

By the time Mina enters the tent, I've gotten used to standing again, though my body still doesn't feel entirely like mine. Every move—every breath—feels like a labor, and every muscle aches. Mina must notice, because she takes one look at me and gives a knowing smile.

"It's normal," she says. "When I came out of the mine, the priestesses said that the gods had broken me and remade me anew. It seemed to sum up how I felt."

I nod, easing myself back to sit on my cot once more. "How long does it last?" I ask her.

She shrugs. "My pain lasted a couple of days, but it varies." She pauses, looking me over. "What you did was incredibly foolish. Going into the mine when you already possessed a measure of power—when you were already a vessel half-full—you were asking for mine madness. You realize that, don't you?"

I look at the ground. It's been some time since I've been chastised like this, by someone concerned about my wellbeing. I rack my mind for the last person; it very well may have been my mother. I suppose Hoa did as well, in her wordless way.

"I understood the risks," I tell her.

"You're the Queen of Astrea," she continues, as if I haven't spoken. "What would we have done without you?"

"You would have persisted," I say, louder this time. "I am one person. We lost far more in the war, far more in the siege itself, including my mother. We have always persisted. I wouldn't have made a difference."

Mina fixes me with a level look. "It was still foolish," she insists. "But I suppose it was also brave."

I shrug again. "Whatever it might have been, it worked," I say.

I show her the same thing I showed Heron, how I can not just summon fire but turn it into an extension of my own self. Mina watches me all the while with her lips pursed, not saying a word until I've finished and am scattering the ash to the ground once more.

"And you slept," she says, more to herself than me.

"Quite heavily, as I understand it," I say dryly.

She steps toward me. "May I feel your forehead?" she asks.

I nod, and she presses the back of her hand to my brow. "You aren't warm," she says before reaching out to touch the single tendril of white in my auburn hair.

"It was there before," I tell her. "After the poison."

She nods. "I remember. Not like the Kaiserin's hair, is it? But I suppose you have Artemisia to thank for that—if she hadn't used her own gift on you so quickly to negate the poison, it would have affected you far more. If it hadn't killed you on the spot, the mine certainly would have."

"You didn't see Cress—the Kaiserin—yourself," I say,

changing the subject. "But you must have heard stories of her power by now."

Mina considers this. "I've heard stories," she says carefully. "Though I find stories are often exaggerated."

I remember Cress killing the Kaiser with just her scalding hands around his throat, the way she trailed ash over the desk with her fingertips. She radiated power in a way that I have never seen equaled. I'm not sure how anyone could exaggerate what I saw with my own eyes.

"It's as if . . . she doesn't even have to call on her gift. She killed the Kaiser in a few seconds with just her hands," I say.

"And you still don't feel strong enough to stand against her," Mina guesses.

"I don't think anyone is," I admit. "Did you ever hear of Guardians killing with that little effort?"

She shakes her head. "I didn't hear anything about Guardians killing at all," she says. "It wasn't their way. If a person's crimes ever warranted execution, it was carried out by more mundane means. Guardians never did the deed with the gifts given to them by the gods. It would have been its own kind of sacrilege, a perversion of something holy."

I think about Blaise going out into the battlefield, knowing he could have died but determined to kill as many Kalovaxians as possible before he did. Was that a perversion of his gift? Or are the standards different now, in times of war?

"The children I saw before, the ones you were testing," I say, remembering the boy and girl with the same unstable power as Blaise. "How are they?"

"Laius and Griselda," she supplies. "They are as well as

can be expected, I suppose. Frightened and traumatized by the horrific experiments the Kalovaxians did on them, but they're strong in more ways than one." She pauses for a second. "Your hypothetical friend has been helpful. They like him, standoffish though he might be. It truly is something, to discover you aren't as alone in the world as you thought."

When I told Mina about Blaise, I only ever referred to him hypothetically, though she saw through that quickly enough. Now, it seems, she knows exactly who he is. But she isn't afraid of him, at least, or of Laius and Griselda, either.

"Have you told anyone else about your findings?" I ask her.

She purses her lips. "I have no findings, Your Highness," she says, shrugging. "Only a hypothesis, and that is not enough cause to get everyone riled up. People fear what they don't understand, and in times like this, fear can lead to dangerous decisions."

If people knew how strong and how unstable Blaise and Laius and Griselda are, they might kill them. It's no more than I already knew, but hearing her imply it like that knocks the breath from my lungs.

"Everyone saw what Blaise did on the ship," I say. "They saw how he almost destroyed himself and everyone around him. They didn't hurt him after that."

"No," she agrees. "In fact, I'd imagine they'll be singing folk songs about that act for some centuries to come, but no one was hurt. He's a hero to them now. A hero who was so powerful, he couldn't control himself, but a hero all the same. Never forget—that can change in an instant."

# IMPASSE

———•———

MINA SUGGESTS A WALK MIGHT do me good, and though my body protests strongly against the idea, I take her advice. I have to lean most of my weight on Heron, and even still my muscles scream with each step, but I can't deny that the fresh air in my lungs and the sun on my skin are worth the pain. And as I walk, my muscles begin to loosen and the aching in my limbs becomes somewhat more bearable.

It's strange to see the mine camp so empty, a deserted city of empty barracks with only a handful still occupied by the ill and the injured. Heron points out which ones are acting as infirmaries when we pass by, but I don't need him to. It's clear in the sounds that seep out from their walls—the hacking coughs, the soft cries, the wails of pain. The sounds threaten to drown me in a sea of guilt.

*So many more are alive and well,* I tell myself. *So many more are free.*

Heron tries to distract me, pointing out other buildings that survived the battle. Food is rationed and served in the old mess hall, he says, and a group of men and women who stayed behind have volunteered to hunt and gather to keep our stores from depleting too quickly. When we leave to catch up with the troops, we'll take more food with us.

Even the old slave quarters have been put to use, though understandably no one is keen to sleep there—instead, they've been cleared of furniture and shackles and repurposed as weapons storage and places to train away from the overwhelming heat of the sun.

"Who is training?" I ask Heron when he points out one of the newly repurposed training rooms to me. "I thought the troops left."

"Not all of them," he replies carefully. "Most of the people we found who'd been blessed in the mines took to the training quickly, and there were a couple of elders who went along to help continue their training, but there were others who needed more assistance."

Blessed. There were over a dozen blessed Astreans the Kalovaxians had been keeping in this camp. Experimenting on, I remember, though the thought makes me shudder. I saw the evidence of it myself: sliced skin, cut-off fingers and toes—one man had even had his eye taken out.

"They trained so quickly?" I ask, surprised. When I went into the cave, none of them had been fit to walk across camp, let alone fight.

"I helped with the physical healing," Heron says, shrugging. "But the mental and emotional wounds are another matter. Many of them viewed  the training as a way of healing. They wanted to. Art, Blaise, and I saw to it, along with a few of the Astrean elders who were familiar with the training, even if they weren't Guardians themselves. They aren't fully trained, of course, but they made good progress during what little time we had. And they should be continuing, even as we speak."

Artemisia once told me what she feels when she kills, how it feels good to take something back. It seems she isn't alone in that.

"I'll have to start training soon, too," I say.

"Let's focus on getting you walking on your own first," Heron replies.

I'm jolted out of my thoughts by a pair of arms coming around my waist and lifting me off the ground, whirling me around. A scream rises in my throat, but before I can let it out, the owner of the arms speaks, and I recognize his voice.

"Welcome back to the land of the living," Erik says, setting me back down.

I turn to face him and throw my arms around his neck.

"Would you believe I missed you?" I ask him with a laugh.

"I wouldn't believe you didn't," he replies, hugging me tightly.

"Careful with her!" Heron chides. "She's a bit fragile at the moment."

Erik scoffs. "Queen Theodosia? I've seen boulders more fragile."

I smile but gently wriggle out of Erik's embrace. "I appreciate that, but he isn't wrong."

As soon as I say it, Erik steps back and looks me over from my head to toes. "You do look like you've been through a hell or two," he says.

"Maybe three," I admit.

"Theo!" a new voice cries out, and I turn to find Artemisia jogging toward me, gleaming dagger sheathed at her hip and cerulean hair streaming behind her.

Unlike Erik, she knows not to hug me. Instead she gives my shoulder an awkward, light pat. "How are you?" she asks cautiously.

"I'm alive, which is more than we had any right to expect," I tell her with a smile. "And it worked."

Her smile broadens. "I should hope so," she says. "Or it would make your new nickname quite unfortunate."

I frown, looking between her, Erik, and Heron. "My new nickname?" I repeat.

They exchange knowing smiles, but it's Artemisia who sweeps into a dramatic curtsy, followed by bows from Erik and Heron.

"All hail Theodosia," she says. "Queen of Flame and Fury."

The three of them rise with matching smiles, but it isn't a joke, no matter how light she tries to make it. Queen of Flame and Fury. It is a hard nickname. A strong one, yes, but brutal as well. For the first time, I understand that, succeed or fail, this will be my legacy. I think of all the paintings of my mother done in soft watercolors, her dressed in flowing chiffon gowns. I think of the poems written in her honor, odes to her beauty and kindness and gentle spirit. The Queen of Peace, they called her. A different sort of queen altogether.

Something sparks in my memory, fighting through the fog of the mines.

"*I died the Queen of Peace, and peace died with me,*" my mother told me. "*But you are the Queen of Flame and Fury, and you will set their world on fire.*"

I don't know what that was in the mine, whether it was my mother's ghost or a figment of my imagination or something else entirely, but I do know that I somehow heard this new name even before it was crafted, and that thought makes me uneasy.

We can't make a plan without Blaise, so I send the others to gather the leaders remaining in the camp, and I make my way to the training barracks where they told me Blaise spends nearly all of his time. Heron didn't want me to go alone, but I assured him I was feeling well enough to make it across camp without leaning on him, and he acquiesced.

Truthfully, I'm not sure I can. Though I'm feeling better, each step is a strain. But I would rather deal with the pain than have Heron or anyone else there when I see Blaise again.

*"Don't do this. Don't leave me,"* he said before I went into the mine, his last words to me not long after I'd made a similar plea to him. Neither of us listened.

Guilt swarms me as I remember how his voice broke, how lost he looked in that moment, as if I'd cut the last rope tethering him to this life. As if he weren't already so determined to leave it.

He left first, I remind myself. He walked into death's reach twice when I asked him—begged him—not to. He can't be angry with me for doing the same.

And now? Against all odds, we're both still here, and now we have to face the consequences of that.

I find the barrack Heron described set apart from the others with the remnants of a fence still buried in the ground.

I remember seeing it during the battle, a great black thing that glinted red in the sun. Søren explained that the fence had been made of iron mixed with Fire Gems, though that's been torn down now.

When I push the door open slightly, I see that the room is dark, lit only by a large candle set in the center, bright enough to illuminate Blaise, Laius, and Griselda. Those two are still mostly bones, but there's a new fullness in their faces, and their skin has lost some of its sallowness—though that may be largely due to the candlelight. Even that isn't enough to disguise the bruise-like shadows under their eyes.

The same shadows Blaise has, proof that they don't sleep.

They're stronger than they were the last time I saw them. That much is evident in the way Griselda leaps through the air, throwing a ball of fire as big as my head at the stone wall. It dies on contact, but it leaves a scorch mark in its wake. The walls are covered with them, more black than gray now.

She lands on the ground an instant later, doubled over and out of breath, but there is a ghost of a smile on her lips, thin and grim but unmistakably there.

"Well done," I say, startling the three of them. Griselda jerks upright, her eyes finding me. She can't be much more than fifteen, not much younger than I am. It occurs to me suddenly that if two weeks passed since I went into the mines, that makes me seventeen now.

"Your Majesty," Griselda says, bobbing into a clumsy curtsy, followed by a bow from Laius a beat later.

"No need for that," I tell them before forcing myself to look at Blaise.

Unlike them, he looks exactly the same as when I saw him

last—the same tired green eyes and hard, angry set to his jaw. But it's the way he's looking at me that really feels like a punch to my gut. He looks at me like I'm a ghost and he doesn't know whether to be frightened or relieved.

*"Are you afraid of me?"* he asked me once, and I was forced to admit that I was. He can't be afraid of me now—not in the same way—but perhaps he is unnerved. About what I might say, what I might do, how I might break him next.

He left me first, I remind myself, but the thought isn't the balm I need it to be.

Blaise clears his throat and looks away. "It's about lunchtime," he says, looking between Laius and Griselda. "Get some food and come back in an hour."

"Actually," I say. "Why don't you take the rest of the afternoon off? I need to borrow Blaise for the day."

Blaise shakes his head. "An hour," he insists.

Laius and Griselda look between the two of us with wide eyes. I may be their queen, but Blaise is their teacher. They hurry from the room as quickly as they can, before I can contradict his contradiction. The door slams shut behind them, and the sound bounces off the walls, echoing in the silence left in their wake. The silence stretches on long after the echo ends, but eventually I force myself to break it.

"We need to agree upon a strategy," I tell him. "We're meeting the other leaders to figure it out. That will take longer than an hour."

He shakes his head, not looking at me. "My time will be better spent here."

"I need you there," I tell him, frustration rising in my chest, hot and stifling.

"No," he says. "You don't."

For a moment, words fail me. This is not how I imagined our reunion. "I thought you would at least be glad I'm not dead," I tell him finally.

He looks at me like I hit him. "Of course I am, Theo," he says. "Every moment you were down there, I begged the gods to let you come back, and I will be thanking them for the rest of my life that you're standing here now."

"I won't apologize for going into that mine," I say. "I knew what I was doing and I knew the risk of it, but it was worth it for Astrea. You must have thought so, too, when you ran into that battle."

"For *you*," he says, the words as sharp as daggers. "I love Astrea—don't misunderstand me—but when I stood on the bow of that ship and pushed myself to the edge, when I ran into that battle knowing I might not come out again—I did those things for you."

The words are both weapons and caresses, but the anger in them adds fuel to my own fury. "If it were truly for me, you would have listened when I told you not to do it," I say.

He shakes his head. "You have a blind spot with me," he says, his voice colder than I've ever heard it. "Your judgment is flawed. Heron and Artemisia and even the *prinkiti* would have told me to do the same thing. I did what you would never be able to ask me to do, and I am not going to apologize for that, either. When the world turns on its head and I'm not sure of anything, I'm sure of you. No matter where we are or who we fight against, I am always fighting for you. And you are always fighting for Astrea, above all else."

I stumble back a step.

"You can't hold that against me," I say, my voice low. "What kind of queen would I be if I put you—put anyone, *anything*—above Astrea?"

He shakes his head, the anger sapped from him. "Of course I don't hold it against you, Theo," he says quietly. "I'm just telling you where I stand."

There's nothing I can say to that, nothing that will change his mind, nothing that will make either of us feel better. After a moment, he speaks again.

"You don't need me to discuss strategy. You'll have Art for that, and Dragonsbane, and the leaders of the other countries. You want me there as a comfort, but you don't need comfort anymore. You don't need me, but Laius and Griselda do."

The words feel like thorns digging beneath my skin, and I leave before I say something I will truly regret. As I step back into the sunlight and close the door behind me, though, I wonder if it was the words themselves that hurt so badly or the truth behind them.

# CLASH

———•———

THE LAST TIME I WAS in the old commandant's office was with Søren, Cress, and the Kaiser, and even though it has been cleaned since then, the echoes of what happened remain. The mahogany desk still bears a line of charred wood from when Cress dragged her finger over it. There is ash trapped in the grain of the wooden chair the Kaiser sat in; there is a burnt red stain on the rug from the poisoned wine I drank. There are some things no amount of cleaning can get rid of. *We should raze the building to the ground,* I think, *when we leave.*

I could have happily gone the rest of my life without setting foot in this room again, but the seclusion and the desk and the array of maps of Astrea and the rest of the world make it the best place to discuss strategy. Still, I have trouble tearing my gaze away from the stain on the rug.

*"It's a simple exchange, Thora. Your death, or your people's."*

All over again, I feel the poison burn its way down my throat, obliterating thoughts of everything else but the heat, the pain. Again, I see Cress standing over me, her gaze distant but curious as she watches me writhe in agony, the same way she used to look at a translation she was having trouble with.

She thinks I'm dead now. What will she do when she finds out I'm not? Maybe we are on something of an even field now, but one thing hasn't changed—she didn't hesitate to try to kill me herself, and I couldn't do the same to her when I had the chance. That alone is enough to frighten me.

"Theo," a voice says, jerking me out of my thoughts. I tear my gaze away from the wine stain to find Dragonsbane perched on the corner of the desk, legs crossed in a way that might look prim if she were anyone else. I know better than to expect any sort of grand reunion with her, but she does give me a small nod that I take to mean she's glad I'm alive.

Erik and Sandrin, the Astrean elder from the Sta'Criveran refugee camp, are there as well, along with a girl who is quickly introduced as Maile of Vecturia, Chief Kapil's youngest daughter and, from the look of her, the opposite of her solemn, peace-minded father. Though they share the same tan skin and long, black hair, Maile has an angrier set to her jaw and a permanent glare that makes her look as if she is constantly contemplating punching someone.

In the coming days, Sandrin and Dragonsbane will leave by sea to bring the Astreans who can't or don't wish to fight to safety. That seems to be all that can be agreed upon.

"We can't stay here much longer," I say when I'm all caught up. "The Kaiserin will send an army here any day now, if one isn't already on the way."

Maile laughs, looking at the others. "She spends two weeks wandering around in the dark, only to deliver us a warning so obvious that a child could have sussed it out," she says before looking at me again. "What exactly did you imagine we were doing while you were going mad in the mine?"

"I didn't go mad," I say sharply. "And from what I've heard, you did little in my absence besides squabble among yourselves."

"The bulk of our troops have gone off to retake the cities along the Savria River. But as soon as we agree on a plan to take the capital, they'll rejoin us," Erik says from his place leaning against the stone wall near the door. He doesn't seem to be paying much attention to any of us, instead focusing on cutting away the skin of an apple with a small knife the size of his thumb.

Maile scoffs. "The capital," she says, rolling her eyes. "You're still on about that foolish plan."

It is a foolish plan. I know that, and I'd imagine deep down, Erik does as well. But with his mother so recently taken from him and the life he knew completely upheaved, Søren is the only family he has left, the only familiar thing in a strange and frightening world. I can't hold his foolishness against him—I can only hope he'll see it for what it is.

"Taking the Earth Mine is a foolish plan, too. That was yours, wasn't it?" I say instead, tracing my finger along the route we would need to take to reach it, the one that passes several large cities and towns, any of whom would send word to Cress as soon as they spotted us. We might as well send her a letter ourselves, announcing our intentions.

Maile grunts but doesn't reply. I look up at Dragonsbane. "What are your thoughts, Aunt? I have a hard time believing you don't have plenty of opinions. Please share them."

Dragonsbane purses her lips. "Maile is right, in a sense," she says after a moment. "Every type of Guardian has their strengths, of course, but in terms of battle . . . if we could liberate the Earth Mine, any Guardians we add to our numbers will have the strength of twenty ungifted soldiers," she says before tilting her head to one side thoughtfully. "But you're right, too, Theo. The Kaiserin would undoubtedly be alerted and would meet us there with the brunt of her forces. We wouldn't stand a chance."

"Those are our opinions," I say. "What is yours?"

Dragonsbane traces her finger along the map, from the Fire Mine to Doraz. "Empress Giosetta owes me quite a significant favor," she says. "She has agreed to take in the Astrean refugees until the war has been won. But perhaps she can be persuaded to lend us some of her troops as well. Perhaps I could take those troops around this way." She traces from Doraz down to the east coast of Astrea, where the Earth Mine is. "It's still a day's journey inland, but the chances of our being spotted go down significantly. Especially if you are causing the Kaiserin problems elsewhere."

I nod. "And can you persuade Giosetta?" I ask, remembering the empress from Sta'Crivero. She was one of the better suitors I met there, but she's still a ruler with her own needs and interests. I doubt she will give us troops out of the goodness of her heart.

Dragonsbane considers this. "After the siege of the Fire Mine, you've become a less risky investment, and there are many who would be glad to see the Kalovaxians brought to ruin—Giosetta among them. She grew up near the Gorakian border, you know. She saw the Kalovaxians lay waste to that land, saw the echoes of it. She'll need compensation, of course, but it's not an impossibility."

"What sort of compensation?" I ask, the words coming out sharp. I haven't forgotten that Dragonsbane once promised the Sta'Criverans the Water Mine without my consent. I'm not about to underestimate her again.

Dragonsbane must hear my suspicion, because she smiles with teeth. "Giosetta has been trying to convert me from pirate to privateer for Doraz. Perhaps I will agree to it. After the war is done, I imagine there will be no more Kalovaxian dragons I will need to be the bane of."

Dragonsbane is as hard to read as ever, but I think it might be an apology for Sta'Crivero. Whatever it is, I'll take it.

"Well then," I say, looking back at the map. "While you do that, where will the rest of us go? The Air Mine is closest—"

"In terms of physical distance, yes," Dragonsbane says. "But we would have to get all of our troops over the Dalzia Mountains and either across or around the Savria River. Not to mention there are several of the same large cities and towns you mentioned that we would have to get past, in the middle of a largely barren landscape with nowhere to hide."

I look at the map, at the large stretch of land at Astrea's center. Dragonsbane is right. We could have made it from here to the Air Mine without detection before we liberated the Fire Mine, but now there are too many of us. We'd be lucky if we even made it to the Savria River before the Kaiserin got word of our actions.

"What of the Water Mine?" I ask after a moment. "It's the farthest, geographically speaking, but we would be able to keep to the coastline, with the mountains for cover. There are some smaller villages we might come across, but we could avoid them or contain them as needed and they wouldn't prove much of a threat. Water Guardians might not have the physical strength of Earth Guardians, but Artemisia is fierce enough, and I can think of a few war tricks to play with illusions."

No one replies right away, but they all exchange glances.

"We received word from the spies we placed in the new Theyn's household," Sandrin says after a moment. "It seems he got word that King Etristo was . . . more than a little displeased that you fled Sta'Crivero, stealing his property."

"You were refugees," I point out. "Not his property." Though I remember how the refugees I met had been given the worst jobs that no one else wanted and had been paid a pittance for the work. In the Sta'Criverans' eyes, they were little more than slaves.

"No," Sandrin says. "But the ships you stole were," he points out. "However, I imagine he's feeling the loss of the refugee camp just as keenly in many respects."

"Right," I say. "I forgot about the ships. How angry is he?"

"Angry enough to conspire with the Kaiserin—more than he already was. We received word that the Sta'Criverans and Kalovaxian envoys will be making a trade in five days' time."

"A trade," I say slowly. "A trade for what?"

"Sta'Criveran troops, most likely," Dragonsbane says. "But whatever it is, Etristo's son, Prince Avaric, will be coming to secure the arrangement in person, so we can assume it's important. The trade will happen at the Water Mine. Our sources say that the Sta'Criverans are on track to arrive around noon in five days, and the trade will happen at sundown. If we were to continue on there, we would be walking straight into them."

Something seems off, but it takes me a second to realize what it is. "They wouldn't send Avaric all the way here to bring troops—he's not a general, he has no experience. And the Sta'Criveran army is subpar at best. You said it yourself, they've never had to fight a war. Why trade at all?"

Maile shrugs. "Bodies are bodies, and we are already out-matched."

I shake my head. "It doesn't make sense. There's more to it. And what is King Etristo meant to be getting out of it?"

"The Water Mine," Dragonsbane says. "It seems our deal might have fallen through, but he's as determined as ever to own it."

With Sta'Crivero facing a deep drought, I'm sure he is. But somehow, that explanation makes even *less* sense.

"So King Etristo is sending his heir all the way here, to a war-torn country, expecting him to return empty-handed, with only a promise? There's no reason for the Prince to be coming in person."

Sandrin tilts his head. "You think there's more to the deal?"

"Yes," I say. "And I don't know what it is, but if both the Sta'Criverans *and* the Kalovaxians want it so badly, then so do I."

I pause, staring at the map, as if I could find answers there instead of just lines and names and paths.

"We could be walking into a trap," I say. "Or we could turn the trap on them."

"How?" Dragonsbane asks.

"Illusions," I say. "The strength of the Water Mine. If the

Sta'Criverans arrive at noon, when will the Kalovaxians meet them?"

Draagonsbane and Maile exchange a look. "It's less distance to cover from the capital," Dragonsbane says after a moment. "They'll be riding, likely a small group. I imagine they would try to get there around the same time."

I nod slowly. "Could we hinder their journey? Put a few hours between the Sta'Criverans' arrival and theirs?"

Dragonsbane considers it. "Yes, we could manage that. Send a few spies to the places they'll stop to rest. Let the horses loose, break some saddle straps, slip something into their food to upset their stomachs. Why?"

"If we're able to take out the Sta'Criveran forces before the Kalovaxians arrive, we could send Artemisia and some other Water Guardians in place of the Sta'Criverans, disguised to intercept whatever they intend to trade. We would have to leave as soon as possible, get there before the other parties do, but "

"And what about Søren?" Erik asks, his voice soft. It's the first thing he's said in a while; I nearly forgot he was here. "Theo, you promised we would do whatever we could."

I bite my lip. Part of me would like nothing more than to march straight toward the capital with fire at my fingertips, burning anything and anyone who stands between Søren and me. But if he were here, he would call me a fool for even considering it.

"The Prinz is the least of our priorities," Sandrin says before I can speak.

"He's likely already dead, anyway," Dragonsbane adds. "You would stage a rescue for a corpse."

"And good riddance, if you ask me," Maile snaps.

Erik's face is etched with frustration, and I imagine he's biting his tongue to keep from screaming. I don't blame him—I don't know what Søren's in the middle of right now, but it can't be pleasant. Still, the others have valid points. It's weighing the life of one against the lives of thousands.

"I know what I promised, but Søren can't be a priority right now," I say, looking at Erik. "He went with Cress to protect the rest of us, and it was a noble sacrifice. Trying to rescue him like this would be a waste of that sacrifice, and I'm sure if we asked him what we should do, he would say the same thing."

I watch the shock and hurt play over Erik's face before it fades to a mask of stone that makes him look alarmingly like the Kaiser, like his father. Without a word, he storms out of the room, the door slamming behind him so hard that I expect it to splinter.

An uncomfortable silence lasts until I break it. "Does anyone have a better plan than the Water Mine?" I ask.

"You don't have a plan for the Water Mine," Dragonsbane points out mildly. "You have an idea."

"One that we need to act quickly on if it's going to work," I say. "We'll leave at dawn, and we can formulate the rest of the plan on our way. Unless anyone has a better idea?"

I look around the room, but no one speaks, not even Maile.

"Very well," I say. "Send word to the troops. Have them meet us in the Perea Forest as quickly as they can. We'll regroup and attack from there."

\* \* \*

I find Erik lingering outside the office barrack, waiting for me.

"You told me we would save Søren," he says as soon as he sees me. "You *promised* me that."

I hold Erik's gaze and nod once before dropping my eyes. "I know," I say. "But they're right, Erik. If we save Søren right now, it's at the expense of everyone else. And on top of that, there is no direct path to the capital that ends with any of us alive. You have to know that."

Erik closes his eyes tightly, shaking his head. "He's my brother, Theo," he says, voice breaking. "We can't leave him to die."

"We don't know that he will," I say, though it sounds naive even to my own ears. "Cress wouldn't take him all the way back to the capital just to kill him. She could have done that here. If she's keeping him alive, it's for a reason."

"A public execution for a traitor prinz is reason enough," he says.

I shake my head. "Her hold on the throne is weak, and there are plenty in the capital who believe Søren is the rightful heir. Her best chance of holding on to the throne is marrying him."

"You're guessing," he says.

I shrug. "So are you," I point out. "But I know Cress. She's too smart to kill him—at least before she's tried to use him to her advantage first."

"If you're right, Søren won't go along with it," he says, his voice dropping.

My stomach twists into knots. Cress isn't as sadistic as the Kaiser, I tell myself, but I'm not sure how true that is. She's a broken girl, and I don't know what she's capable of anymore.

"He can hold up under torture," I say, pushing the thoughts from my mind.

*Torture*. The word hangs between us, sharp and ugly, coloring everything. I feel sick at the thought of Søren being tortured—tortured because of *me*. Because I agreed to Cress's terms and took her poison, even when Søren begged me not to.

"You promised," Erik says again, and the words feel like daggers.

"How would it look, Erik?" I ask, frustration seeping into my voice. "I was the youngest person in that room, and they need to see me as an equal, not a lovelorn teenage girl trying to save a boy. We will find a way to save Søren—I intend to keep that promise—but we have to be smart about it. I am asking you to trust me."

Erik wavers, and for a moment I worry that he'll say no. Instead he smiles grimly.

"It's ironic," he says. "I don't think Søren ever exercised much patience when it came to you."

I feel the words like a slap even as guilt pools in the pit of my stomach. "Maybe not," I say. "But look where that got him. There are too many people depending on me for me to make the same mistakes."

# SPAR

———•—•———

THERE'S AN OLD ASTREAN BALLAD about the sun setting over the Calodean Sea, though it lives in the fray of my memory, fractured and blurred so that all that is left is vague and hazy. Still, I hear the ghost of the melody in my mind now as I watch the vivid orange sun dip below the horizon, casting a warm orange glow on the jagged tips of the mountain range that towers over us, painting the sky in strokes of violet and salmon and turquoise, with the whisper of stars fading into view where the sky is darkest.

*I'm home,* I think, and my chest clenches around the word like it never wants to let it go again.

The surprise takes me aback. I've known I was in Astrea since I set foot on the shore weeks ago, but I don't think I truly appreciated it until this moment. I'm home, and I will never leave these shores again if I can help it.

"If you're done getting weepy-eyed over a sunset, we can start," Artemisia says, though even she doesn't sound unaffected herself.

I turn away from the sunset and toward her and Heron. Artemisia might wear her exhaustion more palpably, wrapped in grumpiness, but I see it on Heron as well—in the slump of his shoulders, the heaviness in his eyes. If they had their way, they would be sitting down in the mess hall now, piling their plates high with food before settling into easy conversation followed by a night of restful sleep. Instead, though, they followed me deep into the mountain range with nothing but a few pieces of hardtack and dried meat to curb their hunger.

And they did it because I asked it of them. Not as a queen—that might have worked on Heron, but I'm sure Art would have suggested some colorful new uses for my crown if I had. No, they're here as my friends, and I'm grateful for that.

It wasn't too long ago that I thought I was incapable of trusting anyone, but here we are, and I would trust the two of them with anything.

Which is why I dragged them out into the middle of the mountains, away from the prying eyes of the others.

I take a steadying breath and look down at my hands, bringing balls of fire to my palms.

Heron has already seen me achieve this much, but Artemisia gives my hands a thoughtful look.

"Decently done," she says. "But you could do that before the mine. Before the poison, even."

Heron turns his attention to her with his mouth hanging open, and I realize I never told him that bit. "She could do *what*?" He looks back at me. "You could do *what*?"

I sigh, closing my hands and extinguishing the flames. "It wasn't the same," I say to both of them. "I couldn't control it then, and it was never this strong—heat, yes, searing heat even, but not full flames. It was never like this."

Heron's mouth is still gaping, but after a second he closes it. "You never told me that," he said.

I shrug. "I didn't tell anyone. Art found out by accident. For a while, I thought I might be going mad or that I was cursed. . . . I don't know. It seemed an easier weight to bear alone."

"Like back in the capital when you didn't tell us the Kaiser wanted to marry you?" Heron asks, shaking his head. "You should have told us. Blaise didn't know, either?"

"No," I say, looking away. "He had enough to worry about. I didn't want to add to that."

Heron nods slowly, weighing his next words carefully. "Is that why he's not here now?" he asks.

I don't answer for a moment, crossing my arms over my chest. "We both decided that some distance would do us good," I say, trying to keep my voice level and free of emotion.

Artemisia snorts. "We'll see how long that lasts. The two of you are the same, through and through. You need one another like the sea needs the moon."

Her words prickle irritation deep beneath my skin. "Well, he told me himself that I don't need him, and I don't have the time or energy to soothe his ego," I say. "Besides, if he's so determined to run headlong into self-destruction, that's his choice, but I'm not going to cheer him on while he does it."

Artemisia and Heron exchange looks that I can't read, before Artemisia sighs.

"All right, so you can summon the flame easily enough, and Heron said that you can change its structure, which is . . . different," she says. "But that alone won't do you much good when you have to use it against an enemy."

An enemy. I appreciate that she keeps it vague instead of saying Cress's name. I wonder if hearing it will ever stop feeling like a knife between my ribs. I push her from my mind and focus on the fire, bringing it back to my hands.

Artemisia beckons me toward her. "Sparring practice all over again," she says with a wry smile. "Try throwing them."

That startles me. "At you?" I ask. "I don't want to hurt you."

Artemisia laughs. "It's charming that you think you could," she says.

I glance at Heron, who looks wary but resigned. He nods. I pull back my right arm and throw, imagining the fire as a ball. It leaves my hand, but as soon as it's airborne, it shrinks and disappears into a cloud of smoke.

"See?" Artemisia says. "I told you it wouldn't hurt me."

I frown, trying again with my left hand, but the same thing happens. "Ampelio could throw fire," I say. "He made it look easy."

"You can make anything look easy if you practice it enough," Heron says. "The farther the fire gets from you, the weaker it becomes. You have to throw not just the flame but your power with it."

"That sounds simple, but I don't know how to do it," I say.

"Focus and practice," Heron says. "Now try again, but send your power with it, not just the fire itself. The gem should help. Imagine you're channeling your power through it."

I touch Ampelio's gem at my neck and take a steadying breath before summoning a ball of fire to my right hand again.

"Do you still want me to throw it at you?" I ask Artemisia.

She grins. "Do your worst," she says.

When I throw the fireball, I feel it in my chest as well as in my arm. Ampelio's pendant throbs against my skin like a second heartbeat. This time, the fire leaves my hand and holds its form, though it grows weaker as it sails through the air. Artemisia throws a hand up before it hits her and water flies from her fingertips, turning the ball of fire into steam.

"Better," she says. "But still weak. Let's go again."

By the time we make our way back down the mountain, every muscle in my body aches. I almost miss the sword lessons. But as sore as I am, I also feel whole and at peace for the first time in recent memory. I feel *right*. I know that it's only the beginning and I'm far from being able to hold my own against Cress, but I'm on the path toward that, and for today, that is enough.

"So, you aren't going to the capital to rescue Søren," Artemisia says as we take the winding path back down toward the camp.

Thinking about Søren feels like walking down stairs and expecting there is one more step than there is. It throws my world off-kilter.

"No," I say, hoping I sound steadier than I feel. "It would be foolish to rush in without enough warriors, without a plan. If Søren were here, he would tell us the same thing."

"It's the right call," Art says with a nod. "And you didn't lose face by prioritizing an enemy prinz in front of allies who are, at best, tentative in their support."

"He's not an enemy," I say with a sigh.

Artemisia shakes her head. "We know that, and maybe

after everything, some others might believe it as well, but there is still a wide chasm between being an enemy and being one of us, and it's a chasm he will never cross."

"I know," I say. "I promised Erik we would save him, though. And we will—when we can."

Something hard crosses over Heron's expression. "Erik is more reckless than you are," he says, his voice low. "He won't be strung along with promises, and we need Goraki's numbers, as meager as they might be, if we're going to stand against the Kalovaxians."

"Erik has a weak hold on Goraki as it is," Artemisia says with a sniff. "He's the Kaiser's bastard son, and now that his mother isn't—" She breaks off, glancing at me, though I'm careful not to give a reaction. "Now that she isn't around anymore, his hold is weaker than ever. If he *does* decide to forsake our alliance and go chasing after his Kalovaxian brother, he would likely do it alone. He can't be foolish enough not to know that."

"He just lost his mother, and Søren is the only family he has left," Heron says. "He's not foolish; he understands the risk. He just might not care about it."

Before Art and I can respond, Heron quickens his stride, outpacing us by a few feet.

"They've been spending a lot of time together," Art says when he's out of earshot, her voice wary.

I'm not surprised. Erik told me he was interested in Heron, and though Heron is far more guarded about his heart, I remember how red his cheeks would get around Erik, how he would turn shy and awkward all of a sudden.

"How long?" I ask her.

She shrugs. "Heron isn't one to spill all the details of his personal life, unlike other people I could name," she says with a pointed glance in my direction. "But I think it started with the *molo varu*. I would catch him with it sometimes, writing messages, reading others, but when I asked him if there was any news from Goraki, he would say no. Whatever it was, after the battle, things seemed to progress quickly. They spend most nights together."

"It's good," I tell her. "I imagine they both need comfort and companionship. They've both faced losses. I'm glad they've at least found something positive in the midst of so much war and pain and grief."

"I suppose it is good," Artemisia allows, eyes narrowing. "But it's moved so quickly . . . and losing Leonidas destroyed Heron. When I met him after he'd escaped the Earth Mine, he was a shadow of a person, all raw wounds and broken bits. He's rebuilt himself slowly over the last year, painstakingly. I think having you and a purpose has been better for him than you realize. It's the strange thing about Heron—most people who have lost as much as he has close themselves off. It's how you and I survived, and Blaise even more so, I think. But Heron is different. He doesn't hold people at arm's length. He holds on to them like a drowning man. It's something I've admired, but it scares me as well. I'm not keen on seeing his heart break again."

I hear the warning in her voice clearly.

"I'll do what I can to keep Erik on our side," I tell her. "But I didn't realize you were such a romantic."

Artemisia glares at me. "I'm not," she says sharply. "I just can't stand moping."

"Of course," I say.

"You aren't moping," she says after a moment. "I thought you would be. You'd grown attached to the *prinkiti*—to Søren. And to Blaise, for that matter. And now here you are without either of them."

I bite my bottom lip. "I'm not going to lie and tell you I don't miss Søren. Of course I do. And I miss Blaise as well, and the people we used to be to one another. But Blaise said that I will always choose Astrea at the end of the day, and right now especially, Astrea needs me. I'm of no use to her if I'm worrying about someone without the sense to worry about himself."

Artemisia glances sideways at me and nods once decisively.

"Good," she says. "And now we don't have to talk about your heart ever again."

A moment passes in silence before I ask a question that has been on my mind for some time. "And your heart?" I ask her. "I haven't seen Spiros in a while. Not since Sta'Crivero."

"Oh, he's around, but I think he's keeping his distance from me, and by extension you," she says with a shrug. "I seem to have hurt his feelings."

"It seemed like he liked you," I tell her. "Not as a friend, but as something different."

Art laughs. "Yes, he wasn't very subtle. Hence the hurt feelings."

"You don't like him?" I ask.

She's quiet for a second. "I do, but it isn't the same. It isn't the way you feel about Søren and Blaise, or the way Heron feels about Erik. I wish it were, even though that would make things so needlessly complicated. But no, I don't like him like that. I've never really liked anyone in that way, even years ago, before the mines, when all the girls my age were getting crushes and swooning. . . . Well, I've never been a swooner, I suppose."

"Oh," I say, uncertain of how else to respond.

She shrugs. "I don't mean that I don't . . . you know . . . *love* people. There are people I find attractive, I suppose. I just . . . I'm not attracted to them in that all-consuming way it seems to affect the rest of you."

"I understand," I tell her, and it's at least half-true.

The rest of the walk passes in a silence that is not uncomfortable. Artemisia is an enigma who has revealed herself to me on her terms, in slivers and shades and hints that have slowly come to form a hazily defined portrait of her. Maybe the image will never be entirely complete, but maybe it's all the more beautiful for it.

# REVERIE

———— ·•·•· ————

WHEN I DREAM, I DREAM of Cress. She stands on the bow of a Kalovaxian ship, near the dragon figurehead, bone-pale hands clasped behind her back. Her gown is made of thick, billowing smoke, curling around her figure in dark swirls that twist and writhe over her skin. Her white hair is cut bluntly at her shoulders, just as it was the last time I saw her and the time before that, the edges singed. It doesn't grow anymore, I realize. It's dead at the roots.

She must feel me there, because she turns, her face sharp and shadowed and bloodless. At first, she looks right through me, but then her eyes refocus and meet mine. Her mouth curves into a grim smile.

"You're here to haunt me," she says, sounding unsurprised. "I confess, I hoped you would be."

I open my mouth to tell her that she's the one haunting me, before I realize what's so strange about the scene—Cress is on a boat, and though it is rocking wildly back and forth as if in a storm, she looks serene.

"You aren't seasick," I say.

She turns her face to look out at the dark and violent

sea. "No," she says. "I don't get seasick anymore. A lot has changed since you died."

"I'm not dead," I tell her.

Her smile turns sad. "When you thought I was dead, did you feel it?" she asks me.

For a moment, I don't know how to answer.

"No," I admit. "But I didn't kill you myself. When I gave the poison to Elpis, I knew there was no turning back. I hated myself for it, but I didn't have time to linger over that. There was so much to do still, so much to plan. I didn't have time to stop and feel your death until after I knew you'd survived."

Cress frowns. "Elpis," she says. "Was that the girl's name? I didn't think I remembered it."

"You wouldn't," I say. "I don't know if you ever thought of her at all."

"But I must have remembered it somewhere," she says, frown deepening. She takes one step toward me, then another, until she's within arm's reach. "I couldn't dream it otherwise."

"This isn't your dream," I tell her, but she ignores me.

"I don't feel your death, either," she tells me, sounding vaguely disappointed. She's close enough now that I can feel her breath against my skin, and that sensation jars me. I can *feel* it as if she's really standing in front of me. "I thought I would. But I don't feel much of anything anymore."

"I'm not dead," I say again, my voice stronger this time. "You didn't kill me. I'm stronger than ever now, and when we meet again, we will end this once and for all. And I assure you, when that day comes, you will feel something."

Her eyes bore into mine, one corner of her mouth quirking

up into a mocking smile. She reaches out to touch my face, but unlike the last time, her hand isn't hot. Instead it feels like ice against my skin. I flinch away from her, but that only seems to amuse her and she keeps her hand pressed firmly to my cheek.

"Do you know why you held your own in our last battle?" she asks me.

I don't answer, but she doesn't seem to expect me to.

"Because you made a patchwork quilt of warriors from different countries with different beliefs, different goals, and though your numbers were impressive, you made a grave mistake. Because in a quilt like that, all it takes is for one thread to be cut, and then the whole thing comes apart. It should make for quite the spectacle. I only wish you could be here to watch it unravel."

My stomach turns. "What do you mean?" I ask her. "What did you do? Did you send troops?"

She smiles. "No, not troops," she says, shaking her head. "Why would I waste troops on a mission when a single messenger would be plenty? Those men and women who rallied around you, they don't deserve a glorious death. It's too noble for traitors like them—like you were once. No, I'm going to let them die pathetically. Quietly. And then their names will be lost to the wind, just like yours. But my name will never be gone. It will live on in history books, and etched into stone, surviving long after I'm gone."

Her voice grows shrill at the end, grating against my mind like the sound of metal against metal. I cringe, wincing away from her, but this time she stops me, bringing her other hand to my other cheek, holding me in place.

"Maybe we will see one another again, Thora," she says, her voice returning to its normal melodic tone. "But not for some time and not in this world. Maybe there are no wars in the next one."

She presses her black lips to my cheek, and the cold left behind spreads over my skin until I can't feel anything else.

# ALARM

———— • ————

THE SOUND OF A PEALING bell drags me from sleep an instant before Artemisia pushes her way into my tent, eyes alight. If there is one thing I've learned about Artemisia, it's this: anything that makes her eyes light up is usually trouble of the highest order. I force myself to get to my feet, reaching for the cloak hanging over the edge of my cot.

"An attack?" I ask her, even as I hear Cress's words in my mind. *"Why would I waste troops on a mission when a single messenger would be plenty?"* But that was only a dream, and this is emphatically not.

"I don't know," Artemisia says. "But I intend to find out, and people tend to be more forthcoming with you than with me."

I can't resist a snort as I pull on my cloak. "That's because I ask nicely."

"It's *because* you're a queen," she retorts.

I put my boots on as quickly as I can, though it doesn't seem quick enough for Art, who taps her foot impatiently. "Well, you can always call yourself Princess Artemisia if you think it will help," I tell her, pulling the last set of laces tight and getting to my feet.

Art looks like she could happily bite me. Technically it's the truth—as the daughter of an Astrean princess, she can claim the title herself, if she wants it. But I think she'd rather claim a swarm of bees.

"Don't even joke about that," she snaps. "And come on."

She turns on her heel and stalks out of the tent, leaving me to trail in her wake. The sky is still dark, the sun a mere hint at the horizon, but the camp has been packed up, ready for our departure in what should have been an hour's time, though perhaps even that was too late. All around, the camp is in chaos, with people running about in a panicked haze. "We'll have to get you a tiara," I continue to Art, hurrying to catch up with her and trying to calm the fear working into my own heart. I have to shout to be heard over the bells and the sound of the crowd. "*Definitely* work on your diplomacy skills."

She ignores my words, taking hold of my arm and pulling me through the crowd toward the mob of warriors already standing at the gate of our camp in a single row, a human wall with mismatched armor layered over their clothing and swords in their hands.

"What's happening?" Art asks them. Not one turns toward her. Instead their eyes stay fixed on the horizon. But Art is not one to be ignored. "Her Royal Majesty, Queen Theodosia, would like to know if her life is possibly in danger, if that isn't too much trouble," she says, pitching her voice louder.

At that, one of the warriors turns around.

"Neither of you should be here," he says, before lifting his helm. Spiros. He barely looks at me, and doesn't meet Art's gaze at all. "You were told to keep the Queen inside her tent."

"And yet I wasn't told why," Artemisia counters. "Don't you think she has a right to know what's happening in her own camp?"

"As soon as we know what he wants, the Queen will be the first to know. But for now, he's a threat," Spiros says, his voice firm.

"He," I echo. In my dream, Cress said she'd send a single messenger. "Is he a berserker?" I ask.

Spiros glances at me, nodding once. "That's our theory, Your Majesty," he says. "But no one is keen on getting close enough to him to put it to the test. He's making his way across the field slowly, and we've got archers waiting on the order to shoot."

"And who's giving that order?" I ask, but Spiros shrugs. "Can you tell if the man is Astrean?"

Spiros shakes his head. "He looks Kalovaxian to me, though I suppose he could be from any number of the northern lands. Pale skin, yellow hair."

"If he's from the North, he couldn't be a berserker," I point out.

"Likely not," Spiros agrees. "But if he gets too close to camp, when he goes off, he could take all of us with him. No one wants to take that risk."

Another warrior turns toward us. "He's yelling something," she says. "Hard to tell what it is."

"He's close enough now for us to make out his face," a third warrior shouts, spyglass raised to his eye.

I step toward him, holding my hand out. "May I?" I ask.

The warrior—another one of Dragonsbane's crew, I suspect—looks to Spiros for permission. He must give it, because the warrior passes the spyglass to me, stepping aside so there is space for me to see. I lift the spyglass to my eye.

It takes a moment to find the lone approaching figure, and a bit longer to focus the spyglass enough for his face to become clear. With shaking hands, I lower the spyglass and pass it back.

"I know him," I say. "One of the Kaiser's messengers."

*"Why would I waste troops on a mission when a single messenger would be plenty?"*

*It was only a dream,* I tell myself again, but doubt nags at me. I push the thought from my mind and turn back to Spiros.

"Let him approach the gate, and hear what he has to say. Then bring the message to me. I will gather the other leaders and we'll decide how to proceed."

Spiros nods. "It'll be done."

"And, Spiros?" I say. "He can't know that I'm alive. If he does, he'll tell the Kaiserin, and she'll bring every battalion she has back here to kill me. We aren't ready for that."

He considers this for a moment. "I'll give the order."

The tension in the former commandant's office is palpable, heavy against my skin like I just walked into a bathhouse. Dragonsbane helped herself to the leather chair behind the commandant's desk, and is leaning back with her boots up. Though she looks perfectly at ease, she clasps her hands so tightly in her lap that they are beginning to turn white at the knuckles.

Maile and Sandrin have taken the other two chairs. Sandrin offers me his chair, but I shake my head. It's hard enough to be in this room. I doubt I'll be able to sit still.

Instead I walk toward where Erik stands beside the window, leaning against the wall with his arms crossed. As soon as I approach, though, he shoves off the wall and crosses to the far side of the room. Part of me wants to follow him, to make him talk to me, but what then? There is nothing new I can say to him. Rescuing Søren is impossible right now; as soon as it isn't, we'll put a plan into motion. The words don't even sound reassuring to me.

No one says a word while we wait for news—a sharp contrast from our last meeting. Then, we were all talking over one another, but now it is silent. I'm not sure which I prefer. The bell has finally stopped ringing, and the camp has gone so quiet that every gust of wind and bird's chirp makes me jump.

The Kalovaxians were never going to let us keep the mine. We knew this. Cress knew it when she promised it, just as I knew when I accepted it. That wasn't really what we were trading—it was my death for the chance for my people to recuperate enough to fight. But I'm not dead, and with most of our troops already departed, we are nowhere near being prepared for a fight, so I suppose neither of us got what we wanted.

She doesn't know I'm alive, though. She can't. Even in my dream she thought I was as much a vision as I thought she was. And now what do I think? Even in the silence of the tent,

I can't sort out an answer to that. The idea that my dream of Cress was anything more than a dream is too ludicrous to entertain.

And yet . . . she told me she was sending a single messenger, and here we are, with a single messenger at our gates.

I know Cress. I know her mind. It's possible that I knew she would send a messenger because I know her. It's a simpler explanation and a more comfortable one, but it weighs on my shoulders like a lie.

Pushing the thought from my mind, I force myself to move any way I can, to pace the small patch of open floor. The stillness and the silence are beginning to drive me mad.

Dragonsbane stares at me, the vein in her forehead starting to throb.

"Do you have to do that?" she asks, each word an icicle.

"Yes," I say, not bothering to elaborate. I stop in front of the desk. "You have some experience in battle. If you had to hazard a guess what is happening, what would it be?"

Dragonsbane exhales, crossing one ankle over the other. "I couldn't begin to guess," she says. "We didn't allow opportunities for messengers on the sea. We fired until they surrendered—no parlays, no talking. This sort of battle is . . . well, it isn't exactly my forte."

It seems to pain her to admit that.

Maile leans forward in her chair. "The simplest explanation is that they are warning us of their return, giving us a chance to flee."

I shake my head. "I don't think the Kalovaxians would waste time on a warning. Besides, they're running low on bodies to work in the mines. Letting anyone leave this camp unchained would be a foolish decision, and the Kalovaxians aren't fools. We all know that too well."

Maile's eyes dart to Erik's and linger there, heavy and a touch accusatory. "What do you think of it?" she asks.

Erik looks at Maile, surprised. "I don't know any more than you do," he says.

But Maile isn't dissuaded. She pushes herself up from her chair and crosses toward Erik. The hair on the back of my neck prickles as I watch them, unsure of what exactly is crackling between them. Nothing good, that's for certain.

"I find that difficult to believe," Maile says. "You are one of them, aren't you?"

Every muscle in Erik's body goes as taut as a pulled bowstring. His eyes narrow, and he looks like he could happily hit Maile—which is exactly what I'm worried about. I open my mouth to speak, but Erik cuts me off with a look before turning back to Maile.

"I have Kalovaxian blood, yes. By force. By violence. But I am not one of them any more than you are," he says, his voice so quiet that I have to strain to hear him. "The only thing the Kalovaxians gave me was skill with a sword, and if you insinuate otherwise again, I will gladly show you as much."

Maile balks, taking a step back. "Are you threatening me?" she asks, her voice rising to a thundering crescendo.

Erik shrugs but doesn't deny it. "Only if you truly are the idiot even your own men say you are," he says, each word acidic. "Are you?"

"That's enough," Dragonsbane says, swinging her legs off the desk and planting them firmly on the ground, as if she's ready to stand at any moment. "You are both idiots if you think it productive to fight each other instead of the enemy quite literally at our gate."

Maile's face flushes red, and her jaw stays clenched tight, but she steps away from Erik, retreating to stand on the other side of the room.

"I'm not saying anything anyone else wasn't thinking," she mutters, loud enough for everyone to hear. "He could be a spy."

At that, Erik laughs. "Of everyone in this camp, you think the Kalovaxians would be simple enough to make a spy out of the only one who shares their blood? They didn't get where they are by making simple choices. I'd be more wary of the servants we turned to spies betraying us, or of the members of Dragonsbane's crew that come from Elcourt, or even the reckless and *idiotic* youngest daughter of a chief who thinks her useless."

At that, Maile lunges at Erik, but Dragonsbane is ready for it. In an instant, she's on her feet and over the desk in one lithe motion, shoving Maile into a chair. Maile must be twice Dragonsbane's size, but Dragonsbane manages it so easily that she only looks annoyed. Maile is as surprised as the rest of us, but Dragonsbane doesn't spare her another glance, instead turning to a wide-eyed Erik.

"And I will thank *you* not to slander my crew, even if it is only hypothetically," she says. "I trust my people just as you trust your own."

Erik is speechless, but manages to nod.

"No one in this room is a spy," I say, my voice quavering. "The second we turn on each other is the second the Kalovaxians win."

As soon as I say it, Cress's words from my dream come back to me, gathering like oil in the pit of my stomach.

"*You made a patchwork quilt of warriors from different countries with different beliefs, different goals. . . . All it takes is for one thread to be cut, and then the whole thing comes apart.*"

"Your Majesty?" Sandrin says, his voice surprisingly gentle in the midst of so much anger and shouting. "Are you all right?"

I blink and turn my attention to him, forcing a smile. "Quite," I say, hoping I sound steadier than I feel. "I'm only impatient to find out what's happening so we can get out of this godsforsaken room."

I almost believe myself—after all, it isn't a lie, exactly. But no one sees the deeper layer of panic working through me. No one hears Cress's words echoing in my mind over and over again until I worry they'll drive me mad.

Because it *would* be so easy for this alliance to fall apart—not just because of Erik and Maile. The ties that are binding us together are flimsy. And without them, we wouldn't be able to make any kind of stand against the Kalovaxians.

# UNRAVEL

———◆•◆———

A N ETERNITY PASSES BEFORE THE door swings open and Heron enters, out of breath from running. In an instant all of us are on our feet and my heart is thundering so loudly that I fear everyone in the room can hear it.

"Was it a trap?" I ask, stepping forward and gripping the edge of the desk tightly.

Heron shakes his head, too winded to speak. After a second of thought, though, he hesitates and nods. "In a manner of speaking," he manages. "Everyone is fine. It was only the one messenger—but the message."

"Søren?" Erik asks, his voice cracking. "Is he all right?"

Heron's gaze catches on Erik. "He didn't say anything about Søren," he says. "I'm sorry."

"What *did* he say?" Dragonsbane asks.

Heron takes a steadying breath. "He brought a very . . . attractive truce offer from the Kaiserin. Granting freedom and land and ships."

"Our freedom is not hers to grant," I say.

"No," Maile agrees. "But it is a very tempting offer all the same, and one with no more bloodshed. We would be fools not to consider it."

Sandrin clears his throat. He's been sitting so quietly in the corner that it's easy to forget he's there, but now he pulls the attention of the room like a flame draws moths.

"There must have been a catch to an offer like that," he says, his voice level and low. "What was it?"

"The peace offer is only good for one country. One group of us," Heron says. "The details the messenger provided were clear, even going so far as to define Dragonsbane's fleet as a country all its own."

A laugh forces its way from my throat, hysterical and shrill and somewhat inhuman. I clamp a hand over my mouth, but that does little to muffle the sound, and once I start, I can't stop. It is the laugh of a madwoman, and that is how everyone looks at me. Like I've gone mad. Maybe I have gone mad. How else could I have dreamed that Cress would do something like this, only to have it proven true?

This is how she pulls the thread, removing one country from our alliance and letting the rest of us fall apart without it. Heron was right—it is a trap, but one that's been alluringly baited.

"Theo," Erik says. He seems to forget he's upset with me, crossing to my side to put a hand on my shoulder. "Are you all right?"

"She's finally cracked," Maile says. "I knew that mine did something to her."

"Perhaps. Why don't we throw you down there and see how you come out?" Dragonsbane replies, stunning Maile to silence.

"Stop it," I manage, straightening up. "This is what the

Kalovaxians want—to break us apart. That's why they're making this offer. It's brilliant, but we can't let it work. We will win together or not at all."

"Pretty words," Sandrin says with a heavy sigh. "But pretty words don't win battles. Neither does loyalty. The Kalovaxians win because they are ruthless, because they have no loyalty. It is deplorable, yes, but they are alive and thriving, while the people under my care are neither."

"You can't truly be considering this," Dragonsbane says, aghast.

"I am," he says. "And you should as well. It is a good offer."

"For one of us," I say. "For a sliver of our army. What about everyone else? You would run and abandon us?"

Sandrin doesn't have a reply to that. He only sets his jaw, his eyes fixed on something far away. My stomach drops. If Sandrin leaves, he'll take the refugees with him. Some might stay with me, but most of the Sta'Criveran refugees followed me because he encouraged it. They would follow him now, too, and we have refugees from the other camps as well. If even half of them followed him, we would feel the loss of them keenly.

Heron clears his throat.

"Not only abandon," he says. "The party who accepts the offer of peace will become an ally of Kalovaxia, fighting beside them in this war. Whoever accepts the peace offering won't merely step out of the war—they'll change sides."

One word catches in my mind, and despite everything, a smile spreads over my face.

"*War*," I say. "Was that the messenger's word?"

Heron looks bewildered but nods. "A direct quote, yes."

I laugh again, but this time it doesn't sound mad.

"Perhaps you have cracked," Erik says to me.

I shake my head. "The Kalovaxians don't have wars," I say. "They have sieges. They have skirmishes. They have battles. If they're calling this a war, it means they believe we're a true threat. It means they see us as something worth fearing."

"Pretty words," Sandrin says again, shaking his head. "But can you promise we will win if we stay with you?"

I want to, but the words lodge in my throat. As much as I wish I could make that promise, I can't. I hope we will win. I believe we can, if we fight wisely. But I don't know what the future holds, and I understand Sandrin's uncertainty. He has tens of thousands depending on him—he needs to do right by them. And so do I.

"The Kalovaxians are not offering freedom," I say. "They are offering to trade your chains for a leash, to fashion you into their attack dogs. And if you believe that they will keep their word and allow you even that much, you haven't learned anything from their past actions."

Sandrin glances away, but Maile holds my gaze and her eyes narrow. "You think you know them better because you saw them up close. We all know what they are capable of," she says. "But perhaps it would be better—safer, at least—to be by their side for once."

I consider it for a moment. "There was a man at court—Ion. Before the Kalovaxians seized Astrea, he was a Guardian, one of the people sworn to use their magic to protect Astrea and my mother. The Kalovaxians offered him a similar deal—die, or use his magic to aid the Kaiser. I'm sure it's a deal that was offered to all of the Guardians, though he was the only one to accept it. I'm sure he thought the same as you do now—that the Kalovaxians would treat him as an equal, that he would be safe. And it's true that as far as I know, Ion is still alive and kept at court, but he is not a free man, and he is certainly not a happy one."

That renders Maile speechless.

"So we don't take this deal," Dragonsbane says, her voice firm. "Are we in agreement?"

"Aye," Maile says, followed a beat later by Sandrin.

Erik, however, says nothing, his expression unreadable for a moment. With resignation, he turns to Heron, and it's only then that he hesitates, and I can see him soften for just an instant. I can see him waver. But it isn't enough. His mind is made up.

"Take me to the messenger," he says, each word heavy. "I would like to accept the Kaiserin's offer."

"Erik," I say, the name wrenching itself from my throat painfully. "You can't."

"I have to," he says, impassive, avoiding my imploring gaze. "I've lived with the Kalovaxians just as you said, been seen as less than human but not quite a slave. I survived it. It wasn't so bad—certainly preferable to death."

"You don't mean that," I say. "I know you're upset, but—"

"But nothing," he says, the words suddenly as harsh and abrasive as a windstorm. "Do you know what's happened since I started trusting you, Theo? I've lost my mother, I've lost my brother, and I've been saddled with responsibility for hundreds of people."

"You would betray everyone because you're angry with me?" I ask.

One corner of his mouth curls up in a sardonic smile. "Your ego is showing, Theo. It isn't about you. Besides, I'm taking a scant few hundred men. Not enough to hobble you."

"Do you expect me to thank you for that?" I demand, my voice breaking.

"Perhaps you should," Erik says before hesitating. "I'll give Søren your regards when I see him."

He steps toward the exit, and I try to follow, to yell at him, to convince him to stay, but before I can make it more than a couple of steps, Maile claps a hand on my shoulder and stops me.

"Let him go," she says, her voice gruff. "He's got traitor blood—it would have won out in the end anyways. Better to have him gone now, before he can truly betray us."

"And he's right," Dragonsbane says. "We can still stand without him. The Gorakians are the smallest number among us."

Heron looks queasy as Erik brushes past him and exits the room. His eyes find mine, desperate and wounded, making my stomach twist. He's lost so many people already, and he was only just starting to let Erik in. This might ruin him.

"Heron," I start, but he shakes his head. All of his emotions seal themselves away behind his hazel eyes.

"I'll bring him to the messenger to negotiate terms. The rest of you should come calm your factions down to prevent an uprising. Theo, stay here so the messenger doesn't see you."

It isn't until the others leave to calm and reassure their people that I let myself break. I collapse into the desk chair that

Dragonsbane abandoned, frustration flooding me until the only way it can come out is in tears coursing hot down my cheeks.

I should have expected Erik to leave—gods know I pushed him to it.

If I had taken his side against Maile . . . If I had come up with a plan to save Søren, even at the expense of everything else . . . If I hadn't let Hoa die . . . But I couldn't do any of that. I failed him at every turn, and now I've lost him.

Just as Cress knew I would lose someone in this ploy of hers, just as she told me in my dream. Was it only a dream?

I don't understand it. I can't begin to guess what has caused it—whether it was the poison or the mine or something older and more deeply seeded that has come awake—but the Cress in my dreams was truly Cress, not a figment of my imagination, but her consciousness.

The thought of it makes me nauseous. I don't want her in my mind, and I certainly don't want to be in hers. I don't want to share anything with her.

*But if you can use it . . .* , a voice in my mind whispers, sounding vaguely like the Kaiser.

And I can use it, I realize with a jolt. Cress thinks I'm dead. She thinks the Theo in her dreams is only her imagination, a ghost of a girl and nothing more. But I know otherwise and that gives me an advantage, if I can figure out how to use it.

It's a grisly advantage, one that I still can't wrap my mind around, but in this war I will take every edge I can.

# SPY

———— ◆ • ◆ ————

H ERON, ARTEMISIA, AND BLAISE COME to fetch me after
the messenger leaves with Erik and the Gorakians.
Though Blaise still brings an air of awkwardness with him, I
can't deny that it's nice to have the four of us together again,
even when the Gorakians' abandonment hangs over us all like
a wool blanket in the dead of summer.

"I'm sorry," I say, mostly to Heron, who won't look at me.
Instead he takes one of the chairs in front of the commandant's desk, his gaze downcast.

Heron shrugs. "He was right—we can withstand the loss
of the Gorakians more easily than that of any other faction.
It's a small blow to our numbers. A surmountable one."

"I know," I say. "But our people will feel the weight of the
betrayal. And I'm sorry we lost Erik."

The weight of just how much I'll miss Erik hits me squarely
in the chest. It's easy to think of it in practical terms. Of the
Gorakians' abandonment as a math equation and nothing
more. But it isn't so simple. Yes, we can survive without their
numbers, but leading this fight without Erik beside me with
his witty remarks and startling bouts of wisdom . . . that

I will miss far more than the number of warriors who followed him.

Heron shakes his head, looking at me with raised eyebrows. "You don't get it, do you?" he asks before reaching into his pocket and producing a large lump of gold—the one Erik gave him when we parted ways in Sta'Crivero. The *molo varu.*

Pieces click into place in my mind. Not the whole picture, not yet, but enough.

"It was a trick," I say. "Erik didn't really betray us."

Heron's smile is grim. "That truth can't leave the four of us," he says, glancing at Artemisia and Blaise and back at me.

Blaise shakes his head. "Does Erik think we have spies?"

"Of course we have spies," Artemisia says with a snort. "The only real questions are how many and who they work for. I have a few suspects—some for the Kaiserin, even some for King Etristo."

Blaise's eyes go wide. "Why haven't we stopped them?" he asks.

It's news to me, too, but I understand immediately. "Because it's better to feed them information than it is to cut off the flow of it entirely. Intercept messages, replace them if we need to. Let them believe we're sloppy. Let them underestimate us. It's better to keep an eye on them than execute them."

Art nods. "For now," she adds.

"We're heading to the Water Mine to interrupt a meeting between Cress and Avaric," I say. "How do you propose we keep that from their spies?"

"I'll have my suspects watched closely," she replies, "and a perimeter of guards set up as well. They'll shoot down any possible messenger birds they see and let no one pass. And no one can know anything about this strategy until we're on the field. All meetings have to be between you and the other leaders and a handful of people you would trust with your lives. That's it."

I nod. "But Heron's right—we shouldn't even tell the other leaders about Erik," I say, thinking about Maile's reaction to him. I don't think she's a spy, but I'm not sure what she would do with the information, and that is enough for me not to trust her with it.

Heron nods. "He didn't have time to tell me much without raising the messenger's suspicion, but he said he would pass us information with this." He inclines his head toward the *molo varu*. "The Gorakians will be staying on the fringe of the capital, but Erik will be inside the palace—an ally and a hostage in one. He's going to play whatever game the Kaiserin wants him to play and try to get Søren free before escaping. You and Blaise know the palace passages better than he does, though, so when the time comes . . ."

I glance at Blaise before nodding. "We'll find the best path, once we know where Cress is keeping Søren."

Artemisia leans back in her chair, folding her hands in her lap. "So we have a few spies of our own now," she says. "The new Theyn's servants, and Erik. It's a start, so long as they don't get caught. I can't imagine that this new Kaiserin will be any more merciful toward spies than the Kaiser was."

"She won't be," I say, before biting my lip. "And I think we have another spy, as bizarre as it's going to sound, though it's one Cress won't be able to catch."

Artemisia leans forward. "Who? I thought I'd accounted for all of our people."

I take a deep breath. "Me," I say, before telling them about my dream last night. When I'm done, the three of them only stare at me, but I can read their thoughts clear enough on their faces. "I know how it sounds, but I haven't gone mad," I say.

"Of course not," Artemisia says quickly, glancing at the other two with raised eyebrows. "But . . . well . . . we all know better than anyone else what that much time in the mine can do to a person. It's perfectly understandable if you might start getting a bit . . . delusional."

"I'm not delusional," I say. "How else would you explain it?"

Blaise shrugs. "Clarity of hindsight," he says. "You dreamed she said a few vaguely phrased things, but you're looking back at it with what you know now, and that's coloring it."

"It's not that," I say, struggling. "I can't explain it, but I *felt her*. I felt her breath. The weight of her presence in my mind—it wasn't ephemeral. It was heavy and solid and *real*."

"It felt that way," Artemisia says, her voice surprisingly gentle. "But that's madness, Theo."

Heron's the only one who doesn't say anything, but his expression is drawn tight.

"What are you thinking, Heron?" I ask him.

He jerks out of his thoughts and shakes his head. "I don't know," he admits. "It does sound like madness, but I've heard madder things. You'll tell us if it happens again?"

I nod. "I'm done keeping secrets from you three," I say. "I don't think it's ever ended up doing me any good. *Yana Crebesti*. I trust you."

It isn't until I have to force the words out that I realize how difficult they are for me to say. I survived for so long by not trusting anyone. It was a necessary lesson to learn, and I wouldn't be alive today if I hadn't learned it, but now I don't think I can make it to the end of this war without trust. There is nothing I wouldn't trust Artemisia, Heron, and Blaise with—not my life and not the future of Astrea, if it comes to that.

The three of them exchange looks before nodding.

"*Yana Crebesti,*" they say.

Artemisia lingers after Blaise and Heron leave, her expression thoughtful but distant so that I can't begin to guess at what is running through her mind. When we're alone, she turns her gaze to me, lips pursed.

"The Kaiserin," she says.

I wait for her to continue, but after a moment it becomes clear she has nothing more to add.

"What about her?" I ask.

"You keep calling her 'Cress,'" she says. "You need to stop doing that. She's the Kaiserin now. Anything more familiar makes it look like you see her as a person—as a friend—instead of the enemy, and you can't afford that."

I swallow. I hadn't even realized I'd been doing it. In my mind, the Kaiserin will always be Søren's mother, with her sad eyes and broken spirit, and Cress will always just be Cress, ambitious and cunning, but not dangerous, not capable of all of the evil she has wrought.

Artemisia's right—I need to stop, but I don't know how to. "I'll try," I say.

"She's not your friend," Artemisia says. "She's not your heart's sister or whatever else the two of you used to say. She's the girl who tried to kill you and very nearly succeeded. She's the girl who sits on your mother's throne and holds our people in chains."

"I know that," I say, each word feeling like it weighs a ton. "Some habits are difficult to break, though. Some things are far easier said than done."

"I didn't say it would be easy," she says. "I said you had to find a way to do it."

I nod, pressing my lips together. "Do you believe me?" I ask her. "That somehow our minds have bridged?"

Artemisia doesn't say anything for a moment. "I believe that you believe it," she says carefully. "And I believe I've seen strange things happen in the mine. But sharing dreams? I've never heard of that."

A thought occurs to me. "The poison she gave me," I say. "Did it come from the Fire Mine?"

She blinks, understanding arriving slowly. "I assumed it had. Encatrio does. Did she say otherwise?"

I shrug. "She said she'd figured it out through torturing Astreans who knew the recipe."

Artemisia tilts her head to one side. "Recipe," she says. "There is no recipe. It's water from the Fire Mine—nothing more. Do you think the poison she gave you was something else?"

"I don't know," I say. "But if she got the poison from the mine, the slaves who were working down there would have to know about it. We can ask them."

Artemisia nods, her mouth twisting into a frown. "I still don't believe you," she says. "But theoretically, if you are sharing dreams, it means she can see inside your mind just as easily as you can see into hers."

"I know," I say, the thought crawling over my skin like the legs of a thousand spiders. "But she thinks I'm dead. As long as she continues to think that, she'll have no reason to think her dreams are anything more."

She considers this for a moment before shaking her head. "It's all ludicrous," she says. "I can't believe I'm even acting like it isn't."

"I know," I say. "I'm not sure I truly believe it myself. Which is why we need answers."

# SEED

———— ✦ • ✦ ————

SOMETIMES, THE TIME I SPENT in the mine filters in like sun-light through a curtained window, diluted and soft-edged and incomplete. But other times, the curtain shifts and light pours in, sharp and jarring. I remember darkness; I remember being cold. I remember my mother.

The memory hurts, forcing its way into my mind like a dagger into flesh. Unlike a dagger, though, it is impossible to pull out again.

*She tended to her gray garden, though nothing grew there anymore.*

*I remember trying to tell her this, to explain that the Kaiser had burned everything, that the dirt is mostly ash and not even weeds are able to force their way through the dry ground, but she wouldn't hear it. She continued to dig with her hands, placing seeds deep in the ground before tucking them in beneath a blanket of dirt.*

*Even in the mine, I knew my mother was dead, though sometimes, when I just saw her out of the corner of my eye,*

*I would forget for just a second. The woman before me with her dirt-caked hands was not my mother—was not a woman at all, really. She was a product of the mine or a product of my mind or perhaps some combination of the two. She was not real. I knew this but I couldn't bring myself to care.*

*Instead I crouched beside her and dug my hands into the dirt as well, feeling it wedge beneath my fingernails. I pressed seeds into the pockets of earth, just as my mother had taught me.*

*She watched me, her eyes appraising, and when she smiled, it was so warm that I didn't miss the sun.*

*"Nothing will grow here," I told her again. "The Kaiser made sure of it."*

*"All it takes is one seed, my love," she told me. "One sprout to push through the earth, to dig its roots deep and wide. If I have to plant a million seeds to find that one, that's exactly what I'll do."*

*Time became liquid, slipping through my fingers whenever I tried to get a grasp of it, but my mother never left my side and I never left hers. We kneeled together in the dirt and ash of her garden, digging and planting seeds. Dirt swallowed my skin, smothered the color of my dress—was it red before? I couldn't recall. My stomach was gnawed by hunger and my throat was so dry that it hurt to speak, but I couldn't complain because my mother was beside me once more and so there was nothing to want for.*

*I plunged my hand into an untouched bit of earth, but this time, when I scooped out a clump of dirt, a quiet sob reached up from the ground and grabbed hold of me. It was pure anguish, reaching into my chest and twisting my heart. I remember how I froze at the sound.*

*My mother began to sing.*

> *"I once knew a girl with hair like night,*
> *With eyes that shone like stars so bright,*
> *Kept the moon on a string round her wrist,*
> *Passed its magic to each soul she kissed."*

*I tore my gaze away from the ground and found her watching me.*

*There was something I needed to be doing, somewhere I needed to be, but that slipped through my fingers as well.*

> *"With each soul kissed, the moon did wane,*
> *And the girl's magic continued to drain*
> *Until naught was left but bones and skin.*
> *The girl was no more but only had been."*

*Something stirred in my memory, pushing through the din of my mind. That wasn't right. It had been some years since my mother had sung that song to me, but that wasn't how it ended. The girl's magic drained as the moon waned—I remembered that—but the ending wasn't so macabre.*

*"Until naught was left but bones and skin," I sang, my voice hoarse and dry. "And once again the world did begin."*

*I looked back down at the patch of dirt before me and began to dig again. Each handful of dirt unearthed a new sob, a wail, a scream. Each one twisted my stomach and dug its* nails into my heart. My hands shook, but I forced myself to keep digging, to find the source of all of that pain.

"My love," my mother said, struggling to be heard over the cacophony. "Stop that now."

I paused, but I couldn't look at her. I knew that if I did, I would falter.

"They need me," I told her. I don't know how I remembered that suddenly, that there were people who needed me, but the certainty was bone-deep.

"You need me," she countered, her voice breaking. "Stay with me and I'll keep you safe."

I looked up at her then, and the sight of her knocked the breath from my lungs. The gash at her throat had grown wider, but the blood was gone, leaving a hole of black nothing. Her bright eyes were dull and sunken, her skin like old paper doused in water and left to dry in the sun.

To keep you safe while your world burns, a voice deep inside me whispered. To keep you safe while those you love die.

"They need me," I told my mother again, but the words were harder to say this time. "They're calling for me. Can't you hear them?"

"Stay with me, my love. Stay safe and never want for love. Stay with me and never want for anything."

I dug more until I reached for dirt and my fingers touched only air. I looked up at my mother, who watched me with wide eyes and a solemn mouth.

"I love you, Mother," I said, swallowing back tears. "And I hope I won't see you again for a long, long time."

And then I pitched myself forward and into the hole I had dug, and fell into a vast nothingness.

# THEORY

———•——

WE HAVE TO PUT OFF our departure for a few hours. It's unlikely that the messenger traveled entirely by himself—if I were Cress, I would have sent spies with him, to monitor our movements. And sure enough, when we send scouts to the mountains, they count twenty men watching us. They're killed instantly—we don't have food to waste on hostages. It's Maile's call, but I can't bring myself to protest too strongly.

As we ready to leave in the afternoon, Artemisia finds me in my tent, her expression as guarded as ever, but with a vague hint of curiosity twisted in the corner of her mouth. I look up from the weathered map spread over the floor—the only thing that hasn't been packed yet.

"Any news from Heron?" I ask.

She shakes her head. "When I saw him this morning, he had that lump of gold clutched so tightly in his hand, I thought he would break it." She hesitates, glancing over her shoulder at the closed flap of the tent, where a figure waits, outlined in shadow. "I did find something, though . . . or, rather, someone. A woman who was in the mines when the Kaiserin came a month or so back."

My spine stiffens. "Cress came here?"

"The Kaiserin," she corrects me, not quite gently. "And yes. The official story was that she was taking on her father's duty of inspecting the mines until a new Theyn could be chosen."

"And the unofficial story?" I ask.

"She was asking a lot of questions," Artemisia says. "About the mine, and specifically about the springs within it."

The words don't surprise me, exactly—I already suspected as much—but the thought still drips down my spine like cold water.

"So she knew about the springs," I say. "This must have been after she'd tortured someone into telling her what Encatrio was."

"Yes, but that's the thing," Art says. "None of the slaves, none of the guards, no one who has worked at the mine since the siege, knew anything about any springs. No one's seen them."

I cross to the other side of the tent, leaning against one of the poles and folding my arms over my chest. "That doesn't make sense," I say. "I heard the springs as soon as I stepped into the mine, even before I lost my memories. And I think I might have seen one once, though I'm not sure. And you . . . Whoever you got the Encatrio from must have gotten it from a mine."

"The source of the poison I got didn't bottle it himself, and I doubt he could have told me who did, or how long ago it was. It might have been sometime before the siege," Artemisia says, shaking her head. "And I don't know what you heard or saw, but every former slave I talked to said the same thing—they never saw a spring, no matter how deep they went. At first I thought maybe they didn't tell the Kaiserin in order to keep the springs hidden, but they told me the same thing just now, and I get the feeling they were telling the truth."

"But you brought someone with you," I say, glancing at the shadow of the person on the other side of the tent. "What do they know?"

"Apparently the Kaiserin wasn't keen to leave empty-handed after all of that trouble," Artemisia says. "So she started asking around about other ways to create a fire poison, something that would have the same effects as Encatrio."

"And this woman helped her?" I ask.

Art shakes her head. "But she knows someone who did, and more important—she knows what that someone said."

At first glance, the woman Artemisia brings into my tent looks to be in her late thirties, with weathered skin, a frail frame, and black hair threaded with gray. Her eyes are heavy and guarded—after she worked more than a decade in the mines, so I'm sure she's seen horrors that I can only guess at. When I offer her a seat, she takes it but sits at the very edge of the chair, hands clasped tightly in her lap. It's then, when I really look at her, that I realize she can't be as old as I originally thought—I would be surprised if she were older than twenty-five.

"Thank you for speaking with me," I tell her. "What's your name?"

"Straya," the woman says, looking up at me with large dark green eyes that skitter away as soon as they meet mine.

"Straya," I repeat, glancing uncertainly at where Artemisia stands behind her, blocking the entrance to the tent to ensure we're not interrupted. "I understand the Kaiserin paid a visit to the mine to gather information."

"No one wanted to tell her anything, Your Majesty," Straya says, her voice shaking. "When she first arrived at the camp, she wore her hair bound up under a silk scarf that wrapped around her neck. Even though the weather was warm, she wore a cloak that covered her from the throat down. All we could see of her was her face. Her mouth was painted red, but I could see that underneath the paint something wasn't right—her lips were flaking and black."

I remember Cress as I saw her last, black lips, charred throat, white hair—she made no attempt to hide the effects of the Encatrio; she wore the disfigurements with pride. But that wasn't always the case, it seems.

"Did you realize what had happened to her?" I ask.

Straya's eyes find mine, and this time she holds my gaze. She swallows, then bites her lip. "There were whispers," she says slowly. "Some of us overheard the guards saying that you'd poisoned her. The night she arrived, I returned to the barracks, and the girl who slept above me—Nadia—said that it must have been Encatrio. She said that when a person survives that kind of poison, it leaves them changed, outside and in."

I sit up a little straighter. "How would Nadia have known so much about it?" I ask.

"Her father was a fire priest before the siege," she says. "She knew all manner of things about the mines that the rest of us didn't. She said she could have escaped, if she'd had any idea about where to go after she did, but she thought that even if she made it out of the camp, she would have wandered about until she starved to death, never mind the execution she would have faced if caught. There were many people I knew who would have taken death over chains, but Nadia wasn't one of them. She planned to live long enough to see the Kalovaxians destroyed."

A sick feeling settles over me. It is not lost on me that Straya is using the past tense to talk about Nadia, and I don't have to guess that she didn't live long enough to see her chains broken.

"The guards knew about Nadia; they knew she understood the mines better than anyone else. So they brought her before the Kaiserin and asked her questions. I never saw her again after that."

"Then how do you know what she told the Kaiserin?" I ask.

"Because she told me what she knew, as soon as the Kaiserin arrived and we'd seen what the poison had done to her. Nadia said that the springs in the mine were elusive, that they moved and sometimes disappeared altogether, but that the springs themselves didn't matter because as long as the Kaiserin lived, the poison was in her blood."

*The poison was in her blood.*

The room lurches around me and I have to struggle to stay upright. A new piece of the puzzle slides into place with a sickening click that I feel all the way in my bones.

"And you're sure she told the Kaiserin this?" I ask her, barely trusting myself to speak.

Straya hesitates. "I can't say for sure. I'd imagine that the only people who could were the Kaiserin and Nadia herself. But the Kaiserin left as soon as she was done with Nadia. The guards had gathered others who might have information, but she didn't want to speak with anyone else. She just left."

I glance over Straya's shoulder and meet Artemisia's gaze. She's trying to make sense of this, trying to process what it means, but it has taken her by surprise, and in a rare occurrence, she looks truly horrified.

"So when she offered me poison," I say slowly, bringing my eyes back to Straya, "she gave me her blood."

"Yes, Your Majesty," she says. "I believe so. It wasn't as strong as what lives inside the mines, you understand. Nadia told me that it's easier to survive the blood poison than the full Encatrio, that there was a time some centuries back when survivors of full Encatrio would sell their blood to those who hoped to attain gifts with less risk than they'd face in the mines. I believe your great-grandmother outlawed the practice."

"That's why it wasn't as strong, why it didn't kill you," Artemisia says to me.

"I thought it was because of you," I say, looking at her. "Because of how you counteracted it."

"Perhaps it was both," Artemisia says.

"It would explain other things as well," I add, giving her a meaningful look. I'm not keen on sharing my dream with anyone else.

Artemisia still doesn't look convinced, but there's doubt in her eyes now.

"Thank you, Straya. You've been more helpful than you can imagine," I say.

Straya nods and stands up, smoothing down the cotton shift she wears. Just as she reaches the tent flap, though, she pauses. "Your Majesty?" she asks, looking back at me over her shoulder.

"Yes?" I say.

"Nadia would have rather taken chains than death, but she was braver than me," she says quietly. "Perhaps it makes me a coward, but if the Kalovaxians try to take me again, I would sooner die."

"It won't come to that," I assure her, though it's a promise I don't know if I can keep. "And I said the same thing during the battle. Would you call me a coward?"

"No," she says quickly. "Of course not. I only meant—"

"There are different kinds of bravery, Straya. Your ancestors are watching you from the After with pride today, and when the day comes for you to join them, they will welcome you with open arms. But that day will not come for a while yet if I have anything to say about it."

Straya ducks her head toward me. "Thank you, Your Majesty," she says, before leaving Artemisia and me alone in the tent.

"You drank her blood," she says after a moment of quiet.

Hearing her say it out loud makes me nauseous. "Yes," I say.

There is a part of Cress in me now, one I don't think I will ever be rid of. The blood pumped by her heart is inside of me, as much a part of me now as it was of her. Heart's sisters indeed.

"That doesn't mean you're truly sharing dreams," Art says, but she doesn't sound as certain about that as she did earlier today.

"We don't know what it means," I remind her. "But we *do* know that Cress has an endless supply of Encatrio quite literally at her fingertips. And she's aware of that."

"If that theory holds, then so do you," Art points out.

The thought hadn't occurred to me, but it strikes me now like a bolt of lightning. The blood in my veins suddenly feels hotter, fizzling with a dangerous energy. I rub my hands over my arms to smooth the goose bumps that have arisen.

"If the theory holds, mine would be weaker," I point out. "Besides, I won't use it."

At that, Artemisia snorts. "Come now, Theo," she says. "There's no need to play the pure and righteous queen, not with me. We both know that when it comes down to it, you'll use whatever weapon you have."

The thought unsettles me, but I'm not sure it's untrue.

"There's something else," I say, recalling the memory from the mine. When I ask Artemisia about it, she bites her lip.

"Everyone I've spoken to who came out of the mine changed said the same thing," she tells me. "At first, we remembered nothing, but over time, three memories returned." She holds up three fingers. "Three tests we passed. That must have been your first."

Three tests. I remember my mother's presence beside me in the garden, how impossible it felt to tear myself away from her. If that was only the first test, I can't imagine what others could have followed. But whatever they were, I must have passed them, or I wouldn't be here now.

"And what were your tests?" I ask Art.

Pain flickers across her face. "You told me one of yours, so I'll tell you one of mine," she says, her voice tight. "You had to walk away from your mother. I walked away from my brother. Sometimes I swear I can still feel his small hands tugging at the hem of my tunic. Sometimes I still hear his voice begging me to stay with him."

I don't know what to say to that, but after a second, Artemisia shakes her head.

"We all had to make difficult decisions, Theo," she says, her voice suddenly soft. "But I'll say this—the first test is the easiest. They'll only get harder. But you passed them; you're here. Remember that."

# DEPARTURE

———◆·◆———

WE ABANDON CAMP JUST AS the sun sets over the Calodean Sea, our group of warriors winding along the Dalzia mountain range by foot and on horse.

Dragonsbane isn't one for goodbyes. When Art and I went to find her before leaving, she had already gone, taking a sizable chunk of her crew with her, along with Sandrin and the refugees who can't or don't want to fight. Though I don't think either of us is surprised, I can see the disappointment lingering in Art's eyes.

"It wasn't goodbye this time, not really," I remind her. "We'll see her again soon enough, after she's taken the Earth Mine."

Artemisia nods, but her expression remains guarded, and it isn't until we're riding away that I realize why that is: she doesn't really know if she'll see her mother again. None of us do. This is war. A million things can happen before it's done and only the gods can know for sure how it will end.

We don't stop riding for the night until the full moon is high in the sky. Though the thought of stopping at all makes my skin itch and my mind whirl with possibilities of being caught, I know that we can't get much farther without at least a few hours of rest.

My small tent is only big enough for a bedroll, two pillows to sit on, and a red lacquer tray that must have been taken from the commandant's office. The tent is just the right size for sleeping and eating, though I can't seem to do much of either. The hardtack and dried venison that served as dinner sit untouched on the tray, and my bedroll is still neatly made. Instead I sit on one of the pillows with my legs crossed and the hastily drawn map of the Water Mine that Artemisia sketched spread out on my lap.

Of everyone in our camp, Artemisia and Laius were the only ones to have set foot in the Water Mine and the camp surrounding it, but both of them only know it from the point of view of a prisoner, and Laius was so young when he was brought to the Fire Mine to be studied with Griselda. He doesn't remember much of anything, and Art only knows the parts she was permitted to see—the barracks and the mine. As such, her map is less complete than Søren's map of the Fire Mine was, seen through the eyes of a visiting prince with insight about guard positions and schedules, entrances and exits, armories and weapon caches. We don't know where the guards are or where the Guardians and berserkers are being kept. We won't know until we're too close to do anything about it.

The Kalovaxians don't go into battles blind. They don't charge into a fight without plans and backup plans and escape strategies. They don't attack unless they're sure they will walk away victorious, which is why they so often are. They would never dream of storming a camp full of warriors with only a ragtag army—not to mention that the Kalovaxians will have Spiritgems aplenty to aid them and we aren't using any, except for the handful that are with our hastily trained Guardians.

Suddenly I miss Søren so much that it feels like a dagger between my ribs, twisting and carving away at my flesh. I don't know if it's the hopelessness and uncertainty of this looming battle or if it's merely being here in this unfamiliar place, alone, but I miss him all the same.

Ever since Cress took him, I haven't let my thoughts linger too long on his absence. I haven't let myself wonder where he is or what he's going through. I haven't let myself remember how we slept those last days before the battle, his body curled around mine, the rhythm of his heartbeat echoing my own. I haven't let myself miss him as an advisor or a friend or whatever else he might have been to me.

But I should have known that the feelings would catch up with me eventually.

I close my eyes tightly, crumpling Artemisia's map in my hands.

If Søren were here, he would remind me that we won the battle at the Fire Mine, that we have more warriors now than we did before. He would tell me that there are thousands of people depending on me and that I can't fall apart and start doubting myself now.

But he's not here—I don't know where he is. I imagine him in the dungeon below the Astrean palace, bound in heavy, rusting chains. I imagine him being kept in a finer room with holes cut into the walls and Shadows who watch his every move. I imagine him dead, his head on a pike at the gate to warn anyone else who might be contemplating treason, like Ampelio's was. I imagine him sitting on a throne beside Cress, unwilling but unprotesting, the way he was for so long during his father's reign.

*Cress.* The thought hits me like a strong gust of wind, enough to bowl me over.

I don't know where Søren is, but I can find out.


I find Cress sitting on a bench in the gray garden, though now it is gray not only because of the stone ground and lifeless trees—everything is covered in a thick layer of ash, and more falls from the sky like a light spring rain. She looks like she's covered in ash herself, but it's only her dress, a gray velvet gown that is simpler than anything I've seen her wear before. There are no gems, no bits of lace, no gold accents. Just gray velvet in a simple silhouette that hugs her torso and bells out at her hips. The neckline is high, but not quite high enough to hide the charred, flaking skin of her neck.

She keeps her hands clasped in her lap and her head bowed, fragile white hair loose and falling forward in a curtain that hides her face. For a second, I think she's praying, but when her head snaps up and her eyes find mine, I realize she was only waiting. Waiting for me.

Her black-lipped smile is brittle and cold, but it is a smile all the same.

"You're late," she says, words light and chiding, as if I've merely overslept and missed the first few minutes of tea.

"Or you're early," I reply, matching her tone. If she's to believe I'm only a figment of her imagination, then I need to act like she expects me to act. It's a strange part to play, but I suppose I've played stranger over the years—I've played helpless, played dumb, played docile. Now I only have to play dead.

She shifts, making room for me on the bench beside her. Though the idea of being so close to her frightens me, I sit. There is only an inch of space between us, and I'm aware of her in a way I've never been aware of a person in a dream— I can feel the warmth radiating from her skin, see the pulse leap in her throat. I wonder if she feels as aware of me, though I hope for my sake she doesn't.

I want to ask about Søren straightaway, but that would raise suspicions, so instead I simply sit with her in silence, waiting for her to speak.

"Do you want to hear the most ludicrous thing?" she asks after a moment.

"What's that?"

"I think I'm jealous of you," she says before laughing. "You're dead in the ground and I'm alive. I'm going to win this war, I have Søren, I have the throne, I have the crown. I have everything and you have nothing—you *are* nothing. And yet . . ." She trails off, shaking her head.

"Is that why you're doing all of this?" I ask her. "Because you're jealous."

She laughs again, but this time the sound is sharper. "You should know me better than that, Thora," she says. "You should know that my father didn't raise me to be led by my emotions. I have a country to run. I have thousands of people depending on me, looking to me for strength. What do you think would happen if I didn't show it to them? How quickly do you think I would join you in whatever afterlife awaits?"

*We both have people depending on us,* I think, and though I don't want to, I can feel myself soften toward her, just a fraction. I push the thought aside and focus instead on the opening she provided.

"What of Søren, then?" I ask her. "Why did you take him if not because you were being led by your emotions?"

"Because he may be a traitor, but he still has the only blood claim to the throne. I need him. For now," she says. "Though he isn't being cooperative."

It's my turn to laugh. "Well, what did you expect, Cress?" I ask her. "That you would drag him back to the palace and he would become your charming Prinz, spouting love poems and threading flowers into your hair?"

Her expression grows sour. "I expected him to have some sense of self-preservation," she says. "Not to sulk in his cell and refuse to eat or drink or speak to me, no matter what I've done to try to . . . convince him."

*His cell.* So he must be in the dungeon. And he's back to the training his father gave him as a child, not eating or drinking when being held hostage. I'm sure they'll force food and water into him sooner or later, if they haven't done so already, but he's making it clear he's a hostage, not apologizing, not begging for forgiveness.

It wasn't until she said it that I realized I was worried he might have done just that. For so many years, he followed his father's orders, even though he knew they were wrong. When he first began to turn toward our side, it was because of me, because he thought he was in love with me and wanted a future where we could be together. Part of me was afraid that now, with him believing me dead, he might go back to who he was before.

But he hasn't. Maybe it was less about me than I thought. Maybe it wasn't really about me at all.

I try not to imagine exactly what she's done to try to convince him. Her father was known for his skill at extracting information and cooperation from prisoners, and the Theyn never had fire at his fingertips to assist him.

"Perhaps he finds his suffering preferable to your company," I tell her.

The thought has already taken up residence in her mind, I can tell, and now she'll hear it again and again in my voice. I hope it drives her mad.

Cress only shrugs. If the thought bothers her, she's careful to hide it. "My father used to say that every person reaches a point where they break."

"I suppose that's true enough," I say. "Though I'd imagine your father thought I reached that point a decade ago, and that mistake killed him."

"I'm not my father," she says. "I don't make the same mistakes—I didn't underestimate you, and I won't underestimate Søren."

She gets to her feet, brushing the ash from the skirt of her gown. Before she leaves, she turns back to me with a sad smile.

"Don't worry, Thora," she says. "Once he's served his purpose, I'll let him join you in death. Won't that be a kindness?"

# BELIEVE

A SCREAM DRAGS ME FROM SLEEP, but it takes a moment to realize that the scream is coming from me. I sit up on my bedroll, out of breath and drenched in sweat, my legs hopelessly tangled in the sheets. The dream clings to the edges of my conscious mind like grains of sand on wet skin—there, but temporary. Already I can feel the details slipping away, no matter how I try to hold on to them.

The tent flap opens and Blaise hurries in, sword drawn, eyes alert and wild. He takes me in, alone and in bed, before relaxing, though he doesn't sheathe his sword.

"What are you doing?" I ask, half-dazed.

"Artemisia needed sleep," he says, sounding out of breath. "I offered to take over as your guard for the night, and then I heard you scream. Just a nightmare?" he guesses, though he doesn't look at me, instead focusing on the ground next to my bedroll.

He's used to my nightmares. He's seen the aftereffects of them since he was one of my Shadows back in the palace. But this wasn't just a nightmare—it wasn't a nightmare at all, really. There was nothing frightening about it, no sense of horror. I didn't see my mother's death, didn't feel my own looming before me. It was only Cress and me, talking in the gray garden like we have a thousand times before. There was a kind of peace to it, almost.

*Because she thinks you're dead,* I remind myself. If she knew I wasn't, she wouldn't be so peaceful. She thinks she's won, that we've reached a kind of truce that has left me with no choices, no voice of my own. The kind of truce that has left me her pet once more.

"I saw Cress again," I tell Blaise, rather than explain all of that to him. The last thing I need is for him to think I'm sympathetic toward her. "She said that Søren is in the dungeon, but she's going to execute him soon."

Blaise lets out a labored sigh, shoulders slumping. "Theo . . . it was a nightmare. That's all." He still doesn't look at me, and when I glance down, I realize why. With all of my tossing and turning and sweating, my cotton nightgown is plastered to my skin, twisted off one shoulder and leaving it bare. I'm sure he's seen me in less—the dresses the Kaiser made me wear in the palace showed more skin—but this is different. The weight of our last conversation alone settles on my shoulders, so heavy that it's suffocating.

I shake my head to clear it, pulling the shoulder of my nightgown back up. "It's not just a nightmare. If you could see it, could feel it, you would understand. I can feel her there, as real as I feel you now."

"It's not possible," he insists.

I bite my lip before telling him about what Artemisia and I learned, about the poison being Cress's blood. When I finish, he's gone ashen. I can't blame him—the thought of Cress's blood in me is one that I doubt I will ever grow used to.

"It doesn't mean anything," he insists. "It doesn't mean you're sharing dreams."

"We don't know what it means," I say. "But Søren is being kept in the dungeon. He's not agreeing to marry her, to solidify her claim to the throne, which makes him a threat to that claim instead. She isn't planning on keeping him alive for much longer. I need you to bring Heron to me so we can get word to Erik."

Even before I finish, Blaise is shaking his head. "No, you can't risk ruining Erik's cover for a hunch that you can't prove. He'll find Søren himself when he's inside the palace."

"There might not be time for that," I reply. "Cress knows Erik. She knows he and Søren are friends; she might even know they're brothers by now. She'll know that it's a large part of why Erik changed sides, and so she'll keep Søren's location from him for as long as she can. She'll bait him with it, use it as leverage to get him to do whatever she needs done."

"You don't know that," he says, shaking his head.

"I know her," I remind him. "I know how her mind works better than anyone else does."

He's quiet for a moment, though he finally looks at me, green eyes meeting mine. "Is it what you would do?" he asks me.

I don't have to think about it for more than a second. "Yes," I say. "It's the smart move to make. She'll know better than to trust a turncoat. She won't bring him into the fold right away. She'll use whatever information and force he brings with him—which won't be much on either count, hopefully—but she won't trust him. He'll be treated barely better than a hostage. And more than that, I can't imagine the Kalovaxians will be keen to accept the Gorakians as allies. She made this truce and so she has to stand by it, but she'll be looking for an opportunity to go back on it. It's the only way she can keep the respect of her people, and that's something she's struggling with as it is."

"Did she tell you that as well?" Blaise asks. It's difficult to miss the mocking in his voice.

Something shifts inside me. My hands grow hot, and though that in and of itself is nothing new, this time it's followed by a loud pop as flames jump to my fingertips, setting the sheets on fire. It happens slowly, then all at once. I quickly extinguish the flames on my hands, and Blaise takes the glass of water from my tray and throws it onto the sheets so that they're put out as well.

A beat passes in silence.

"Are you all right?" he asks me, his voice softer. I should prefer it to his mocking tone, but I don't. It makes me feel like an invalid.

"I'm fine," I tell him, my voice coming out cold. "I asked you to bring Heron to me. You might not agree with me, but I don't need you to."

For a moment, Blaise doesn't move, staring at me in disbelief. Finally, he nods, his face smoothing over into impassiveness.

"I'll find him," he says before hesitating. "Your power is strong, but you don't know how to use it."

My cheeks warm. "Artemisia and Heron are helping——"

"Artemisia and Heron are very good at controlling their own powers, but they don't understand yours, not the nature of it or the strength of it. It is like trying to fit a horse bridle over the head of a moose." He pauses for a second. "I can help, though. You aren't on the edge of mine madness like I am, but in terms of strength, it's closer to mine than theirs, and fire is closer to earth than it is to wind or water."

Annoyance prickles at my skin, though I know he has a point. The few lessons I've had with Heron and Art have helped, but they have never felt quite right.

"You said I would be fine without you," I point out.

He glances away, pressing his lips together. "Maybe you will be," he says. "But I'd like to help if I can."

I hesitate for a second before nodding. He might have hurt me and I might have hurt him back, but I've missed him. "After I speak with Heron," I tell him. "Before we set off toward the Water Mine again. We'll only have half an hour or so, but——"

"It'll be a good start," Blaise says.

When I tell Heron what I saw and ask him to pass the information on to Erik, he doesn't protest like Blaise did. Instead he looks at me with solemn eyes, clutching the *molo varu* in his hand tightly.

"You don't believe me," I say when he remains silent.

Heron shakes his head. "I don't know what I believe," he says. "But I do know that Erik is playing a dangerous game in the palace. If he's caught or the Kaiserin begins to even suspect that he's a spy, he'll be killed. If you tell me that you're sure enough to take that risk, I'll let Erik know. But I'm asking you to be sure, Theo."

I open my mouth to tell him I'm sure, but the words don't come out. I can't lie to Heron, not about this. "I'm not sure about anything," I tell him instead. "I haven't been sure of any choice I've made since I decided to meet Blaise in the kitchen cellar all those months ago. But if I'd waited to be sure, I would still be there, under my Shadows' watch, waiting for a rescue that would never come."

He doesn't say anything at first. "Do you think it's worth the risk?" he asks.

"I don't know how to answer that," I admit. "But I think Erik will find it is. Tell him what I said, at least. Give him the information; let him do with it what he will."

Heron still looks worried, but he nods.

"It'll take some time to tell him everything," he says, looking down at the *molo varu*. It's the size of his palm, its gold surface smooth and unblemished. He nods toward the unlit candle resting on my tray. "Do you mind?" he asks.

I reach for the candle, pinch the wick between my thumb and index finger. The flame comes as naturally as breathing, catching on the wick and turning into a small, steady burn. I release it and shake my hand, extinguishing the fire that clings to my fingers.

Heron sits down beside the candle, turning the *molo varu* over in his hands before setting it down on the tray and digging into the pocket of his trousers. He pulls out a silver needle and holds the tip to the flame of the candle.

"You miss him," I say, breaking the silence.

Heron gives a snort of laughter, not looking up from the candle. "Don't ever tell him that," he says. "His ego doesn't need the boost."

I hesitate. "Erik's all false bravado," I tell him. "Don't take his swagger too seriously. I'm sure he misses you as well."

The tip of the needle begins to glow orange, and he pulls it from the flame, then presses it to the surface of the *molo varu* and begins to write.

When he speaks again, his brow is creased in concentration, his eyes glued to the *molo varu*. "I didn't want to have to miss anyone again, after Leonidas, but some people have a way of forcing their way into your life. When they go, it becomes a void you can't fill," he says before glancing up at me. "But I don't have to tell you about missing people. Don't you miss the *prinkiti*?"

I hesitate. Heron's feelings about Søren are complicated, to say the least. I doubt they will ever call each other friend, but at least they seem to have reached a truce of sorts.

"Yes," I tell him. "Do you think badly of me for that?"

He's surprised at that, the needle freezing on the stone's surface. He looks up at me, holds my gaze. "Why would I think badly of you?" he asks.

"Because missing him makes me look weak," I say. "Because of who he is and what he's done. I know his sins. I know how much blood covers his hands—I know you do as well. But he saw me. He understood parts of me that no one wanted to acknowledge existed. Like you said—he left a void behind."

"It doesn't make you look weak, Theo," he tells me, going back to writing on the stone. "It makes you look human."

I laugh softly. "Maybe. But I'm not meant to be human. I'm meant to be a queen."

"No one's saying you can't be both," he says. He must have finished his message, because he sets the needle down on the tray. "You miss him and you're allowed to miss him, but every time you've had to choose between him and your country, you've chosen Astrea. You always choose Astrea, no matter what it costs you. If that doesn't make you a queen, I don't know what does."

Blaise said the same thing to me—that I always choose Astrea over him. I don't think he meant it as a condemnation, but he's right: what I have left over isn't enough for him. Maybe it will never be enough for any person. Maybe that's the reason why my mother and all of our foremothers never married. That sort of commitment requires more of us than we have to freely give. Maybe being a queen means being alone. The thought leaves me cold and hollow.

# MAILE

I FIND BLAISE ON THE OUTSKIRTS of the camp, a tin cup of coffee in hand. The sun is just barely peeking over the horizon, and most of the camp is only just waking up. We'll have maybe half an hour while everyone gets ready and packs up before we'll set off. But as Blaise said, it will be a start.

"What did Heron and Art teach you?" he asks when he sees me, wasting no time with preamble.

"Fireballs," I tell him.

"Show me."

I take a steadying breath, focusing on a large rock about ten feet away. I summon the fire to my fingertips, and when I throw it, I throw my power with it, just as Artemisia told me. The fire hits the stone before falling to the grass in a clump of ash. It is the same as it ever is, and I think it was impressive, but Blaise frowns at the stone before looking at me with pursed lips.

"That's it?" he asks.

"It's only been a couple of days, a few scattered lessons when we had some time to spare," I say defensively.

"You're aiming too small for the size of your power," he says.

I shrug. "How else would you start out? Heron says that you start small, then grow."

"Normally that's the case, yes," he says. "But when a person's power is as strong as yours—as strong as mine, even—it is more difficult to restrain it to something so small than to use it for something larger." He pauses, searching around the small clearing. "There," he says, motioning to a large tree on the far side, at least fifty feet from where we stand. "Hit that."

"I don't want to kill it," I tell him.

"Rot has already done that," he assures me. "It's all but dead. Go on, hit that. And don't think of it as a ball of fire. Think of it as . . . as a wave."

"A wave," I say slowly, frowning.

"Just try it," he says.

I sigh, turning toward the tree. Then I take a deep breath and let the fire build inside me, gathering in my hands until it isn't only a ball, small and manageable. I let it build until it becomes so great, it feels like it might consume me.

And then I let it go, throwing it like Artemisia taught me, not just with my hands but with my chest, a deadly blast of fire and power. A wave, as Blaise said.

The blast of fire hits the tree, and it erupts into flames, a towering inferno.

For a moment, all I can do is stare at it. I did that. Me. As proud as I am, it also frightens me. This power is inside me, after all.

Blaise brings a swirl of dirt up from around the tree, surrounding the flames and suffocating them before letting the earth settle once more. The tree is blackened and bare now, a skeleton of what it was.

"Better," he says, offering me a rare smile. "How do you feel?"

I'm not sure how to answer him at first. But he's Blaise, and if there is anyone I can be honest with, isn't it him?

"Powerful," I say. "Fearful and fearsome all at once."

He nods. "Good," he says. "Try again."


The sun is fully in the sky when Blaise and I make our way back. Everyone is awake and fed now, and bustling around the camp to get it packed so that we can leave as soon as possible. Dragonsbane sent a pigeon with a message that reached Art early this morning, letting us know that Sta'Criveran ships were spotted heading our way. If we hurry, we'll arrive at the Water Mine a day before they do, and hopefully that will be enough.

After training so hard with Blaise, I can barely keep my eyes open as I help Artemisia pack up the tent. Though I could have done with more blankets and pillows last night, I'm grateful for the sparsity now. There's less to pack, and though drowsiness makes my whole body feel heavy, I'm already anxious to get moving again.

The rest of our camp seems to feel the same way, everyone moving through their assigned tasks in a kind of tense silence, barely looking at one another.

They're afraid, I realize, doubt tying my stomach in knots. They should be afraid—we all should be—but this is the right move to make.

Maybe if I tell myself that enough, I'll start to believe it.

I don't think I can feel worse, until I spot Maile approaching, three tin cups clumsily held in her hands.

"You look like you could use some coffee," she says to Artemisia and me, with a smile that I suppose she thinks is charming, though it mostly just annoys me.

Art seems to feel the same way. She tightens the tie holding our bedrolls to our horse, before looking Maile up and down with a scornful gaze.

"Are you saying we look tired?" Art asks her, each word dripping with derision.

Maile blinks. "Well, we're all tired—"

"Some of us didn't go to bed early to get our beauty sleep. Some of us were up most of the night strategizing. We're fighting a battle in a few days, in case you've forgotten," Art continues, her voice acidic.

It takes Maile only a second to regain her wits. "I offered to help yesterday, if I remember correctly," she says. "You said there was nothing to do."

Artemisia and I exchange glances. Maile has not proven to be anyone's favorite person in the camp. Truth be told, I'm not sure why Chief Kapil sent her to us. She lacks her father's knack for diplomacy, and she hasn't offered up any strategic suggestions apart from insulting Erik and laughing at any ideas the rest of us offer up. As far as I can tell, she's little more than blistering bravado and a hot temper.

I search for an excuse to provide for leaving her out, but Artemisia beats me to it with the blunt truth.

"You haven't been particularly helpful in any other meetings," she says with a shrug. "And since the Emperor is no longer here for you to levy insults at, we didn't think you would get much out of it, either."

That seems to render Maile silent for the first time since I met her, though she recovers quickly enough.

"Well, it's not as if I was wrong about him, is it? He showed his true colors in the end," she says with a smug smile.

I have to bite back a retort. It's important for everyone to believe that Erik truly abandoned us.

"I'm sure your behavior toward him made that an easy decision," I say instead.

Maile stares at me in disbelief. "You can't hold any sympathetic feelings toward him, Your Majesty," she says. "First the Prinz and now the cowardly Emperor? It seems you have a type."

"And it seems you have all of the oafishness of an ogre," Artemisia retorts.

Maile's brow furrows. "What's an ogre?" she asks, before shaking her head. "Never mind. I don't want to know. Do you want coffee or not? It's quite hot, so if you don't mind taking a cup."

Artemisia rolls her eyes and takes two cups, passing one to me. "Don't expect a thank-you," she tells Maile matter-of-factly. "We may like coffee, but we still don't like you."

Maile looks at me. "Is she always so rude?" she asks.

"I don't know what you mean. She's being awfully polite

by her standards," I say with a shrug, bringing the coffee to my lips and taking a small sip. It's steaming hot, with a touch of cinnamon to cut the bitterness. Milk is a luxury we don't have, but the coffee is still good without it. "If Artemisia really didn't like you, she'd introduce you to her sword. We don't seem to be there yet."

"Don't tempt me," Artemisia says, before walking back around to the collapsed tent to continue packing, sipping at her coffee as she goes.

Maile watches her go and then looks back at me.

"I think I'm justified in my hatred of Kalovaxians and my mistrust of those who share their blood," she says. "Besides, the Emperor was fighting with them when they attacked Vecturia."

That catches me off guard. I've thought about the battle at Vecturia often, even held it against Søren for leading his army there and taking countless Vecturian lives. I knew Erik took part in that battle as well, but I hadn't really connected it to him. I certainly hadn't connected it to Maile. Suddenly her behavior toward Erik makes more sense. It isn't an excuse, but I understand her a bit better.

"In many ways, Erik was as much a prisoner of the Kalovaxians as I was," I tell her. "Not following orders would have cost him his life, and there was also the risk that the Kaiser would take it out on his mother."

Maile is unmoved. "He's a traitor," she says. "He was a traitor to the Kalovaxians, and now he's a traitor to you."

I can't argue with that, so instead I force myself to nod. "I don't mean to defend him. I'm just telling you what I know," I say.

"I'd also rather you didn't leave me out of any strategy

meetings in the future. My father sent me here because I've proven my worth in battle, more so than any of my siblings. I can help," she says, her tone sour.

"I hope so," I tell her. "But Artemisia is right—thus far, you've done very little to show that. Mostly you've put everyone on edge."

Maile doesn't say anything for a moment, looking down at the coffee in her hands.

"I don't like that my father sent me here," she says finally. "I don't like that he sent his strongest warriors to help you when it's left us defenseless against any outside attacks. I want the Kalovaxians gone, too, but this isn't our war. We have our own problems. I don't have my father's sense of honor or his sentimentality."

"I didn't ask him for help. He offered it," I tell her. It had been a way to repay me for sending Dragonsbane to protect Vecturia against Søren's army, a way to make up for the fact that when Astrea was besieged by the Kalovaxians all those years ago, he chose not to help.

"I know that," she says. "I'm only saying that it wouldn't have been my choice. But I'm here now and I've got warriors invested in this fight, and I intend to do everything in my power to ensure that I get them home as quickly and safely as possible."

"Then we're on the same side," I say. "And with the Prinz gone, we need as many strategic minds as we can get. It was largely to his credit that we were able to take the Fire Mine with as few casualties as we did. Whatever you might think of him—and you're certainly entitled to your opinions—his advice was invaluable."

Maile shrugs that off. "Prinz Søren can do a lot with a large army. I won't deny that. But it doesn't impress me. He has the numbers and the weapons and every other advantage. I managed to hold him off with less on every front. We'll discuss strategy more tonight, I'm assuming," she says.

I nod. "Considering the fact that we didn't land on any concrete plans last night, we'll have to."

"Bring me in, then," she says. "I'll do what I can to help, and I'm sure you'll find me at least as valuable as he was."

"Fine," I say. "But if you pick any more fights, I'm not going to defend you."

"I don't need you to," she says. "But with the Kalovaxians all gone, I can't imagine that will be an issue."

*Erik isn't Kalovaxian*, I want to protest, but I have to hold my tongue, so I merely nod.

"I thought she was a strange choice of guard," Maile says, glancing over my shoulder to where Artemisia is loading up the horse's saddlebags with one hand, holding her cup of coffee in the other. I certainly couldn't do both at once, but she manages it with an enviable amount of grace. "She doesn't look tough enough to hold off a swarm of wasps, let alone a human assassin. But I have to admit she's surprisingly ferocious."

Artemisia doesn't respond but her shoulders go stiff, and I know she heard Maile.

"If you want to find out how ferocious she is," I tell Maile, "by all means, keep acting like a condescending ass. Though it would be in your best interests to wait until she's not holding a cup of scalding liquid."

For a beat, Maile looks genuinely concerned. Then she

shakes her head. When she walks away, I think I hear her laughing under her breath.

"I don't like her," Artemisia says when Maile is out of earshot.

"Neither do I," I say. "But she's right—we need her."

# WATER

—————◆·◆—————

IT TAKES THREE DAYS TO make the trek to the Perea Forest.
Three mornings of training with Blaise. Three nights of arguing with Maile, Artemisia, and Heron about what to do
when we actually arrive at the Water Mine. The rest of our
troops are lying in wait in the cover of the forest, but our numbers won't be enough to take the mine with pure force—at
least, not without heavy losses that we can't afford.

It would help if we had a better idea of what to expect, but
the more anyone tries to push Artemisia for details about the
mine, the more frustrated she gets.

"I never thought I would be back there," she finally snaps.
"When I eventually left, I tried to put it as far from my mind
as possible."

The only plan we come to agree upon is a flimsy one: hit
their weak spots as hard as we can.

We stop at the place where the Perea Forest meets Lake
Culane, giving our horses a chance to drink, a couple at a
time, while the rest of the army takes cover in the woods.
From the shaded shore, I can just make out the walls of the

camp and the Water Mine on the other side of the lake. Unlike at the Fire Mine, these walls are made of sheets of cold metal—iron, if I had to hazard a guess. It seems to be the Kalovaxians' metal of choice when gold is too impractical. The walls don't look particularly strong, but when I mention as much to Art, she shakes her head.

"That isn't what they're there for. There was no wall around the Fire Mine because it was better protection against fire magic to have miles of sand around it. The wall isn't here to shield from attacks from outside—it's there to smother the water magic of those within."

She stands barefoot, ankle-deep in the lake, the cuffs of her trousers rolled up to below her knees. It's astonishing the change the water has made in her. Summoning water for horses and humans alike took its toll, making her tired and crankier than usual, but now the life has come back to her. She looks at peace, though *peace* is never something I would have associated with Art.

"At least we still have the element of surprise," she says. "If word had reached them, they would have a patrol out. But they don't expect an attack, certainly not from this direction."

"It's too bad we *can't* approach from this direction," I say, frowning. I cross my arms over my chest and survey the lake. "But we don't have the boats for it and we can't get the ships from the ocean here."

"No," Artemisia agrees with a sigh. "But if we *could*, it would make things an awful lot simpler."

"*Simpler* would be a nice change of pace," I say.

"But what about the risk? The complex plans that don't fall into place until a moment before it's too late? Admit it, you would miss that," she says wryly.

I snort. "I really wouldn't," I tell her. "I honestly thought we would have figured something out by now. We're here, the rest of our troops have gone unnoticed, but we still don't know how to attack."

"Never tell Søren I said this, but he knew what he was doing," she says. "He was useful in that, at least."

I glance sideways at her. "You say that like we're going to see him again," I say.

She pauses. "I hope we do. Has there been any word from Erik?"

"No," I say, looking back out at the lake's placid surface. "Heron said he would tell me when there was. There hasn't been any word from Erik at all, though. I think Heron is starting to worry."

"Erik is strong," she says. "And we've got enough problems right in front of us."

I spy a figure making her way down the shore toward us and immediately recognize Maile.

"Speaking of problems," I murmur to Artemisia, nodding toward Maile.

Art exhales, long and low. "Do you think it's too late to pretend we didn't see her and take refuge in the forest?" she asks, and I'm not entirely sure she isn't kidding.

"The least she could have done was bring more coffee," I say, though I lift my hand and wave at her.

"You're awfully diplomatic," Art says, though from her lips it doesn't sound like a compliment.

I want to respond, but Maile is too close now and would doubtlessly overhear.

"I've been looking for you," Maile says to me, though her eyes flicker warily toward Artemisia. "What is she doing?"

"I was *trying* to relax and rejuvenate," Artemisia says, her voice testy. "It isn't easy, you know, summoning water for everyone when I haven't been near it in some time."

"Oh," Maile says, frowning. "I assumed that was just . . . how it worked for you."

"I don't have a never-ending supply," Art says, before wrinkling her nose. "Though I would have offered you a couple of buckets full if it meant you could have bathed. You're riper than a bushel of apples."

"I'll add that to my list of priorities," Maile replies, and turns back to me. "We've sent half our troops to hide in the caves along the shore, and they'll be waiting for further instruction. But I noticed something strange—no guards patrolling outside the wall. And the wall—it doesn't look built to sustain an attack."

"It's not," Artemisia says, explaining to Maile what she'd just explained to me. "They don't expect an attack from outside—their defenses are more aimed at protecting them from their prisoners."

Maile considers this, her eyes sparkling. "Then I think I might have an idea about how to approach without losing the advantage of surprising them."

Artemisia and I exchange glances. "Really?" I ask Maile.

"Yes, but I don't think you're going to like it."

\* \* \*

As it turns out, I approve of the plan, though when we share it with Heron and Blaise, I seem to be the only one who does.

"You want us to hide," Blaise says to Maile slowly, crossing his arms over his chest. The sun is low in the sky now, just grazing the horizon. Blaise had Griselda use her gift to build a campfire while Heron used his own gift to dispel the smoke in the air to avoid drawing attention. Now, though, we stand a bit away from the camp we've built, with Heron keeping an eye on the smoke in the air, waving a hand and using his gift to dissipate it whenever it starts to thicken.

"No," Artemisia says with a scoff. "She wants us to be *distractions*." The word drips with derision.

Maile holds her ground. "This is not a war that will be won with the gifts of four people, as talented as you might be."

"Twelve," Blaise corrects. "Including the Guardians we liberated from the Fire Mine."

"My point stands. Of the twelve of you, you three are the only ones with any substantial training," Maile says, motioning to Blaise, Heron, and Art.

"Theo's been making a lot of progress these last few days," Blaise offers. "She could hold her own in a fight. And Laius and Griselda are some of the strongest I've ever seen."

"Strong, but not stable," Artemisia adds softly.

"And four is not much better than three," Maile says, before she motions to me. "And she's too valuable to risk losing on the front lines of battle. As soon as you show the Kalovaxians what you are—what you can do—you'll become their target. The rest of us will be an afterthought."

"So instead," Blaise says slowly, "you would rather we hide in the woods."

"Instead," Maile counters with a surprising measure of patience, "I would rather you hide in the woods *and* cause them as much trouble as you can. While they're running around trying to figure out what's happening behind them, we'll storm through the front gate and attack with the brunt of our force. It won't buy us much of an advantage, but it's something."

"You want us to be distractions," Artemisia says again.

Maile looks to me for help. "It's not *just* a distraction," I say. "We'll be attacking from another direction, just from afar. I've seen the three of you use your powers at such a scale that we'll still be able to help. Heron, you can throw a windstorm at them. Artemisia, you can buy our troops even more time. This close to the water, you can summon waves to hit at the mine's walls. You said yourself—they aren't built to withstand an attack. We might not be able to send men across the lake, but that doesn't mean we can't attack from here in a different sense."

That makes Artemisia grin. "One big wave would certainly be enough to destroy the walls, and a good chunk of the camp as well."

"We do need to remember that there are innocent people in the camp—more innocent people than there are guards," Heron points out mildly.

"Right. Small waves, then," Artemisia says, looking put out.

"And, Blaise," Maile continues, "I heard that you destroyed three ships from a greater distance than we'll be at."

I wince, remembering how Blaise used his gift to rip the Kalovaxian ships outside the Fire Mine apart plank by plank, how the effort very nearly destroyed him—destroyed all of us—until Artemisia knocked him unconscious and saved his life.

"That may not be the best example to use," I say.

What we're talking about—the distance, the scale—it requires a good deal of power. Too much power. Again, I imagine a pot boiling over, the way Mina described Guardians like Blaise, Laius, and Griselda, whose powers aren't quite stable, though they aren't quite berserkers, either.

My stomach ties itself in knots. Before he destroyed the ships, he said that he wouldn't push himself if I asked him not to. Now, though, I don't think I could stop him.

"You'll leave after supper," I tell Maile. "There's a narrow part of the lake just to the west of us that is shallow enough to wade across. Take our soldiers to join up with the others. The twelve of us with gifts will stay and start our attack just before dawn. As soon as we begin, you'll attack as well."

Maile nods, eyes measuring me in a way I don't appreciate. I can't help but feel that she's keeping a running tally in her mind about me, and I'm not sure what to make of that. "Which means you should eat now," I say pointedly. "And bathe. Artemisia's right—you are starting to smell."

# STRIKE

——•——

MAILE LEAVES WITH HER LEGION as soon as the sun sets completely, wrapped in the cover the darkness provides. I stand on the shore with the others, watching them go. I wonder how many I'll see again. Suddenly I wish I'd gotten to know them better. I think I spoke to only a handful of them, and even so, their names and faces blur together in my mind.

Søren remembers the names of those he has killed, even nine years removed. Even if we have the numbers to win this battle, we won't do it without casualties. Their blood will be on my hands. And I don't even know their names.

I turn away and walk back toward the small camp we set up—just a scattering of bedrolls under the open sky, and a dead fire.

Twelve of us total but even that seems like so many. Besides my friends, I know only Griselda and Laius, and the two of them have been too frightened of me to mumble more than a few words in my presence. But it's more than I've heard from the other six. Two men and four women, their ages difficult to surmise. Some might be teenagers, others could be in their forties, but the years of malnourishment and physical labor make them all look both older and younger. Sallow skin and skittish eyes and hair already threaded with gray. Their arms are more scar tissue than unblemished skin, not unlike my back. I suppose that no matter how old they are, they've all lived through far too much pain and suffering.

And yet, here they are. Lining up to risk still more.

Artemisia and Heron sit together near the dead fire, bowls of lukewarm stew in hand, the *molo varu* between them, still smooth and unchanged. Heron waves me over, but I shake my head. I don't feel like I'm good company just now, and I certainly don't think I could keep any food down. Instead I walk around the perimeter of camp, crossing my arms over my chest to ward off the humid chill in the air from being so close to the lake.

The woods are peaceful, the murmur of voices from the camp barely loud enough to be heard over the sounds of crickets chirping and the wind ruffling the leaves overhead.

"You do remember that you have the Fire Gift now, right?" a voice says, startling me. I turn to see Blaise sitting at the base of a tree, cross-legged. Though I know he's speaking to me, his eyes remain downcast, focusing on the dirt gathered in the palms of his hands. I watch silently as he levitates it from one palm to the other and back again. A child's party trick, nothing useful, but his hands don't shake at least. When I step toward him, he looks up at me. His eyes remain his own and the dirt falls back to the ground.

"I don't want to waste my gift," I say. "I'll need all the fire

I can spare for tomorrow. You should try to restrain yourself as well."

He shakes his head. "We're surrounded by earth, and that alone recharges me, but even if we weren't . . . it doesn't work that way for me," he says. "Like a well that can go dry. The power is just . . . me. It doesn't run out."

"*You* run out, though," I say, but he only shrugs.

"We don't know that for sure, do we?" he says. "We've never tested that theory."

The way he says it—so offhandedly—unnerves me.

"Tomorrow," I say slowly, "I'm going to hold on to your gem. We won't need your gift."

He exhales slowly, eyes dropping away from mine again. "Theo, we're at war," he says. As if I don't know that. As if I ever have the luxury of forgetting that. "I have no illusions of living to see the end of it, and I don't care that I won't. As long as you're on the throne at the end, I'm happy to watch on from the After."

I sit down beside him, careful to keep a proper distance between us. I want to argue with him again, to tell him the same thing again. I need him. I can't do this without him. I don't know what to do if he's not here.

But suddenly I'm not sure how true that is. I love Blaise, and I know that I would feel his absence like a hole in my chest for the rest of my life—a void, as Heron said. I don't want to lose him. But I don't need him, not the way I did a few months ago. Back in the Astrean palace, he was my tether to a life I barely remembered and to the person I wanted to be. But now I'm here, I'm standing, I'm Queen Theodosia, and

I know who I am. I may want him, but I don't need him the way I used to.

"I love you, you know," I say.

"I know," he says.

The words hang between us, neither comforting nor wounding, just a fact that, while undeniably true, doesn't mean as much as it should in comparison to everything else. I wish it did. I wish saying those words stopped time and put everything in the world right once more. I wish they had the power to save him and Astrea and even me, but they're only words. They don't do anything.

"I'm keeping your gem, but I'll have it if we need it. It's a last resort," I tell him after a moment. "If we need you, we need you. But we won't. Not tomorrow. As long as we distract them long enough for Maile to get enough warriors through the gate, it'll be an easy battle to win. There's no use sacrificing yourself for it."

He doesn't reply for a moment, but finally he nods, keeping his eyes focused straight ahead. His dirt-streaked hand inches toward mine before he thinks better of it and brings both of his hands to rest in his lap. "It's a last resort," he says, his voice level and sure. As if we're talking about what we're having for dinner instead of his death.

When the sun bleeds over the peaks of the Dalzia Mountains, Heron and I make the first strike. I spin a ball of fire in my hands, stretching it bigger and bigger until it's larger than my head, before I throw it across the lake with all of my might. It shouldn't make it more than a few feet, but that's where

Heron comes in, sending a gust of wind strong enough to carry it but gentle enough to keep it aflame. Instead of burning the fire out, the air nourishes it, growing it even larger, so that by the time it finally hits the wall of the camp, the sound of the impact echoes through the woods behind us like a clap of thunder.

For a moment, the world is quiet. The ball of fire spreads slowly across the wooden cross supports of the wall, melting the iron as it goes. Then, all at once, chaos erupts. Shouts pierce the air, carrying over the surface of the lake, loud but indecipherable. Water falls over the burning parts of the wall but it's too far away to tell what—or who—is the source of it.

"Again," I say, my voice firm. I look to where Griselda stands beside me and nod to her. Though she and Laius, like Blaise, are pots close to overflowing, he vouched for their control. Theirs hasn't been pushed to the edge yet, the way Blaise's has been. Today won't require much effort from them; it won't be too much.

A smile blooms on Griselda's wan face as she summons her own ball of fire, holding it between her hands just as I did, before she hurls it across the lake. Again, Heron guides it to hit the target—the south corner of the wall, far from where the Kalovaxians have gathered.

More shouts. More panic. But before they can put out that fire, the other six Fire Guardians throw their fireballs, and Heron pushes the balls toward the target until the entire wall is aflame.

"They'll need some water to put those out," I say, looking at Artemisia, who grins. Beside her, Laius looks more nervous than excited, but he manages a small, tight smile as well.

I've seen Art in battle before, seen the light that comes into her eyes, the way she fights like she's not entirely in her body. This is different—it's personal.

With the grace of a dancer, she lifts her arms over her head, and Laius mimics her movements, watching her to make sure he gets them just right. The once-placid surface of the lake rises as well, higher and higher, until it blots out the sky overhead.

"Careful," I say to them. "There are innocent people there. Many of them in chains. You don't want to drown them."

Artemisia gives a huff, and they reluctantly lower the height of the wave. "Where do you want it?" Art asks me.

"North wall," Blaise says, before I can. His interruption annoys me, even though it's exactly what I would have said.

Artemisia looks to me for confirmation and I nod.

With force, she and Laius bring their arms down, falling into matching crouches and slamming their hands to the ground. As they do, the tall wave crashes down as well, destroying the northern wall.

The chaos multiplies, and through the holes that Griselda and I melted into the iron wall, I see figures running to and fro in a panicked frenzy.

Blaise steps toward me but I put a hand out, rest it on his arm.

"Not yet," I say, though I feel the weight of his Earth Gem heavy in the pocket of my dress. "They're distracted enough."

As I say it, a new sound joins the cacophony, a single battle cry that repeats a thousandfold.

"Our warriors are coming through the gate now,"

Artemisia says. "We've distracted them, but it'll only work as long as we seem like the larger threat."

"Well then," I say. "Let's threaten some more. Fireballs again in five, four, three . . ." I summon another fireball along with the others, except for Griselda, and again, Heron carries them over the lake, igniting one of the few intact parts of the wall.

"Another wave, Artemisia," I say, my voice winded.

Art nods, though she looks worn as well. These are not the easy tricks we've gotten used to practicing. This is larger, heavier work, and it is taking its toll. Laius is unfazed and I know that he could easily summon more water, but like with Blaise, I don't want to use him more than necessary. As Art brings up another wave, I look at Heron, who is doubled over, hands on his knees, catching his breath.

Raising her arms once more, Artemisia summons her strength, and the lake rises for her, spiraling into a tall spindle. It reminds me of a sword's blade, thin and sharp and precise. She doesn't ask where to aim it, but I know she's thinking about the armory in the very center of the camp.

"Can you do it?" I ask her quietly.

Her concentration is focused on the spire of water, but she nods once, her expression drawn tight and sure. I open my mouth to remind her of the others, of what will happen if she misses, but I quickly close it again. She knows what will happen. She knows the risks. If she's sure of it, I have to be sure of her.

"Do it," I say.

She doesn't need to be told twice. As soon as the words

are out of my mouth, she's bringing her hands down again, eyes closed tightly and hair writhing wild around her shoulders, tips flashing a blinding blue. When her hands hit the ground, the sound of it rings in my ears so that I can't hear anything else. All I can do is watch as the perfect spiral of water arcs over the iron wall to the center of camp, the tail of it following.

By the time my hearing returns, the lake's surface has gone placid once more, as if nothing happened at all, but I know that's not true. Water is flooding out from the camp, pushing its way through the fractured bits of leftover wall, pulled back to the lake.

Beside me, Artemisia is crumpled, on one bent knee, hands braced on the ground as her shoulders heave with each labored breath.

"Did you do it?" I ask her.

With some effort, she lifts her head, her wild eyes finding mine. "There's no way to know until it's over and we can see for ourselves."

I nod, surveying the rest of our group. Apart from Blaise, Laius, and Griselda, everyone looks winded. Those of us with the Fire Gift could do more, but without Heron to carry our flames across the lake, there isn't much good in it.

"That's it, then," I say. "Let's gather our things and head for the rendezvous point. Whoever meets us there should have an update for us."

"I can do more," Heron says. "We'll send more fire."

I shake my head. "Artemisia has drenched most of the camp by now—there's not much that would catch. And what little more we *could* do would not be worth having to drag your unconscious body over there. No, we've done all we can."

"Not all we can," Blaise says, his voice quiet and on edge, like the air before lightning strikes.

"You were our last resort," I say, my hand slipping into the pocket of my dress. I know his gem bracelet is there, but suddenly I need to reassure myself of its presence. The hard, cold metal of it is a comfort, its edges digging into my palm as I grip it tightly.

"There's no sign that we need you," I say. "Maile didn't give the signal, which means she got her army in without incident. Once they're in, the camp is ours. Especially with Artemisia destroying their armory."

"*If* she destroyed their armory," Blaise says, taking another step toward me. There's something unfamiliar in his eyes, something wild and desperate.

"Maile hasn't signaled for more help, so there is no reason to believe your gifts are needed," I say, keeping my voice calm.

"Or Maile is dead. Or she's otherwise occupied trying *not* to die. Are you willing to pin Astrea's hopes on one person's ability to do what she said? On *that* person's ability to do what she said?"

I cast my gaze around at the others, finding ten pairs of eyes watching me warily. Though she's drained of energy, Artemisia still looks ready to force herself between us if she needs to, but I don't want it to come to that. I grip the bracelet tighter in my hand.

"Don't talk to me about Astrea's hopes," I say. "I'm perfectly aware of what's at stake and who I trust. Maile knows battles. This is not her first. If she needed help, she or one of her warriors would have sent the signal. I know that you're eager to sacrifice yourself for your country, but I'm afraid it's going to have to wait for another day."

For a moment, Blaise is frozen in place, but there is something in his eyes that unsettles me, a frantic urgency, a glazed distance. It is not so different from the way he looked when he stood on the deck and destroyed the Kalovaxians' ships—like he wasn't quite himself. He doesn't even seem to see me—all of his attention is focused on the gem in my hand, his expression focused and starving.

"It's my gem and my choice and I'm choosing to fight," he says, his voice fracturing around each word.

"Blaise, you promised me," I say, careful to keep my voice level. I'm not sure what has come over him, how he can be verging on an outburst without a gem. It scares me, and I'm not the only one. Artemisia and Heron are watching him warily, neither of them seeming to breathe, while the others look merely bewildered.

Blaise doesn't say anything to that, and for an instant, I think I've won. I think I've gotten through to him. But before I can even exhale in relief, his hand snakes out toward me, toward the hand holding his Spiritgem, and latches on. I try to pull away from him, but his hand is clasped around my forearm, the skin of his palm scalding hot.

Berserker hot.

"It's mine," he says, but he doesn't sound like him, not entirely. He sounds feral and not quite human, too desperate and hungry and angry to be the Blaise I know. Yet he is.

"Blaise," I say, but he doesn't respond. His grip on my arm is painfully tight, his fingers digging into my skin. I cry out, but he barely seems to hear me.

"I can feel it," he says, tugging hard at my arm, trying to drag my hand—and the gem—out of my pocket. "I need it, Theo."

Before I can respond, Blaise is yanked away, his hand wrenched away from my arm. The imprints of his nails remain on my flesh. When I look up, Heron is holding Blaise, arms pinned behind his back while he tries to jerk himself free. Tired as he is, Heron can barely keep a hold on Blaise.

"You have to knock him out," I say, but the words don't feel like they belong to me.

Heron's eyes meet mine, and though he looks anguished at the thought, he nods. He fights to get the palm of his hand flush against Blaise's head, but as soon as he does, Blaise's body goes slack, falling to the ground like a marionette whose strings have been cut.

Even that small bit of power takes its toll on Heron and he sways on his feet. Artemisia hurries to his side and helps to keep him upright, though she looks unsteady herself.

For a long moment, no one moves and we all stare at Blaise. The others look frightened—and understandably so. Blaise's condition wasn't known to anyone but Art, Heron, and me, but now it will be difficult to keep it quiet. And to them, it must look an awful lot like mine madness.

Truthfully, I'm not so sure it's not—that the line between whatever he is and a berserker hasn't been too blurred to keep them separate.

"By the time he wakes up, he should have recovered his wits," I say loudly, glad my voice doesn't waver. "I'm sure he will feel quite embarrassed about this outburst."

Even to my own ears, the words sound insufficient. When I look around at the others, they seem wary and uncertain, except for Griselda and Laius. Neither of them looks at me. Instead their gazes are focused on Blaise's unconscious form. Their mentor, their teacher, their future.

# BRIGITTA

M AILE MEETS US AT THE rendezvous point herself. She's
already waiting at the place where the lake, mountain
range, and forest all meet, standing alone, slumped against
a tree with her arms folded over her chest. When she sees us
approach, she straightens up, a giddy grin spreading over her
face, but it quickly fades when she notices Heron carrying an
unconscious Blaise.

"What happened?" she asks. "Were you attacked?"

I glance at the others, expecting someone to jump in, but
the ten of them are silent, waiting for me. Though Blaise
might have frightened the other Fire Guardians, he's still the
one who's led them and trained them and supported them
over the last few weeks. Though they don't know what to
think of him now, they know that he is still one of us. They
know that if anyone else finds out what happened, they might
try to hurt him. So they hold their tongues, and for that I'm
grateful.

"He overexerted himself," I say, but that only makes
Maile's frown deepen.

"How?" she asks. "There were no earthquakes. Fire and

waves and hurricane winds, yes, but nothing remotely earth-related."

I force a dismissive shrug. "It didn't make it past the lake," I lie. "He tried as hard as he could to get it there, but . . . well . . ." I trail off, nodding toward his unconscious form. "But it turns out it was unnecessary. I'm assuming we took the camp?"

Maile nods, her grin returning. "As soon as we made it through the gate, it was easy enough. Especially once their armory was destroyed," she says, turning her gaze on Artemisia. "Well done."

Art is thoroughly unaffected by Maile's praise. "And civilian lives?" she asks.

"There were some injuries," Maile admits. "But they all look to be easily treatable—nothing fatal. We already have some healers making their way around. We had some casualties on our side, but all in all, we made it through with far more warriors than I was anticipating. In large part thanks to you lot."

"And how many Astreans were there?" Heron asks.

"I didn't exactly take the time to count," Maile says. "But I'd guess about the same as the Fire Mine, more or less. Enough that we'll be able to take the next mine with ease, so long as word doesn't reach the capital before we get there. We shouldn't stay here for more than a day."

I frown. "We came here to intercept the Sta'Criverans. Is there any sign of them?"

"I have scouts waiting in the cliffs that overlook the sea, but so far no word," she says. "Are you sure you want to risk staying for this? We don't even know what they're trading."

"We know it's important to the Kaiserin," I say. "That's

good enough for me. But there's no reason for all of us to stay. You should continue on with half of our troops, meet us back where we camped in the Perea Forest—there are a couple of villages not far north of there that could use liberating. As long as you don't get caught—"

"We won't," Maile interrupts. "Are you sure you want to be here with diminished numbers when the Kalovaxians and Sta'Criverans arrive?"

"Leave me the Water Guardians, and I'll be just fine," I say.

Maile nods once. "We should bring Water Gems with us," she says, and though her voice is conversational, the idea stops me in my tracks.

"Gems?" I ask. "Why would we do that?"

She shrugs. "There are quite a lot of them stockpiled in a storeroom. If I had to guess, well over a thousand gems. It's power we could certainly use as we go forward."

It takes a moment for me to understand what she's saying, what she's suggesting. Artemisia understands quicker than I do, though.

"You suggested the same thing at the Fire Mine, and you were told no," she says, her voice soft but with a dangerous edge to it. "Those gems are not to be misused by people who aren't meant to wield them. The answer hasn't changed now, and if you prove foolish enough to ask a third time—"

"I expected the sentimentality from Heron," Maile interrupts. "But the two of you are too practical for that. Those gems can be the extra weight we need to tip this scale. You can't put superstition over logic."

"What are you talking about?" I ask, their argument sinking in. "What gems at the Fire Mine?"

Maile and Artemisia exchange looks but Artemisia speaks first.

"We found them when you were in the mine—an underground stockpile with hundreds and hundreds of gems. There was a discussion about what to do with them. Some—like Maile—thought we should use them in battle, the way the Kalovaxians do, that it would level the playing field. Others disagreed."

"Heron," I say. Of course he would have disagreed—I'm not sure what I believe as far as the gods go, but Heron believes in them absolutely. He believes that someone who hasn't been gifted by the gods shouldn't use a gem, the way the Kalovaxians do. That it's sacrilege. "Who else?"

"Blaise, me," Artemisia says, and then pauses. "My mother as well. And though you weren't there to speak for yourself, we all knew how you felt about the gems. How you refused to use one yourself until . . ." She trails off, her eyes falling on the Fire Gem pendant around my neck. Ampelio's gem.

"So what was done with them?" I ask her.

"We left them where they were," Artemisia says, shrugging. "Sealed the entrance to the underground storeroom so no one could get them."

I nod. "Good. We'll do the same thing here."

Maile frowns. "But—"

"It's a settled decision," I say. "One that has already been agreed on."

"It's superstition," she says.

"Maybe," I say. "But it's one that Astreans believe. And Astreans still make up the bulk of our troops. If our beliefs—our superstitions, as you so condescendingly put it—are disrespected, people will begin to rebel. We cannot be splintered now, not with Goraki already gone."

For a second, Maile looks like she wants to argue, but Artemisia speaks before she can.

"Astrea was conquered for those gems," she says, her voice soft. "Many of us were forced to pry them from the earth until our fingers bled and our minds became frayed at the proximity to them. Nothing good will come from distributing them widely."

Maile nods, but she still looks annoyed. "There's something else," she says after a second.

"I swear to the gods, if you don't let it go—" Artemisia says.

"Not that. Something else."

A frown tugs at my mouth. "A good something else or bad?"

Maile rubs the back of her neck. "Hard to say, to be honest. Perhaps it's better to show you than to try to explain. Follow me."

I remember seeing the Water Mine only once before the siege, before it was a mine at all and was just a cave with a temple standing, tall and proud and shining, around it. Those memories are distant and faded at the edges, but I remember the priestesses in their pale blue silk gowns that flowed around their bodies like water. I remember my mother standing in front of the temple, small and humble before it. I remember thinking it was the most beautiful place I had ever seen, even more beautiful than the palace.

But that temple hasn't stood for ten years now, and the camp the Kalovaxians erected in its place could never be called beautiful. Its layout is similar to that of the Fire Mine camp, with rows of barracks that resemble blocks of gray stone— one of which Heron carries Blaise to, where he can rest until he wakes up. The Fire Guardians disperse to the dining hall, the twin of the one at the Fire Mine. We even pass the same Fire Gem–infused iron gate that surrounds the area where the Guardians and berserkers would have been kept. I want to ask Maile how many people she found there, but I can't form the words. My mind is too busy turning over what she could possibly be leading me to.

Artemisia is quiet as well, though I'd guess that she's less distracted about where we're going than about the camp itself. I wonder how it looks through her eyes, years after she thought she'd left it behind for good. I wonder if she's searching the faces of the former slaves we pass, looking for someone familiar. If she finds anyone, her expression doesn't give it away.

"Are you all right?" I ask her, softly enough that Maile can't hear.

She turns her dark eyes to me, though it takes her a moment to focus. "It's strange," she manages finally. "Being back here. The girl I was when I left is not the girl I am now, but I can't help feeling like her all over again. I don't care for it."

"That girl survived," I remind her. "That girl became strong enough to save the other people here."

Her smile is sad. "Not all of them, though," she says. "How many do you think have been killed since I left?"

"Their blood isn't on your hands, Art," I say. "It's on the Kalovaxians'."

"I know that," she says, her hand idly finding its way to the hilt of the dagger at her hip. "And I'm ready to make them pay." She quickens her pace to catch up with Maile. "How many guards are left alive?"

Maile glances at her, uncertain. "A hundred or so," she says. "We're holding them in a couple of the barracks, under heavy watch. We thought they'd be more valuable alive than dead."

Artemisia looks put out at that, but she quickly recovers. "For now, maybe," she says. "I want to see them after this. Wherever you're taking us. Where are you taking us?"

Maile glances over her shoulder at me before looking forward again, nodding toward a building I recognize as the commandant's office, just next to what must have been the armory, though there's little left of it now. Artemisia's aim was certainly precise.

"There were a couple of people here we were . . . surprised to find, to say the least."

"Kalovaxian or Astrean?" I ask her as she opens the door and ushers us inside.

"Neither," she says.

It takes my eyes a moment to adjust to the dim lighting, but when they do, I have to stifle a gasp.

There are two people waiting, their hands bound behind their backs. The man looks Gorakian, with the same golden skin and dark hair as Erik and Hoa, but the woman—at first glance, I think it's Cress. She has the same porcelain doll's face, the same gray eyes, the same yellow hair wound into two braids that hang down to her waist. But this woman is older, her expression lined around her eyes and mouth. Though her face is thinner than Cress's, it's softer somehow—at least, softer than Cress's has been the last few times I've seen her. Instead this woman resembles the Cress I used to know.

There is something else about her, something familiar that prickles at my memory.

"Who are you?" I ask her, ignoring the Gorakian man entirely.

The woman's eyes search my face, recognition sparking in her eyes. I don't know her, but she knows me.

"My name is Brigitta, Your Majesty," she says, lifting her chin. Her voice is like Cress's used to be, too, melodic and soft, but the kind of voice that demands to be heard.

It takes me a moment to place the name, but when I do, the world shifts beneath my feet and I remember where I've seen her before—a small painting, no bigger than my thumb, that Cress kept as a charm on one of her bracelets, a token of her dead mother, who, I found out later, wasn't dead at all.

Brigitta is the name of the previous Theyn's wife, the woman who ran away with a Gorakian man before the Kalovaxians came to Astrea. Brigitta is the name of Crescentia's mother.

# TRAP

---•---

BRIGITTA'S HANDS SHAKE AS SHE brings the porcelain teacup to her lips before replacing it upon its saucer with a rattling clink. We're alone in the commandant's office, her hands unbound, though Artemisia is waiting outside in case Brigitta tries anything foolish. I don't think that will be an issue— there is not much fight in the woman. Even now, dressed in a rough-spun cotton shift, with weather-beaten skin and frizzy hair barely contained in its braids, she looks every bit the Kalovaxian noblewoman she was raised to be.

"Where did they take Jian?" she asks, gray eyes settling on mine.

Jian must be the name of the man she was with. The man I assume she left the Theyn for.

"We thought it best to question you separately," I say. "To ensure you're both being truthful."

She arches her blond eyebrows the same way Cress does. "Truthful," she echoes. "We were being held here, prisoners as much as the others."

It isn't that I don't believe her. All signs say she's telling the truth. But sitting across from her now, I can't help but think about Cress, about one of the last conversations we had as friends, when she told me that her mother had left her. I can't help but wonder how different things would have been—how different *Cress* would have been—if she hadn't.

"You can't blame us for taking precautions," I say instead, sipping my own coffee. "You are Kalovaxian, after all."

I expect her to protest, but she only lifts a shoulder in a shrug. "What would you like to know?" she asks.

There are so many things I want to know. Why did she leave Cress? What has she been doing in the last decade? Who is that man—Jian—to her? Why is she here? But those are not the most pressing questions to ask.

"Have you had any contact with your daughter since she became Kaiserin?" I ask.

She blinks, surprised into silence for a moment. "How do you know who my daughter is?" she asks.

I consider lying, but I don't see what that will get me. "She told me her mother left her, ran off with a Gorakian man. I knew her mother's name was Brigitta. And I've seen a miniature painting of you—Cress wears it on her bracelet. Besides, you look just like her."

She flinches from the name like it was a physical strike. Her eyes drop from mine, focusing instead on her hands.

"I've had no contact with her since I left," she says, her voice wavering. "I've heard things about her, how she's faring, over the years, but she's heard nothing from me. I thought it would be better that way. . . ." She trails off, shaking her head. "No. That's a lie. I kept my distance because I feared her father would use any communication I sent her as a way to find me, and Jian. I've spent the last twelve years looking over my shoulder, waiting for the day he did."

At that, I feel a pang of sympathy. After all, I know something about fearing the Theyn. The man was a constant fixture in my nightmares for a decade.

"The Theyn is dead," I tell her.

Her smile is grim. "Yes, I heard that. I suppose I owe you a debt of gratitude. He was not a good man."

"I'm well aware," I say curtly. "You still left your daughter with him easily enough."

"There was nothing easy about it," Brigitta says, her voice taking on a sharp edge. "I left her because I had to. You must believe me, it was the best thing for everyone."

"I have a hard time imagining how it was the best thing for her," I say. "You let him shape her, raise her into a monster. If you had stayed, she would be a different person now."

"If I had stayed, the world as you know it would be little more than a pile of ash," she says sharply.

When I'm too surprised to respond, she shakes her head.

"What was the rumor?" she asks me. "That I left my husband for another man? That I fled the Kalovaxians for love? Maybe there is some truth in that—I did love Jian, *do* love him. I wouldn't have left my child for that, but it was an easier rumor to spread than the truth, I suppose."

"And what is the truth?" I ask her.

She smiles, but there is no mirth in it. "You'll forgive me if I don't trust you, Queen Theodosia, but I've seen how power corrupts, and what people are willing to do when they become desperate."

I want to disagree, but I know there is at least some truth in her words. "I can't help you if you don't help me," I say instead.

She considers this for a moment, lifting her teacup to her lips to take another sip.

"Are you familiar with alchemy, Your Majesty?"

The word is familiar, but only distantly. It's a Gorakian practice, a blend of science and magic that created the *molo varu*, among other things.

"Vaguely," I tell her.

"Jian was considered the best alchemist in Goraki before the Kalovaxians came. As with your Spiritgems, the Kalovaxians wanted to find a way to use alchemy for their own gain. My husband, the Theyn, took Jian into his household, where he could be watched, studied. Where his skills were to be used to create weapons that the world had never seen before. Jian refused, of course. For years, he gave them only trinkets, little bits of alchemy that were just enough to keep him alive—swords that could cut through anything, even muscle and bone, cannons that never missed their targets, a battering ram with the strength of a thousand men."

My mouth goes dry. "I've never seen weapons like that," I tell her.

She smiles. "You wouldn't have. Jian was smarter than the Kalovaxians thought, and alchemy isn't like your Spiritgems. It is more akin to a living thing—it needs tending to, nurturing, in order to last. In a matter of months, the weapons he created were useless."

"I imagine the Kalovaxians weren't happy about that," I say.

"No," she says, anguish flashing across her face. "But in those few months, the Theyn had set Jian to creating a new kind of weapon, one that would only need to work once, but that would have the power to bring thousands to their knees. Quite literally."

I sit up a little straighter. "What weapon?" I ask.

She doesn't answer right away. "Jian called it *velastra*. In Gorakian, the word's combined roots mean something close to *dream taker,* but there's a translation error. In Gorakian, a dream isn't only something that happens when you sleep, or even a distant hope for the future. It's closer to the soul itself, to *want.* Created properly, velastra takes away a person's wants, their desires—their dreams."

My mouth goes dry. The Kalovaxians have always had their slaves, but it seems even chains are not enough for them.

"How?" is the only thing I can think to ask.

She shakes her head. "A gas—expanding to fill whatever space it can, but a single inhalation is enough to render a person little more than a marionette. Their lives will revolve around the smallest suggestions made to them: clean the kitchen, take off your clothes, jump off a cliff. The victim would have no choice. Jian figured the formula out quite quickly, all things considered, but he kept it from them. I only discovered he knew by accident—I caught sight of some of his scribblings, and he didn't realize that I understood enough Gorakian or science to make sense of them. We both knew what a dangerous weapon it was, that Jian couldn't keep it from my husband forever and that when the Theyn discovered it, the world would crumble. So we hatched a plan to escape."

"That was why you left Cress," I say.

She hesitates, then nods. "I left Cress to protect the world," she says. "It was not an easy decision, but it is one I stand behind."

"And Jian still knows how to make velastra?" I ask.

She pauses. "If you had the chance, Your Majesty, to bring the Kalovaxians to ruin in a matter of moments, would you take it?"

"Of course," I say, without hesitation.

"You could, using the velastra. Take away a person's autonomy, their choices, what makes them human," she says, tilting her head to one side. "Would you do it?"

That gives me pause. On the one hand, it's hard to imagine there is anything I wouldn't do for my country, but that? I was the Kaiser's puppet for ten years, though even when it felt like I had no choices, I did. That was the only reason why I was eventually able to say no, to stand up, to escape. If he'd had access to velastra then . . . The thought of it makes me sick to my stomach. I'm not sure I would wish that fate on even my enemies. "No," I tell her after a moment.

"I might believe you," she says. "But, you are still only one woman, queen or not, and I'm unsure the others in your rebellion would feel the same. I won't risk it."

I almost protest, but then I think of Maile, who I don't doubt would use such a weapon if she could. Heron wouldn't, I know that, but I'm not sure about Artemisia. And the other leaders who aren't here, Dragonsbane, Sandrin—what would they do? No, Brigitta is right. Jian should keep it to himself. Whatever it is, it's dangerous, and Cress cannot be allowed to get her hands on it.

"So you left to keep the plans for this weapon away from the Theyn, away from the Kalovaxians," I say. "But that doesn't explain why you're here."

Brigitta takes another sip of her coffee. "Jian and I settled in Sta'Crivero a few years ago—not in the capital. A small, nameless village near the eastern coast. It seemed easier to avoid attention that way, though I suppose a Kalovaxian woman and a Gorakian man will draw attention no matter where they go. One of our kind neighbors alerted the King to our presence in exchange for extra water rations sometime last month. They've had us ever since."

Something clicks into place in my mind.

"You're part of the exchange," I say. "You're the reason Prince Avaric is coming here in person—to oversee your trade for . . . what? The Water Mine? King Etristo must think her a sentimental fool, trading so much for a few hundred troops and her mother and the lover her mother abandoned her for. He likely has no idea who he really holds."

At that, she shrugs.

"Speaking as little Sta'Criveran as I do, I couldn't understand everything my captors said. But it seems King Etristo and my daughter reached an agreement after he warned her and the Kaiser about your plans—and yes, that's the gist of the trade. Sta'Crivero gets access to the Water Mine in exchange for troops to help quash the Astrean uprising once and for all. Capturing me and turning me over to my daughter is meant to be the King's gesture of good faith ahead of the official trade, which Crescentia and Prince Avaric are meant to seal in person just outside the mine. Jian and I were sent early with a small group of guards to validate our identities with a Kalovaxian guard who had been part of the Theyn's household in Goraki. Crescentia's scout left just a day before you arrived."

My heart drops. "Cress is coming here," I say slowly, having trouble wrapping my mind around anything else she said.

"Yes. This evening," Brigitta says, brow furrowing in confusion. "Didn't you know?"

I shake my head. I knew about the Sta'Criverans, I knew about the trade, I even knew about Prince Avaric coming in person to seal the treaty. Maybe I should have known that Cress would come in person as well, but the Kaiser always hid behind the palace walls, always sent others to do his bidding. He would never have risked his own life coming to meet a stranger whose loyalty he couldn't rely on.

Or maybe I did know, deep down. Maybe I just didn't want to accept it. Maybe I knew I wasn't ready to face her again.

"She won't be coming alone," I say finally, looking up at Brigitta. "She would be a fool to meet a foreign prince and his army with only her guards. She's not a fool. She'll be coming with an army. A large one, I'd imagine. The Sta'Criverans worked against her so recently, she won't trust them. And besides, she'll want to show off so they never think of crossing her again."

We came to the Water Mine expecting to ambush a simple trade—we aren't nearly prepared to step into a full-blown war.

"We could run," Maile says, breaking the silence that's hung over the commandant's office for the last few minutes.

Barely a moment after Brigitta's revelation, Maile stormed back into the commandant's office, Heron and Jian following in her wake. Jian had told them the same thing Brigitta had told me. We called for a guard to bring Jian and Brigitta somewhere secure, and surmising that her presence was needed as an advisor more than a guard, Artemisia joined the rest of us in the office, closing the door firmly behind her.

We just got word from the scouts that ships are visible on the horizon now and they'll be here before sundown.

"We can't run," I say, my voice level even though fear is coursing through my veins, hot and panicked. "We have a Sta'Criveran army approaching offshore to the south and the Kalovaxians coming from the north by land. With as many people as we have—many of them still injured or malnourished—we won't be able to move fast enough to avoid getting caught in between."

Maile doesn't back down, though. Her eyes meet mine, hard and sure. "We can run," she corrects me. "Us and the people who can keep up."

"You can't be serious," Heron says, spitting the words out.

"I'm not saying it's ideal," she says. "But I won't be shamed for suggesting the only reasonable way out of this. Some of us can survive this, or none of us will."

"It isn't as if we would get far," Artemisia puts forth. "Once the Kalovaxians arrive and see the mess we've left, they'll follow us, and since the only way to avoid detection and keep from running headlong into their army is to travel around Lake Culane, they'll catch up with us in a matter of hours."

Their bickering continues, but I barely hear it. This attack was my idea. I'm the one who read the situation wrong, who didn't get enough information before making a decision. Perhaps I should have waited, but that might have left us still at the Fire Mine, waiting and vulnerable.

I turn over what Brigitta said before. Cress will be here tomorrow, and she and her army expect to find the Water Mine in its usual condition. They will meet with Prince Avaric to seal a deal, and then both parties will be on their way once more. It's such a lot of fuss for such a short meeting. If only there were a way to drape a curtain over the mine, to hide that we've been here.

As soon as the thought occurs to me, an idea follows on its heels.

"How many Water Guardians do we have?" I ask, but my words are drowned out in the bickering. I clear my throat and try again, loud enough to be heard.

Maile looks at me as if she forgot I was here. She shakes her head. "Twenty," she says.

"Actually, none," Artemisia says. "No *trained* Water Guardians. Twenty people with raw power but no training."

"Twenty, though," I say slowly. I think of what Artemisia has done on her own, then multiply that by twenty. I understand what she's saying. I understand the difference, I do, but I also remember what I could do even before I started my training. My power was a wild, untamed thing, yes, but it was strong. And we don't have any other options.

"We aren't going anywhere," I say to Maile before looking at Artemisia. "And we aren't fighting, either. With the number of troops Cress will have with her, and our own forces recovering from this morning, it is a fight we would lose. So instead we're going to hide in plain sight and wait for this to pass. Then we will continue on our way without the Kalovaxians any the wiser."

"And the Sta'Criverans?" Heron asks.

"We can take them out before they even set foot on shore. They aren't experienced warriors, and they are less experienced sailors. With the help of a few Fire and Water Guardians, we can destroy the fleet."

"That's all well and good, but the Kalovaxians will still find a destroyed camp," Maile says.

"No they won't," I tell her. "They'll see the camp exactly as it was, exactly as they expect to. And Prince Avaric and the Sta'Criverans will be on the shore, waiting and ready to strike a deal."

The others frown, confused, but Artemisia meets my gaze. "You're talking about using untrained Guardians," she says. "You know better than most, Theo, how raw power is different from trained power."

"I do," I say. "And under different circumstances, I wouldn't suggest it. But as it is, I have to ask: Can it be done?"

She hesitates before nodding. "In theory, yes."

"In theory will have to be good enough."

"And what about the trade?" Heron asks. "Cress wants Jian and Brigitta, but if what Brigitta told you is correct—"

"She can't have Jian," I say, shaking my head. "Whatever happens tonight, that much I know. We'll tell her he died on the journey here."

"She won't be happy about that," Artemisia says.

"I'm sure she won't be," I say. "But I'd rather deal with her temper than put that weapon in her hands."

"And Brigitta?"

I hesitate, biting my lip. "If we don't have either of them, she'll grow suspicious," I say. "And Brigitta isn't dangerous to trade. Cress's interest in her is sentimental, not strategic."

"She'll kill her," Heron points out.

She will, I know, but not right away. I'm sure Cress has more in store for her. Perhaps I'll retake the capital before Cress can kill her; perhaps it won't make a difference. But Brigitta was right: I am a queen, and I will do what needs to be done.

"We'll trade Brigitta, but the Kalovaxians cannot be allowed to find Jian. If this plan doesn't work . . ." I trail off, but Artemisia catches my meaning.

"They may take the rest of us, but they won't take him alive," she says.

# STORM

H ERON WORKS ON HEALING THE Water Guardians as quickly as possible while Maile herds the former slaves and anyone injured in battle into their barracks, where they will remain out of sight until the Kalovaxians leave.

While those preparations are being made, Artemisia, the other Fire Guardians, and I make our way to the seashore, a couple of miles from the camp.

"Could you kill her if you had to?" Art asks me as we walk.

I look at her, surprised. I don't have to ask who she's talking about.

"That's not part of the plan," I say. "Today we just need to survive and keep their army from growing. Killing Crescentia would accomplish nothing. If we do, someone else would take her place quickly enough. I'd guess the nobles have had contingency plans ready since the Kaiser died. Longer, even—if my dreams are to be believed, she already thinks they're planning some kind of coup. We just need to survive this so that we can win another day. Sometimes surviving is enough."

I don't realize I quoted the late Kaiserin until the words are out of my mouth.

"If you had to, though," she asks again, and I realize what she's actually asking. Not whether I physically could do it—I'm not sure either of us really knows the answer to that—but whether I could stand before the girl I once called my heart's sister and end her life.

I open my mouth to say that yes, of course I could, but no words come out. It's easy to remember that Cress is my enemy when I think of her as she was the last time I saw her in person, but the Cress in my dreams—or whatever they may be—has her claws in me as well. Could I kill Cress?

I don't reply, but Artemisia must hear my answer anyway because she doesn't press it.

The sun is high in the sky by the time we make it to the shore, where we linger in a copse of cypress trees, out of sight from the Sta'Criveran ships lying in wait about three miles offshore. It's hard to tell their size from this distance, but I have to assume they're large enough to carry not just Prince Avaric and his guards, but also the army he promised Cress.

"They won't come closer until it's time to meet," I say. "But if they see Kalovaxians on the shore with prisoners, they'll assume the Kaiserin arrived early, and we can lure them in."

Artemisia nods. "Into positions," she says, loud enough to be heard by the Fire Guardians.

The eight of us cluster into two groups, six of us to be Kalovaxians and the other two to be the Sta'Criveran guards who escorted Brigitta and Jian. Facing us, Artemisia closes her eyes and lifts her hands, weaving them through the air in a set of intricate patterns. As she does, it feels as if a net of air falls over us, covering us head to toe. Finished, Art opens her eyes and nods once.

"You'll do from a distance," she says.

I look at the others in my group, their tawny skin now pale white, various shades of dark hair turned blond. She took my own appearance a step further, altering my plain shift into a flowing gown of slate-gray silk, though when I touch the material, it still feels like cotton.

The others stare at me, their eyes lingering on my neck. The skin there feels like my own skin, but I assume Artemisia changed that too. She made me into Cress, or a close enough approximation. The Sta'Criverans have never met Cress, but they must have heard enough stories about her.

"You're wearing a crown as well," Artemisia tells me. "You have to hold your head like it."

"How close are we letting them get that they can see that?" one of the Fire Guardians asks—a woman named Selma.

"Not too close," Artemisia says. "But they'll have telescopes. More advanced versions than the ones you're used to. I don't want to take any chances. That's why I wanted to see the bodies of the guards, since they're the only ones who might be recognized."

I glance at the two Fire Guardians designated for those roles and have to restrain a gasp. While the others retained their own faces with different coloring, these two have been changed completely. I didn't go with Artemisia when she went to inspect the bodies, but I can still tell she did a thorough job of it.

"You have to do yourself as well," I say. "With your hair, you'll be recognized instantly by anyone on board who met you at the palace."

Artemisia's eyes narrow, but she nods. She closes her eyes

again, and this time I watch as her own appearance ripples like the surface of a lake, shifting and changing. When she's done, she looks like any Kalovaxian shieldmaiden with ivory skin and golden hair cut bluntly at her jaw.

"Good," I tell her. "Now it's time."

We file out in a procession. When we reach the shore, Artemisia waves her arms in the air so wildly, she looks ridiculous.

"What are you doing?" I ask her.

"To them, it looks like I'm holding a Kalovaxian flag," she explains.

At first, nothing happens, but then the ships begin a slow trudge forward. We could fire on them now, but without Heron to use his Air Gift to drive the fire farther, there's a significant chance we would miss and then the ships would flee. No, we have to ensure that all six of them sink. Otherwise, they'll come back, and we have enough to worry about at the moment.

We have only the one chance, so we can't fire too early, but if we wait too long, we run the risk of Artemisia's magic fading. That can't happen, either.

Again I wish Søren were here. He would be able to tell us exactly how close the ships would come to shore before dropping anchor. He would be able to anticipate exactly how the crew would react to the attack. But instead he's locked in a dungeon.

An eternity stretches out around us as the ships inch closer, painfully slow. I know that I need to wait, but fire itches at my fingertips, begging to be used, and it's all I can do to hold back. The others are growing restless as well, fidgeting and talking among themselves. The sun overhead beats down on my shoulders, hot and heavy.

"All right," Artemisia says. "They're too close now to turn away. The tides are on our side."

The ships are closer than the camp was from the other side of the lake, but not by much. I would feel better if Heron were here again to guide our fire, but he's too weak now. That kind of effort would fully drain him. I swallow my doubts and brace myself, drawing my hands up. The others do as well, following my lead.

Artemesia drops our disguise, and I let the first ball of fire fly, throwing it as hard as I can at the closest ship, but it misses by fifty feet at least, landing in the ocean with a splash and a sizzle. My heart sinks like lead.

The others around me try, but though some get closer than I did, no one manages to hit a ship. Seeing the attack, the ships begin to panic. From this distance, I can make out crew members running, can hear the dim shouts of captains giving orders. To turn around, I imagine. To flee. The tides are on our side, Artemesia said, but if we can't reach the ships, tides won't help us much.

"Art!" I shout, a new idea taking shape. "Bring those ships closer. Wreck them on the shore if you have to."

Artemisia acts before the words are fully out of my mouth, slashing her hands violently through the air. She throws her arms wide before bringing them in front of her and pulling them into her chest. As she does, a wave rises behind the fleet, then rushes forward and pushes the ships with it as if they were no more than child's toys floating in a bath.

"Again!" I shout to the other Fire Guardians.

This time, when I throw a ball of fire, it strikes true, hitting the front ship's hull with a thwack that echoes across the expanse of sea. Fire catches the hull and begins to spread quickly.

Many of the other Fire Guardians' blows find their targets as well, though a few fall harmlessly into the sea instead. Enough hit to cause damage. The lead ship is already sinking.

I glance at Artemisia, winded and doubled over, hands on her knees.

"Can you do it again?" I ask her. "We can't have any survivors."

She looks up at me, still out of breath, but her eyes are hard and determined. She nods, straightening and squaring her shoulders.

"If you weaken them more, I'll finish it," she says, her voice tired but sure.

I nod and ready myself for another strike, aware of Ampelio's Spiritgem glowing and hot around my neck. I focus my energy on the front ship and throw another ball of fire toward it. The sails catch fire this time, quick as tinder.

Fireballs fly through the air one after another, thrown by the other Guardians. After that, not a single ship remains unlit. They burn bright against the afternoon sky, and crew members begin to jump off, abandoning ship before they, too, end up burnt.

People. Sta'Criveran sailors who are only following orders, only doing what their king told them to do. People with lives and families.

People, I remind myself, who are standing between Astrea and her freedom.

"Now," I tell Artemisia, my voice coming out more level than I feel.

She doesn't hesitate. This time, the wave she builds is bigger than any I've seen from her, taller than the highest tower in the palace, taller even than some of the spires in the Sta'Criveran capital. When she brings it crashing down, screams pierce the air, loud enough to deafen, loud enough to shake the very earth.

But when the waves turn calm once more and floating planks of wood are the only remnants of the Sta'Criveran fleet, there are no more screams, no more shouted orders, no sound at all apart from our own labored breathing and the erratic pounding of my heart.

*Guilt* is not the right word for what I feel as we trudge back to the camp under a heavy blanket of silence. I'm not a stranger to guilt—how it gnaws at your insides until you feel sick with it, how it plagues your nightmares until you think you'll go mad. This is not that. Thousands of people are dead by my hand, on orders I gave, yes, but I have no regrets about it. If I had it to do over again, I wouldn't hesitate to do exactly the same.

*"I'm tired of death,"* Søren said to me when we first escaped Astrea, and though I didn't fully understand him at the time, I do now. Because that's how I feel. Tired. So tired that I feel the exhaustion deep in my bones. I could sleep for a thousand years and still feel it, I think.

I'm tired of death, yes, but tired of fighting as well. Tired of leading. Tired of making difficult decisions. Tired of bearing the responsibility for those decisions.

One day, maybe I won't feel it anymore. I'll be able to wake up in a world not smeared with blood. I'll go a whole day—maybe a whole week—without worrying that my people won't live to see another sunrise. I'll be able to make choices without life-and-death consequences attached. What to have for breakfast. What color dress to wear. Who to dance with.

In all of my questing for victory, I never yearned for the simpler life that would come along with it, but now the idea makes my whole body ache with want.

# ILLUSION

———◆•◆———

B Y THE TIME WE RETURN to the camp, the bodies have been cleared away but most of the buildings are still waterlogged and burnt, the ground still blood-soaked. I've never seen what kind of illusions a group of Water Guardians can accomplish, but I hope it's enough to make this place appear whole again to the Kalovaxians when they arrive.

In all of the chaos of people running about, preparing, Blaise is the only person standing still. He leans against the wall of one of the barracks, arms crossed over his chest, in fresh clothes. His eyes are heavily shadowed—more so than usual—and his skin is sallow even in the afternoon sun. When his eyes meet mine, I hold his gaze, but neither of us makes a move toward the other.

Eventually we'll have to talk about what happened to him, about the feral, desperate energy that came over him, like a drunk fighting for just one more sip of ale. How he grabbed my arm so tightly that I can still feel the ghost of it. How he disobeyed a direct order and could have killed not just himself but all of us in the process.

I have tried so hard to keep him close, to protect him

however I can, to try to save him. But I can't control Blaise; I can't control what he does. I can't help him if he won't let me. His wanting to destroy himself is not something I can fix, but I can ensure he doesn't drag the rest of us with him.

I tear my gaze away from Blaise and look at Artemisia instead.

"I'm going to find Heron," I tell her. "You check in with the Water Guardians and see how they're doing. We need them as strong as possible by the time the Kalovaxians arrive. And find Laius," I say. "Just don't ask him to do anything too strenuous."

Artemisia nods, but her eyes are distant. I wonder if all of that death has taken its toll even on her. She looks like she wants to say something, but holds back. Instead she turns away from me and looks at the group of Fire Guardians.

"Get some rest," she tells them. "We may need you again if this plan doesn't work."


I find Heron in the commandant's office, guarding Brigitta and Jian, whose hands have been bound once more. When I first see them, I want to protest, before realizing it's the right call. They have no loyalty in this war, no reason not to sneak away while we're busy. And if we don't have at least one of them, there's no telling how Cress will react.

"You're going to turn us over to her?" Brigitta asks me.

I meet her eyes for an instant—the same cold gray as Cress's—before looking away and nodding. It's better for her not to know we'll be separating them. I don't think Brigitta has any reason to be working against me, but I don't trust her, either. It isn't personal—I don't trust many people anymore.

"We have no choice," I say. "She wants you both for a reason, and she wants it enough to come here personally."

Brigitta looks to Jian, who murmurs something to her. "She'll torture us," she says.

I hesitate before nodding. "Yes," I say.

Brigitta considers this and exchanges a few more words with Jian.

"He says he's stronger than he looks," she translates. "We won't tell them anything."

Easy words, but I doubt they know what Cress is capable of.

"We will retake the capital," I tell her, infusing my voice with a surety I'm not sure I feel. "When we do, we'll free you. I'm not sure how long it will be—weeks, months—but we will free you."

Brigitta frowns. "Why are you telling me this?" she asks.

"Because," I say. "When I was held by the Kaiser, tortured and tormented, the only way I persisted was by believing that one day, someone would come for me. No one made me any promises, but I'm making you one. We will take the capital back. I will free you. But I will be able to do so more quickly if your daughter continues to believe I am dead."

Understanding flashes in her eyes, and she nods once.

"I will keep the secret as long as I am able," she tells me.

It's as much as I can hope for. And besides, if Brigitta does tell her under pain of torture, I'm not sure Cress would believe her. It would seem too outlandish, something Brigitta was making up to save herself.

The thought makes me sick. I can't look at her anymore or I will go mad with guilt. Instead of dwelling on her and Jian, I move away, toward Heron, who is still holding the *molo varu* in his hands, focused on its smooth gold surface.

"No news from Erik?" I ask him quietly.

He looks up at me only long enough to shake his head before focusing on the stone once more. "Nothing in four days, Theo," he says, his voice rough. "Something's wrong. I know it."

"You don't know it," I say. "He's likely just waiting until he has news to share. With Cress gone, there must be precious little information worth sharing."

Heron meets my gaze again. "If Cress is gone, and her best soldiers with her, why hasn't he taken the opportunity to free Søren?" he asks. "If everything is truly fine, there would be no better chance."

To that I have no reply. My stomach ties itself into knots at the thought of Erik caught, of him joining Søren in that cell or worse—dead, his head on a pike just like the Kaiser used to do to traitors. The way he did to Ampelio.

"He's fine," I manage finally, but it doesn't sound convincing even to my own ears.

Before Heron can respond, the door to the office opens and Maile steps in, then closes the door firmly behind her.

"We sent scouts north, to see how far away the Kalovaxians are," she says, wasting no time. "We heard back moments ago—they'll be here before sundown."

"They'll be planning on spending the night," I tell her. "We should draft a letter in Kalovaxian urging the Kaiserin to return to the palace, to convince her to leave as soon as possible. Tell her the nobles are planning a coup. She'll believe it easily enough, and she's already paranoid. She would ride day and night in order to get back there to stop it, and she wouldn't give her men any choice but to accompany her."

Maile nods. "Consider it done."

A question lingers on my lips. It's not something I want to ask Maile. I can imagine what she'll say, and I doubt it will be what I want to hear. But that's all the more reason why I need her answer.

"Will this work?"

Maile considers it for a moment that seems to last an eternity.

"I don't know," she admits. "But it's the best plan we have."

Hardly reassuring, but at least it's honest. I'll take that over blind optimism any day.

"It's a rigid plan, though," I say carefully. "There is no room for unpredictability."

"No," Maile says, brow furrowed as she tries to suss out my meaning.

I look between her and Heron, biting my lip. "Blaise has become an unpredictability," I say.

Heron lets out a long exhale, though he doesn't look surprised that I'm bringing it up. "What would you have us do?" he asks.

"When we evacuate those who are too weak to face a fight if it comes to it, he should go with them."

"He won't go easily," Heron points out.

"I know. I trust that you will do what you have to do to keep him safe and out of the way."

It isn't a command, not exactly, but Heron gives one sharp nod.

On my way out of the office, I nearly run into Artemisia and Laius, standing in front of the door, ready to come in. Artemisia blinks at me for a second before lowering her arm.

"One more thing to discuss," she says. "About Brigitta and Jian."

I close the door and lead them down the walkway. "I don't like turning her over, but we have to," I say. "Of the two of them, he's more valuable—we can't let the Kalovaxians have access to a weapon like the velastra."

"I'm not arguing that," Artemisia says. "But the Kaiserin must know about the velastra. She wouldn't have given up the Water Mine easily, and you said it yourself: the Sta'Criveran army isn't—*wasn't*—very strong. When we don't have him, she'll be angry. As unpredictable as she is, the whole plan could fall apart."

"It's a rigid plan," I agree, the same thing I just told Maile and Heron. I shake my head. "But I would rather risk her fury now than put that weapon in her hands. The rebellion can rise again—you told me that once. But if the Kaiserin has the velastra, there will be no rebellion, not from anyone, ever again."

Artemisia doesn't say anything for a moment, looking at Laius, whose mouth is pressed into a thin line as he stares straight ahead with heavy brown eyes.

"But if there was a way to give the Kaiserin both Brigitta and Jian, while not giving her Jian at all? No risk of raising her suspicions or inciting her temper? A way to ensure that she and her troops are long gone before she realizes anything is amiss?" she asks. When she sees my confusion, she turns her gaze to Laius. "Go ahead. Tell her what you told me."

Laius swallows. He looks so young—sixteen, maybe—but that's only a year younger than I am. He's the same age I was when I killed Ampelio, when Blaise came and offered me a chance to fight back. He has that look about him now, the look of someone ready for a fight. That is what scares me, even before he speaks.

"I've gotten good at disguising myself," he says, his voice level. "I can hold an illusion on myself for long periods of time. It doesn't drain me the way it does the others, and with Blaise's training, it doesn't make me lose control, either. It's not big enough magic for that."

I frown. "What exactly are you saying, Laius?" I ask him.

"The man, Jian, he has information the Kaiserin wants. Information we don't want her to have," he says. "So send me in his place. I don't know anything."

"No," I say, almost before he's finished talking. "Absolutely not."

"I'm not a child, Your Majesty," he says. "I'm not naive. I know what life has in store for me. I saw what happened . . . what happened to Blaise. That is my future. I know that I don't get to see the end of this war. But if I can help in ending it, that will be enough."

"We aren't only talking about your death, Laius," I say. "We are talking about torture first, about her trying to pry information from you however she can, until you wish for death."

He doesn't say anything for a moment, pulling his bottom lip between his teeth. Finally, he looks at me, his eyes somber.

"Did you wish for death, Your Majesty?" he asks quietly.

"Pardon?"

"We've all heard the stories of the things you endured when you were held by the Kaiser, how he tried to get information from you that last night, how you were tortured both physically and mentally. How you persisted through it and that's the only reason I was freed, the only reason we are here at all today."

For a moment, I can't speak. I remember standing in the throne room, watching as my own blood trickled to the tile below, knowing that death was inevitable but that I would do everything I could to protect the rebellion. I remember how Elpis made the same choice when she swallowed the last of the Encatrio and burned up from the inside before my eyes.

*He's too young,* I think, but he's not. He's the same age I was. He's older than she was.

I look at Artemisia and find my own thoughts mirrored on her face.

"Are you sure, Laius?" I ask him, my voice low. "You need to be sure."

He considers it for only a second before nodding. "I'm sure," he says. "For Astrea, I'm sure."

# TREATY

———•———

IT IS A STRANGE THING, to wear Princess Amiza's face. I barely remember what she looks like, only having met her briefly in Sta'Crivero, the night we first arrived. She didn't speak much, except to ask about the punishments I'd suffered at the hands of the Kaiser. Artemisia must have gotten a good look at her at some point, though, because when she shows me my reflection in a small hand mirror, I recognize the Princess's face at once.

When I look down at my bare arms, they're the same burnished bronze color as King Etristo's daughter-in-law's.

"I could only do so much," Artemesia says, giving me the once-over and taking the mirror back, tucking it into her pocket. "So try to remember that you're a twenty-something-year-old woman who's led a soft life. All curtsies and fluttering and grace."

I wish I could remember more about Amiza, but I only met her the one time. Suddenly it strikes me as strange that I never saw her again, but perhaps, like the rest of the pretty things in their possession, the Sta'Criverans kept her for display only, never letting her do more than look beautiful and birth heirs.

I hope that she wasn't really on one of those ships with Avaric.

"You don't have to do this," Heron says, though he doesn't look like Heron. Instead he wears Avaric's face. He was the only one tall enough to pass as the crown prince, and he hesitated for just a second before agreeing. He didn't want me to take the risk with him, though. He urged me to evacuate with the others, to keep Blaise calm when he woke up from the magic-induced slumber I asked Heron to put him under.

"I need to see her," I say, though even to my own ears, that sounds foolish. I shake my head. "I don't know how to explain it. I just . . . if someone is going to face her, it needs to be me. Besides, I know her better than anyone, how she'll react to certain things, what she'll want to hear. It needs to be me."

After the Kalovaxians are spotted approaching, Heron and I set out to meet them, bringing a handful of disguised Fire and Water Guardians with us, including Artemisia. When Art took Brigitta to relieve herself earlier, Heron and I switched Jian and a disguised Laius. Jian was understandably confused and panicked, but time was of the essence, so Heron had to use his gift to knock him unconscious. Jian was taken far from camp after that, across the lake to where the infirmary has been set up. The guards stationed there have orders—if the plan goes awry and it looks like the Kalovaxians are going to take the camp, Jian will be killed before the Kalovaxians can get to him.

The thought horrifies me, but not as much as Cress's having access to velastra.

So now Brigitta and Laius are bound together, both gagged. The gagging seemed unnecessary at first, but I don't trust Brigitta any more than she trusts me. I don't know what she'll say to Cress, or how she will react when she learns Jian is no longer Jian. All I can do is hope that Cress and her men are long gone before Brigitta's gag is removed.

I don't know what is going on in Brigitta's mind, but her steps never falter. Her gray eyes—the same as Cress's—stay focused straight ahead. There's nothing I can do for her, I remind myself, but it does little to ease my guilt.

I focus on holding myself like Amiza would, hands clasped delicately in front of me, shoulders squared, head bowed. Delicate and deferential.

Heron seems to be having a harder time pretending to be Avaric. He looks decidedly uncomfortable, unsure of how to stand, what to do with his hands. It's lucky that Cress has never met Avaric. Besides, no one has any reason to suspect imposters. We are barely one step ahead of the Kalovaxians, but we are still ahead.

We stop a good half mile away from the camp in hopes that we can keep the Kalovaxians from setting foot in the camp at all. The other Water Guardians are ready to disguise it if Cress's soldiers do enter, and I arranged for the letter I wrote to be delivered as soon as we have need of it, but I would rather it not come to that.

It's only a moment before the cluster of horses approaches, pulling a single golden carriage. Fifty guards, I would guess. A good quarter of a mile behind, I can make out the army she brought with her, though I can't begin to count how many warriors there are. Too many, certainly, if it comes to a fight.

I can't imagine they were brought to serve much purpose except to intimidate the Sta'Criverans and remind them who holds the reins in this partnership.

The guards dismount in what looks like a single choreographed motion, one stepping up to the carriage to open the door.

Cress emerges slowly, each move a deliberate show of power from the instant her heavily jeweled hand extends from the carriage, glinting in the late afternoon light. When she does finally step out, her silver silk gown pools out around her in a glittering puddle that makes her look ephemeral. She made no effort to cover the charred skin of her throat with cosmetics or cloth, instead bearing the wound with pride.

Her cold gray eyes take Heron and me in, raking over us from our heads to our feet before her mouth curves into a tight-lipped smile.

"Prince Avaric," she says, her voice melodic but loud enough to carry over the distance that separates us. "Princess Amiza. I'm so glad that you could make the trip yourselves. How were your travels?"

She lifts her skirt and steps toward us, her two strongest guards not even a half step behind her.

I wait for Heron to speak first, but when he says nothing, I step forward and smile, holding my hand out.

"The seas are lovely this time of year," I say, pitching my voice a few notes lower so that she doesn't recognize it. "It was a fine voyage and quite worth it for the splendor of the Water Mine."

Cress's pale eyebrows arch high. "Have you already seen

it, then?" she asks, looking put out. "I had hoped to show it to you myself."

"We arrived earlier than expected," Heron says, finding his voice. "Your men were quite hospitable. The mine is everything we hoped for and more."

"I'm glad," Cress says. "And as to your own part of our bargain . . . Are my ships waiting?"

Heron nods once. "Just off the coast. Send your men to see for themselves, if you like."

Cress turns over her shoulder and nods at a couple of her soldiers, who quickly mount their horses once more and take off toward the coast, where they will hopefully find a fleet of ships, or rather, the illusion of one. Several of the Water Guardians we found will be on the shore to hold the illusion in place and disguise the wreckage from the real ships.

"And it will be enough to eradicate the rebels at the Fire Mine?" she asks, turning back to Heron.

Heron's nod is jerky. "As soon as we're done here," he continues, saying the line we practiced. "I'll give the order to bring them there. Between your troops and mine, I'm sure we can wipe out this infestation of rebellion once and for all."

"I certainly hope so," Cress says with a brittle smile. "But I'm afraid I'm finding rebellions to be like cockroaches—there are always a few survivors. Speaking of which, where are the cockroaches you brought me?"

It takes me a second to understand what—or rather, who—she's talking about. "Ah," I say, snapping my fingers and gesturing to the Guardians behind me.

A disguised Artemisia brings Brigitta and Laius forward,

bound and gagged. Laius stumbles a bit, and I have to stop myself from cringing. Even though he wears Jian's face now, I can almost see beneath the illusion to the boy he is, a boy making his way toward certain death. But his gaze doesn't waver. His shoulders are square, his head held high. Still, I want to stop it, to pull him back, to call off the plan. But it is too late now. I can't stop his sacrifice, but I can make certain it isn't in vain.

Beside him, Brigitta eyes her daughter like she is seeing a ghost—and I suppose she is. The ghost of the child she left, the monster that girl became. Does Brigitta feel regret now, or is there only fear left?

Cress barely glances at Jian, her eyes lingering on her mother. Her smile widens and her eyes glint with cold joy as she steps toward the woman. Cress is taller than her mother by a couple of inches, and I wonder what Brigitta thinks about that, about the woman standing before her and how different she is from the small girl Brigitta left behind.

"Mother," Cress says, reaching out to touch her mother's cheek. Brigitta flinches from the touch, from the burning fingers that leave delicate trails of red behind on her skin. "We have so much to catch up on."

Cress jerks her head toward the guards, and two of them step forward to pull Brigitta and Jian toward them. The guards replace the prisoners' binds with heavy iron chains, though they keep the gags on.

"What will you do with them?" I ask her, letting my voice waver, as Amiza's surely would.

"Some wounds are deeper than others," Cress says, glancing at her mother one last time before looking back to us, her gaze lingering on me. "Some wounds demand to be repaid without delay, by your own hand. Surely you have some idea what I speak of."

I do. I understand her need for vengeance so much that it frightens me, but Amiza doesn't. Amiza doesn't hold those sorts of grudges; she doesn't have those sorts of wounds. Cress must realize this, because she shakes her head.

"You must think vengeance is ugly," she says with a small smile. "I envy you that. I did, too, once. Shall I bring out the other part of our bargain?"

I struggle to hide my excitement. *The other part of our bargain.* I was right. There was something more to the arrangement, something worth Prince Avaric's coming all this way personally.

Gold is of little value to the Sta'Criverans, but the Theyn had an extensive collection of art and relics that they might find valuable. Perhaps that's it.

Cress snaps her fingers, and one of her guards opens her carriage door once more. At first nothing happens, but then the guard reaches in and roughly drags out a figure wrapped in so many chains that he can't move so much as a finger. His hair is so matted in blood and dirt that it's difficult to tell the color, and his face is a mottled mess of bruises and broken bones, but I still know him as surely as I know my own name. *Søren.*

The guard throws him roughly to the ground before reaching into the carriage again and pulling out another chained figure, this one slightly less roughed up, though his face is still marred by cuts and bruises, with a thick strip of white cloth tied to cover his eyes. Still, I know him right away, and with a sinking stomach, I realize why Erik hasn't sent us a message. Suddenly it seems foolish to have expected anything else.

I told Heron that Erik was fine, that he was likely just too busy saving Søren to write. But I must have known deep down that wasn't the case. Seeing him now, like this, feels like a punch to my gut.

I push past the emotions, focusing on the reason. Why would Etristo want Søren and Erik, and why would Cress be willing to give them up? The first answer comes quicker—Søren was arrested in Sta'Crivero for murdering the Archduke. It didn't matter that he was innocent. King Etristo believed him guilty, and that was enough to doom him to execution. The Sta'Criverans give no leeway with crimes of any kind. Etristo must have been furious when Søren escaped. And Erik . . . well, maybe Etristo thinks that Erik broke Søren out. Or maybe Erik is wanted merely because he's Gorakian—that seemed to be crime enough in Sta'Crivero.

"Wonderful," I manage to say, my voice coming out level. "King Etristo will be very pleased to have these criminals back in his dungeons."

Cress's eyes are dispassionate on Søren and Erik before she looks back at me. "I suppose," she says. "Though keeping them alive seems to be a waste of resources that Sta'Crivero can't spare, if you ask me. Better to kill them now, save yourselves the trouble of carting them back. They are horribly misbehaved prisoners, in my experience. The Emperor made a deal to align Goraki with me but had the gall to try to steal Prinz Søren the night he set foot in my palace." She pauses, tilting her head to one side thoughtfully. "Of course, I was already planning to give him to King Etristo as a peace offering, but still, it was terribly rude."

"I wish we didn't have to bring them back alive," Heron says, shaking his head. "But my father was quite insistent about it."

Cress lets out a dramatic sigh. "I suppose I understand," she says. "I'm sure your father is looking forward to seeing their deaths firsthand, or else he would have asked for their return to him dead or alive."

"It is the way of Sta'Criveran justice," I say, remembering what I was told upon first entering the city. It's a struggle to tear my gaze away from Søren's and Erik's battered forms, but I force myself to meet Cress's cold gray gaze. "The public deaths of criminals serve as deterrents to others who think about breaking our laws."

Cress purses her lips. "Well, then I'm sure the public deaths of a prinz and an emperor will be deterrents indeed." She pauses a second before continuing. "There are those in my court who would still rather have a traitor prinz on their throne than a woman, those who were planning a coup to free him. I'd hoped that the Prinz and I could form an alliance, but he's been quite stubborn about it, and if he's not by my side, he's a threat. I trust you will not show him any kind of mercy."

As diplomatic as her words are, I understand the meaning plainly enough.

"Of course," I say with a smile. "He'll be executed as soon as we get home, and you will be able to sleep a little easier, with one less threat."

Heron is growing more uncomfortable with each passing second. I can tell by the way his eyes keep darting toward Erik and Søren, and the beads of sweat forming on his brow that have nothing to do with the balmy evening weather.

I need to end this, quickly.

"We should be going," I tell Cress. "Our ship captains wish to set sail this evening in order to take advantage of the tides. King Etristo's health is declining, and it is quite a chore for my husband to be away from his father during this tumultuous time."

I loop my arm through Heron's, giving his a squeeze that is both reassurance and warning.

"Oh dear," Cress says, brow furrowing. "Of course. Though the way the tides have been this season, you are far better off waiting an hour. Otherwise they will simply beat you back a foot for every inch you gain. Come—spending the last few days surrounded only by soldiers has me missing the company of other women. You and I will have a glass of wine together before you depart."

She extends her hand to me, and I have no choice but to let go of Heron to accept it, though my heart pounds in my chest. When her fingers wrap around mine, they are hot and dry. It doesn't feel like I'm touching something human, but rather a marble statue that's been standing in the sun. She doesn't feel feverish, like Blaise does, but the sensation is disconcerting all the same.

"I would enjoy that," I say, managing a smile. "Avaric, dear, will you secure the prisoners to their place on the ship so that we're ready to leave when the Kaiserin and I are done?"

Heron's eyes are wide, darting between Erik and me, but

he manages to nod. "Very well, my love," he says. "I'll see you in an hour's time."

There's an undercurrent of fear to his words, and I hope I'm the only one who notices. He kisses my cheek goodbye and lingers a second longer than necessary, his hold on my shoulder bracing. Though he says nothing, I feel the warning in the silence between us, though I hardly need it.

*Be careful. Don't get caught. Come back.*

# ALLIANCE

———•———

I HAVE TO REMIND MYSELF TO breathe as Cress and I approach the camp. Suddenly it feels impossible that the Water Guardians could have succeeded—the camp is bigger than anything I've seen disguised before, and though there are many Water Guardians, they are untrained. I fear Cress will be able to see right through the illusion, and I can't stop thinking that this was a foolish plan that will only delay the inevitable. I was a fool to ever believe otherwise.

A disguised guard opens the gate and ushers us through, giving me a wink as he does. In that moment, I know it's Maile, but I'm too preoccupied to pay her a second thought. Instead my attention is focused on the camp—standing undamaged, and populated by hundreds of uniformed Kalovaxian guards.

It is not a perfect illusion. When I search for the flaws, they show themselves clearly, like seams in a dress when the fabric is pulled taut. I know that the northern fence was burned entirely, and though it stands whole now, when I stare hard at it, I can make out a shadow of the charred wood, the blank space where the sky shows through, the light haze of smoke that lingers in the air. The same goes for the waterlogged buildings and the streets that were flooded only hours ago.

But Cress does not know to look for the illusion, so the details are lost on her. She sees only the tall, proud fence, the clean, sharp-edged buildings, the dry, packed dirt ground. She sees Kalovaxian soldiers with cropped yellow hair, clean-shaven jawlines, and pristine uniforms instead of bedraggled rebel warriors with hungry eyes.

Her personal guards keep close behind us, though they, too, seem taken in by the illusion, not seeing beneath the magicked exterior. Still, I can't calm my thundering heart. I won't be able to breathe freely until Cress and all of her men disappear into the distance.

"It smells strange, doesn't it?" Cress asks me in a conspiratorial whisper. "A bit like death."

It's difficult not to think of all the times Cress and I walked arm and arm, all the times she used to trust me with her whispers. It's difficult to remember that I am not Theo right now, that I am not even Lady Thora. I am Princess Amiza, and Cress is a stranger to me.

I force my voice to come out evenly. "I suppose so, Your Highness," I say. "Is that not how it always smells here? As I understand it, there is a high turnover rate for workers."

"The slaves, you mean," Cress says, frowning. "I suppose that's true, but it's terribly unpleasant, don't you think?"

"It is," I agree. "Perhaps we would be better off enjoying a glass of wine outside the gates, where the air is clearer?"

For an instant, Cress appears to consider it, but she quickly shakes her head. "No, we'll drink in the dining hall. Hopefully the smell of dinner cooking will drown out this stench."

I have no choice but to follow as she instructs a guard to lead the way and have a table set for two.

When we enter the dining hall, Cress tells the guards to stay outside, with the same charming smile I'm used to from her, though with her soot-black lips, it hardly has the same effect. Instead of getting flustered and red the way men used to get around her, the guards merely look unnerved.

"It's only going to be some talk between girls," she tells them. "Nothing at all to worry about."

She doesn't give them a chance to respond before pulling me into the hall toward the single table that has been set with a crisp white tablecloth and a gold, jewel-encrusted carafe with two matching goblets.

The room is drafty, raising goose bumps on my arms, though I hope Cress doesn't think it strange. I hope the illusion holds long enough that she doesn't realize that the southern wall of the dining hall has been completely destroyed, letting in the chilly evening air.

"How do you like living in Sta'Crivero?" Cress asks me, pulling my attention back to her. "Is it very different from Doraz?"

The question catches me off guard before I remember that Amiza was born in Doraz, the daughter of the Emperor there, though Doraz rulers choose their successors, so she became a princess only when she married Prince Avaric.

"Sta'Crivero is truly unlike anywhere else in the world," I tell her, hoping she doesn't ask more about Doraz. I don't know the first thing about that country, beyond what Søren and Artemisia told me of their power structure. "It's indescribable, really. I do hope you'll come to visit sometime, once all of this unpleasantness is behind you."

"My father always enjoyed his visits there," she says, sounding wistful. "He said that you all live in towers so tall, they touch the sky, all painted the most vibrant colors. I confess, I can't quite imagine it."

"Neither could I, before I saw it with my own eyes," I say, which is true enough. "Sta'Crivero is a desert country, so hot that it's unbearable, but the capital sits on a natural spring, so it keeps the temperature more mild."

But Cress doesn't care about natural springs. I can tell in the way her eyes glaze over. She reaches for the gilded carafe, and pours red wine into both of our goblets. I stare at her hands as she does, remembering the last time she poured a glass of wine for me, laced with Encatrio that nearly killed me.

She catches me staring and sets the carafe down again, then tucks her cracked gray tinged hands under the table. She thinks I was staring at that, I realize. She thinks I was noting her charred skin. She's self-conscious about it still, at least with someone like Amiza. She might wield her fearsomeness like a weapon in front of her warriors because they need her to be fearsome, but Amiza . . . Amiza is her peer, living the kind of life that Cress always thought she would live, a life of handsome royal husbands and elegant ball gowns and beauty.

She's intimidated by Amiza—by me. The idea is ludicrous, but there it is.

"May I ask what happened?" I ask her carefully. "There have been rumors, but I'm not sure I believe them."

Cress's eyes flash. "Did *she* tell you any of those rumors?" she asks, each word biting. "While she stayed in your palace as your guest?"

I don't have to ask to know that she's talking about me—Theo, that is. I flinch away from her and drop my gaze.

"Yes," I say, choosing my words carefully. I need to tell her what she wants to hear, nothing more. "Queen Theodosia said that she poisoned you but you survived it, that it gave you certain gifts in return."

Cress relaxes slightly. She reaches for her goblet, takes a long sip of wine before speaking.

"Encatrio is a gruesome poison," she says, her voice low. "Do you know exactly how it kills?"

I do, but Amiza doesn't. I shake my head, and Cress smiles grimly.

"It's a fire potion, brought from the deepest parts of the Fire Mine. Scentless. Tasteless. As soon as it touches your lips, though, it begins to burn its way through you, down your throat, into your belly. It burns you alive from the inside out. I saw it happen to my father—it killed him in a matter of minutes, but those minutes were agony. I never thought I would see my father cry, but he sobbed like an infant, voicelessly begging for mercy. I couldn't cry at all. I felt the pain of it, the burning, but unlike with my father, my agony didn't end after a few minutes. It stretched on for hours, and I kept hoping—begging—for death to save me from it. Yet death had other plans for me, and when the pain finally did subside, the poison had left me quite changed."

"That does sound gruesome," I say, barely trusting myself to speak. "I'm very sorry that you had to endure such misery."

For a long moment, Cress doesn't say anything. She takes another sip of her wine before replacing the goblet on the table with a thud that echoes throughout the room.

"I'm not," she says finally. "You see, I used to be like you, Amiza—may I call you Amiza?" I nod, and she continues. "I thought power was something that could be attained through marrying the right man, through impressing the right people. Through being *liked*. No one likes me now."

"I'm sure that's not true—"

"Oh, it doesn't bother me," she says with a hard laugh. "I suppose it did, once, but not anymore. Because I realized that power—real power—isn't attained through winning the approval of others. The only kind of power that matters is when you're the one doing the approving, making the decisions. The kind of power that comes from being feared, not liked. You understand, though, don't you?"

I nod because there is nothing else to do or say.

"It's a shame about your father-in-law's health," Cress says, leaning back in her chair and surveying me. "But it's a shame, too, that when he is gone your husband will be the one who will rule in his place and you will only be queen consort—a role without any power at all."

There is something dangerous hiding under her words that I cannot quite place. Something Amiza would not hear at all because she doesn't know Cress as I do. She does not know the focused look Cress gets when a thought takes root in her mind.

"I don't mind," I say, forcing a smile.

"Of course you do," Cress says, reaching across the table to take hold of my hand, her skin still warm but lifeless. "You can't tell me that you don't want to rule in your own name, as a true queen instead of a mere vessel for future princes and princesses."

I bite my lip, aware of my heart beating rapidly in my chest. *Tell her what she wants to hear,* I think.

"And if I did want that?"

Cress's smile broadens. "Then I think you and I could help one another. I think that we could be true allies—beyond this farce of a truce. Let's not pretend, between you and me, Amiza. King Etristo has no plans of keeping this alliance for more than a few months. As soon as the rebels have been subdued, he will try to take advantage of the fact that the Kalovaxians have—to his way of thinking—a weak ruler. He will try to take my throne from me, and with it Astrea's magic."

I don't know how much of her rambling is founded on facts and how much is sheer paranoia. It sounds ludicrous. King Etristo is greedy, it's true, and he underestimates women in all of their forms, but he doesn't know the first thing about waging war, and he is too lazy to try.

It doesn't matter, though, what is true and what is Cress's imagining. All that matters is that Amiza tells Cress what she wants to hear.

"I believe that we could arrange that," I say slowly. "What would you need from me?"

Cress draws a vial from the pocket of her gown. Encatrio. My breath catches as the pieces of her plan come into focus.

"I need for you to take the power you so desperately want," she says. "Even if it costs you dearly."

"What is it?" I say aloud because Amiza has never seen the poison before.

Cress slides the vial across the table toward me.

"Encatrio," she says, as easily as she might say *honey* or *water*.

"You want me to kill Etristo?" I ask, hoping that playing dumb will buy me time.

"I want you to drink it," she says.

"But—but that will kill me," I stutter.

Cress shrugs. "Perhaps. It isn't pure Encatrio—that has become elusive these days, so it's diluted a bit. Less lethal. Most of the time, at least."

Diluted with her own blood, I think, with a nauseous lurch of my stomach.

She continues, oblivious to my discomfort. "It's a risk, yes, but isn't the risk worth it? For that kind of power?"

She pushes the vial closer toward me.

"Now?" I ask, casting my eyes around the room desperately, searching for something—anything—that will give me a reason not to once more find myself drinking Encatrio forced upon me by Cress. This time, it will kill me. I know that with a crushing certainty.

"I need to know that I can trust you, Amiza," Cress says, her voice level. "So now it is. We'll tell your husband you aren't feeling well, that your journey home will be postponed for a day. And if it does go poorly, I'll blame the poisoned wine on the rebels. The alliance between our countries will stand."

That hardly reassures me, and I can't imagine Amiza would take any comfort in it, either.

"I have a child," I say. "He needs his mother."

Cress doesn't even blink. "He needs a mother he can be proud of," she says, nodding toward the vial. "Go on. From what I understand, Sta'Crivero is on the cusp of a crisis. It's only a matter of time before its walls fall, before its people riot. You can save them. You can be the queen they deserve. Take it. What is fleeting pain compared to a lifetime of power?"

She takes my hand and wraps it around the vial, then unstoppers it, like I am a doll she is playing with, controlling my movements, making my decisions. And what's worse, I let her. I am in a state of shock, speechless and still.

A knock on the door interrupts us, and Cress yanks her hand away from mine as if my touch burned her.

"What is it?" she snaps, glaring at the guard who enters clutching a roll of parchment in his hand, its seal unbroken.

"Apologies, Your Highness," he says, bowing. "It's a letter from the palace. I think you'll want to see this for yourself. It's urgent."

With a huff, Cress gets to her feet, stalks toward the guard, and snatches the letter from him. She reads it with her back to me, but I see her shoulders tense. When she finishes, she crumples it into a ball in her fist.

"Ready our horses," she says, her voice tight. "We'll leave at once."

The guard bows again before departing, leaving Cress and me alone once more. She turns back to me, but now she is all taut fury, any glimpse of the Cress I knew gone once more.

"Something has come up, I'm afraid," she says, shaking her head. She takes the vial from me and stoppers it again. "We will stay in touch. When your father-in-law is on his deathbed, take the poison. In all of the chaos surrounding the shift in rulers, you'll be able to seize the throne easily."

I can only nod and take the poison from her, but when I

do, she clasps her hands around my own. Her gray eyes search mine like she's seeing straight into my soul. "You remind me of someone, you know," she says. "A friend I had once. I hope that you will prove to be a better friend than she was, Amiza. Together, you and I could conquer the entire world, I think."

I don't let myself relax until the Kalovaxians disappear over the horizon. When they are finally out of sight, I sag with relief, leaning against Heron, who brings an arm around my shoulders.

"We did it," I say, but the words taste strange. I can't quite believe they're true.

"We did," he agrees, but his voice sounds distant. "The delivery took longer than we expected—we had to get the messenger around the Kalovaxian troops in order for its arrival to be believable."

"It came at the perfect moment," I assure him. "I'm fine. You're fine. Our people are safe. And what's more, we got Søren and Erik back."

Heron nods, but his eyes are troubled. "And the Gorakians Erik brought with him to the capital? What do you think happened to them?"

I don't know. I don't *want* to know.

"Come," I say to Heron, pushing the thought from my mind. "Let's go see Erik and Søren."

# SIGHT

———•———

INFIRMARY TENTS HAVE BEEN SET up across the lake, hidden past the edge of the Perea Forest, in case the Kalovaxians decided to do any exploring during their visit. Those injured in the battle are there, as well as the former slaves who were too ill or malnourished to stay in the camp. It's also where I had Heron bring Blaise to keep him from doing anything foolish. When Cress turned over Søren and Erik, it made sense to send them there as well.

It's a short boat ride across for Heron, Artemisia, and me—especially when Art and Heron use their combined gifts to propel us across the lake's surface. The trip takes less than an hour but feels like it drags on for an eternity. Søren is *here*. He may be hurt, but he's alive. He's safe. It isn't until now that I realize there was a large part of me that believed I would never see him again.

"What happened with the Kaiserin?" Heron asks me, voice low.

I swallow, aware of the vial of Encatrio in the pocket of my dress, warm through the thin material. My first instinct is to keep it to myself, but I promised I wouldn't keep any more secrets, so I tell them everything.

"She's lonely," I say when I finish. "She's isolated. There's no one else like her, no one who doesn't see her as a monster. So she's decided to create a monster of her own."

"She's deranged," Artemisia corrects. "She must have known she was offering death, not power. Even diluted, that much Encatrio would kill most people."

"I think she's beyond caring," I say, shaking my head. "She's so desperate to not be alone that she'd have let Amiza die on the off chance that she could survive it. And the way she offered it . . . it didn't seem to be her first time."

Artemisia frowns. "Where's the poison now?"

I draw it out and show them. "I'll get rid of it once I figure out how. I don't want to start a fire by accident."

"Or you could keep it," Heron says.

Art and I both stare at him, and he shrugs. "I'm just saying. Encatrio is rare, and it could come in handy."

"It's not real Encatrio," I tell him. "She told me as much. It's the kind she made herself, with her blood. I don't like carrying it with me."

Artemisia sighs. "Heron's right, though," she says. "We need all of the weapons in our arsenal that we can get. That poison is a weapon. It might be diluted, but it's stronger than whatever you have in your own veins."

I hesitate for only a second before tucking the vial back into the pocket of my dress.

Artemisia steers the boat onto the shore, and the three of us clamber out. Though the camp is hidden behind the tree line, this close I can make out the signs of it—the bright white cloth of the tent through the trees, the hushed voices, the smell of sickness and blood. It's enough to make my head spin.

"There are five tents total for the wounded, plus two more for the ill," Heron explains. "You'll have to avoid those. Many of the illnesses I can't name, so I don't know how contagious—or how deadly—they are. They're my first priority after checking on Erik and Søren." Though he tries to hide it, I can tell he's exhausted.

"The Air Mine should be our next stop," I tell him, placing a hand on his arm. "We can find more Guardians there so you won't be the only healer."

He nods, but his eyes are distracted.

"Come on," Artemisia says, leading the way through the trees.

"I didn't know you were so fond of Søren and Erik," I say, following her.

"I'm not," she snaps, so forcefully that I'd guess it's not the truth. "But they must have learned something in that palace, and I want to find out what it is."

We have to walk through two of the tents in order to get to the one Søren and Erik are being kept in. It was decided that keeping them separate from the others was the best idea. Søren is Kalovaxian, after all, and as far as most people are concerned, Erik turned his back on us. No one wants to risk a fight breaking out, so they set up a small separate tent for them.

The smell of blood intensifies the instant I step into the first tent, so thick in the air that it is nauseating. Bedrolls cover almost every available inch of space, lined side by side. Close to twenty in total, I would guess, most occupied. Some of the men and women are only bandaged but look all right otherwise, but others are in worse shape. A few are missing arms and legs, the wounds covered only by bandages already been soaked through with blood that shows no sign of stopping anytime soon. One man has a gash that cuts across his face so deeply that his jawbone juts out.

I want to look away from all of the carnage, but there is nowhere to look. It's everywhere, inescapable.

Perhaps even worse than the wounds and blood and people in pain, though, are the empty bedrolls, still rumpled and stained by those who occupied them so recently. People who didn't survive. I count five in this tent alone.

Heron's hand comes to rest on my shoulder, steadying me.

"There are fewer injuries—fewer casualties—than there were in the last battle. And far fewer than there would have been if not for your plan to fool the Kaiserin," he says, his voice soft but insistent. I know he means well, but it does little to reassure me.

I don't let myself relax until we reach Søren and Erik's tent, and even then, it's short-lived. I don't know what to say to either of them, but I have no choice other than to push open the flap and step inside.

It's smaller than the other tents, only big enough for the two of them. Søren is sitting up on his bedroll, but Erik is asleep, rolled over so that his back is to us and all I can see is his hair. It used to hang down past his shoulders, but it's been shorn so hastily that there are gashes on his scalp that have only just begun to close.

Søren and Erik have been cleaned up, but soap and water have done little to mitigate their injuries. Søren is shirtless, baring wounds over every inch of his exposed torso, arms, and even his face. He keeps his eyes down when we enter, though his shoulders tense and I know he's aware of our presence. I'm not sure what he's been told—or what he believes—about his rescue, though Søren is perceptive enough to realize that he wasn't taken to a ship like he was meant to be, perceptive enough to recognize that people are speaking Astrean and not Sta'Criveran. He might not have the whole picture, but I would be surprised if he hasn't pieced most of it together by now.

When I step closer, I realize that his wounds are actually burns, traced in elaborate patterns of swirls and lines and—in some places—words. Words written in a familiar hand.

I can't help but let out a gasp, and that is when Søren looks up at me, shock and disbelief and relief taking turns playing over his face. He looks at me like I'm not real—some figment of his imagination, summoned forth and made flesh. He looks at me like he thinks I'll disappear if he so much as blinks.

"Theo." The word is barely more than a breath, but I hear it. It reverberates through every inch of me, thrumming through my blood.

"Hello," I say. It's a painfully insufficient greeting, but it's the only word I can make my lips form. I try to look him in the eye and not let my gaze wander to the burns, not read the words that Cress has branded into his skin, words that I don't think even Heron will be able to erase.

He forces himself to his feet, eyes somber on mine. I think for an instant that he means to embrace me, here, in front of everyone. I don't even know that I would be able to hold back if he did. Instead, though, he falls to a knee, head bowed.

"My Queen," he says. "It is good to see you again."

"None of that," I tell him, struggling to keep my voice from wavering. I crouch in front of him so that we're eye to eye. This close, I can see the word *traitor* branded above his heart in Cress's looping hand. I reach out to touch his cheek. His gaze meets mine and a thousand words pass between us unsaid.

"I thought you were dead," he says, choking the words out. "Even when Erik said you weren't . . . I couldn't believe it. But you're alive."

"I'm alive," I tell him. "Cress doesn't know, though, and we have to keep it that way."

Søren nods. "If she knew, she would burn this whole country to the ground to finish what she started."

I nod, pressing my lips together tightly. I glance at Erik's sleeping figure behind him. "How is he?" I ask Søren.

Søren looks away from me, his eyes finding Heron and Artemisia instead. "Cress was always planning on betraying him," he says. "But she was very angry when she learned he'd betrayed her first."

My stomach sinks. "The Gorakians he brought to the capital. Did she kill them?"

"No," he says, and I let out a breath of relief before he continues. "Not most of them, at least. With the mine turnover as high as it is, they're running out of bodies to work there. She sent any who were strong enough to the Earth Mine. They have the lowest numbers. Any who were too old or young or weak she had killed."

I close my eyes tight and shake my head. "I'm so sorry," I say.

"It's not your fault," a voice says. Erik, though he keeps his back to us. His voice is barely recognizable, full of anguish and raw from screaming or crying or perhaps both. "It was my foolish plan. I'm the one who put them in danger. I'm the one who killed them as sure as if I'd cut their throats myself."

"Erik," I say, reaching toward him. When my hand comes down on his shoulder, he draws away from me, curling in tighter on himself. "You made a judgment call. You thought it was the right one. You thought it was the only one."

"I was wrong," he bites out. "My mother told me I had to lead them, and I did—straight to their graves, one way or another."

"There's no changing that now," I say. "But we can focus on saving those who were sent to the mine. Dragonsbane is on her way there—she'll free them. All isn't lost."

Erik doesn't reply but his shoulders shake with silent sobs.

Heron kneels down beside me, his own expression tight and unreadable.

"We'll avenge them, Erik," he says softly. "We'll save the ones who can be saved, and we'll make sure those bastards feel every ounce of pain and death they've inflicted tenfold. With the two of you leading our army, we'll make them pay."

"That's just it," Erik says, his voice hoarse. "I won't be leading any armies."

He rolls over to face us, and I can't help but let out a cry. His hair isn't the only thing the Kalovaxians took. One eye is swollen shut, red and ugly, but where the other should be, there is only a gaping hole of seared flesh, still raw and fresh. I know without asking how it happened. I can imagine Cress with her burning fingers, digging out Erik's eye like a lychee from its rind, cauterizing the wound as she did.

*"She was very angry,"* Søren said, but even then I never imagined this. I feel sick all over again.

"I'm sorry," I say, bringing my hand over my mouth. "I'm so sorry, Erik."

Erik shakes his head. "I'm useless to you now," he says. "I have no army for you, Theo. I can't lead a battalion. I'm not even sure I could lead the way out of this tent."

"You're blind," Heron says, finding his voice again finally.

"Half," Erik says, motioning to the swollen eye. "This one should heal, I think. But with no depth perception and a narrower field of vision—"

"No," Heron says. "I mean you're blind—you aren't dead. You want to help, you want to save your people, then do it. You don't have to lead an army to do that."

I don't think I've ever heard Heron speak to anyone so harshly, apart from Søren. Even Erik seems taken aback.

"He's right, Erik," Søren says. "What would Gormund say to see you giving up so easily?"

"Gormund?" Heron asks, frowning.

"A Kalovaxian warrior of legend," I explain. "They said he was half god, that he could freeze a person where they stood with a single look. But his human brother grew jealous of him, and while the warrior slept, the brother cut out Gormund's eye."

"Gormund still had one magical eye," says Erik. "I'm not even sure how well my nonmagical eye will heal. It isn't the same thing."

"It's settled, then," Heron says, his voice strangely cold. "When we leave here, you'll bring up the rear with the other wounded, with the elderly and the children. And when we meet with Dragonsbane, you'll join them on her ships and wait for the war to be over. And when we save your people, you can tell them how easily that witch managed to cow their Emperor by taking his eye. See how many of them will still call you Emperor after that."

Erik flinches from the words, but his mouth tightens. "It isn't that I don't want to stay," he says. "Of course I do. But I won't be of any help to you now. It's better for you to send me away."

"If you want to stay, then I want you to stay," I tell him. "You aren't useless. You have your mind, you have your determination. You can still probably wield a sword better than half of Cress's army, I'd bet, depth perception or no. Stay and fight and show her that she didn't ruin you."

Erik swallows. For a moment, he says nothing, but eventually he nods his head. "I don't suppose you could heal me, Heron?" he asks, though he sounds like he already knows the answer.

"I can't make you a new eye," Heron says, his voice pained. "But I can try to help with healing your other one."

"What about you, Artemisia?" Erik asks. "Any illusion you could cast to hide it?"

"Nothing permanent. I'm sorry," she says. "And nothing that would give you back your vision."

"Ah well," Erik says, his voice still quavering. "I had a few good years of being handsome. It's more than most get."

It's an attempt at a joke, but no one laughs.

"You're still handsome," Heron says quietly.

Erik laughs, the sound hard. "I'm monstrous," he says.

"You're brave," Heron says, louder this time. "And steadfast. And you fight for your people—for what you know is right no matter what it costs you. You are, without a doubt, the handsomest man I've ever seen, and if you try to say otherwise one last time, I will break your nose as well, you vain ass."

The proclamation is followed by silence. I don't think I've ever heard Heron curse, let alone threaten violence, and the thought of it is so ridiculous that I can't fight a smile, as small and frail as it feels on my lips. After a moment, Erik shakes his head and I see he has a smile of his own—not a full one. Not the one I'm used to from him. It is a fragile thing, likely to break if anyone breathes the wrong way. But it is a smile all the same.

It strikes me suddenly that we are all together again, in a way I never imagined we would be. We are here and we are alive against all odds. Cress has taken so much from us, and I know that this is war and she will likely take much more before all is said and done. But today, we are here and together and victorious, and that is enough.

# WOUND

———— • ————

I WAS RIGHT ABOUT SØREN'S WOUNDS—Heron can't fix them with his magic. They'll have to heal on their own, and even then, he'll likely always carry the scars. Heron offers to heal them as best he can, but Søren refuses.

"There are too many others here who need you more than I do," he says. "This won't kill me—it just hurts."

"It will kill you if they get infected," Heron says. "But you don't need me to prevent that. The worst ones just need to be sterilized and bandaged. I can try to find someone who knows how, but it may be a while."

"I'll do it," I say before I can stop myself.

Heron looks at me with raised eyebrows. "Do you know how?" he asks.

I shrug. "I was on the other side of it often enough after the Kaiser's punishments. I'm sure I can figure it out."

Heron nods. "All right, then. I'll get you some supplies. Art, can you help Erik outside? Get him used to finding his way around?" He looks at Erik. "The last thing you're going to do is wallow. You're going to get back on your feet and figure out how to adjust. Trust me, you'll thank me for it later."

Erik grimaces but nods. "I'm sure I will," he says, forcing himself to sit up, and groaning as he does. "But right now, I'd like to say some far less savory things to you."

"Keep a list," Heron says with a small smile. "You can tell them to me over dinner."

For an instant, Erik is shocked and flustered—a look I've never seen on him before. He recovers his wits quickly enough. "It's a deal," he says.

Artemisia looks between the two of them, eyebrows raised so high they almost disappear entirely into her hair.

"We are at *war*," she says with a sigh. "Surely there is a better time to flirt than when death is around every corner?"

"Truth be told, I'm hard-pressed to think of a better time to flirt," Erik says, pushing himself to his feet. "You very well may never get another chance."

Artemisia rolls her eyes.

"Just because I can't see you doesn't mean I don't know you're rolling your eyes, Art," he says, holding an arm out to her, which she takes. She guides him a couple of hesitant steps. "Just because you don't know how to flirt—"

"I know how," she snaps indignantly as she leads him out of the tent, the two of them continuing to bicker as they go.


When Heron leaves us with the ointment and bandages, he takes all of the air in the room with him. Alone with Søren, I'm aware of every breath he takes, standing on the opposite side of the tent—the rise and fall of his bare chest, marred with scars and wounds. I'm aware of him being aware of me, his gaze careful and wary, like he still doesn't trust that I'm really here. I don't blame him—some days I can't quite believe it, either.

"I really thought that you were dead," he says, breaking the silence. The words are a confession, whisper-quiet, as if saying them out loud might negate the miracle.

"I know. I thought you were as good as," I reply. "I didn't think I would see you again before she . . . I wanted to get you back, I swear I did. I would have done everything I could to rescue you, but . . ."

"But storming the capital before you had enough warriors would have been to doom your rebellion," he says. "I know. You couldn't do that. I never expected you to."

"You would have done it for me," I point out.

He hesitates but doesn't deny it. "Maybe I would have," he says softly. "But it would have been a foolish decision. You are many things, Theodosia Eirene Houzzara, but you aren't a fool."

I bite my lip. "Erik thought I wasn't acting because I didn't care. He thought I was indifferent to your suffering. I wasn't," I say. "I'm sorry I didn't do more. Maybe if I had, he wouldn't have lost his eye."

He shakes his head, dropping his gaze. "You don't owe me any apologies, Theo. You don't owe them to Erik, either. You aren't responsible for his faulty plot," he says. "Besides, you've saved me plenty of times before, and you did so again today. I don't think it's a debt I'll ever be able to repay."

"There are no debts," I tell him quietly. "Not between us, Søren."

His eyes find mine again, and without a word he holds

out a hand to me and I take it, stepping into his arms as if it's the most natural thing in the world. He buries his face in my neck, and I hold him as tightly as I dare to, carefully avoiding his wounds. Somehow, beneath the blood and sweat, he still smells like the sea, and that makes him feel a little more real to me.

For a moment, neither of us moves. We just stand there, holding one another, and I wish that the moment would last a lifetime, but eventually Søren pulls back, fixing me with an imploring look.

"Your skin is warm," he says slowly. "Not hot. Not feverish. But warm—warmer than it used to be." He pauses, weighing a question he knows he doesn't want the answer to. "What did you do, Theo?"

"What I had to," I say, stepping out of his arms to retrieve the ointment and bandages that Heron left, though it's also an excuse to not have to look at him when I say the words. "I went into the Fire Mine."

He gives a sharp inhale, like he's been hit. "And here I was, saying you weren't a fool," he says, shaking his head. "It could have killed you."

I shrug, but I still can't meet his gaze. "Cress could have killed me. The Kaiser could have killed me. There were times when I think even King Etristo wanted to kill me back in Sta'Crivero. Believe me, the mine was a less frightening prospect after all of them. Besides, I trusted that the gods had other plans for me. They wouldn't have let me die like that, not in their domain."

He doesn't say anything for a moment. Instead he watches

as I open the jar of ointment and spread it over his wounds, starting with the ones on his face. The second the cool salve touches his skin, he flinches.

"I know, it hurts," I say. "It's the same kind Hoa would use on me. But the pain will go away in a moment, and then it won't hurt at all."

He relaxes slightly and I move on to his chest, tracing Cress's handwriting on his right clavicle. *Betrayer* she wrote there, the lines of her script hard and inelegant. Angry.

"What was it like?" he asks me. "The mine?"

My hand stills and I realize that no one ever asked me that. Most people don't want to know, and the only people who would have asked already know from their own experiences. I take a deep breath, the mint from the salve stinging my nostrils.

"I don't remember most of it," I tell him. "It comes back in flashes sometimes, but there are still parts where I don't know if it was real or not. I saw my mother, as real down there as you and I are now. Some days, I'm not sure I ever left the mine at all. It feels like I'm still there."

His hand comes to rest on top of mine on his chest. "But you did make it out," he says. "And you came out stronger, didn't you? Gifted?"

I nod. "I'm not as strong as Cress, but I'm stronger than I was. I hope it'll be enough when we meet again."

He drops his hand and lets me continue my work, wrapping the rolls of white gauze bandages around his shoulders. I leave them off his face for now—in part because they will be uncomfortable but also because I think if I can't see his face, I'll be less able to believe he's here.

"What—what about you?" I ask him, stumbling over the words. "What did . . . what did she do to you?"

I'm not sure I want to know the answer, and Søren doesn't seem inclined to give it, but after a moment he speaks.

"Her claim on the throne is weak. Many of the nobles were in awe of her power to begin with. They feared her, and that was enough that she was able to seize power after my father died. But the novelty of it wore thin quickly. As powerful as she is, she's still a woman, and Kalovaxia has never had a female ruler. There have been whispers about overthrowing her, plots even to free me and put me on the throne instead. She thought that if she married me, she could consolidate power, that no one would question her claim to the throne then. But she couldn't control me, she knew that. She could have forced it, but that would have backfired—as soon as I was out of the dungeon, she would have been assassinated and I would have been crowned Kaiser. She seemed to think I wanted that. So she endeavored to convince me to marry her willingly—though *willingly* isn't an apt term when it comes after torture."

I flinch, picking up the jar of ointment again and dabbing it onto the *traitor* branded over his heart, then the *weak* scrawled over his ribs.

"And since she couldn't make you an ally, she got rid of you," I say. "Better to have you far away, to have you dead, so your supporters couldn't use you against her."

He nods, not speaking for a moment.

"I thought of you, you know," he says quietly. "When I thought I might break. I thought of you and how you'd survived worse. I thought that you were watching me from the After you believe in, and that if I broke, you would be ashamed of me."

I shake my head. "There's no shame in breaking," I tell him. "Gods know I did often enough. You just have to put yourself back together again."

His torso is more burns than it is unmarred skin, and I use almost half of the jar of ointment there alone.

"Turn around," I tell him. "I have to get your back."

He does as I ask and I have to stifle a gasp. However bad I thought it might be, it's worse. Though the lines of the burns are thin—done by one of Cress's fingers, I would guess—she's crafted what looks like an elaborate spider's web from his shoulders to his lower back. Lines are layered over one another, some going so deep that his flesh peels back like pages of a book.

I dig into the tub of ointment and take a steadying breath, willing my stomach to settle.

"It's going to hurt," I warn him.

"It already hurts," he admits. "Just . . . keep talking to me. It'll distract us both."

I nod before remembering that he can't see me. "I think Cress and I are sharing dreams," I tell him. It still sounds ludicrous to say out loud, but he doesn't laugh like I expected he might.

"What do you mean?" he asks instead, through clenched teeth, emitting a low hiss of pain after the words.

"In my dreams, she talks to me, as clearly as we're talking now. The things she says . . . I couldn't make them up. She told me she was keeping you in the dungeon. She said that she was trying to convince you to marry her—essentially she told me exactly what you just did. It could be a coincidence, a few lucky guesses, but . . . it doesn't feel like that."

"You think you're really speaking to her in your dreams?" he asks. The subject must be distracting him, because this time he doesn't even react when I smear ointment over one of the rawer burns.

"The poison she gave me was made from her blood," I explain. "I know it sounds ridiculous, but I know what I know. It's her."

He doesn't say anything for a moment, and when he speaks again, his voice is low.

"But she still thinks you're dead."

"She thinks I'm haunting her," I tell him. "But it's strange. In these dreams, she talks to me like a friend. Like we used to talk. Even when we talk about the things we've done to one another, she doesn't sound angry. She just sounds tired."

"She isn't well," Søren says. "There were rumors that made their way down to the dungeon—noble girls found dead in the palace after they were seen with her. Their throats were always charred, lips black. Like . . ." He trails off.

"Like they'd drunk Encatrio," I say, pieces beginning to fall into place.

He nods. "Everyone knew that she was responsible, but she's untouchable—at least for now. They were too frightened to accuse her out loud, but everyone knew."

I think about her offering the potion to me—to Amiza— how she'd hoped that in taking it, Amiza would become like her. That they could be rulers together in a changed world.

I tell Søren about that as I finish up with the ointment on his back.

"She's trying to build an army," I say when I'm done, reaching for the roll of gauze. "An army of women like her, placed high in society. Here and abroad. She doesn't just want Astrea; she doesn't just want to rule the Kalovaxians. She wants a new world."

Søren shakes his head. "As I said, she isn't well," he says. "It's a delusion—she'll keep killing girls."

"Most of them, yes," I say, wrapping the bandage around his torso until there is no skin showing through at all. "But not all. A fraction must have survived, just like she did. Just like I did. And they have that poison in their veins now as well. Weaker poison, yes, but maybe still strong enough to turn others, who could turn others."

"It can spread like a disease," he says, looking at me. "Killing almost everyone it infects but changing the few it doesn't."

I nod. "The Kalovaxian court doesn't want her for a Kaiserin, so she's creating enough loyal followers to cow those who would dethrone her."

Søren doesn't say anything at first, but I can see his mind whirring.

"At this rate, the Kalovaxians will weaken themselves," he says. "There's a chance, if we let them carry on like this, fighting one another, that in a few years they won't be a threat at all."

"A chance, just as there's a chance they'll grow too strong to ever stop," I repeat. "And besides, we don't have years."

I don't meet his gaze as I start spreading ointment over his arms. The muscles there have softened in his three weeks in the dungeon.

"Do you pity her?" he asks me quietly.

If anyone else asked me that question, I would deny it. Of course I don't pity her. She has committed more atrocities than I can possibly count. She's ruined lives. She even tried to take mine. I know who my enemies are.

But it isn't just anyone asking. It's Søren, and Søren has always understood the darkest, most conflicted parts of me.

"Yes, I pity her," I admit. "And I hate her and I love her, too. I don't know how all of those things can be true at once, but they are. It doesn't matter, though, because soon the time will come, and this time I won't hesitate to destroy her. I can't."

He absorbs my words, nodding slowly. "And I'll be right there, at your side," he says solemnly.

His eyes meet mine, and I realize how much I missed those eyes. I forgot how bright a blue they are, bluer than the sea itself. They aren't his father's eyes anymore, not in my mind. They are all Søren. I touch his right cheek, the just-healed wound pressing into my palm.

"I know you will be," I say softly. "I missed you, Søren. So very much."

He leans into my touch and closes his eyes.

"I missed you too," he says.

I softly brush my lips over his, aware of how fragile he is, though it seems laughable to think of him that way. But he is—I can feel it in his sharp intake of breath before he kisses me back, his hand resting on the nape of my neck, anchoring me to him. It feels like a revelation, like waking up after a long sleep. It feels like we're making up for what we've lost.

I want to keep kissing him for hours, to celebrate the fact that we are here and we are alive and we are together even though neither of us thought we would be again. I want to lose myself to his touch and forget about everything else. But that isn't what he needs right now—he needs rest and food and water. And we need to figure out where we go from here, where we strike next.

Besides, we have time.

So I break the kiss and instead I just hold him and he holds me and we try to convince ourselves that we're real and here and together until we begin to actually believe it.

# PEACE

———•———

I LEAVE SØREN SO HE CAN get some rest. I barely make it to the tent's entrance before his snoring begins, and I know he'll likely sleep for some time. He needs to, after all he's been through—and I'm sure he didn't tell me everything. I only hope that Cress doesn't plague his sleeping mind the way she plagued mine, even before whatever connection between us was forged.

It's nearly midnight by the time I get back to the camp, and I would like nothing more than to fall into a bed of my own. After today, every muscle in my body yearns for sleep, but I know my mind won't let me find that kind of peace. There is still one more thing left to do.

So instead I ask after Blaise, and a kind warrior I dimly recognize as one of Maile's men points me toward the northern edge of the camp, just outside the gates.

There's a chill in the air, and as soon as I step through the gates, it gets even colder. I pull my linen shawl tighter around my shoulders and look around for Blaise. In the dark, he should be difficult to find, but instead he is impossible to miss.

He stands alone on the lake's shore, the moon shining

down on him, illuminating his tawny skin and making it look like brown topaz. He moves like there's no one watching, sword in hand. He slices the blade through the air one way, then another, never stopping even to breathe.

Blaise is not a great swordsman, though I don't think I ever realized that until this moment. He could likely defend himself if he needed to, could possibly even hold his own in battle for a time, but Artemisia would defeat him in an instant and so would many others. It isn't a skill that comes naturally to him, and I don't think he's put enough practice in to truly excel at it.

He also doesn't know how to pace himself, and within minutes he is out of breath, his sword arm falling and the blade dropping unceremoniously into the rough sand in a way that would make Artemisia scowl.

It's then that he sees me, his eyes widening for an instant. He stands a little straighter, dropping the sword altogether.

"How long have you been there?" he asks me.

"Only a minute," I say, stepping closer now that he's no longer waving his sword through the air. "I wanted to see how you were. After earlier."

For a second, he doesn't say anything. He looks to be at war with himself, but the battle only lasts the span of a breath. "After I tried to attack you in a fit of desperation, or after you had Heron knock me unconscious to keep it from happening again?" he asks.

I take a step back and ready myself for the fight I knew was inevitable. It seems like all we ever do is fight these days, and I am so tired of it.

"Both, I suppose," I say, keeping my voice level. "And if

you're looking for an apology for keeping you out of the mirage plot, you won't get one. Tensions were already high, and I couldn't risk you becoming volatile again and ruining the entire plan. You're unpredictable, and today you weren't worth the risk."

He stares at me for a moment, expression unreadable, before he shakes his head. "I'm not looking for an apology from you, Theo," he says with a sigh. "I don't expect one and I don't deserve one. You made the right choice and I'm glad it all went smoothly. I can't say with any certainty that it would have if I had been there."

"Oh," I say, taken aback. I've gotten so used to Blaise being hotheaded and reckless, I forgot how it used to feel when we were on the same side of an argument. "Good, then. And I hope you know that I'll keep doing it, so long as you pose a threat."

"You won't have to," he says. "It won't happen again."

I laugh, but there is no mirth in the sound. "Of course it will, Blaise. And I think we're done pretending otherwise," I say.

"No," he says quickly. "I mean that I won't be losing control again because I won't be using my gift again. At all. Not in battle, not casually, not even when it's begging to be unleashed."

Whatever I expected Blaise to say, it wasn't that. I expected anger, I expected a fight—I always do now, whenever we speak. I came with battle armor on, sword at the ready, and here he is waving a white flag, and I don't know how to respond.

"Why?" is all I can ask.

His jaw clenches and he looks toward where the sea laps

peacefully at the shore. When he speaks, his voice is level and sure. "Because when we stood by that lake and I . . . I grabbed you like that—it wasn't like it has been before, when I lost control. It wasn't the power consuming me, taking control of my actions. I can't blame it on my gift. It was me, so desperate to give in to the temptation to use my gift that it overwhelmed me, that it defined me, that it made me a person who would hurt you. And that scared me more than any battle. I don't want to be that person. I knew that this power came with a cost and I was happy to pay it myself, but not like that. Not through you."

It's all I've wanted him to say for months, and though the words send relief washing over me, they are somehow not quite enough. I still feel his hands on me, his fingers digging into my skin, hurting me.

"I'm glad," I tell him, which is more or less true.

He glances away, chewing hard on his bottom lip, as if he hears the words I don't say. Maybe he does. In some ways, Blaise knows me better than anyone else in this world. He's the only soul alive who knew me before all of this, before the rebellion and the siege, back when we were children and the world was so much simpler.

"All I ever wanted to do was protect you, Theo. I hope you know that," he says.

"I do," I say, considering my words carefully. "And there was a time when I wanted that—needed that, even. But I don't anymore. What I need is for you to trust that I know what I'm doing and I know what I'm risking. I need you to have faith in me the way I've had faith in you."

He looks down at the sand between us. Only a foot separates us, but it feels like an uncrossable ocean.

"Do you think you can ever forgive me?" he asks, his voice barely loud enough to be heard over the wind.

It's a loaded question that I can't begin to answer. I want to say, *Of course. You're my closest friend and I love you and you are my past and my present and my future. You're already forgiven.* But that wouldn't be the truth. The truth is he betrayed me, he hurt me, and that will leave a wound of its own, and there is no telling how long it will take to heal or what kind of scar it will leave behind when it does.

"I think you need to forgive yourself, Blaise," I tell him. "I think that if you've truly decided you want to come out of this war alive, you need to make sure you build a life worth living. I can't do that for you. Only you can."

Blaise swallows and nods, lifting his head to meet my gaze again.

"Do you know what Ampelio said to me—the last thing he said—before he let the Kalovaxians catch him, to spare me? He said that it was his time, but it wasn't mine."

The words prickle at my memory.

"He said something similar to me," I tell him. "When he asked me to kill him, he said that it was time for the After to welcome him, time to see my mother again, but that I had to live and keep fighting." I pause before forcing myself to say the words buried deep in me. "Sometimes I resent him for that. He got peace, and I got . . ."

Blaise understands what I mean. "You got me, showing up and throwing your life into chaos."

I shrug. "It isn't as if it was a good life. It needed the chaos. It needed you in it. But it was a much easier life, in so many ways. It was a much simpler thing, to be a princess of ashes instead of a . . ." I trail off.

"An Ember Queen," Blaise says. I must look confused, because he continues. "It's what I've heard some of the people call you. It started with the former Fire Mine slaves, but it's caught on. A bit less of a mouthful than 'Queen of Flame and Fury.'"

"It may be less of a mouthful, but it still feels too big for me," I admit.

He shakes his head, taking a step closer, though he doesn't reach out for me. I almost wish he would—but I'm even more relieved that he keeps his hands to himself.

"Ampelio gave up his life for us," he says, his voice soft. "I think that no matter what comes of this rebellion, he would be proud of what we've done with his sacrifice."

I blink away the tears forming behind my eyes and try to smile. "I think that when the time comes, he'll greet us in the After with open arms."

"Yes," Blaise says. "But that time is not going to be for many, many years, Theo. Not for either of us. Not if I have anything to say about it."

# FREE

———— • ————

I SAW AMPELIO, IN THE MINE. I remember this as I finally settle into bed that night in one of the tents that have been set
up in the camp. As soon as that shard of memory returns,
piercing painfully into my mind, the rest of it follows, bleeding in like watercolors as sleep drags me under.

*After leaving my mother in her dead garden, I hit hard ground
with a thud that reverberated through my bones. The floor felt
like dirt and stone beneath my fingers but it was too dark to
tell, too dark to see anything at all but black. It was the sort
of dark that I never knew existed.*

*And then the hands were on me, dirty fingers with ragged
bloody fingernails, grabbing at my skirts, my skin, anything
they could reach.*

*Panic rose in my chest and I summoned a flame to my
hand. It was buried deep inside me then, smothered by layers
of bone and flesh and sinew, but it was there. I pulled it forward to the tips of my fingers. It wasn't much, but it allowed
me to see.*

As soon as I could, I yearned for blindness once more.

A girl stood before me, grabbing at me desperately, hungrily, her face covered with a long tangle of dark brown hair.

"It's all right," I told her, trying to catch her hands with my unlit hand, to calm her. "I can get you to safety."

The girl went still and quiet. "Safety," she repeated, tasting the word.

I knew that voice. It spilled over my skin like a shock of cold water. The flames at my fingertips responded and expanded, casting a brighter glow around us.

"Haven't you learned better than to promise that by now?" She looked up at me, her hair falling away from her face. She had the same wide brown eyes, the same freckles on her cheeks, but now her lips were black and patches of her skin were charred. From the Encatrio the Kaiser made her drink.

"Elpis," I said, my voice shaking. "You're dead."

She smiled, revealing black teeth. "And whose fault is that?"

The words were a slap, though it was nothing I hadn't thought myself. After it happened, I would have given anything to be able to apologize to her, to have a moment just like this one to admit my mistake and tell her how much I regretted putting her in danger. Now that I had the chance, though, I froze.

"The Kaiser's," I told her finally.

She laughed, but it wasn't the laugh I remembered from Elpis—it was high-pitched and grating and sharp-edged.

"Was the Kaiser the one who turned me into an assassin at thirteen?" she asked me. "Knowing I could be killed? That even if I survived, I would be a murderer?"

I stumbled backward a step. "I gave you a choice," I said, but my voice wavered.

"I was a child," she bit out. I tried to move away from her, but her hand grabbed my wrist, her burnt black fingertips crumbling to ash as soon as they touched my skin. "And now I will never be anything else."

I pulled away from her, only to hit something else. I turned, holding up my burning hand, and found myself face to face with another ghost.

"You killed me," Hoa said, her eyes just as glassy and lifeless as they'd been the last time I saw her.

"You killed me," Archduke Etmond said, his face purple and swollen.

"You killed us," the Guardians from the prison said, their voices harmonized as one.

"And us," added warriors—so many warriors, dressed in so many different uniforms.

"And me." That was Laius. Impossible as it should have been. The memory was so long ago now, he shouldn't have been here with the dead, but he was.

They surrounded me, pressing in on all sides. The smell of decay and burning flesh permeated the air, their breath hot against my skin. I tried to scream but it died in my throat. I couldn't scream, I couldn't speak, I couldn't even breathe. I did this to them, I ended lives, either by my own hand or through my actions. I did this and I could never undo it.

"I'm sorry," I managed to choke out, the words mangled. "I'm so sorry. I wish I could take it back."

"Do you truly?" A single voice broke through, silencing

all of the others. The crowd of spirits parted, making way for one man.

The last time I'd seen him, he had been in chains, but now he walked free, his only injury the one I'd caused—the sword wound in his back that was bleeding through his stomach, marring the white robe he wore.

"Ampelio," I said, the name little more than a breath on my lips.

His smile was grim. "You killed me," he said. "Would you take that back?"

"You asked me to," I told him.

Ampelio shook his head. "The choice was yours, Theo," he said. "If you could go back, would you make it again?"

A sob wrenched itself from my throat, and the flames at my fingertips flickered, threatening to go out, but I managed to keep hold of them.

"Yes," I said finally. "You were a dead man as soon as you were caught. If it hadn't been me, it would have been someone else. And your death allowed me to fight back, to escape, to liberate this mine. It's why we're going to take our country back. I wish I hadn't had to do it, but yes, I would do it again."

Ampelio said nothing and I looked around at the others. So many faces, so much blood and death. Too much, yes, but all of it a necessary sacrifice. Ampelio stepped toward me, his hand reaching out to take hold of the pendant around my neck—his Fire Gem.

"Then you need to let us go, Theo," he told me, his voice quiet and soft. He released the Fire Gem and took hold of my wrist instead. His skin was warm against mine, pulsing with life. He was not real, I told myself, but I wasn't sure I really *believed that. His eyes locked on to mine as he brought my flaming hand toward his chest. "You know what to do."*

*I shook my head, but I knew he was right. He gave me an encouraging smile, and so I summoned what strength I had left and pressed my flaming hand to his chest.*

*He slipped into smoke, gone in an instant.*

*The other spirits closed in around me, but now their wails and accusations didn't wound as much as they had before. I still felt their cries acutely, but they didn't incapacitate me.*

*"Your deaths were necessary," I said, to them and to myself. I looked at my warriors, the Guardians, Elpis, Laius. "Some of you knew this; some of you chose it. Some of you were bystanders," I added, looking at Archduke Etmond and Hoa. "But you died honorably and I hope that you have found peace."*

*Hoa's wailing quieted first, and for just an instant, there was a spark in her lifeless eyes. She brought a hand up to my cheek, and I felt her touch again.*

*"My Phiren," she murmured to me.*

*I touched my flaming hand to her cheek and let her go.*

*Archduke Etmond followed, then the trio of Guardians. Elpis. Laius. Each of them bowed their head to me before I set them free. My soldiers were next, a seemingly endless line of them in their mishmash of colors. Astrean, Gorakian, Rajinkian—no matter where they'd come from, I kissed their forehead, placed my hand on their cheek, and set them free.*

# QUARREL

———————— • ◆ • ————————

HERON WAKES ME THE NEXT morning when the sun is a mere suggestion in the sky, the barest hint of dawn light bleeding through my tent.

"Theo?" he says, shaking my shoulder.

I force myself to breathe in, breathe out as the dream slowly loosens its grip on my mind. Artemisia was right—that memory of the mines was even more difficult than the first. I can still feel their hands on me, still hear their shrieks, still feel the guilt like lead in my chest. But I set them free, I let them go, I honored them the only way I could. It was a test I passed.

"Are you all right?" Heron asks.

I'm not sure how to answer that. "Another memory from the mine," I tell him softly.

He understands and doesn't press the matter.

"You're here," he says instead. "You survived. You're all right."

I nod once. I survived, but that isn't what hurt so much about that memory—it was all the people who hadn't. But

Ampelio was right. We wouldn't have come this far without their sacrifice, and I owe it to them to honor it.

"What's wrong?" I ask him, pushing the thought from my mind.

He shakes his head, lips pursing. "We thought it best that Erik speak with Jian—as terrible as his Gorakian is, we thought he'd be able to explain what happened with Brigitta better than the rest of us."

"And? Was he?" I ask.

In truth, I all but forgot about Jian, in the chaotic day we've had. I wonder how Laius is doing, though I know I'll drive myself mad if I keep thinking along those lines. He knew what he was choosing when he volunteered to take Jian's place. All I can do now is honor his sacrifice.

Heron doesn't answer right away. He takes me by the arm and steers me toward one of the guard barracks by the dining hall.

"Best if you hear for yourself," he says.


Erik and Jian are waiting in the barracks, and when I enter, they both get to their feet. A swath of black fabric has been tied over Erik's eyes—both the one that's missing and the one that's swollen shut—but I see his forehead furrow.

"Theo?" he asks.

"It's me," I say as Heron closes the door behind us. "Heron said there was something urgent?"

Erik glances in Jian's direction before looking back toward me.

"The weapon Jian developed. The velastra," he says slowly. "That was why you kept him here, yes?"

"Yes," I say. "An alchemical weapon—a gas that takes away the will of anyone who inhales it. You see why we couldn't trade him to Cress."

Heron clears his throat behind me. "Apparently not an alchemical weapon," he says. "At least not entirely. A combination, of sorts, with Spiritgems."

"Spiritgems?" I ask. "But this was long before the Kalovaxians thought to invade Astrea."

"Apparently some gems had . . . leaked out over the years. Were traded and re-traded until no one knew where they'd come from. It would seem the Theyn had a couple of them."

I remember how the Theyn liked to collect things from other cultures, how the rooms he and Cress had in the palace were so full of artifacts that they resembled a museum.

"The velastra was used only once, according to Jian," Erik says. "That was when Jian and Brigitta decided to flee. They knew if the Kalovaxians had access to a weapon like that, they would be able to hold the entire world on a leash."

I nod. "Brigitta told me as much. But we have Jian—so the velastra is out of the Kalovaxians' grasp."

No one responds right away.

"We do have Jian," Erik says finally. "But as it turns out, he didn't make the weapon alone. Brigitta wasn't only his paramour; they were partners. She developed it with him."

Jian looks between all of us. He might not understand much of what we're saying, but he understands his name and Brigitta's.

"We destroyed the prototype," he says, stumbling over the

Kalovaxian words. "But she has the plan, here." He points to his head, his expression grave. He points to his heart as well. "And here," he adds.

"In her heart?" I ask, frowning.

He shakes his head. "In her blood."

I swallow, the nausea returning tenfold. "The subject the velastra was used on," I say slowly.

Jian nods, his frown deepening as he searches for the words. "The effect . . . it lasted months after we fled. And we ran tests—the effect wore off, but the poison never left her."

My legs give out beneath me, and Heron helps me into a chair.

"So even if she doesn't break under the torture," I say slowly, forcing the words out, "the secret of it is right there for the taking."

"Cress won't know that," Erik says. "Even if she found out her mother was a test subject for the velastra, she won't know it lingered. Jian only knew because of the tests they ran tests there's no way for Cress to have any idea about."

I wish that reassured me, but it doesn't. I know Cress too well to make the mistake of underestimating her, and I know there is nothing Cress loves more than a good puzzle. And here I've hand-delivered her a puzzle that will destroy the world if—*when*—she manages to solve it.

After word of the velastra is passed on to Artemisia, Søren, Blaise, and Maile, they meet Heron, Erik, and me in the commandant's office, where we proceed to stare at the large map of Astrea painted on the wall, and argue.

We have to get to the capital before Cress figures out how to replicate the velastra. Everyone agrees on that point. What no one can seem to agree on is how we should go about doing it.

"The Air Mine is the closest to us," Søren says, pointing it out on the map that takes up the bulk of one wall. It's a fine map, but even at first glance, it's clear that it's missing a few geological features—Lake Trilia, for instance, and part of the mountain range. It seems to have been used mostly for decorative purposes, but it's enough to get the point across at the moment.

"It's the obvious choice," Søren continues. "We can't waste any time, and once we free the slaves there, we should have enough men to take the palace."

Maile nods along, arms folded over her chest. "You're right," she says after a moment, and even Erik looks shocked to hear those words come from her mouth. "It *is* the obvious choice, and so it's the one the Kalovaxians will expect. In all likelihood, we'll be walking into a trap."

"Cr . . . The Kaiserin doesn't know we're already here at the Water Mine," I point out. "We have at least another two days before she gets back to the palace, provided she rides all night. We're a step ahead of her. We can make it to the Air Mine before she knows we're heading there."

"In an ideal world, yes," Søren says. "But in order to reach the Air Mine, we have to travel past the Ovelgan estate, which is right around here." He points to an unmarked place on the edge of the Perea Forest. "As soon as the Ovelgans see us, they'll alert the Kaiserin and she'll put the pieces together."

"We'll take cover, then," Erik says.

Søren shakes his head. "It's flat land, and once we're out of the forest, it's barren as well. No trees. No mountains. Nowhere to hide."

"The cover of night, then," Erik replies.

That gives Søren a second of pause. "It would be a large risk to take," he says. "Especially if we have other options. I think we'd be better off heading to the Earth Mine instead. You said Dragonsbane was going to attack there after bringing the refugees to Doraz?"

I nod. "One of her carrier pigeons found us just yesterday—she just left Doraz and should arrive at the Earth Mine in two days' time."

"Perfect," Søren says. "We'll get there a day or two after she does, and with the added forces we'll be able to take the capital directly. We'll still march past the Ovelgan estate, but we'll make them think we're going to the Air Mine. It's a more roundabout path, so it'll take a few days longer to reach the palace, but it might be worth the risk. You have spies?"

"Our spies or her spies?" Artemisia asks. "We have both. Our spies are in the capital, but they aren't close enough to the Kaiserin to have access to any pertinent information about this weapon."

"But her spies here?" he asks.

"We had a few," Artemisia says, the corners of her mouth pulling down into a frown. "We were using them to pass misleading information to the capital, but they became liabilities at the Water Mine, so we had to do away with them."

"But the Kalovaxians don't know that," Blaise points out. "We could still send information, pretend it's from them."

"Exactly," Søren says with a brief grin. "We'll make sure the Kalovaxians think we're going to the Air Mine. So they'll set the trap there, like Maile said, but they won't catch us."

Maile shakes her head. "It's still too risky," she says. "Say we didn't execute all of the spies. Even if a single rogue missive makes it to the capital . . . We aren't a small army anymore, and we can no longer avoid notice like we did before you let yourself get captured, *Your Highness*."

The temperature in the room drops several degrees, and Søren's shoulders tense. I open my mouth to scold Maile, then close it again. Her eyes are alight and fixed on Søren as she waits for his reaction. She's baiting him, I realize. She *wants* Søren to snap, but nothing good will come of that, so I clear my throat.

"I have to imagine you have an idea if you're so quick to shoot down everyone else's," I say to her instead.

Maile stands up, approaches the map. She points to the gold-painted star that represents the capital.

"Time is of the essence; you said so yourselves," Maile says. "So why not stop worrying about them catching us and go after them instead?"

I can't help but let out a snort. "Because we don't have the numbers for an attack like that. And besides, they'll have the advantage of fighting on their own ground, with their own resources. The lookouts at the capital walls will see us coming for miles. We won't even make it through the gates."

Maile shrugs. "You asked for a plan—that's my plan," she says. "Maybe we don't have the numbers or the resources, but at least they won't be expecting it. With a little finagling, we could even trick them into sending the bulk of their troops to the Air and Earth Mines, leaving the capital relatively un-defended."

"That just sounds like more maybes to me," I tell her, shaking my head. "It's all maybes. Every choice is risky. So the question is, which option gets us the most?"

"That's easy," Maile says. "Take the capital and the war is over. It's checkmate."

"Not necessarily," Søren says. "In your plan, the bulk of their army will be outside the city walls, with thousands of chained Astreans—and now Gorakians—at their mercy."

"And as we know, the Kalovaxians don't have mercy," Erik adds. "I was only two when we left Goraki, but I'll never for-get the sight of them burning it to the ground on our way out. When they get word the capital has been taken, they'll flee and destroy everything in their path as they go."

"The Air Mine," I interject. "That's the risk that's worth the most. It's the clearest path to the palace, so we'll be able to go there next. Besides, we need healers, and more warriors. That's where we can get both."

"It's the obvious choice," Maile says again.

"Maybe," I allow. "But it's the one that makes the most sense. And we can take precautions to mislead the Kaiserin and her armies. Make them think we're going to the Earth Mine, or even back to the Fire Mine—we can send them so much conflicting information that they don't know what to make of any of it."

"And the Ovelgan estate?" Søren reminds me. "They'll send word to Cress as soon as they see us."

I bite my lip, staring at the spot on the map where Søren indicated the estate stood.

"How well do you know the Ovelgans?" I ask him. "How well do they know you? They weren't at court—I barely heard their name mentioned—but they're clearly wealthy enough for an estate of their own."

Søren's brow furrows. "They don't like court," he says, shaking his head. "They hosted me at the estate when I was young, but they didn't talk about politics. I got the feeling they didn't want to say anything that would get back to my father."

"That's not exactly earth-shattering, is it?" Erik asks. "Everyone was afraid of your father."

"What if we didn't approach them as an army?" I ask. "If we approached as a small group there to negotiate passage?"

"You want to negotiate with Kalovaxians?" Maile asks, disgust dripping from each word.

"I want to get us past their estate without the Kaiserin finding out. If they were mistrustful of the Kaiser, I would imagine they're at the very least ambivalent about the Kaiserin," I say, looking at Søren. "Do you think it's possible we could win them over?"

Søren considers it for a moment before shaking his head. "They may not like the current ruler, but they're still Kalovaxians, loyal down to the bone." He pauses. "But, I think they're at least smart enough to hear us out before they make that decision."

We make plans to leave at dawn, which gives us just enough time to get the injured and those who can't or don't wish to fight settled in at the camp, where they will be safe until Drag-onsbane can make it down the coast to collect them, and to do an inventory of supplies to decide what to take and what to leave behind. All twelve Water Guardians have decided to join us, adding to the eight Guardians from the Fire Mine, which means that we won't have to carry water.

As the camp packs up, I lead Erik through the streets. He still leans heavily on me with each step, but at least he's try-ing. Heron tied a new strip of cloth around his temples, this cloth bright red, made from one of the Kalovaxian flags that were torn down and desecrated as soon as the camp was ours.

"You're doing well," I tell him.

He snorts so hard, he throws us both off balance and I very nearly topple to the ground.

"Sorry," he says, helping to right us. "It's just that *well* doesn't seem to fit how I feel at all."

"I know," I say. "But you're alive, Erik."

"I am," he says. "But so many others aren't because I made a mistake. I should have stayed in the camp. I shouldn't have risked their safety just because I was worried about Søren. You were right—the better choice was to wait and see how it would play out. And look, Cress brought him right back to you without realizing."

"That was a stroke of luck," I say, shaking my head. "I truly didn't think I would see him again. I thought he was lost. I just . . . I thought that if I asked him what he wanted me to do—"

"He would have told you not to risk it," he finishes. "Søren tends to be calm and level-headed like that, doesn't he?"

"But you were right—if our positions were reversed, he wouldn't have hesitated to come after me," I point out. "The guilt of it was difficult to bear."

"You made the right decision," he says.

"Maybe," I say. "But I'm not so sure you made the wrong one. Maybe it looks like that now, but at the time, I thought you'd made a smart choice. Maybe a few years down the road you won't regret it anymore. Who can say for sure?"

He doesn't reply for a moment.

"Heron said something peculiar," he says hesitantly. "He told me that you think you and Crescentia are sharing dreams."

I stop short, giving him no choice but to stop as well. "Yes," I say. "I know how it sounds, but—"

"I believe you," he says, cutting me off.

I stare at him, unable to hide my surprise, though I realize he can't see it. "You do?" I ask.

He licks his lips, weighing his words carefully. "She said something I thought was strange at the time, but if what you're saying is true, it makes sense," he says. "She kept shouting your name—well, she kept shouting *Thora*. Things like *'Do you hear that, Thora?'* and *'What do you think of this, Thora?'* She's not well, Theo, but there was something about her rambling that didn't seem insane. It only seemed . . . I don't know. Desperate."

# ALIVE

W E LEAVE JUST AFTER SUNRISE and I ride on the back of
Artemisia's horse as usual. When we reach the other
side of Lake Culane, just before disappearing into the forest,
Artemisia pulls the horse to a stop and turns around to take
one last look at the Water Mine.

"I never thought I would come back here after I escaped,"
she tells me softly. "It was a place that haunted my nightmares. It was a place of pain and misery and death in my
mind. Maybe in some way it always will be. But I'd like to
remember it like this. Broken down to almost nothing."

"Soon we'll build something new in its place," I tell her.
"The next time you see it, it will be beautiful."

She pauses. "No," she says. "I don't think so. I don't want
to see it again at all. To me, it will always be an ugly place and
there's no changing that. I'd just rather remember it ugly and
broken—broken by me in places. That's the best memory I
can have of it, I think."

She turns back away from the camp and digs her heels
into the horse's side, spurring him forward into the cover of
the woods.

As we ride in silence, I think about her words. Though it takes some time, I think I come to understand them. After all, the Astrean palace was a place I loved once, but now there are so many awful memories there that I wonder if it will ever feel like home again. I wonder if some places are so haunted with terrible memories that they are better left in ruins than built anew. I wonder if I have it in me to do that to the only home I've ever known.

We stop to make camp in the middle of the Perea Forest, and after a mostly sleepless night before, I turn in early, retreating to my tent just after a quick dinner. The dull sound of conversation leaks from the campfire, but I don't mind the noise. It's soothing, in a way, to know I'm not alone, and it helps to keep my thoughts occupied as I crawl onto my bedroll and draw the threadbare quilt up to my chin.

The last few times I've slept, I haven't dreamed of Cress at all, but with Erik's words lingering in my mind, I wonder if tonight will be different. The idea both terrifies and thrills me, and I know that the very prospect will make it difficult to fall sleep, no matter how exhausted my body feels.

After what seems like at least an hour of trying, the sound of a throat clearing interrupts my roaming thoughts. It seems like it's coming from just outside my tent. After a second, there's a tentative whisper.

"Theo?"

"Hello?" I call out warily, sitting up.

"It's me," a voice says, a little louder. It takes me a second to recognize Søren.

"Oh," I say. "Come in."

The tent flap opens and Søren slips inside before closing it again, leaving us in the pitch dark. He bangs into something—my tray, I think—and lets out a curse.

"Sorry," he says. "Do you have a candle I can light?"

"I've got it," I say. I call on my gift, and a ball of flame pops to life in the palm of my hand, illuminating the room and Søren's surprised face along with it. It's one thing to tell him about my gift, I suppose, but another thing altogether for him to see it with his own eyes.

I try to read his expression. Is he horrified? After what Cress did to him with the same power, I'm not sure I would blame him. But he doesn't look horrified, not exactly. He looks surprised, yes, but that's all. He swallows, his eyes fixed on the flame in my hand, processing.

"Can you pass me the candle?" I say, nodding toward the black taper candle in the brass candlestick that rests on the ground by his feet.

With fumbling hands, Søren takes the candle and brings it to me. As soon as it's lit, I close my hand and extinguish my own flame. Søren places the candle on the ground by my bedroll, but he doesn't seem to know what to do afterward. His hands fidget and he doesn't look at me.

"Is everything all right?" I ask him. "It's late."

"I know," he says, shaking his head. "I didn't wake you up, did I? I was waiting so that no one would see me come in, but it took longer than I thought."

"No, I couldn't sleep," I admit, motioning for him to sit down next to me, which he does.

It feels strange and a bit dangerous to have him here, sitting with me on my bedroll, but before he was kidnapped, we were spending most nights together. It was only a few weeks ago, but it feels like a whole other lifetime. "Who's on guard? Did they see you?" I ask.

"Only Artemisia," he says. "She let me through and rolled her eyes, but she didn't say anything. I think she might have missed me."

"I think she just really can't stand Maile, and it's making her like other people a bit more by comparison," I say.

"Either way, I'll take it," he says with a shrug. "I couldn't sleep, either."

"Does Erik snore?" I ask him.

Søren shakes his head, a small smile playing on his lips, though it fades quickly. "Terribly, but I got used to that ages ago," he says before hesitating, looking down at his hands and licking his lips. "I've seen a lot of terrible things, Theo. This wasn't the first time I've been held captive, beaten."

I wince. "And all of them were because of me," I point out. "I'm sorry."

He shakes his head.

"No, I don't mean that," he says. "And please don't apologize for it. I'd go through it all again to be here now, with you, as the person I am. I just mean that this time was different."

I frown. "What do you mean?"

He considers his words carefully for a moment. "The first time—on the *Smoke*—I was still so full of guilt. I deserved to be in that brig; I deserved what was happening to me. I don't think I was ever angry about it. I wasn't angry in Sta'Crivero, either. I felt . . . I don't know. Resigned. It was a misunderstanding because of who my father was, and that seemed . . . strangely appropriate. Besides, I think I always knew that you would find a way to get me out of there. There was always a light at the end of that tunnel."

He pauses, his fingers playing with a run in the comforter. There's still dirt wedged under his fingernails, still thin cuts on the backs of his hands, closed up but red.

"But this time . . . it was my own people holding me there. It was a girl I've known my whole life, someone I might have even liked and respected at one point. It was a world that I was a part of, once, a world that I was supposed to end up ruling. And you . . . you were dead. So this time, I was angry. And that anger felt like it was going to eat me alive, but it was also the only thing that kept me going. I think you understand that better than most."

I say nothing, only nod.

"I thought that anger would go away, now that I'm here and alive and safe again, but it hasn't. It's just festering, like an open and untreated wound. I don't know what to do with it," he says. "I don't know how to make it go away."

"You don't," I tell him after a second. "You learn to live with it, and you learn how to let it push you forward. The anger is always going to be there, but you can give it a direction and a purpose and turn it into something good."

He nods, his eyes still far away. "I'm with you, Theo," he says. "I know I said that before, and I meant it then, but it was different. I knew what you were fighting for and I supported it and I wanted to do everything I could to help you succeed. But now . . . I'm in it with you. And I'll be with you until the very end, whatever that might entail. Because those are my people, and whether I like it or not, they are my responsibility. And they need to be stopped."

I bite my lip. "We've never talked about it, Søren," I say quietly, "about what happens at the end, if we're victorious. What that victory looks like and what it means for the Kalovaxians who survive it."

"We haven't," he says carefully. "But I can't have a say in that. What I faced in the dungeon was a mild inconvenience compared to what the Kalovaxians have done to millions. And I trust your judgment."

I can't begin to think about what judgment that will be. It's so far away, with so many variables. But it's a decision Søren trusts me to make, and so I hope that when the time comes, I'll be able to do just that.

His hand tentatively reaches for mine, and when I entwine my fingers with his, we both just stare at them until he breaks the silence.

"I really thought you were dead," he says, his voice quiet. "This still feels like a dream, like I'm going to wake up and none of it will be real."

"I'm real," I tell him, but I know exactly what he means. He doesn't feel entirely real to me, either, more like a figment of my imagination that I somehow made corporeal. "We're alive," I add, for both of our sakes. "We're here."

# GHOST

———•———

I DON'T REMEMBER FALLING ASLEEP, BUT when I find myself in the Astrean throne room, I know I must be dreaming. Light from the waning moon filters through the stained-glass ceiling, casting the large room in an eerie, otherworldly glow.

"There you are," Cress's voice says, and I whirl around to see her, standing mere feet from me in a gown of ink-blue silk, with a wide neckline and gossamer bell sleeves studded with diamonds, making her look like the night sky itself. Her white hair is loose, falling just to her shoulders, still brittle and frayed at the ends. Her lips are blacker than they were when I saw her last, but when she steps closer, I realize that it isn't all natural—she's painted them with black lacquer.

I wonder if she's trying to make it into some kind of style, something strange and beautiful instead of a flaw. I wonder if the court is now full of noblewomen with painted black lips, if merchants are charging absurd prices for a lacquer shade they likely made using nothing more than coal and grease.

"You've been forgetting about me. I haven't seen you in days," she accuses.

I feel the old urge to apologize, and have to hold myself back. I don't owe her apologies. I don't owe her anything.

"I'm dead," I tell her with a shrug. "I have better things to do than entertain you. In fact, perhaps I should go."

I make a move to leave, though I'm not sure where I *would* go or how I'd make myself wake up, but the bluff works. Cress grabs my hand roughly, her fingers hot against my skin.

"No, don't," she says, her desperation leaking through before she hastily adds "Please," her voice small and childlike.

I pretend to hesitate. "Fine," I say. "I suppose I can stay for a bit."

She releases my hand and instead loops her arm through mine, squeezing it and smiling broadly.

"Exciting things are happening, Thora," she says. "Very exciting things. I had to give up Prinz Søren to set them in motion, but it was a price worth paying, I suppose," she adds with a pout.

My stomach turns as I think about Brigitta and Laius. Has she already discovered that Laius isn't Jian? Has Brigitta broken so soon?

"What sort of things?" I ask. "It must have been something for you to give up the Prinz."

She scoffs. "I'd hoped Prinz Søren would be useful to me, but he proved far more trouble than he was worth. I was glad to see him go. And what I got in return was far better, I assure you."

I swallow. "And what was that?" I ask.

But instead of answering, she frowns and leans in to sniff my hair. "You smell like him. Did you know? Like driftwood and sea salt. I suppose if he's joined you in death so soon, he didn't survive the journey to Sta'Crivero. Pity—I think King Etristo had quite the execution planned. You'll give him my regards, won't you?"

"I think he's had enough of your regards," I tell her.

She only laughs, throwing her head back. "No need to be so dramatic, Thora. It's *war*. Surely Søren understands that, even if you don't. And besides, I gave him back to you in the end. Shouldn't you be thanking me for that?"

"You tortured him," I remind her. "You burned your words into his skin. What part of that should I thank you for, exactly?"

She blinks languidly. "Well, he's dead now, isn't he? What does any of that matter?" she asks with a laugh. "I suppose it's the least you could hope for. Both of you failed, but at least you're together in death."

*No,* I want to tell her. *We're together and alive and we are coming for you.* But I hold my tongue.

"What did you trade him for?" I say instead, focusing on what matters.

She laughs again. "I traded him for an end to this war, an end to any future rebellions. You could say, Thora, that I traded him for control of the world itself."

My heart beats so loudly in my chest that I fear she can hear it, but I proceed cautiously. "A weapon, then?" I ask her, as if I don't already know the answer.

But Cress is unbothered. Instead she raises a thin, ashen eyebrow. "Don't think so mundanely, Thora," she says. "It's unbecoming and I expected better of you. A weapon. What I have planned is so much greater than that. Come. I want to show you something."

Without waiting for my response, she pulls me out the throne room door and down the palace hallway. It's exactly as I remember it, down to the details on the stained-glass windows we fly past. It even smells the same, like the lye and lemon soap they use to clean the floors. She rounds a corner, then another, and I realize where she's taking me—to the main balcony, the one that overlooks the rocky coastline.

When we arrive, the balcony isn't empty. A lone girl stands by the railing in a black, billowing gown that glistens in the moonlight. When she hears us approach, she turns, her sharp-angled face illuminated. Dagmær. In the months since I last saw her, she's grown more gaunt; her limbs are barely more substantial than bits of string. Her blond hair is paler, cut bluntly like Cress's—perhaps another trend Cress has started. But as Cress pulls me closer, I realize that isn't it at all. Dagmær's lips aren't painted black. They're charred, just like the skin of her neck. Just like Cress's.

And she looks at me the way Cress does, as if she can truly see me as clearly as I see her. In this dream, she is every bit as real as Cress and I are.

"Oh, Dagmær," I say quietly. "What's happened?"

But Dagmær gives a feral smile.

"I've been saved," she tells me, before shifting her attention to Cress. "I did it, Your Highness."

Cress smiles and peers over the railing. "So you did," she says. "Well done. I knew you could. And now you're truly free."

I force myself to lean over the railing to see what they're talking about, and when I do, I can't muffle a gasp. Sprawled out on the rocks below are bodies. I count ten of them altogether, some of them too small to be fully grown. Necks snapped, limbs at unnatural angles, pools of blood around them.

"You see, Thora?" Cress says, pulling me back from the edge, her grip on my arm so tight, I feel her nails digging into my skin. "Dagmær is free now and justice has been served, just as it was for me."

"I did to my husband what he did to his wives before me," Dagmær says, her voice thin and far away. "What he will never be able to do to me now. And then I killed his sons, too. Now no man controls me. Only I do. And my Queen, of course."

She looks at Cress with fawning eyes, a loyal devotee. And why shouldn't she be? Cress saved her, let her liberate herself from a husband who beat her, who would have killed her if she hadn't done it to him first. But his sons? Lord Dalgaard's youngest was only six. I think of the small body I saw on the rocks below and feel sick.

"There are so many women in the world, Thora," Cress says, cutting through my thoughts. "So *many* who suffer at the hands of the men who think they can control them. My father controlled my life for years, but at least he was a kind jailer. The Kaiser wasn't kind, though I don't need to tell you that, do I? And he's not the only one. He may not even have been the worst. But I won't let them do it anymore."

I push my nausea aside and face Cress.

"And what of the Astrean women who suffer at your hands?" I ask her. "If you want to save women, what will you do for them?"

Cress's face contorts in fury as quickly as I blink. "It's never going to be enough for you, is it?" she snaps. "I'm doing good, Thora. I'm helping people with this curse you forced upon me, and you can't even appreciate that."

"Why do you care so much what I think?" I ask her, my own voice rising. "Why are you showing me this? Why can't you let me rest?"

"Because," she all but shouts, her voice shaking. "Because I am making a new world, Thora. Because you weren't strong enough to be a part of it, but I want you to see it anyway."

Before I can formulate an answer, the dream world begins to flicker, tearing itself apart until I am left in the darkness of my tent once more, the only sound Søren's steady breathing next to me.

One thought stays with me, forcing its way past all of the others. Cress knew I would likely die when she gave me that poison, but she hoped I wouldn't. She didn't want to kill me; she wanted to change me. And she still has no idea that she did.


I don't find sleep again, and I don't really yearn for it. I don't want to see Cress again, but maybe more than that, I don't want to see Dagmær. I don't want to remember that Cress wouldn't have had to save her from her wicked husband if I hadn't meddled to have them married in the first place. That crime was mine, and so in some ways, the crimes that followed in its wake are mine as well.

And now she's like us, like Cress and me. It must be the blood that binds us together, Cress's blood now a part of all of us, allowing our dreams to cross over like this. It makes me sick to think about. How many others are there?

I scratch at my arm idly for a moment before noticing there is something off about it. It itches, yes, but the skin there is raw and almost painful. I sit up in bed, careful not to wake Søren, though I don't think an earthquake would be enough to do that, as heavy a sleeper as he is. I summon a small flame to my fingertips, just enough to see my arm. When it's fully illuminated, I gasp.

The skin from my wrist to my elbow is bright red—the color of a fresh tomato—and there, in the soft underside of my forearm, are four small crescent-shaped indents from Cress's nails.

The place burns and itches horribly, but it's proof.

I clamber out of bed as quickly as I can and change into the clean white cotton shift dress that was left out for me, folded neatly at the foot of the bedroll. When I sit down again to pull my shoes on, Søren stirs, rolling toward me, blue eyes barely open.

"It can't be time to get up yet," he says.

I shake my head. "I had another dream about Cress—well, not a dream. And I can prove it this time."

That banishes all remnants of sleep from his eyes. He sits up quickly.

"What happened?" he asks.

"You were right," I say. "She's building her own army, using the Encatrio made from her blood. It might be killing most of them, but not all. I saw one of them. Dagmær—Lady Dalgaard. I don't know if you remember her—"

He has to search his memory for only a second. "I remember *you* were very nearly Lady Dalgaard, until I persuaded my mother to make other arrangements. That poor girl."

"Not such a poor girl anymore. She's changed. Like Cress. Like me," I tell him. "And the first thing she did was to rid herself of her boor of a husband and all of his sons."

I see the realization dawn on him. "And his daughters?" he asks. "He had a few of those as well."

"I'd imagine that those young enough to still be under Dagmær's care will be the next victims of Cress's poison, or her newest recruits," I say.

"Recruits for what?" he asks.

I shake my head. "I don't know. But she has something planned, something she wouldn't tell me. She thinks she's doing something good—liberating women, empowering them. But she has a very limited idea of which women qualify for her kind of empowerment."

"She thinks Amiza is on her side," he reminds me. "She thinks she'll have all of Sta'Crivero."

"She'll learn soon enough that she doesn't," I point out. "But it seemed like more than that. She said I would see before long."

"Does she still think you're . . ." He trails off. I suppose this soon after thinking as much himself, he can't say it out loud.

"She still thinks I'm dead," I tell him. "But you were wrong earlier—we all were. She didn't want me dead, not entirely. She wanted me changed. Somehow, even after everything, she thought that I would be on her side, a devoted disciple like Dagmær."

He frowns, thinking it over. "Maybe it does make sense," he says slowly. "To her way of thinking, you were corrupted. Isn't that what she said? That you'd been swayed by rebels, brought over to their side? Maybe she thought that by giving you powers, she would make you strong enough to come back to her."

The thought of it makes me sick. It's so convoluted, but then Erik and Søren both said that she wasn't well. I saw it myself when she thought I was Amiza—her blind desperation, her lack of logic. The Cress I knew always operated like a dagger, precise and exact in every sense of the word, but these latest moves are more erratic. She's become a rogue cannon, firing in every direction and hoping something strikes true.

I knew her mind well enough to see her dagger strikes coming, to prepare for them, but this new Cress is something I can't begin to understand. She's unpredictable, and there is nothing more dangerous in war than that.

"You said you have proof?" Søren asks, dragging me out of my thoughts.

I summon the flame to my fingertips again and show him my arm. When he sees it, he inhales sharply, reaching out to touch the tender skin, but as gentle as he tries to be, it still hurts and I pull away.

"Sorry," he says. "What happened?"

"She grabbed my arm in the dream and dragged me back from the balcony's edge. It hurt then, but I didn't really feel it. Now I do."

"I've never seen a burn like that," he tells me. "And those nail marks are deep. I'm surprised there's no blood. Heron might be able to help."

"Hopefully," I say. "And I need to show him and the others. You believed me from the beginning, but they need the proof of it."

He nods, throwing the blankets off and grabbing the boots he shucked last night. "Then let's go," he says.

I glance toward the door. "There's one problem with that," I say. "Blaise has been taking over guard duty for Art at night so she can get a few hours of sleep."

Understanding dawns on him. "You don't want him to see me coming out of your tent at this hour," he says.

"I know that there are more important issues at the moment, but we left things a bit raw the other day," I say. I hesitate before continuing. "We ended it—whatever it was. For good this time."

He pauses, hands on the laces of his boots, and looks up at me.

"You didn't have to do that because I'm back," he says. "He means a lot to you. I know that. I've known it as long as I've known he existed."

"He does," I say, choosing my words carefully. "But I think that kind of love—it's not good for either of us. It's more destructive than not."

For a second, he looks like he wants to ask more, but he doesn't and I'm grateful for that.

"You go, then," he says. "I'll wait a minute before following and I'll meet you at Heron's tent."

# PROOF

———•—

"IT DOESN'T CHANGE ANYTHING," MAILE says when I finish recounting the dream again for her, Heron, Erik, Artemisia, and Blaise.

She's the first one to speak after a lengthy pause, which I suppose makes sense because she knows the least about Cress and about my fraught and tangled relationship with her. I didn't want Maile to be here at all, but since she and Heron are sharing a tent, she insisted on joining for fear of being left out of another strategy meeting.

"Are you joking?" Heron asks. I don't think he's lost the look of shock on his face since he first saw my arm. "She's sharing dreams with the Kaiserin and they aren't just dreams. That's a physical injury. Which means Theo can be hurt in these dreams."

"Theoretically," Art says softly, "it also means that the Kaiserin can be hurt in them."

It's a possibility I hadn't considered until now, but Art is right. If Cress can hurt me through our dreams, why can't I hurt her? Or worse? If I managed to kill Cress in a dream, would it kill her in real life? It's a question I can't begin to

+ 241 +

know the answer to, though I remind myself that it doesn't matter either way. Cress is only the face of the problem—with her dead, the Kalovaxians would just replace her, but things could very well get worse. At least I know Cress. At least I understand her, to some extent.

"No," Blaise says before I can answer. "It's too dangerous. We don't know *what* would happen, and if the Kaiserin learns that these dreams are anything more . . ."

He doesn't finish, but he doesn't have to. The implication hangs in the air. They think she would try to kill me, but they don't know what I told Søren—that Cress didn't want me dead. That there is a part of her that thought she was saving me. From them. From the life I chose, which she thinks was forced upon me. I glance at Søren, who seems to be having the same thought. But when I don't correct Blaise, he stays quiet.

I don't know why I keep that bit of information to myself. Maybe because it feels like a vulnerability they would judge me for, a tie between me and Cress that hasn't been severed—that may not ever be able to be severed.

"She doesn't suspect," I say instead. "She seems to know they aren't dreams somehow, but she thinks I'm dead. She thinks I'm haunting her."

"If she thinks you're dead, why wouldn't she just tell you her plan?" Maile asks.

I have to think for a moment, turning over possibilities in my mind until I strike on one that feels undeniably true.

"Because she wants to make sure I keep coming back," I say. "She was angry that she hadn't seen me in a few days. She's holding that information so that she knows I'll return."

"But you can't," Blaise says. "It's too dangerous. Heron,

you can make some kind of medicine, can't you? Something that will give her dreamless sleep?"

Heron frowns but nods, his eyes finding mine. "I could," he tells me. "It's an easy enough draught, if you want it."

Do I want it? The prospect of dreams that aren't plagued by Cress is a tempting one. Not just to avoid her finding out the truth but because of Cress herself, how she talks to me, how she makes me feel. I don't like remembering that she's a real person, someone I hurt. It's easier to think of her as my enemy when she's far away, monstrous and threatening.

"No," I tell Heron. "This bond is our best chance at staying a step ahead of her, and we need to keep an eye on her progress with Brigitta and the velastra. We don't have many advantages over the Kalovaxians—we must use every one we can."

"Theo . . . ," Blaise starts, before breaking off and shaking his head. "Are you sure?" he asks instead.

I'm not sure of anything. I haven't been for quite some time. But I nod all the same. "It's the best chance we have," I say.

"Speaking of the velastra," Maile says, her voice already wary. "I'm going to go ahead and suggest the thing that no one has wanted to suggest. Instead of waiting for the Kalovaxians to create this magical alchemical weapon, why don't we beat them to it? We have Jian—"

"No," I say before she can get any further. "Brigitta was right not to trust us with that. A weapon that takes away a person's will should not exist."

"But if it has to exist, if it has to be *used*," Maile points out, "better by us than by them."

Heron shakes his head. "If we use the velastra, we *become* them," he says.

Maile looks toward Søren. "And you, Prinz? Your hands are already dirty; you know what war is. You can't have these same moral hang-ups."

Søren holds her gaze for a few seconds. "Are you familiar with berserkers?" he asks her after a moment.

Maile's eyes narrow. "You used them against my people. I would say I'm familiar enough with them."

Søren shakes his head. "From the one side of it," he says. "But from my side of it . . . do you know how we got the berserkers to do what we wanted, to walk to their own deaths without a single protest?"

Maile doesn't answer, but I do.

"You drugged them," I said, remembering what Erik told me back at the palace, when he first explained to me exactly what berserkers were.

Søren's eyes cut to mine, and a flash of anguish crosses them, but he nods. "It was the only way to do it, to convince them to do what we wished, to destroy themselves for our gain. But it wasn't convincing, not really. I saw their eyes go blank, saw how they moved like marionettes on strings, dazed and not of their own accord. To take away someone's will is to take away their very soul. I did it before and I will regret it for the rest of my life. I won't do it again, no matter the circumstances."

For an instant, I think Maile will argue, but eventually she clenches her jaw and looks away. "So nothing's changed," she says again. "In the immediate sense, at least. We're still marching toward the Air Mine. You lot still want to go through with this foolish plan at the Ovelgan estate?"

"You only think it's a foolish plan because you didn't come up with it," Erik points out.

"That doesn't change anything," I say, ignoring their snark. "We'll continue on our way as soon as we can get everything packed again. The sooner the better."

The others take that as the direction it was, and they quickly file out of the tent, Heron last. He lingers by the entrance, watching me scratch at my arm only to wince in pain.

"Maybe Cress's grand scheme is to drive me insane with this," I say, looking down at my wound. It's just as red as it was when I woke up, but at least it doesn't appear to be getting any worse.

Heron walks back toward me, holding his hand out. I show him my arm, and he examines it closely, careful to avoid touching the raw parts.

"It's definitely a magical wound," he says after a moment. "But I can heal it."

I pull my arm away from him. "I'd rather you use your gifts to heal the people who need it more," I say. "It's irritating, but it won't kill me."

Heron nods, looking a touch relieved. I'm sure with all of the healing he's been doing, he's feeling drained. "Put some salve on it and keep it clean and covered, and it should heal on its own in time," he says.

"Thank you," I say.

He lingers for another second. "I'm sorry I didn't believe you," he tells me. "About your dreams. I should have."

I shake my head. "It sounded insane—even to me. I almost didn't believe it myself."

"I'm going to make the dreamless-sleep potion," he tells me. "You don't have to drink it, but you might want the option one of these days. And if she does begin to realize . . . well, it'll be good to have some on hand."

I can't disagree with that. "Thank you," I tell him.

He nods, smiling tiredly before ducking out of the tent.

# FOREST

———◆•◆———

THE PEREA FOREST IS A dense expanse of olive trees and cypresses and a few other types of trees that I can't put a name to. I remember my mother telling me about it, how when the gods made Astrea, Glaidi made the trees from her own fingers, pushing them up through the earth and leaving a bit of herself behind in the roots so that the forest would always grow strong and thrive.

As a child, I was perplexed by the idea that Glaidi could have so many fingers, but now that part of the story doesn't bother me. It was only a story, and the truth of it wasn't in the details—it was in the heart. Maybe the trees aren't really Glaidi's fingers, but there is a part of her in them, somehow. I feel it now as we pass through the forest. I feel her presence all around me like the comfort of a heavy blanket over my shoulders. I feel her watching over me—watching over all of us—and I feel safe.

The forest is also bursting with birds the deeper in we go, birds with wings in a jewel-box array of shades—from ruby to citrine, pearl to obsidian. When a group of them flies overhead, they are a watercolored blur.

"I used to hear them," Artemisia says to me after an hour passes in silence. The ride is slower than I'm used to, but I'm grateful for it. The last thing I want to do is go galloping through a forest with no inkling of what awaits ahead. Artemisia clears her throat before continuing. "Across the lake, in the camp. I could hear their songs sometimes, early in the morning or late at night. I never really imagined what they looked like, or how many there were. I just thought their songs sounded sad. Like they were crying."

"They don't sound that way anymore," I tell her.

And it's true. The birds that fly overhead let out caws so loud that they hurt my ears, but they sound like shouts of joy. They sound like laughter.

"No," Art says. "Don't mention that to Erik, though. The last thing we need is some clever rhyme about how even the birds are celebrating our victory."

Though I can practically hear her rolling her eyes, there's a touch of affection in her voice as well, and I know that she's glad to have him back. My arms are wrapped around her waist to help me stay upright, but the horse's gait is slow and gentle, unlike the rides we took together in Sta'Crivero.

Behind us, Søren urges his pitch-dark horse into a canter coming up beside our horse. He looks better than he did even this morning, though his arms and chest are still covered in bandages. His skin isn't as sallow; the shadows beneath his eyes are less pronounced. It's a wonder what food and sleep will do. When his eyes meet mine, he smiles, and I smile back like it's the most natural thing in the world.

Our horse—a mild-mannered dappled mare—gives a

jump when his approaches, kicking her front legs in warning. I tighten my grip on Art's waist.

"Did you want something?" she asks him. "Or are you *trying* to spook my horse?"

Chastened, Søren steers his horse to the right, giving ours a bit of a wider berth.

"We'll be at the estate by sundown, which means the Ovelgans will likely invite you and me to eat supper with them," he says.

"Why would they want to eat with you?" Artemisia asks. "You're their enemy, aren't you?"

"Because diplomacy demands it, and the Ovelgans are more diplomatic than the Kalovaxian courtiers. They can afford to be, this far from court politics and schemes. They'll take the chance to hear us out."

I nod. "Good. How much do you know about them?"

He exhales, considering the question for a moment. "Lord Ovelgan was a commander in the war, but he hasn't fought since the siege of Goraki. He was injured in combat and retired to the country with his young wife. They have four children. Their eldest will be fifteen now, but I don't think he lives with them. He's off training to follow in his father's footsteps."

"What about Lady Ovelgan?" I ask. "What about her family?"

That takes him a moment more to consider. "The Stratlans," he says finally. "Do you remember them at court?"

"Vaguely," I say, frowning. The courtiers seemed to exist on a wheel to me, always turning. One family never stayed on top for long, and it was often difficult to keep them all straight. But I remember Rigga Stratlan, a girl a little older than me who Cress was friends with but who never said more than a couple of terse words to me. She was pretty in the conventional Kalovaxian way, with pale blond ringlets and a round face with a nose that turned up sharply at the tip.

When I mention her to Søren, he nods. "A cousin, I believe," he says, though I think we're pressing his area of expertise. Battle strategies and diplomacy he might know, but the tangled web of the Kalovaxian court is beyond him. "Lady Ovelgan was considered a great beauty—there was actually a rumor about her being one of my father's consorts for a time. Hard to believe there wasn't some credibility to it, knowing him."

He says the words casually enough, but they sour my stomach. "It's no wonder Lord Ovelgan was hasty to get her away from court when an opportunity arrived."

"If we're lucky, they'll still hold animosity toward the royal family for that," Artemisia says.

I shake my head. "*Or* they'll be far more likely to be sympathetic toward the Kaiserin," I point out.

Søren catches my eye. "Do you think Cress has already gotten to Lady Ovelgan? Offered her the Encatrio? Killed her or changed her?"

The same thought occurred to me, but I shake my head. "Cress has grown up in the court; she's never left it for more than a few days. I doubt she's thinking about anyone outside. It's practically another world to her."

"The Kaiserin," Art corrects me sharply, glancing back at both of us. "Not Cress. *The Kaiserin.*"

"I know, I know," I say with a sigh, even though she's right. Even if there is no one around to judge me for my familiarity, the distinction does help to keep them separate in my mind, but they never manage to stay that way for long. I look at Søren again. "What about the staff? How many people are on this estate? Are they Kalovaxian servants or Astrean slaves?" I ask him.

"Maybe three-quarters slaves, one-quarter servants," he says. "Plus, there's a Kalovaxian village just outside the estate."

A Kalovaxian village. It's a strange thought—I'm so used to Kalovaxian courtiers, the wealthy and privileged, that I often forget that they can only be wealthy and privileged if there are others who are beneath them. But the villagers are still Kalovaxian, I remind myself. Poor as they may be, they're still far more privileged than my people in their chains.

"How many of each, if you had to guess?" I press.

He exhales slowly, considering. "Maybe a couple hundred slaves working the estate. Maybe fifty, seventy-five servants. Plus a thousand in the village," he says. "If I had to guess, but I haven't been there in years. I really have no idea what to expect."

Artemisia grunts. "So we can fight them if we need to," she says, a surprise burst of optimism from her. "The numbers are on our side, and most of them won't be trained warriors, like most Kalovaxians we've fought."

"But as soon as that fight breaks out, they'll send word to the Kaiserin," I point out. "And then she'll know where we're headed. We'll have shown our hand, and the element of surprise is the only thing we have on our side."

"And if they send a messenger as soon as they spot us?" Art asks. "We should send our fastest group around to block off the other side in case they send someone."

I nod. "Yes, let's do that. And then we should only have a small envoy meet the Ovelgans," I add. "Not so many as to seem aggressive, but enough that we can hold our own if we need to."

"A group of twenty," Søren suggests. "And the others should stay close enough to pose a threat in case they think about striking out."

"The three of us," I say, counting off on my fingers—a struggle while sitting on top of a jostling horse. "Maile will likely insist on coming with us. Plus Erik. He has the status to be impressive to them, royal and also half-Kalovaxian. And his eye is an example of Cress's deranged cruelty. The other fifteen should be Fire and Water Guardians, though the Ovelgans don't need to know that. They'll be there and ready if we need them, but hopefully we won't."

"And Blaise?" Artemisia asks with a dose of hesitation. "Will we be needing him?"

I shake my head, feeling Søren's eyes on me as well. "I don't think Blaise will have any interest in that," I say. "He doesn't want to use his power anymore. We came to an agreement about it."

That surprises Artemisia. She looks at me over her shoulder with eyebrows arched high. "He said that?" she asks.

"He did," I say. "What happened at the Water Mine changed things for him. He doesn't want to risk that again."

Artemisia turns back around, looking at the forest ahead.

"He says that," she says. "Maybe he even thinks he means it, but words are one thing. Actions are another. And Blaise isn't the sort of person to sit contentedly on the sidelines."

"You're wrong," I say, though her words wedge under my skin. "You didn't see him when we talked about it. He was set on this path."

She doesn't say anything for a moment. "I hope you're right, Theo. But only time will tell for sure."

I don't know what to say to that, so I hold my tongue. She doesn't know what she's talking about, I tell myself, but there's a small voice in my head that whispers that she's only giving voice to thoughts I've had myself.

"Søren, pass along our plan to the others ahead," I say. "Get volunteer Guardians to round up our envoy. Artemisia, is there a stream nearby? I should clean up before we get there, and change into something more regal. If these people want a queen, I'll give them one."

Artemisia finds a stream nearby to clean up at, Heron tagging along. While I splash cool water onto my face and run my fingers through my hair to loosen the knots and mats that have formed, Heron pulls an emerald-green silk dress from my saddlebags. We found it in one of the barracks at the Water Mine, though no one was sure where it had come from. It was too big in some areas, too small in others, but Heron tailored it to fit me.

I pull the dress on and let Artemisia braid my hair again, this time twisting it into a bun on top of my head—a simple style, but one that looks regal.

"There," she says when it's done.

I glance at my reflection in the stream and can't help but frown. The girl staring back doesn't look like me—her face is sharper, eyes harder, jaw stronger. I used to think I looked like my mother, but there is precious little of her left in me now, though it isn't quite Ampelio's face, either. Instead I think I merely look like myself.

# ESTATE

———•———

THE OVELGAN ESTATE RISES INTO view as soon as we're out of the forest, a tall structure that shines gold in the light of the morning sun. Because of the name, I was expecting something characteristically Kalovaxian, something gray and sharp-edged and daunting, but the design of it is unmistakably Astrean, with the same rounded towers and stained-glass windows and domed roofs as the palace. I wonder what it was before the siege, and I look around for Blaise because if anyone would know, he would, but I can't find him in the crowd.

"Who are you looking for?" Heron asks, riding up beside me and Artemisia.

"Blaise," I say. "I wanted to ask if he knew what the estate was before."

"He rode ahead with a group to the far side of the village to cut off any messengers they might send out. Just in case Søren's hunch about the Ovelgans hearing us out first was wrong," Heron explains, glancing at the estate with a furrowed brow. "But I can answer that for you—it was the Talvera estate."

I glance sideways at him. "How do you know that?"

He doesn't answer right away, instead shrugging his shoulders. "Because it was Leonidas's—his family's, at least. He was supposed to be the future Lord Talvera."

"Oh," I say, suddenly speechless. Leonidas was the boy Heron knew in the mines, the boy Heron loved and lost to mine madness. "You didn't say anything when we were making the plan."

He shrugs again, his eyes focused straight ahead. "What was there to tell? I had nothing to contribute to the discussion—I've never been, know nothing of the layout. All I know of it is what he told me. He painted such a lovely picture of it when everything else seemed so impossibly dark and ugly. He told me about how he used to run down the tiled halls, how the mosaics shone like gold in the noon sun, how it was the most beautiful place in the world. He told me someday we would live there together, when this was all over."

He swallows and turns his face away, but there's no hiding the catch in his voice.

"And the rest of his family?" I ask. "You said there was no one left. No one with a proper claim to it?"

He shakes his head. "Leo was the last one."

I consider this for a moment before coming to a decision. "Then if we make it through this, it's yours," I say. "If you want it."

That takes him by surprise. "Mine?"

I shrug. "He made you a promise," I say. "He might not be able to see it through himself, but there's no reason it shouldn't hold. Besides, it looks like a place you would be happy in. Peaceful, away from the capital, close to the Air Mine—what will be the Air Temple once it's rebuilt. You could oversee that, if you want to."

For a moment, Heron stares at me, mouth gaping. Finally, he smiles. "I think I would. Want that, I mean. It's a very grand house, though, Theo," he says, glancing back at the estate.

"You're a very grand man," I reply.

"Don't let anyone else hear you promising things, or they'll start lining up," Artemisia says. "And besides, you won't have anything to benevolently parcel out if we don't actually win. Let's focus on that."

"I know," I say quickly. "But sometimes it feels like this war will go on forever. It's nice to imagine what comes next."

Artemisia, Heron, and I ride to the front of our formation, where Søren and Maile are already leading the troops. When Maile sees me approach, she gives me a critical once-over.

"That's not a very practical dress," she tells me matter-of-factly, eyes lingering on the emerald gown.

"The Kalovaxians don't expect women to dress practically," I tell her. "They won't listen to a word I say if I don't look the way they expect a ruler to look."

Maile frowns. "And me?" she asks, gesturing to her own outfit—close-fitting brown leather trousers and a white cotton tunic that looks like it needs a good wash. "As a Vecturian princess, should I change into something more conventionally regal?"

I consider my words carefully for fear of insulting her, before I remember that Maile would likely be more offended by my trying to protect her feelings.

"No," I tell her honestly. "It isn't about impressing them. It's about giving them what they expect. They expect Vecturians to be dirty and ill-mannered and bedraggled. Honestly, you could stand to rough yourself up a bit more. Don't speak; pretend you don't understand their language. They'll assume you're a simpleton and underestimate you, which will no doubt come in handy."

For a beat, Maile looks offended, and I open my mouth to apologize, but before I can, she throws her head back and laughs loudly enough to startle the horses.

"Very well," she says when she recovers. "You trusted my plan to take the Water Mine. I'll trust your plan here, as diabolical as it might be."

By the time we're halfway across the open field, the gates of the estate open and the Ovelgans' battalion of guards pours through them to meet us, carrying yellow flags to match ours. Parley.

The last parley I held with the Kalovaxians ended with me half-dead. I hope this one will go better.

I take a steadying breath as Artemisia pulls the horse to a stop to wait for the Ovelgans, and the rest of our troops follow suit behind us. Søren dismounts in one easy, fluid motion before helping me down from my own horse in a far less graceful manner. Once both of my feet are firmly planted on the ground, I straighten out the skirt of my gown and force myself to stand up straight.

The thunder of the approaching hooves matches my rapid heartbeat. Søren seems to sense it, glancing sideways at me. He moves to reach out to me but thinks better of it here, in front of my army. I'm grateful for his discretion, but part of me wishes I could entwine my fingers with his and sap some of his unwavering strength. I could use a dose of it right now.

The Ovelgans and their army stop a good distance away, two figures I assume must be the lord and lady themselves dismounting.

"We'll meet on foot from here, just us and just them," Søren tells me, his voice low.

I follow him into the open field, away from the security of my army, though I know I still have Søren, at least, with his sword sheathed at his hip. The Ovelgans follow our lead, the two figures on foot advancing to meet us.

As they get closer, I can better make out their features. Lord Ovelgan must be in his late thirties, with collarbone-length blond hair and a strong jawline accentuated by a well-groomed beard. His wife, Lady Ovelgan, is only a few years younger—thirty-five, maybe—with a round, open face and an expression as smooth as polished stone, utterly unreadable. It's easy to see why she was considered a great beauty when she was at court, though I know that beauty in the late Kaiser's court was more curse than blessing. She has the look about her of someone at sea, praying to all of her gods that the waters stay calm and a rogue wave doesn't overturn her small boat.

I almost pity her before I remember that I never asked for this war, either. It barged into my world unprovoked, and all I've done is try to put an end to it.

Søren speaks first, bowing his head in a show of respect. "Lord Ovelgan, Lady Ovelgan," he says to them in turn. "I hope we're finding you well."

"I'd be a lot better if you weren't trying to march a rebel

army through my lands," Lord Ovelgan says, his voice deep and gruff, before reluctantly adding, "Your Highness."

As forced as the address might be, it's promising that he used it at all. It means that Søren is right—Lord Ovelgan still sees him as royal, someone to be respected. It means that he is willing to hear Søren out before he makes any decisions and sends word to Cress. He doesn't spare me so much as a glance.

Søren doesn't miss a beat. "We can be out of your way in an hour's time if you'll let us pass in peace," he says.

Lord Ovelgan gives a short burst of laughter. "You know I can't do that," he says. "You were always a brave boy, and headstrong."

The words send a jolt through me, and I glance at Søren. In all of his talking about the Ovelgans, he made it sound like he barely knew them, but Lord Ovelgan sounds so familiar with him.

Oblivious to my confusion, Lord Ovelgan continues. "I thought you would prove to be a better Kaiser than your father was, but I see you've chosen a different path at the feet of a girl."

At that, he looks at me, and I wish he would go back to ignoring me, because there is so much hate in that final word that even Lady Ovelgan flinches.

I force a smile. "It's a pleasure to meet you, Lord Ovelgan. Lady Ovelgan," I say. "I think we can cut the theatrics. We all know that you'll agree to let us pass through. It's only a matter of what your price will be, and since you've been kind enough to meet us, I imagine you have your price in mind already. The sooner you tell us what it is, the sooner we can come to an agreement and be on our way."

Lord Ovelgan doesn't seem to be an easy man to stun, but I think I've managed it. He stares at me with his mouth open for a few seconds, until Søren coughs in a poor attempt to hide his laughter at the ridiculous expression.

Lady Ovelgan places a delicate, bejeweled hand on her husband's arm and smiles graciously at me, though I'm familiar enough with her type to notice the tension in her jaw, the irritation in her eyes.

"You'll join us for supper tonight," she says, more a command than an invitation. "What matters we have to discuss can be done so more comfortably. And I know the children would like to see you again, Prinz Søren. You'll both stay the night as well—it's nearly dark, after all. Your men will stay here so as not to alarm our village."

There it is again, the warm familiarity leaking through the polite courtesy. Søren knows these people better than he let on. He knows their children. Why would he have kept that from me?

"We'll arrange for our troops to remain outside the estate gate," Søren says smoothly. "But close enough for our security. And we'll be bringing twenty guards inside, ten for each of us, plus Emperor Erik of Goraki."

Lady Ovelgan's eyes widen, though it seems to be more act than genuine surprise. A more natural smile curves her mouth. "Do you not trust us, Prinz Søren, after everything we've done for you?" she asks, a mocking note in her voice. "How ironic, when it's you who betrayed us."

Søren doesn't acknowledge the barb but keeps his gaze leveled on Lady Ovelgan. "Your husband trained me to be wary of anyone who meant harm to myself or my crew," he says, now looking between the two of them. "I don't believe you would hurt me, but Queen Theodosia is the crew I've chosen, and I don't doubt that if she stood before you alone now, you wouldn't hesitate to harm her however you could. So no, Lady Ovelgan, it pains me to say that I don't trust you. Perhaps you should bring that grievance up with your husband for training me as wisely as he did."

Silence follows his declaration, and for a moment, I'm worried that Søren has offended them so deeply that the Ovelgans will rescind their invitation for dinner and we'll have to turn back. Instead Lord Ovelgan surprises me by laughing, the sound booming and clear and loud enough to be heard by the troops on either side.

I all but sag with relief as Lord Ovelgan steps forward, clapping Søren on the shoulder.

"Whatever happens, boy," he says, "it is good to see that you haven't changed."

Søren returns his smile, but it doesn't quite reach his eyes. "I have to disagree, sir," he says. "I've changed quite a bit since I was your pupil." He steps out of Lord Ovelgan's grip. "Thank you for your hospitality," he says to both of them. "We'll get our troops settled and gather our guards. We'll see you at sundown."

As Søren and I make our way back to our troops, I grab his arm, forcing him to look at me.

"You didn't tell me you knew Lord Ovelgan so well," I say. "The way you talked just now, it was like you were family."

He shrugs, but doesn't meet my gaze for more than a

second. "I told you I knew him," he says, but that isn't an answer and he knows it.

"You implied that he was a casual acquaintance. It's more than that. He *trained* you. You respect him. You might even like him."

At that, he does look at me, his eyes heavy. "What do you want me to say, Theo?" he asks. "That I spent a year at this estate four years ago, with the man and his wife and family, being treated like one of their sons? That I admired them, liked them? Of course I did. After growing up with my father, this place felt like paradise. But it doesn't change anything."

"Doesn't it?" I ask. "You aren't their surrogate son anymore, Søren. No matter what agreement we come to with them, we are on opposite sides of this. I need to know that you know that."

For a moment, he doesn't speak, his eyes focused straight ahead. "*Yana Crebesti*," he says finally. "I trust you, Theo. Do you trust me?"

The words do little to calm my mind, but I know he has a point. Søren has had countless opportunities to turn his back on me, countless opportunities to take someone else's side, countless opportunities to choose an easier path, but he never has. At the end of the day, he has always chosen to stand by me, and I have no reason to believe that this time will be any different.

I squeeze his arm before releasing it. "*Yana Crebesti*," I tell him.

# OVELGAN

FROM FAR AWAY, THE ESTATE was a thing of beauty, but as our group approaches, it looms larger and darker. With the sun fully set, it no longer shines like gold. Instead it looks like a shadow, a ghost of what once was.

The Ovelgans are waiting just inside the manor, at the base of a sweeping marble staircase, joined by two of their daughters—neither older than ten. Both have golden hair and somber wide-eyed expressions; both are laced into stiff velvet gowns that look too tight for them to breathe in.

The younger one stares at the plush carpet at her feet, but her sister's eyes survey us, taking in our large group of twenty-three crammed into the entryway. They catch on me for a second, then linger on Erik. With a little time and Heron's healing, his swollen eye is open again, but he has a red scarf tied diagonally over the missing one. He keeps one hand on Heron's arm for guidance. The girl stares unabashedly at Artemisia's blue hair, her small mouth gaping. But when she sees Søren, a smile stretches over her face and she can't resist lifting her hand and waving at him.

"Søren!" she says, rolling onto the balls of her feet in

excitement, before her mother shushes her, taking hold of the hand she was waving and holding it tightly in her own.

For his part, Søren gives her a smile, like everything is normal and we are just going to have a normal dinner together, discussing normal things like the weather.

"Welcome to our home, Prinz Søren," Lord Ovelgan says, inclining his head toward Søren. He pauses, long and deliberate, before turning to me and adding, "Queen Theodosia."

I smile, satisfied. Small a thing as it is, hearing my true name in the mouth of a Kalovaxian feels like a triumph all its own. Not *Lady Thora*, not *Ash Princess*, but *Queen Theodosia*. There is power in names, after all, and his calling me that would be nothing short of high treason in Cress's eyes. It's a good sign.

"Have you met Emperor Erik of Goraki?" I ask, motioning to Erik. He takes the cue and bows with more grace than I could manage even with my full sight. Somehow, the scarf tied around his missing eye doesn't make him any less handsome, especially when he's dressed in his Gorakian brocade robe. Instead it lends him an air of mystery and roguishness, like a tragic hero in a ballad. He doesn't look at all like he did when I first met him, in his ill-fitting Kalovaxian clothes, an outsider who never felt comfortable in his own skin.

"Emperor," Lord Ovelgan says, with some hesitation. "It is good to see you again."

"I wish I could return the sentiment, my lord," Erik says with a grim smile. "But as you can surmise, I can't see very well these days."

Lord Ovelgan shifts uncomfortably, eyes darting around as if he's looking for help.

"I noticed," he says carefully. "I'm sure it's quite a story."

Lord Ovelgan gestures around the entryway. The room is only lit by the chandelier overhead, and it's just bright enough for me to make out the ornate stairway, the deep red carpet, the walls painted in gray and gold. "Welcome to our home. Your guards are welcome to wait here in the foyer, but dinner will just be us," he says before looking at his daughters, placing a hand on each of their shoulders. "Karolina, Elfriede, off to bed with you. Say good night to our guests."

"But, Father," the older one says, her bottom lip jutting out in a pout. "It isn't fair. I'm ten years old now, and that's old enough to stay up. I want to talk to Søren."

"The Prinz," Lady Ovelgan corrects gently, taking hold of her daughters' hands and passing them to a waiting Kalovaxian servant woman—their nanny, I would imagine. "And there will be time for that another day. But we need you to be good girls and go straight to bed. All right?"

In a huff of protest, the girls let their nanny lead them off.

"Where is Fritz?" Søren asks, watching them go. "He was only a baby the last time I saw him, but he must be almost five now—"

"He's ill," Lord Ovelgan interrupts brusquely. "Shall we adjourn to the dining room and settle this matter?"

Søren takes a step back, as if Lord Ovelgan physically struck him. He nods. "I apologize, my lord. You're right. We have much to discuss."

"Wilhelmina, you should check on Fritz. There's no need for you to join us," Lord Ovelgan says to his wife.

Lady Ovelgan glances at the stairs, a hint of longing in her otherwise stoic expression, before she turns back to us. "No, I'll stay," she says quietly. "Come, before the meal gets cold."

She leads the way down the hall, giving the rest of us no choice but to follow.

"If we need help," I say to the guards before we leave, "I'll scream. Otherwise, you know what to do."

Heron nods, unlatching Erik's fingers from his arm and helping him lean on Søren instead. His eyes are heavy on mine.

"Be careful," he says to me.

"And you as well," I reply.


The dining table has been set with golden plates and utensils and crystal goblets studded with Water Gems. The candlesticks are covered in Fire Gems. Lady Ovelgan's blond braid is threaded with Air and Water Gems, and even Lord Ovelgan's jacket has Earth Gems instead of buttons. Just stepping into the room with so many Spiritgems is overwhelming. I feel the weight of them pressing down on my shoulders, on my chest, calling to my blood and making it difficult to breathe.

No one else seems to be as affected, so I try to keep my expression neutral as the Ovelgans' servants usher us to our seats. I find myself between Søren and Erik, directly across from Lord Ovelgan.

As soon as everyone is settled, a slave girl approaches with a carafe of red wine and pours some into each of our goblets. I watch her pour the wine, her eyes downcast. It's the same wine going into each goblet, so it can't be poisoned, but the goblets . . .

"Will you switch glasses with me?" I ask Lady Ovelgan, holding my goblet toward her.

"I beg your pardon?" she asks, taken aback.

"I don't mean to offend," I tell her with a smile. "But I've learned the hard way to be wary of drinks offered by those whose motivations I'm not sure of."

Lady Ovelgan frowns, glancing toward her husband, who nods, keeping his eyes fixed on me.

"Ridiculous," Lady Ovelgan says with a huff, though she takes my goblet and offers me hers. "As if I would ever poison a guest."

"One can't be too careful these days," I say. "Søren, Erik, Lord Ovelgan—if you don't mind doing the same."

There's some shuffling as the three trade glasses. In the end, no one has their original glass of wine, though Erik has Søren's because he seems to be the only one of us the Ovelgans would like to keep alive. All of us take a hesitant sip.

The wine is fruity with a good dose of spice, and I can't discern any poison. I set the glass down again. That doesn't mean much, though—I couldn't taste the bolenza poison that Coltania slipped into my tea in Sta'Crivero, either.

Perhaps I will always be wary of strangers offering me drinks now, but I would rather be too wary than even slightly careless.

"So," I say, looking to Lord Ovelgan. "You know what we want from you, and I can't imagine you would have agreed to host us tonight if you didn't want something from us in turn. What is it?"

Lord Ovelgan barely glances at me before shifting his attention to Søren. "An alliance," he tells him, as if Søren asked the question and not me. "When this is all over, someone will need to sit on the Kalovaxian throne. The obvious answer is you, Prinz Søren, and I am not the only Kalovaxian to believe that. There are many—perhaps even *most*—who would rather see you on the throne than the bitch who sits there now."

I'm the last person who would defend Cress, but the way Lord Ovelgan talks about her rubs me the wrong way, and I have to bite my tongue to keep from saying anything.

"When this is all over, Lord Ovelgan," Søren says carefully, "there may not be a throne left to hold, not by me or any Kalovaxian."

Lord Ovelgan snorts. "Not here, perhaps," he says. "If you ask me—which your father didn't—we shouldn't have come to this country in the first place. There was nothing wrong with Goraki, nothing wrong with Yoxi before that, or any of the other countries we've conquered. Why put all of the work into conquering a country, only to abandon it a decade later?"

"Why put all the work into conquering a country at all?" I say before I can stop myself. "Erik is the rightful ruler of Goraki and there's no place for you there. I imagine Yoxi and every other country you've attacked will feel similarly."

"Then what would you have us do?" Lord Ovelgan asks, finally looking at me. "Kalovaxia is a wasteland—barren. It can't sustain us. Let's say, by some miracle, you actually manage to triumph and retake your throne, *Your Highness*. What would come next for all of the Kalovaxians who have made this land our home?"

"It's *Your Majesty* in Astrea," I tell him, keeping my voice firm. "And the answer to that question is entirely up to you, my lord. Personally, I see no reason to show you any more mercy than you've shown my people over the last decade. But seeing as how you are in a position to change my mind about that now, I could be persuaded to seek other options. There are refugee camps set up in Sta'Crivero and a couple of other countries that you haven't yet made enemies of. Perhaps they would be kind enough to take you in."

Lord Ovelgan's jaw clenches. "I suggest you tread carefully, *Your Majesty,*" he says, each word a dagger. "You do still need my help, after all."

I lift my eyebrows. "And here I thought we were helping one another," I say.

"Theo," Søren warns, before turning his attention to Lord Ovelgan. "What would you like from me, then?" he asks them. "You want me on the throne—a throne, wherever our people end up going when this war is over—but that can't be all."

I feel like I'm no longer in the room. I've been forgotten entirely, and Erik has as well. It's only Søren and the Ovelgans.

The Ovelgans exchange a look. "As we said—an alliance. The most permanent sort," Lady Ovelgan says. "We want Karolina to be the Kaiserin."

That takes Søren by surprise. "She's a child," he says.

"Of course," Lord Ovelgan cuts in, "it would only be a betrothal, until she comes of age. But we want a promise, from you, in writing."

"You're assuming that I have any eye toward taking my father's throne," Søren says.

"I know you, Søren," Lord Ovelgan says. "You have always done what is needed of you. And right now, your people need you to lead them."

"What you mean by that, Lord Ovelgan, is that I have always been good at following orders," Søren says, choosing his words carefully. "You want someone on the throne you can control, and you think that I will be easily controlled."

Lord Ovelgan doesn't deny it. Instead he takes a sip of his wine, unbothered. "Do we have a deal, Søren?" he asks.

Søren shakes his head. "I'm not easily controlled anymore," he says. "I'm afraid I can't make that deal."

I look sideways at him, taken aback. This was not part of the plan. The plan was for me to be prickly and stubborn—every bit their idea of what an Astrean queen would be—while Søren would be their kind savior Prinz, there to support them and give them whatever they asked for in order to let us pass. He was supposed to be agreeable, not antagonize them further.

"But there was never going to be a deal, was there? Not really," Søren continues, glancing at the door. "Where's Fritz?"

Lady Ovelgan's eyes widen, and she looks to her husband before answering. "We told you," she says, but there's an edge of panic in her voice now. "He's ill. Sleeping upstairs."

"They're stalling us," Søren tells Erik and me. "But what I can't figure out is why."

I glance between our two hosts, knowing that Søren is right, but there's something else. . . . Lord and Lady Ovelgan don't look smug or proud or triumphant. They look afraid.

"If you think you sent a messenger, I have some bad news for you," Erik says, leaning forward. "Our men were ready, patrolling the northern perimeter of your village. They would have intercepted anyone who left the estate."

"Oh, but not all missives require messengers," a voice

says from the doorway, soft but rough around the edges like a plume of smoke.

With a sinking stomach, I turn to see Rigga Stratlan standing there in a draping gray silk gown that shows off the charred black skin of her throat. The last time I saw her, she had long hair the color of rose gold, but now it's dull and ashen, the brittle ends stopping at her sharp collarbone. When her eyes meet mine, her black lips curl into a pleased smile.

"Lady Thora," she says, though there is no real surprise in her voice, merely amusement. "Oh, Cress will be so interested to learn you're alive."

# RIGGA

⸻·⸻

SØREN IS ON HIS FEET in an instant, drawing his sword from its sheath, but Rigga's smile only broadens.

"Would you really hurt me, Prinz Søren?" she asks, tilting her head to one side. "Not very chivalrous of you, is it? To hurt a woman?"

Søren doesn't lower his sword. "If I thought you were harmless, I wouldn't dream of it," Søren says, matching her casual tone. "But you aren't harmless, are you, Lady Rigga?"

She laughs. "No, I'm not. And it is a wonderful feeling, to be neither harmless nor helpless." She turns to her left and reaches for something I can't see, but a second later, she pulls it into the light—*him* into the light. A small boy no older than five with pale blond hair and large, frightened green eyes that are red around the edges, like he's been crying. At the sight of him, Lord and Lady Ovelgan are on their feet as well.

"Fritz," Lady Ovelgan cries out. The boy tries to run to her, but Rigga has a tight grip on his arm, holding him like a shield—which I suppose is precisely what he is to her.

"What exactly is going on, Theo?" Erik whispers to me,

his voice casual enough, but with an underlying edge. "It's too dimly lit and my good eye is straining—I can't see much more than vague shapes."

I open my mouth to try to answer, but there is no time for the kind of explanation the situation requires.

"Nothing good," I tell him instead, taking hold of his hand and squeezing it. "Just don't move, don't speak. Listen."

Erik frowns, and I half expect him to protest, but he nods.

"Let the boy go," Søren says, lowering the tip of his sword.

"Fritz and I are only playing a game," Rigga says, tracing one black-tipped finger along the boy's cheek. He flinches away from her touch, closing his eyes tightly.

"Please, Auntie," he says, so quietly that I almost don't hear him. "Please let me go. I'll be good, I promise."

"Oh, soon, Fritz," she coos to him. "Just as soon as everyone does as they've been told."

"And what is that, exactly?" Søren asks through gritted teeth.

"Well, first of all, you're going to put that sword down before you hurt somebody," Rigga says, stepping into the dining room and dragging a shaking Fritz with her. "And you," she adds, turning to her cousin, "are going to summon the servants to bring dinner like nothing is amiss. I'm quite starving. And then we are going to wait here, together, until the Kaiserin arrives."

With that, she sits down at the foot of the table between Søren and Lady Ovelgan, pulling Fritz into her lap and keeping an arm wrapped around him in what might look like a protective gesture if she weren't holding him so tightly. One of his hands reaches out to grab his mother's.

"We intercepted all messages leaving the estate," Søren says again. "The Kaiserin isn't coming."

Rigga laughs, and dread pools in the pit of my stomach as I understand.

"She didn't need to send a message, not really," I say. "The Encatrio she was given was made from Cress's blood—it binds them. Just as I can see Cress in my dreams, just as I saw Dagmær, Rigga can see them as well. Communicate with them. Cress knows we're here."

"All it took was a drop of a sleeping draught and a quick nap as soon as we received word that your troops were approaching, though I didn't know you were alive at the time. That will be a wonderful surprise for her, don't you think?" Rigga says, barely able to contain her glee. "Imagine—she only sent me here to give my cousin and my nieces the same choice she gave me. I was so disappointed when they refused. Wilhelmina actually had the nerve to throw the potions I'd brought out the window—caused a nasty little fire. I was dreading having to tell my Kaiserin that I'd failed her and wasted the Encatrio. But alas! Here you are, and I can't imagine she will see me as a failure now. She will be here in roughly two days, so we have quite a wait ahead of us. Call for dinner," she says, looking to her cousin.

Lady Ovelgan keeps her eyes on her son, wide and frightened, as she clears her throat.

"Dinner," she calls, her voice ringing out like a bell, without any hint of fear or wavering.

A moment passes in silence, but nothing happens. The door to the kitchen hallway remains closed. There is no sound of footsteps or voices. Only silence.

Søren and I exchange a loaded look.

Lady Ovelgan looks at the door, her brow furrowing.

"Dinner!" she calls out again, louder this time. Still there is no response.

"Well," Rigga says through clenched teeth. "Go check on them."

Lady Ovelgan doesn't move, her eyes locked instead on her son, her hand clutching his back.

"I'll go," Lord Ovelgan says, pushing his chair back.

"No," Rigga says, eyes narrowing. "You'll stay where you are. Wilhelmina, see what's keeping them."

With a pained expression, Lady Ovelgan pries her son's fingers from her hand and stands up, then walks toward the kitchen hall door with shaking shoulders.

Søren and I exchange another look. We both know what she'll find in the kitchen, and we can both guess at what will happen when she does.

"So," I say, an idea taking shape in my mind. "Cress made you powerful, more powerful than you ever could have been on your own."

Rigga turns to me, a single eyebrow raised. It's the same way she used to look at me back at the palace, like I was a bug beneath her shoe, hardly worthy of her attention.

"Yes," she says slowly.

"But not as powerful as she is," I say. "Isn't that right?"

The words hit home. The corners of Rigga's mouth pull down slightly before her expression smooths out.

"I don't know what you're talking about," she says coldly. "She put fire in my veins and vengeance in my heart. She made me strong."

I let myself smile. I give her the same contemptuous, pitying gaze she used to give me when I was only the Princess of Ashes.

"But not strong enough," I say. "I've seen Cress; I've seen her power; I've seen what she can do with it. She gave you her gift, yes, but she made you a shadow of what she is, nothing more. She doesn't see you as her equal; she sees you as a servant."

This time, Rigga flinches, her grip on Fritz tightening until the boy cries out in pain.

"Theo," Søren says. "Don't."

I ignore him and push forward. "I'll bet she only gave you a few drops of the Encatrio, barely a taste of what she had."

Rigga's lips purse. "It's a poison," she says calmly. "It has to be dosed out by the drop, or else it could have killed me."

I lift my eyebrows and laugh. "By the *drop*?" I ask, shaking my head. "Gods above, I gave Cress an entire vial and she survived that. A drop. She must think so little of you."

"It was enough," she says, lifting her free hand and summoning a ball of fire barely the size of her pinky nail.

I laugh louder. "I'm sorry," I manage to get out. "I shouldn't laugh; it's rude. I just . . . Is that really all she gave you? How much can you really do with that little power? Why, Dagmær had enough power to kill her husband and all of his sons. What can you do? Light a few candles?"

She grits her teeth, bringing the fire in her hand close to Fritz's face. He tries to squirm away from it, but she holds him tight. "You see?" she asks me. "I can do enough."

"Theo," Søren says, more insistent now, but still I ignore him.

"Yes, it's very impressive," I say, lifting my hand and summoning my own flame, so large that I can barely contain it. Just as quickly as I summon the flame, I close my hand and snuff it out. "You will let me know if you grow bored of threatening children and want to make yourself a little stronger, won't you?"

Rigga's eyes glint, but before she can answer, Lady Ovelgan enters the room again, expression bewildered.

"The servants—" she starts, her voice high with panic.

"Hush, Wilhelmina," Rigga interrupts, not sparing her so much as a glance. Instead her eyes are focused on me, hungry. "What are you talking about?"

I force my hands not to shake as I draw the vial of Encatrio from the pocket of my dress.

"I was saving this for myself, in case I needed another dose," I tell her, before pausing. "*But* I could trade it for the boy. Let him go, and I'll give it to you."

Her eyes dart around, but there's a manic sheen in them. She's more than tempted by the offer. "And what's to stop me from just taking it from you?" she asks me.

I hold out my arm, holding the glass vial over the tile floor. "If you try, I'll drop it," I say.

"That could kill us all," Lord Ovelgan says, panicked. "Don't do anything rash."

"I'm not," I say, keeping my eyes on Rigga. "I'm merely giving her the choice. Let the boy go be upstairs with his sisters, out of the way. We'll stay here, with you, until Cress gets here. You'll lose your child hostage, but you'll have enough power to keep us here without one."

Rigga considers it, licking her cracked black lips.

"No," she says softly, though the word seems to cost her. "There's a trick somewhere. It's not an even trade for you otherwise."

I shrug. "I have no qualms about staying here with you, Rigga," I say before gesturing to Erik and Søren. "We were on our way to confront Cress at the palace. In bringing her here, you're doing me a favor. My only concern just now is that you're going to hurt that boy. You don't want to do that. So do us both a favor and let him go, and I'll give you the potion. Think of how pleased Cress will be, to realize that you're stronger than she thought you were, that you're her equal."

Rigga leans forward, her eyes intent, fingers digging into Fritz's skin until he cries out in pain. After what feels like an eternity, she releases him, pushing him off her lap. He scrambles for his mother, wraps his arms around her waist, and buries his face in her dress, crying.

"Shh," Lady Ovelgan says, smoothing his hair. "Go wait with your sisters, all right, my love? I'll come find you soon."

With some reluctance, Fritz obeys her, skittering out of the room as quickly as he can. When he's a safe distance away, I pass Rigga the vial of Encatrio.

"How did you get it?" she asks me, inspecting the opalescent liquid in awe. "It's exactly the same as what I drank."

There's no reason to lie, so I tell her the truth. "Cress gave it to me. She thought I was someone else, someone she wanted to turn. I held on to it in case I needed it."

The answer seems to be good enough for her. With wild eyes that seem to glow in the candlelight, she unstoppers the poison and pours it into her cousin's full wine goblet.

"Don't drink too much," I tell her, trying to sound

concerned. "You don't know what will happen. Cress and I both managed to drink it all, but you might not be as strong as we are."

Rigga waves my concern away, taking the words as the challenge I intended them to be. She takes a deep breath and then tips the goblet back and drinks the poisoned wine in a few gulps, before slamming the goblet down again on the table with a thud that echoes throughout the space.

With a rasping, quiet scream, she crumples to the ground, her body writhing in agony as the black mark at her throat begins to spread, burning the skin as it goes.

The only other person I saw drink Encatrio was Elpis, and though I feel no pity for Rigga, I can't help but think of that now, watching as Rigga's neck, her chest, and the rest of her body begin to burn from the inside out, turning the air rancid with the smell of charred flesh. It's difficult to watch, but I don't let my eyes leave her body until she finally stops moving, well and truly dead.

In the silence that follows, I hear Lord Ovelgan let out a breath of relief.

"Thank you," he says to me, sounding sincere. "You have our gratitude. You're free to pass through our lands."

He says it so magnanimously that I can't stifle a laugh.

"Of course we are," I say to him. "After all, they are no longer your lands. They're mine, property of the Astrean crown, which means that you are the trespassers."

It takes a moment for my words to register, but when they do, Lord Ovelgan rises to his feet once more. "Guards!" he calls out, but no one comes.

"No one is there," Lady Ovelgan says, her voice quavering. "That's what I was trying to say. There are no guards, no servants, no slaves. No one at all in this house."

"They've all been gathered in the village," I say, before beginning to recount the second half of our plan. Back at the Water Mine, Søren said that the Ovelgans would hear us out, that they would invite us into their home. From then, it became a matter of what we would do once we got here. "Those who put up a fight were killed on the spot, with the weapons my soldiers smuggled in to arm your slaves. Many of my soldiers are Water Guardians, and their weapons were hidden with their illusion gifts. Those who surrendered will be staying here in the village, under close watch of your former slaves, until we can decide what is to be done with them. You are welcome to stay with them, and with your children, so long as you cooperate."

Lord Ovelgan turns to Søren. "You can't allow her to do this," he says, his voice rising. "I'm no ally of the Kaiserin's. Surely there is an arrangement to be made."

For an instant, Søren wavers, but he pushes his doubts aside just as quickly. "I don't allow Queen Theodosia to do anything, my lord," he says. "You are no ally of the Kaiserin's, that's true, and that will be taken into consideration, but you and your wife are still war criminals in the eyes of the Astreans. You have still taken their lands and held the people as slaves, and there are consequences for those actions."

"And what of you?" Lord Ovelgan demands, his voice becoming a roar. "What are your consequences?"

That gives Søren pause, but after a second, he finds his

answer. "I think I've begun to pay them," he says. "And I will continue to do so until the day I die, however my Queen decides I should."

"But what of the children?" Lady Ovelgan demands. "They're too young; they've done nothing wrong."

"What if I said we would treat them as kindly as you treated our children when you came here?" I ask, unable to keep my voice from rising. It gives me some satisfaction to see the horror cross their faces at the prospect. "Lucky for you, we are not so monstrous. They'll be taken care of. Fed and clothed and cared for—given far better treatment than you gave the children of Astrea. I can assure you of that."

Søren draws his sword again, and Lord Ovelgan's hand immediately goes to the pommel of his sword, but his wife places her hand over his, stopping him.

"No," she says, her voice barely louder than a whisper. "No, we'll surrender. We'll come quietly and do as you say. So long as the children are safe."

For an instant, Lord Ovelgan looks like he might argue, but he only drops his head and releases his sword, raising his hands in surrender and allowing Søren to disarm him and bind his arms behind his back without a protest.

# AFTERMATH

———◆•◆———

WHEN WE REACH THE VILLAGE square, it is aglow with bonfires and torches, and frantic with an energy that is half terrified and half triumphant. I spot familiar faces in the crowded square from the troops we brought in, but plenty of strangers as well, with a haunted and disoriented look about them that I've grown familiar with over the last few months— the look of people who can still feel the weight of chains against their skin even after they've been removed.

Søren leads Lord and Lady Ovelgan to what used to be the slave quarters. He's arranged for them to remain separate from the other Kalovaxians, with only their children, though that is less of a kindness and more of a precaution. If I learned anything from the Kaiser, it was the necessity of keeping my enemies isolated, to keep them manageable and unable to conspire with others like them.

The children will be taken care of—I truly meant that. I've seen enough to know that hate is something learned, not something inherent. I saw it firsthand in Cress, in how she treated me when we were children and how she treated me once her father and her world convinced her that I was less than her.

Perhaps there is hope that Fritz and Karolina and Elfriede and all of the other children from this village will be able to grow up differently. I have to hold on to that hope or else I don't know what it is I'm fighting for—to be the same as the Kalovaxians? To treat their children the way they treated ours, treated me? To give them all of the hate we've stored up until one day they strike back at us the same way we're striking now?

That cycle would have no end. There has to be a better way.

"Theo."

I turn to find Blaise, Artemisia, and Heron coming toward me, each looking worn but with no injuries, as far as I can see. I let out a breath of relief.

"Any complications?" I ask them.

All three shake their heads.

"It was just as Søren said—altogether, there were more slaves than there were Kalovaxians. Once we got them weapons and helped them use them to take control of the village, it was all rather easy."

"The manor was the same," Heron adds. "As soon as you and the Ovelgans were in the dining room, the other guards and I went through the house, arming any Astrean we saw with the weapons the Water Guardians had disguised. We left the children and their nanny upstairs, just as you said."

"It wasn't only the nanny with them," I tell him, before explaining what happened with Rigga. When I finish, they're all silent.

"You're sure she's dead?" Blaise asks.

I nod. "There was nothing left of her by the time the

poison had done its work. Just ash. But we have a bigger problem now—Cress is on her way. She should be here in two days—which means that this victory was a temporary one. Even if we leave, she and her men will simply reclaim the village and return the Astreans here to chains, if she doesn't just kill them."

"We could stay here and fight," Artemisia says. "It's as good a place as any, and since we have more information than she does going into this, there's a good chance we could win."

I shake my head. "It would be a temporary win, even if we do manage it," I say. "No, send a message to your mother. Have her change course and meet us at the Savria River before she goes to the Earth Mine. We'll send the prisoners and a group of Astreans who can't or won't fight to her while we continue to the Air Mine as planned. By the time Cress arrives, there will be nothing here."

They all consider it for a moment.

"We could buy ourselves more time if we leave a handful of Kalovaxians here," Heron says. "Give them a message to relay to the Kaiserin, lead them to believe we're marching toward Etta Forest to prepare for a siege on the capital."

I purse my lips. "Lord Ovelgan," I say. "We'll leave him, and him alone. We'll have his wife and children, and I'm sure he'll say whatever we ask of him in exchange for some measure of clemency."

"You aren't going to pardon him?" Artemisia asks, brow furrowing.

"Gods, no," I say. "But I don't think he'd believe us if we offered that anyway. No, we'll agree to spare his wife and his children, to send them away somewhere to live in peace. If Cress doesn't kill him and he manages to survive the war, he'll stand trial for his crimes and pay whatever price is agreed to be fair, just like every other Kalovaxian. If he lives long enough to atone for his crimes, he'll be able to join his family."

The three of them exchange looks.

"It doesn't sound like enough," Artemisia says after a moment.

"I know," I say. "But what would you do? Kill them all?"

Art doesn't answer, and I have a feeling that's exactly what she was about to suggest.

"I understand the temptation," I say. "Believe me, I do. But all that would do is keep this vicious circle moving. Those children would grow up thinking of us as the enemies who slaughtered their families, building up anger until they've built a rebellion all their own to avenge their loved ones, just as we're doing now. I want to end this for good."

Heron nods. "I'll tell Søren. If anyone is going to convince Lord Ovelgan to cooperate, it will be him."

I give him my thanks and watch him leave, before turning back to Artemisia.

"I don't think there is any punishment, any measure of vengeance, that will ever be enough to make up for what they've done to us—to you," I add, thinking about her time in the Water Mine, her brother's death, her rape at the hands of a guard. "Even death seems like it is too good for many of them. But there are others who were only complicit. It's enough of a crime on its own and it will not go unpunished, but there are shades to it, levels. If we slaughter them all, we're no better than they are. What will we even be fighting for?"

Artemisia looks away, but she nods. "I'm not the only one who will disagree with you on this," she says. "You know that. There are others who will want to bury every Kalovaxian, some who might not even want to spare the children."

"I know," I say, the pool of dread in my stomach deepening. "But this is the only way to have peace—not for their sakes, but for ours. I would like to live a peaceful life after all of this is done, and I can't do that if this war keeps being reborn with each new generation."

She doesn't protest, but she doesn't agree, either.

"I'll get a message to my mother and start dividing those who want to stay with us and those who want to go with her," she says finally, before walking toward the village center and leaving me alone with Blaise.

"You were quiet," I say. "Do you think it was the right choice to make?"

He pauses before shrugging. "I don't think any of us can say that with any certainty, Theo. I don't know if we'll really have the answer to that for years. Decades, even. But I understand your reasoning, and if I were in your position, I like to think I would make the same decision."

I nod, biting my bottom lip. "Thank you," I say finally. "For that, and for staying out of the battle."

"I didn't do it for you," he says before the weight of those words fully settles over him. He laughs. "It's strange. I don't think I've been able to truly say that in a while, not since we were in the palace. Since then, everything I've done has been for you."

"Blaise—" I start, but he cuts me off.

"No, it's a good thing," he says, looking at me. "This time, I acted for myself, because I know it was the best thing for Astrea. And that knowledge . . . it feels good."

# TRUST

———•———

WE LEAVE AT DAWN THE next day and ride until the sun is high overhead and it's time for lunch. Before I can get my rations and quiet my rumbling belly, Blaise pulls me aside.

"You haven't practiced in a while," he points out. "We should take advantage of the break. Art can grab you an extra ration to eat afterward."

My stomach gives a loud protest to that, but I know he's right. Blasts of fire are one thing, and it was enough back at the Water Mine, but controlling my gift is still difficult, and I know there will come a time when I will need to wield it as a dagger instead of a cannonball.

"Are you sure it's wise?" I ask him. "Someone else can teach me—"

"I thought we'd established that wasn't the case," he points out with a wry smile. "And you were getting better with me, weren't you?"

I can't deny that. Artemisia and Heron tried, but the way they talked about their powers felt nothing like mine; it was like an archer trying to teach a swordsman.

"You aren't supposed to be using your gifts," I point out.

"I know," he says quickly. "But I don't need to use my gifts to help you control yours."

My skepticism must be clear because he sighs. "I'm managing, Theo. It isn't easy, but it's getting better. I wouldn't throw that progress away for the sake of showing off here and now. If you'd rather eat or rest, by all means, but I think you could use some more practice before we get to the Air Mine."

I think back to what happened with Rigga at the Ovelgan estate. I was able to get through that without actually attacking her, but that won't always be the case. And it's only a matter of time now before I'll have to face off against Cress.

"Fine," I tell him, ignoring my grumbling belly.

He leads us away from my troops until we find a stretch of space far enough away that we won't be seen. There are no trees to practice on this time, only flat, barren earth interrupted by a pile of rocks.

"You've got the distance," Blaise says, crossing to the rocks. He reaches down and picks up a small stone the size of his palm. He tosses it into the air a few times, catching it with ease. "Precision, though, is off."

He holds the stone up, opening his hand so that it's resting on top of his palm. "Can you hit the stone?"

I stare at him, my mouth agape. "I'll hit you," I tell him.

He shrugs. "I'd rather you didn't, but that's up to you."

"Put the rock down and I'll try to hit it," I say. "Same target size, less risk."

"You need the risk," he says, shaking his head. "If we had

more time—months, years, even—we could start small. But we don't have time. Do it. I believe in you."

"You shouldn't," I say, choking out a laugh. "I've never tried anything like this before. I haven't practiced or trained enough—"

"The fire is a part of you," Blaise says. "All of the Guardian training, all of the lessons, it's about finding that bond. You've found it, Theo. You wouldn't be able to wield it like you do if you hadn't. Now it's about finding the limits of that connection."

"Surely there are better ways," I say.

"Safer ways, maybe," he says. "But you work best under pressure."

I sigh. "You're going to get hurt," I say again.

"It wouldn't be the worst pain I've been in," he says with a shrug. "And Heron isn't too far. He'll be able to heal it if need be, but I don't think we'll need him. Go on, stop stalling."

"I'm not stalling; I'm trying to make you see reason," I snap, but he gives me a level look and I shake my head, lifting my hand and summoning a flame. This one is small, just the size of my thumbnail.

Blaise is about ten feet from me. The target isn't so small, all things considered, but if I miss . . .

*Then don't miss,* I think.

I focus on the stone, letting everything around it fade away until Blaise and the clearing cease to exist altogether. And then I let it fly.

The flame hits the stone, but as soon as it touches, Blaise drops the rock with a cry, shaking his hand out.

"I'm sorry," I shout. "I told you it was a bad idea."

"No, you did it all right," Blaise says, shaking his head. "You didn't burn me, but it was still hot." He picks up another small stone and takes a few steps backward so there is now closer to fifteen feet between us. "Go again."

We continue on for about half an hour, until Blaise's hands are bright red and I start to feel dizzy. I begin to understand what he meant, though, when he said the fire was a part of me. I feel it now even more than I did sending the balls of fire toward the Water Mine. With the smaller bits of magic, it feels more personal, more a part of me.

The last few times I do it, I can almost feel the hot stone against my fingertips in the instant the fire hits it.

Blaise seems satisfied as well, though his expression is closed off, more so than I've ever seen it. He passes me a canteen of water, and when I take a swig, he speaks.

"It's strange," he says slowly. "I thought that being around magic, seeing you wield it, would make me miss it."

I wipe my mouth with the back of my hand, my stomach already tying itself into knots.

"And?" I ask, passing the canteen back to him. "Did it?"

"Yes," he admits. "But not in the way I thought it would. I crave it, sometimes, especially here, in the woods. I can feel it calling to me, reaching out. I don't know how to explain it."

I bite my lip. "I think I understand. Before I went into the mine, before Cress gave me the poison even, I felt something similar. Anytime I was around Fire Gems, they called

to me. And when I was angry, I felt it, too. Impossible to ignore, sometimes."

I think about my burning hands, how I once charred my
bedsheets after a nightmare. I wasn't able to control myself,
but I hope it's not the same for Blaise.

He nods once, his brow furrowed. "But the strange thing
is, I don't actually *want* to use it again. Since the Water Mine,
my mind has been clearer. It's felt like my own again. This
voice that used to live inside me, whispering about power
and craving magic . . . it's gotten quieter. I can hear my own
thoughts again. I've missed that."

"You seem better," I tell him. It's true—the circles beneath
his eyes are still there, but they're less pronounced. The color
has returned to his skin. He's still hot; I can tell that without
touching him. It radiates from him so that even standing a few
inches away, I feel it. "You seem more yourself."

"I'm sorry, Theo," he says, the words seeming to cost him.

I shake my head. "We've been over that already. You apolo-
gized for the Water Mine—"

"No, not that," he says. "I'm sorry that I didn't listen to
you, even before that. You tried to tell me there was something
wrong, but I wouldn't hear it. That whispering in my mind I
mentioned . . . it was terrible, but it also felt like I needed it.
Like it was me. Like without its presence, without the feel
of magic coursing through my veins, I wouldn't really exist
anymore."

"You didn't know who you were without your power," I
say, recalling a conversation we had about it when I first asked
him to give it up in Sta'Crivero.

He nods. "I do now, though," he says, smiling tentatively. "I'm still me," he says. "I still have value. I can fight in other ways. But I owe you an apology. Several dozen apologies. If I'd listened to you in Sta'Crivero, things would be different now, between us. You wouldn't look at me the way you do. With a touch of fear."

I want to deny it, to tell him that of course I'm not afraid of him. He's changed, I can see that. What happened at the Water Mine won't happen again. But that old fear lingers. I wish it wouldn't, but fear isn't something that is easily controlled.

"One day, I won't anymore," I tell him instead.

"One day," he agrees. "We'll get there, both of us."

I chew on my bottom lip. "Do you remember when we were children and the castle was preparing for my mother's birthday? I stole two lemon cakes from the kitchen and gave one to you. When the cook found us, I was the one with crumbs all over my face and she was going to tell my mother, but you took the blame for it."

His brow creases and his eyes get faraway. "I remember."

"And do you remember when Ampelio brought us both back those wooden dolls from Vestra? Mine broke within an hour and I was so devastated, but you let me have yours."

He nods. "I remember," he says again, looking more confused.

"And do you remember," I continue, "when you risked your life to break into the palace to rescue me? And when I made it more difficult for you, when it meant risking your life time and time again, you stood by me. You fought beside me. You trusted me."

"Theo—"

"There are a lot of versions of you that live in my memory, Blaise," I tell him. "Not all of them are pleasant, but most of them are. In most of them, you are my closest and dearest friend, someone who has always been steadfast and true. Someone I would trust with my life. And one day, the version of you from the Water Mine will be so small and distant compared to all of those other versions that it won't matter anymore. I believe that."

He looks down at his hands, his eyes beginning to turn red, as they always do just before he cries. He glances away, wiping his eyes hastily with the back of his hand. He opens his mouth to speak, but no words come out. Instead, quiet tears work their way down his cheeks.

There is nothing to say between us, not now. So I take him into my arms and let him cry.

# JOURNEY

———◆·◆———

I T'S ONLY A DAY'S JOURNEY to the Air Mine, but we don't want to attack until sunrise, in order to best take the Kalovaxians by surprise, so at sundown we make camp a good mile away. Unlike the Fire and Water Mines, the Air Mine has no mountains around it, no lakes, no forests. It stands in the middle of flat earth, interrupted only by the occasional thicket of olive trees, which means that our choices for cover are limited and we can't take our chances with any kind of fire, for risk of being detected.

We split evenly into three groups and spread out through three different olive groves to the east, south, and west of the mine. Tents are pitched. Rations are passed out. There is some grumbling about the lack of fires, and thus the lack of cooked meat, but the complaints are halfhearted at most. In truth, the relatively easy siege of the Ovelgan estate has lifted everyone's spirits.

For the first time, we don't feel like a scrappy group of warriors trying their best and getting lucky enough to make up for our weaknesses. For the first time, we feel strong and capable. For the first time, there is a light at the end of this never-ending dark tunnel, and it is looming closer and closer with every passing day.

I go with the southern camp group, along with Artemisia, Heron, Blaise, Søren, and Erik. We pitch as few tents as we can to save space in the grove, and instead of taking one to myself, the five of us share a single large tent, with six bedrolls lined up side by side, like a group of children at a slumber party.

Even when we turn in for the night, the energy is too much to allow for sleep. It makes us giddy and optimistic and excited for the day to come, the day when we get yet one more step closer to victory. And when Erik produces two bottles of fine Astrean wine from the Ovelgan estate, we get all the giddier.

"How did you manage to steal these?" Blaise asks him, using a knife to uncork one of the bottles.

Erik shrugs. "No one pays much attention to the half-blind fellow fumbling around the wine cabinet amidst chaos," he says. "And second of all, it technically isn't stealing because everything on that estate now belongs to Theo. Do you consider it stealing?" he asks me.

"You would have to ask Heron," I say. "I told him if we took the estate, it would become his."

Heron's eyebrows rise. "You were serious?" he asks. "I assumed you were just making grand promises to hide how frightened you were that we wouldn't succeed."

"Yes, well, that too," I say with a sigh. Blaise hands me the bottle and I take a swig. It's a dark red, warm and spicy. I wipe whatever is left on my lips away with the back of my hand in what I'm sure is a very regal fashion. "But I meant it. Gods know you could use something nice and quiet when this is all done. And it's what Leonidas wanted."

"Artemisia was right, though," Heron says. "If you start giving things out, everyone will want something."

"I know," I say, looking around the tent. "But this is just between us. I suppose it's assumed that Blaise will take on his father's old title, and his land holdings along with that. Artemisia is always welcome to call herself a princess of Astrea and take whatever jewels and houses that come with that title, but I have a feeling—"

"I would rather not," Artemisia cuts in, wrinkling her nose and making me laugh.

"Where will you go, then?" Blaise asks. "When this is all over?"

Art shrugs, taking the bottle of wine from me. "I figure I'll stay in the palace for a while," she says, drinking some before passing it on to Heron. "Someone's got to make sure Theo keeps her head long enough to actually wear that crown, after all. After she's secure and in good hands . . . who knows? Maybe I'll take over one of my mother's ships. Maybe I'll make sure the Kalovaxians we exile stay out of trouble."

It shouldn't surprise me, coming from Art, but it isn't a life I can imagine anyone wanting after all of this war.

"Won't you be tired of fighting?" I ask her.

She frowns. "I think I'd sooner grow tired of breathing. It's who I am." She turns to Heron. "We can't keep calling it the Ovelgan estate if it's yours," she points out.

"Well, it isn't as though I have a family name," he says. "Besides, it was Leonidas's family's before. The Talvera estate. I'd like it to stay that way."

"Then would you like to be the new Lord Talvera?" I ask. "It was what Leonidas wanted, wasn't it?"

Heron goes quiet for a moment before nodding. "Yes. I think I'd like that. I think he would have too."

"It's a fitting tribute," I say. "Restoring his family's estate and putting you in charge of it."

Heron nods, though his eyes are faraway. "Lord Talvera," he says, mostly to himself.

"Very well," I say, getting to my feet and gesturing for Heron to rise as well. Uncertainly, he does, letting go of Erik's hand. The tent is so low that he has to hunch over when he stands.

I hold my hand out to Artemisia. "Can I borrow your sword for a moment?" I ask her.

She gawks at me like I just asked if I could borrow her lungs or her heart, but after a second, she reluctantly unsheathes it, passing it to me hilt first. I take it and hold it before me, the silver of the blade glinting in the low light.

"Kneel," I tell Heron, and he does, looking perplexed. I realize that he's never seen a Guardian ceremony. I only re-member them dimly, mostly how bored I was during them, watching as Guardian after Guardian came before my mother to receive her blessing and whatever reward she saw fit for their service. I try to recall the details now—what she said, exactly, the words themselves a kind of binding magic. But there might not be a person in the world left who knows what those words were, so I suppose I have to make up my own and give them magic myself.

I clear my throat. "Every Guardian is brave," I say, glanc-ing around the room. "Every Guardian is strong. But it is less common to find a Guardian as kind as you are, Heron. Especially in this world, in this time, a Guardian with a heart as pure and balanced and forgiving as yours is a rare thing. Not only have you helped to reclaim our country, to save our people, but with your judgment and guidance, we will ensure that when the smoke clears and we stand free on the other side of this war, the world we rebuild will be a better one."

I look around the room to see the others watching me. Artemisia nods along with me. Blaise wipes away a tear. Søren leans forward, eyes glowing. Erik smiles.

I tap Heron with the blade once on each shoulder. "Rise now, Heron, Lord Talvera. I will forever turn to you for your fair mind and good judgment."

Heron rises again on shaking legs and smiles at me. "Thank you, Your Majesty," he says, his voice low and gruff with what might be tears. "I hope I serve you well."

I shake my head, passing Artemisia her sword back before laying a hand on Heron's shoulder. "I hope *I* serve *you* well," I tell him.

Heron pulls me into an embrace, wrapping his arms around me. I bury my face in his chest and hold him tight, listening to his heart beat. Without any warning, he lifts me up, spinning me around until we are both laughing. When he sits down next to Erik again, he takes the bottle from Blaise and holds it up high.

"To Queen Theodosia," he says, his voice clear.

"To Queen Theodosia," the others echo, and the bottle makes another round before coming to Søren last. I watch as he lifts the bottle to his lips and drinks deeply, finishing the last of the wine.

"What will you do when this is all over?" I ask him.

He lowers the bottle and meets my gaze. He considers the question for a moment before shrugging.

"I don't know," he admits. "I think it depends on a lot of things. But I still have a debt to repay you and your people, Theo. I still have a lot to make up for."

"When Astrea is ours again, I think you can consider your debt more than repaid," I say.

"Hell, I considered it repaid after you managed to survive the Kaiserin's torture," Blaise says.

"Before that even," Heron adds. "The Fire Mine. We couldn't have taken that back without you."

"Honestly, I considered our slate clean after we left Sta'Crivero," Artemisia says. "I figured you had been punished enough by then."

Søren looks down at his lap, a smile tugging at his lips that doesn't quite reach his eyes. "Thank you," he says. "But I don't think I'll ever truly feel like I've made up for the hurt I've caused. I intend to keep trying until I do."

# MOURNING

CRESS WEARS A BLACK SILK gown with swirls of onyx beads that move over her body like plumes of smoke. Though it covers her from throat to wrists to ankles, her bone-white skin shows through in more places than not. It is the kind of thing she once would have mocked Dagmær for wearing, but now she wears it as comfortably as if she were born in it.

She surveys me over the rim of a golden wine goblet, sitting in my mother's throne with one leg crossed over the other, jewels ringing each of her fingers—each one set with Fire Gems of different shapes and sizes. There is a Fire Gem at her throat as well, set into a gold choker that doesn't hide the charred skin of her neck but rather highlights it.

Slowly she lifts the wine goblet to her black lips and takes a sip.

"Oh," she says, her voice almost bored. "There you are."

Disinterested as she tries to sound, there is a hunger in her eyes so ferocious that I want to take a step back, though I force myself to hold my ground. I'm here for a reason, I remind myself. Cress has had her mother and a disguised Laius in her clutches for a few days now. I need to know where she's gotten with them.

*She doesn't know I'm alive,* I remind myself.

"Here I am," I tell her, matching her tone. "What would you like to show me today? Your prisoners, perhaps? The mother who abandoned you, like I did?"

She flinches at that but she doesn't rise to the bait. Still, there is nothing triumphant in her eyes, nothing gleeful. Instead her eyes are cold even as her mouth spreads into a wide smile. She gets to her feet.

"No. Tonight, we're going to a party," she says, lifting the skirt of her gown primly as she steps down from the dais and onto the marble floor.

I look down to see that I'm in a gown of my own—no longer the worn nightgown I wore to bed. This gown is an incandescent white, crafted from light chiffon, with tiny pearls sewn into the bodice in ornate floral designs. My shoulders are bare, but for the first time in my memory, I'm not aware of the scars on my back, though I know I should be. They aren't there, I realize. There is no tightness, no twinge of pain. It just feels like skin.

Cress loops her arm through mine and tugs me out of the throne room, her skin hot.

"You're late, of course, but only fashionably so," she says as we wind through the palace hallways.

She's leading me toward the ballroom, I realize. To the party being thrown there. But when she shoves open the door, the cavernous room is very nearly empty. Every other time I have been here, it has been overflowing with people in glittering gowns of every shade, twirling under the light of the chandelier. Now, though, I count only half a dozen other girls, all under the age of twenty, with a couple as young as eight, all dressed in black silk. All with the same charred throats, black lips, and white hair as Cress.

The sound of harp music floods the room, though I don't see its source before Cress pulls me into a dance, taking both of my hands in hers and spinning me across the floor. As soon as we're dancing, the other girls join in, an unending whirl of black silk unfurling across the dance floor. Except me—I am the only one dressed in white.

"It's meant to be a somber occasion," Cress tells me conversationally, her voice carrying over the music. "But Rigga did love dancing, so it seems appropriate, don't you think?"

The name digs under my skin, but I force myself to keep my expression neutral as I search for something to say. The smell of fire and smoke is heavy in the air, making me cough.

"I can't say I knew her very well," I say when I recover, looking around the room for the source of the smoke, but there is no sign of fire. Something is wrong, something is off, yet I cannot put my finger on what it is. "But I remember how much she cared for you."

She tilts her head, eyeing me thoughtfully, a small smile tugging at her lips. "Is that what you remember?" she asks. "I would have thought that watching her die after you poisoned her would have left far more of an impression."

She says the words casually enough, but ice slides down my spine. I try to pull away from her, but she holds my hands fast, so tightly that I feel my bones strain beneath her grip. The other girls have stopped dancing. They form a circle around us, watching with hungry eyes and black-lipped snarls. Gone are the pretty, giggling court ladies I remember from the palace—now they are feral beasts, watching and waiting to pounce. The smell of smoke grows stronger, making my eyes water.

I look back at Cress, who is still calm and smiling like nothing is wrong.

"Cress—" I start, but she doesn't let me finish.

"I know that I will never forget feeling the life leave her body, even miles and miles away. I felt it as soon as she slipped into unconsciousness, saw your face in her mind's eye, watching her die. You looked so satisfied, so relieved, so *alive*. Is that how you looked when you thought you'd killed me?" she asks.

"No," I manage to get out. "I don't know what you think you saw—"

"Shh," she says, releasing one of my hands to bring a finger to my lips. Her smile grows broader, showing her teeth. I half expect them to have grown into fangs, but they haven't. "No more lying, Thora. It's unbecoming."

I see only the brief flash of silver slide from the sleeve of her gown before she sinks the blade into my stomach, up to the hilt. I look down to see it protruding from me, the white silk gown blossoming with dark crimson, which spreads farther with each passing second.

A scream pierces the air, and I know, distantly, that it's my own, but I don't feel it. I don't feel anything but the pain flooding through every inch of my body, yet the sound only makes her smile wider. She pulls me close, pushing the dagger even deeper into my stomach as she leans in to my ear. The smell is coming from her, I realize. She smells like fire, like smoke, like burning wood and burning flesh.

"I'll see you again soon, Thora," she whispers, her voice soft and delicate. She twists the knife. "In the meantime, I hope you enjoy my little surprise."

Then she kisses my cheek and releases me altogether, pulling the dagger from my stomach and letting me fall to the cold marble floor in a heap of bloodstained white silk.

I wake up with a gasp, the sharp pain of Cress's dagger still as excruciating as it was in my dream, the smell of smoke still thick in my lungs. I cough, sitting up and grabbing my stomach, only to feel a new wave of pain. My fingers come away sticky and wet, stained a bright red that is visible even in the pitch-dark.

It takes my brain a few seconds to drag itself from the tendrils of my dream enough to realize that I am awake, I am miles and miles away from Cress, but the wound she created is very real.

The scream that rips its way out of my throat is not entirely human, not entirely mine. I fall back onto my bedroll, clutching my stomach.

In seconds, the others are awake and alert and gathered around me, all panicked words and hands touching the wound, but I barely hear them. The agony is unbearable, made worse with every breath, every touch.

"It's deep," one voice says. Heron. "But not fatal. I can fix it."

No sooner does he say the words than the wound goes

numb, like an icy wind has brushed over, freezing it. The pain is still there, but it is a dull thrum beneath my skin. It no longer feels like I'm being torn apart from within.

I open my eyes to five concerned faces staring down at me. Heron's hands are covered in blood—my blood.

"What happened?" Blaise asks. "Were you attacked?"

He's on his feet, searching our small tent for any sign of intruders, but I shake my head.

"Not here," I manage to get out. I sit up carefully and cough. The smoke is still in my lungs. If anything, it's getting stronger. "In my dream. Cress. She knows I'm alive; she knows I killed Rigga. She stabbed me, and I woke up . . ."

"You woke up stabbed," Artemisia says quietly.

"It isn't possible," Blaise says, still pacing the tent, searching for some other explanation, but there is none.

"And yet . . ." Artemisia trails off, her eyes trained on my wound.

"It's not possible," Blaise says again, stopping his pacing to stare at us. "You can't really believe this madness."

"I've seen madder things than this," Erik says, turning his face toward Blaise. "Yourself included, if you don't mind me saying so. The real madness would be in ignoring the truth when it demands to be acknowledged."

Blaise doesn't have a response to that. He only scowls before turning to me.

"Are you all right?"

It's such a ridiculous question that I can't help but laugh, but the movement makes the dagger wound ache all over again.

"Here," Heron says. "Lie down and I'll heal it completely."

I do as he says and bring the blanket up to cover my hips so that Heron can lift my nightgown and bare my stomach. There is so much blood, though the wound itself is still frozen.

"I have to unfreeze it first," Heron says. "It'll hurt for a few moments—badly—but then it'll be fully healed."

I take a deep, bracing breath before nodding. "Go ahead," I tell him.

Søren reaches for my hand, squeezing it tightly in his to distract me, but it doesn't work. As soon as Heron begins working, pain floods through me again, blurring my eyesight and turning my mind into a whirl of bright colors and agony. I hear myself scream, though the sound feels far away, not quite a part of me.

"Breathe," Heron says, his voice low. I feel his hands on me, warm and soothing but always gone too quickly. I can feel the skin closing, feel it knitting itself together again, excruciating and slow. "It won't leave a scar," he continues, which I suppose he means to be a relief, but the idea doesn't faze me—what's another scar, after all?

After what feels like an eternity, the pain begins to ebb and I find I can breathe normally again, though I can't rid myself of the smell of smoke. It lingers in my lungs, like Cress's fingers, refusing to let me go completely.

"There," Heron says, lifting his hands from my stomach and pulling the blanket up to cover me. "Good as new, or thereabouts."

"What happened, exactly?" Søren asks me.

"I thought I could find out how she was progressing with Brigitta and Jian—Laius, rather."

"Did you?" Artemisia asks.

"Not in so many words, but when I mentioned her mother, Cress frowned. She looked annoyed. I don't think she's broken her yet. I don't know about Jian."

"What *did* she say, then?" Heron asks.

I find my voice and tell them about the dream, the half-dozen other girls Cress has turned. I tell them about the moment when I knew that she knew I was alive, and the moment she slipped the dagger into my flesh, as easily as a knife through a pat of butter.

"She called it a surprise afterward," I say, shaking my head. "'*I hope you enjoy my little surprise.*' That's what she said. And she smelled like smoke, like burning. I still smell it now," I admit, wrinkling my nose.

Søren frowns, looking around the room. He sniffs at the air, and the others do as well.

"I smell it too," he says quietly. "Smoke."

Blaise shakes his head. "It's a hallucination," he insists. "She said she smelled smoke, and now all of us can smell it."

But when the screams sound from outside the tent, I realize that Blaise is wrong—it isn't a hallucination. It isn't a stubborn remnant of my dream, either. An instant later, Maile bursts into the tent, still dressed in her own nightclothes, red-faced and winded.

"The camp at the Air Mine," she manages to get out between gulps of breath. "Our scouts just returned. It's on fire. The whole thing."

# SMOKE

—————•—————

OUTSIDE THE TENT, THE SMOKE in the air is thick enough to choke me, and I hold the sleeve of my bloodied nightgown up to cover my nose and mouth to filter some of it out. All around our small camp, people are panicking, running in one direction or another, half-asleep still and trying to determine what's happening.

Maile leads us to the northern edge of the olive grove, where the Air Mine is just visible rising over the pale pastel horizon. At first glance, I could mistake it for the sun itself rising. The whole thing is ablaze, the brightness of the flames so intense that I have to shield my eyes to look at it.

"How?" Artemisia asks behind me, unable to manage more than the single word.

I can't bring myself to answer, though in my gut I know exactly how, and exactly why. I remember Cress leaning in, twisting the knife in my stomach.

"*I hope you enjoy my little surprise,*" she whispered. I thought she'd meant the stabbing, but that wasn't it—Cress had another trick up her sleeve. She knew what had happened at the Ovelgan estate and so she knew exactly where we would go next.

Maile was right when she said it was the predictable course to take.

"They're burning all of it," Søren says, pulling me out of my thoughts. "The mine and the stores and the slave camp—everything. Why would they do that?"

"Because she knew we were going to take it and she couldn't get warriors there quickly enough to protect it," I say. "And she would rather destroy it all than lose it to me."

Without waiting for a response, I turn around and walk back toward our camp. Horror and fear duel in my mind, but I force myself to speak loudly enough to drown them out.

"I want everyone on the move now," I say to the gathered men and women. "We need to get word to our other groups as well—especially the Fire and Water Guardians. We'll extinguish and control the fire as best we can while the rest of our army fights off the guards—I'm sure many of them will still be lingering about, waiting to ambush us."

"You can't be serious," Maile says, matching my pace. "It's a trap; you must know that."

"I do," I say. "But there are people in there."

"Good as dead already," she replies. "What's the point of losing more people in the process of trying to save them?"

I know she's making sense, but I barely hear her. Blood pounds in my ears, pushing me forward, demanding action.

"You don't have to take orders from me," I tell her. "But that's the order I'm giving my people, and given that most of them could have very easily found themselves in a burning mine, I can't imagine anyone will decide to sit it out. You, however, are welcome to."

For a beat, she doesn't say anything, but then she quickens her pace and jogs ahead. "Like I'm going to let you take all of the glory," she shouts over her shoulder. "I'll get word to the eastern group."

"Then I'll take the west," Blaise says before running off in that direction.

Heron catches up with me, Erik beside him. "There are Air Guardians in there," Heron reminds me. "I should go in as well. If I can get to them, we might be able to coordinate enough wind to help extinguish the fire."

"Or you'll feed it," I point out. "Stay outside. There will be injured slaves coming out, and they'll need your help when they do."

"And me?" Erik asks.

"Stay in the camp with Søren," I tell him.

"Theo—" Søren says, coming up on my other side.

I shake my head, already anticipating his protests. "It's dark and we don't know what sort of trap we're getting into. The last thing we need is you getting mistaken for a Kalovaxian guard. Stay here with Erik and keep watch. If you see anything new heading our way, get word to us."

Søren doesn't like being a lookout—I can see it in the twist of his mouth—but he nods.

"Go," he tells me, and in the dim light I can see the worry outlined clearly on his face as he looks at me. "I don't need to tell you to be careful, so I'll just say to come back safe, all right?"

\* \* \*

I know that Artemisia is riding as fast as she can, but as I stare at the flames blazing in the distance, it doesn't feel fast enough. Screams whip through the air, raising goose bumps on my skin and sending my heart thundering. I don't realize I'm holding Artemisia too tightly until she delivers a gentle but solid elbow to my side.

"Get a hold of yourself," she shouts at me over her shoulder. "You aren't good for anything if you're a panicked mess."

I know she's right, but it's hard to stay calm and collected when the dying screams of innocents are ringing in your ear.

We get as close to the camp as we can before the horse begins to panic, and we go the rest of the way on foot. I don't look over my shoulder—all of my focus is on what's left of the burning wall that surrounds the camp—but I know the others are behind me. Up close, the fire is even bigger than I expected; there doesn't seem to be an inch of the camp left untouched.

Standing before the inferno, even Artemisia looks frightened.

"Where do we even begin?" she shouts to me.

I don't know how to answer her. I feel frozen myself. But I steel my nerves and raise my hands. I focus, feeling Ampelio's pendant warm against my heart.

I press my palms together, then pull them apart, throwing my arms wide. As I do, the flames of the camp part as well, mirroring the motion. It is barely a crack, barely enough to show the remnants of where the wall once stood, but it's large enough to create a path into the camp, and that is all that matters.

"You and the other Water Guardians start from the outer

edge and work your way in," I shout to her. "The other Fire Guardians and I will make paths to get people out."

Artemisia nods and lifts her arms, but I can't stay and watch. I turn back to the path I made and start down it, careful to keep my concentration steady. Narrow as the path is, one slip and it could close in on me, and though fire has never burned me in small doses, I'm not about to test how much that protection can withstand.

The screams are louder now, so loud and piercing that the hairs on my arms rise. I follow the closest scream, widening the path ahead and letting it close behind me until I come to a break in the flames where one of the barracks stood, but now all that's left is the skeleton of the structure. I step inside and lower my arms before bringing my sleeve to my nose and mouth to filter out the smoke thick in the air, along with a smell that I would rather not put a name to.

"Hello?" I call out in Astrean. It's impossible to see anything through the curtain of smoke, but the screams are even louder, underscored by soft crying.

"Hello?" a voice calls back, frightened and hoarse.

I step toward it, stumbling over something on the ground that has the distinct feel of a lifeless body. I crouch down to see if it's alive, but the voice stops me.

"Dead," it says before I can reach out to touch the body. "Over here, please."

My stomach twists and I straighten up. The voice is younger than I thought at first, speaking halting and uncertain Astrean.

"Are you alone?" I ask, but when no one responds, I ask again in Kalovaxian.

Instead of an answer, I hear a sharp intake of breath, before a loud exhale forceful enough to knock me back a step. In that gust, the fire nearby roars larger, but the room clears of smoke and I find myself face to face with five frightened people. The youngest can't be older than six, and the eldest— the Air Guardian who blew away the smoke—is a woman around twenty.

I want to ask if they're all right, but anyone can see that they aren't. They're frightened and covered in ash and soot, to say nothing of the burns on their skin. They were huddled on the ground, but now that the air is clear, they scramble to their feet.

"Come on," I say, holding a hand out toward them. "Follow me and stay close."

The Guardian woman nods, though she eyes me warily. She reaches behind her and takes the hands of two of the younger ones before following me. All of them have cloth wrapped around the lower halves of their faces, covering their mouths.

When we reach the wall of fire again, I take a deep, steadying breath before using my gift to part the flames once more, trying to keep the space wider and deeper to fit everyone. It's a struggle to hold a space that large, but I manage and I lead them through.

"Who is she?" a voice whispers behind me, but it's quickly shushed.

I focus in front of me, in what I'm almost positive is the way I came in, though I can't say for sure. On fire, everything looks the same. There are more screams, loud and close, but I force myself to ignore them. For now, I tell myself. I can come back, but I need to get these people to safety first.

The smoke in my throat is so thick and hot that I can barely breathe, even through the sleeve of my dress. It feels like drinking the Encatrio all over again, burning down my throat.

Just when I think I can't stand it anymore, I walk straight into a wall of water, soaking me head to toe. I gasp for air, shocked and relieved all at once.

I hear my name, dim and distant, and the water dies down to reveal Artemisia in front of me.

"Are you all right?" she asks me before noticing the others I brought out. She lets out a curse below her breath and turns her attention to them. She shouts for Heron, who comes running, a case of gauze and ointment ready.

"I'm going back in," I say. "There were so many others."

"Theo," Artemisia says. "It's out of control. You can't risk it."

Heron doesn't protest, though. Instead he takes a rag from his case and holds it out to Artemisia. "Douse this with water," he says. "It'll make it easier for her to breathe through."

Artemisia looks ready to argue, but she does as he says and Heron passes the wet cloth to me.

"You're breathing too much smoke, even with this," he tells me. "When you're out, find me right away, all right? And don't go in more than you can. You know your limits, Theo. And you know you can't help anyone if you're dead."

"I know," I say, taking the rag from him and tying it around my head so that it covers my nose and mouth.

The wet rag helps the second time I go into the flames, but it does nothing to keep the smoke from burning my eyes. I follow the screams and manage to find another group of four men and women huddled together in what looks like it might have been the dining hall. They follow me out just as the others did, and I only rest a few seconds before going back in again.

With the Water Guardians working from the outside toward the center to extinguish the fire, the trip gets easier every time. There is less smoke, less fire to cut my way through, but my body aches with every step, and my lungs burn so badly that breathing is agony. Yet the screams are still there, still crying out for help, and so I keep going back.

"Theo, it's enough," Heron says after I bring out the fourth group. He's hard at work healing a boy of ten, his hands on the boy's chest, helping to clear the smoke from his lungs. "Rest for a few minutes. Drink some water. There's time."

But the screams in the air pull at me, dragging me back into the flames without even a moment to rest.

"Just once more," I say, and I let Artemisia douse me head to toe with water again before stepping back into the flames.

I hear Heron calling my name just as I step inside, but then he's lost to me and all I hear is the crackling of the fire and the unending screams. I stumble blindly toward one, dimly aware of how much every inch of my body aches and burns and drags with the effort of putting one foot in front of the other. The world around me spins, the roar of flames becoming a blur. I close my eyes and take a deep breath to steady myself, opening them only when another scream sounds, clear and close.

I take off toward it. *Just one more,* I remind myself. *Then I can rest.*

Flames lick at my skin as I run, but I barely feel them

anymore. All I feel is the blood pounding in my brain, urging me on.

There's a break in the flames and I step into it, looking around for the source of the scream, but all I can see is fire and smoke. I hear the scream again, this time coming from behind me, and I whirl around but there is nothing there.

"Hello?" I call out. "Is anyone there? I'm here to help you, but I need to know where you are."

Another scream—this time from right beside me. But as soon as I turn toward it, the scream morphs into a laugh, shrill and high and raspy.

I search the smoke, searching for the source, even as that laugh works its way beneath my skin, itching with a familiarity I can't place it until a figure steps through the smoke and comes into a hazy, blurred focus.

Dagmær, dressed all in black, just as she was in the dream I had of Cress in the ballroom. And she isn't alone. Flanking her are two other ladies in the same type of mourning dress, their faces covered with funeral veils.

"Hello, Thora," Dagmær says with a pointed smile. "I'll be sure to tell Cress how much you enjoyed her little surprise."

# INFERNO

—•—

M Y VISION IS A BLUR, my mind spinning. They aren't
real—they can't be real. But of course they are. Of
course this isn't a normal fire, caused by the strike of a few
matches. Of course Cress had a grander plan in mind. I can almost imagine it, the three of them leaving the palace as soon as
Cress got word of where we were headed, riding day and night,
unencumbered by weapons or other supplies. They would
have arrived at the camp an hour ago, getting the guards out
before using their powers to start fires, growing them larger
and larger until the entire camp was caught aflame.

Cress couldn't have come herself, not with the threat of a
coup hanging over her head, but I imagine this is the next best
thing.

It's a struggle to focus on Dagmær—to focus on any of
them. My vision keeps blurring, my eyes burning and tearing
from the smoke. Still, I call on my gift and summon a ball
of fire, and throw it at Dagmær, who doesn't even have to
dodge it. It sails harmlessly past her, a good foot to the right.
She watches it, bored almost, before turning back to me with
raised eyebrows.

"Oh my. Someone isn't in good shape," she says, clicking her tongue as she steps toward me. The train of her black gown has caught fire, dragging flames behind her with every step she takes, but she doesn't seem concerned by it. "Are you tired?" she asks, her voice saccharine, the way one might speak to a child.

She reaches out to touch my cheek, her fingers scalding hot. I bat away her hand and—lacking any weapon—do the first thing that comes to mind. I ball my hand into a fist and punch her as hard as I can. The movement feels heavy and weak, but it's enough to elicit a nauseating crack when my knuckles collide with her nose.

Dagmær stumbles back a few steps, bringing her hand up to touch her broken nose. She pulls her fingers back, and with a distant sort of fascination examines the blood that coats them, before turning her gaze back to me. The blood gushing down her face makes her look even more frightful than she did earlier.

"I suppose there's still a bit of fight left in you after all," she says, her mouth curling into a vicious smile. "Good. That'll make this fun."

She summons fire to her fingertips, and the two girls behind her do the same. Then they advance toward me, each step agonizingly slow.

I push through my aching bones, my burning lungs, my dizziness, and I force myself to focus, calling on my own power to draw fire. That, at least, doesn't cost much effort. Here, surrounded by so much of it, my magic is one thing that is strong. It feels like I have an unlimited supply of it.

Dagmær eyes the fire in my hands thoughtfully. "Not bad," she says. "I'll be sure to tell Cress that you died well."

"We aren't supposed to kill her," one of the other girls says.

"Hush, Maeve," Dagmær hisses at her. "Of course we'll try to capture her alive but . . . well . . . accidents do happen, don't they?" She turns toward me. "And I can't imagine you'll come with us peacefully."

For an instant, I consider what would happen if I did. I could get back into the palace, face to face with Cress in reality this time, not in dreams, not wearing someone else's face, and . . . and I would be there alone, with no plan, no allies, nothing but myself and my power. And it wouldn't be enough. Even if I managed to kill her, I would still be trapped in a palace surrounded by enemies, with no way out.

No. I can't do this alone. I thought I could through our dreams, but that was a mistake—one that cost so many lives. I need to get back to the others, I need to make a plan, I need to do this right.

Instead of answering, I throw the fire in my hand at Dagmær, who sidesteps it with ease.

"Fine, then," she says with a smile. "I'd hoped you'd make this difficult."

She throws fire at me, and I try to duck out of the way, but it hits my hip, causing the nerves there to explode in pain. Luckily, my nightgown is still soaked through and the fire dies quickly. I pause, doubled over.

"Is that all you have, Dagmær?" I ask her, straightening up. "I suppose I'm not as easy to kill as your six-year-old step-son. Did that make you feel strong and powerful?"

She doesn't flinch. "You know nothing about power, Thora," she says. "How could you? With your crown of ashes, always relying on others to help you. First it was Cress, then whatever rebels you had. Then it was Prinz Søren, wasn't it? All of your power is secondhand, given by others on their terms. Even this—what you are—was given to you by Cress. You didn't want it, didn't even try to take it."

She conjures more fire, throws three small flames at me. I dodge two of them, but the third one hits my shoulder, and I cry out in pain.

Somewhere in the distance, someone calls my name, but I can barely hear it, barely hear anything besides the blood pounding in my ears.

"Cress did not give me this," I tell Dagmær, each word coming out sharp and sure. "If you see Cress again, you tell her that. The power she gave me was nothing, a shadow of a shadow, barely enough to light a match. I chose this power as I was meant to, in the Fire Mine. I fought for it. I *earned* it."

Dagmær laughs, advancing on me again, flames in both of her hands.

"Well. We'll see if that makes a difference, won't we?" she taunts, eyes bright, the flames around us reflecting in her pupils.

I steel myself, summoning my own fire and preparing to attack. But before either of us can strike, there's a loud cry behind me and a blast of water that hits Dagmær in the chest, knocking her backward and into the other two girls, extinguishing the fires in their hands.

The three of them splutter, clambering to their feet and looking around, bewildered, as Artemisia steps out of the flames, appearing at my side with her sword in one hand and the other hand poised and ready for another blast.

"You were taking too long," she tells me. "I thought you could use a bit of help."

"Perfect timing," I say.

"Someone else coming to your rescue, I see," Dagmær snarls, her mocking smile washed away entirely. She's no longer smug—she's angry, and seeing her fury only ignites mine.

"I'm sorry, I can't properly explain the concept of friendship," I say, throwing a ball of fire at her. It hits her in the stomach, sizzling against her wet gown, and she lets out an ear-piercing scream before charging toward us, the other two at her heels.

Artemisia throws another gust of water at them, but this time they're ready for it and it only knocks them back a step; Artemisia is ready, charging forward with her sword.

It's all I can do to stay out of her way, though I try to work a few blasts of fire in as well, when I'm sure they won't hit her. Most of them go wide, serving to frighten more than anything else, but a few hit true, sizzling against their wet gowns and, on occasion, finding a patch of bare skin.

But for every strike we make, it feels like they make two. There is a never-ending barrage of fire coming toward Artemisia and me, and her use of her Water Gift manages to block only most of the fireballs. Many still make it through, burning skin and singeing clothing.

A larger flame, thrown by Dagmær, hits me so hard in the shoulder that I fall backward and land on the ground with a thud. Sensing weakness, one of the other girls—Maeve—advances on me, her grin feral and hungry, knowing that I am a sitting target. Artemisia is busy with the other two girls; I don't even think she notices me.

*"Always relying on others to help you."* Dagmær's words echo in my mind. It's true, I can call on fire, but so can Maeve, and right now Maeve has the upper hand. The flames behind Maeve shift, ever so slightly, and in that instant an idea comes to me.

I hold my hand out, and Maeve flinches before realizing I hold no fire.

She laughs. "Out already, Thora?" she asks me. "All that talk about being stronger—"

Before she can finish, I yank my hand back to me, and from behind her a tendril of fire reaches out like a hand, wrapping around Maeve's waist, and dragging her into the flames. Her screams are deafening before they die out altogether.

Artemisia glances my way, her eyes lit up like they always are in the heat of battle, her expression beatific.

"Amazing, Theo—" Before she can finish, Dagmær pounces, all of her feline grace gone as she tackles Artemisia to the ground. She wraps her hands around Artemisia's neck, squeezing and burning her at once.

"No!" I scream. I try to do the same thing I did with Maeve, but Dagmær lunges out of the way, losing her grip on Artemisia as she does, and the flames take the other girl, swallowing her into the wall of fire before she even has the time to scream.

Dagmær moves toward Art again, but this time I'm faster. Without thinking, I throw my body over Art's, shielding her. I call on every remaining ounce of my power, drawing the flames larger and larger and larger, imagining the entire camp as nothing but fire, every inch burning. As soon as I think it, I hear the roar of it in my ears, feel the lick of flames against my skin, feel Dagmær's scream vibrating in the air. Then I push the fire down in my mind. I shove it deep into the ground until there is no fire left, only ashes.

Then all there is is silence and smoke and the world gone still. But I can feel Artemisia's heart beating, feel the steady rise and fall of her chest, and that is enough.

I force my head up, force my eyes open to see only charred ground around me, the remains of burnt buildings, patches of a destroyed wall. And bodies—too many bodies to count, including one mere inches from me that I somehow know in my bones is Dagmær's, though there's not enough left to truly recognize.

I hear someone shout my name, and a cacophony of voices, but then my vision goes dark and I don't hear anything at all.

# DARK

————— ◆•◆ —————

DARKNESS SURROUNDS ME, A NIGHT with no stars, no moon, nothing at all to see by. I feel it wrapping around my limbs, slithering over my skin like a dozen snakes. I feel it in the air, in every frigidly cold breath I take.

There is no ground beneath my feet, nothing at all around me except pitch-dark air. I open my mouth but no sound comes out, even when I scream at the top of my lungs.

Perhaps this is what death is—no After, no reunion with my mother and Ampelio and Hoa and Elpis and all of the others I've lost. Perhaps I didn't deserve that, perhaps they turned me away. I dimly recall why they would, how I let Cress into my head and how thousands of Astreans at the Air Mine paid the price for it. Perhaps this is what I deserve—an eternity of conscious nothingness.

Time is immeasurable, an unending expanse where an hour could just as easily be a second which could be a week, and I would have no way of knowing. It is both infinite and infinitesimal at once.

I close my eyes, and when I open them again, I am no

longer alone in the darkness. Cress is a few feet before me, her white-blond hair floating around her head like she's suspended in water, her black lace gown billowing in an invisible current. For an instant, she looks at peace, her eyes closed and her expression relaxed, but then her eyes snap open and lock on to mine and I see the cold seething fury I've grown more accustomed to from her.

Maybe this is the After I deserve, an everlasting nothingness with only Cress for comfort. Maybe this is what we both deserve.

I thought once that by the time we saw one another in the After, we would maybe have forgiven each other, but that was before the trespasses piled up. Now, looking at her, I know that there is no forgiveness waiting, no grace, only a hate that will sustain us for eternity.

She reaches out a hand but can't fully extend her arm before she hits some sort of barrier. The sound of the collision echoes around me, like a thud against a thick pane of glass. I reach out as well, feeling it for myself, cold and hard and solid.

Cress frowns. She opens her mouth, and I can see her forming words, speaking, but I can't hear a thing. She must realize this as well because her frown deepens and she places both hands against the barrier that separates us. She leans in close, her features becoming distorted through it. She takes a deep breath and opens her mouth wide, and this time, I can hear the scream, deafening in my ears. It raises goose bumps on my arms and makes the hairs on the back of my neck stand up straight.

She screams so loud that the barrier between us quivers and cracks, a spiderweb of fractures spreading over the surface before it shatters altogether.

I come to with a gasp, the air in my lungs no longer ice cold. It hurts to breathe, each inhale agony, but it's a reminder that I'm alive, and so I savor it. With some effort, I force my heavy eyes open. At first, the brightness blinds me, but when I blink a few times, I realize that the only light is coming from a single candle set up beside me in an otherwise dark tent.

When I try to sit up, my head throbs and I have to lie down once more with a groan, throwing an arm over my eyes to block out the light, though even that small movement sends a wave of pain through my whole body.

"Theo?" a voice asks, barely louder than a whisper. I lower my arm, squinting into the dark to see Heron sitting nearby, between my bedroll and another one. Though the occupant's back is to me, I can just make out the spill of cerulean hair. Artemisia.

"Is she all right?" I ask. My voice comes out raspy and rough, barely intelligible, but every syllable hurts, but Heron understands.

"I fixed everything I could," he says, looking at her. "She's alive. She's breathing. But she hasn't woken up yet."

I swallow, but that only makes the pain in my throat worse. "How long has it been?" I ask.

"Just over a day. It's almost sunrise," he says. He pauses before asking the inevitable question.

"What happened, Theo?"

I close my eyes tight, memories filtering back in slowly, then all at once. "The scream—that last one I went in for—it was a trap," I say, before telling him about Dagmær and the other girls, about how Dagmær grabbed Artemisia's throat, choking and burning her at once.

"She was going to kill her," I tell him. "So I . . ." I break off, unable to say it, but I force myself to tell him. "I tried to cover Art and then I caused the explosion. It was the only thing I could think of to stop Dagmær."

For a second, Heron doesn't say anything. "It did, though. Stop her."

I nod, looking at Artemisia again. I force myself not to think the worst—that it might not have been enough to save Art.

"What about the others?" I ask instead. "Was anyone else hurt in the explosion?"

Heron pauses before shaking his head. "Not in the explosion, no. By then, we'd gotten everyone out that we could," he says, but doesn't continue. He won't look at me, either, his eyes focused on the flame of the candle.

"Tell me, Heron," I say, quiet but firm. "I need to know."

He takes a steadying breath. "Our best estimates say there were three thousand people in the camp, not including the guards who abandoned it when the fire started. All in all, close to five hundred survived."

I close my eyes tightly. Twenty-five hundred people, dead. The thought is unfathomable, but Heron isn't done.

"And we took losses of our own," he adds. "There were

guards lying in wait, ready to fight, as you thought there might be. And some who went into the fire to help didn't make it out again."

I don't want to know the answer, but I have to ask the question anyway.

"How many did we lose?" I ask.

"A hundred altogether," he says. "At first, only the Guardians went into the fire, but there were unblessed people going in as well. They saved lives, all of them, but . . ." He trails off. "We lost Guardians and non-Guardians alike."

My mind is a blur of thoughts, but only one works its way past my lips.

"It's my fault," I say.

Heron must have expected me to say as much, because he doesn't miss a beat. "It was their choice, Theo," he says, moving closer and grabbing hold of my hand. My skin is still raw and my bones ache, but I don't pull away. "They could have stayed in the camp; they could have found other ways to help. They *chose* to go into that fire, knowing perfectly well that they were risking their lives. It's not your fault."

I turn toward him and shake my head. "Not just that," I say. "The fire itself. She did it to taunt me, because she was angry about Rigga. *A little surprise,* she called it. If I'd listened to you, or Blaise, or anyone who'd told me to take a dreamless potion and block my mind from her—"

"We still might be here," Heron interrupts. "She might have still sent her ghouls here. She might not have taunted you about it, she might not have made it personal, but you said it yourself. If she couldn't have the mine, she wanted it destroyed. Nothing about that would have changed."

I know he's right, but it doesn't help ease my guilt. Twenty-six hundred lives lost.

Heron squeezes my hand tightly in his. "You made the best decision you could with the information you had. You couldn't have seen this coming."

"I *should* have," I say, a sob leaking into my voice. "I know her, I should have known what she would do."

Heron lets out a loud exhale. "What you should do is get some more sleep. I got some of the dreamless potion into you as soon as I could after you passed out, but I have more here."

I think about my dream, of Cress on the other side of that glass wall, unable to break through, until she did. Heron digs in his pocket, pulls out a vial of blue liquid, and I hesitantly take it. It's cool in my hand. I want to tell him that I'm not sure how much good it does, but I can't. He would only worry. Besides, it held well enough, and when it didn't, I woke up.

"What do we do now?" I ask him.

He pauses. "While you were asleep, we made some decisions," he admits. "We got word to Dragonsbane, and she's heading to the Savria River now—she'll meet us there in two days' time to take our wounded before leaving for the Earth Mine."

"But if Cress sent her ghouls to the Earth Mine, too—"

"Blaise said the same thing. We're sending a group there, in case something similar is happening, but we don't want to send everyone in case we're walking into another trap."

I nod. It makes sense, and at this point, I don't think there's anything Cress isn't capable of.

"Blaise is going to lead them," he adds, almost hesitantly.

At that, I force myself to sit up, ignoring the throbbing in my head. "Blaise," I echo. "The same Blaise trying to avoid using his gifts is going to wander into an area with tens of thousands of Earth Gems, begging for him to use them?" I ask.

Heron doesn't look happy about it, either, but he nods. "He's the only one who's been there," he says. "He knows the camp, knows the layout. It's necessary."

I want to argue, but I know he has a point. "And what about the rest of us?" I ask. "Where will we go after we meet Dragonsbane?"

"That's up to you," Heron says. "Of course, Maile has been very vocal about a lot of ideas. Most of them revolving around storming the palace, despite the fact that our numbers are depleted."

I sigh, shaking my head. "It would be a death strike," I say.

Heron frowns. "Death strike?"

I realize that the term is a Kalovaxian one, so I explain. "It's what the Kalovaxians call it when they wage a battle they know they'll lose—either to weaken the enemy or make way for a larger victory or whatever the end game is. But it's a sacrifice for the greater good. Usually the commandants throw their lower warriors at it, knowing they won't survive it, but so that the more important ones will live to make the next battle count."

"We don't have lower warriors, or more important ones, for that matter," he points out. "It wouldn't be a death strike; it would just be death."

I nod, but the truth is that I don't know what to do now, where to go from here. It's hard to believe that just two nights ago, we were celebrating what we thought was an imminent victory. How did everything change so quickly?

I tuck the dreamless-sleep potion into the pocket of my nightgown. "I'll have to sleep later," I tell him. "Now there's too much to do."

"You really should rest," Heron cautions. "I healed you as best I could, but there are some things your body has to do on its own."

"I'll rest soon, I promise," I tell him. "But we can't stay here. You know that. We're sitting ducks and Cress knows exactly where we are. Can you bring the others? We need to discuss our options."

"Theo—" Heron says.

"I'll rest after," I tell him. "And I'll keep an eye on Artemisia while you're gone. When she wakes up, you'll be the first to know."

I don't say *if.* I try not to even think it, but Heron must hear it all the same because his brow creases with worry and he looks back at her sleeping form.

"All right," he says with a sigh, dragging himself to his feet. "I'll get some food as well. You need to eat something."

# GOODBYE

---

I DON'T TAKE MY EYES OFF Artemisia for a second while Heron is gone. I barely blink. Every rise of her chest, every subtle movement she makes while she sleeps, I notice all of it.

*Wake up,* I think. *Wake up, wake up, wake up.*

But she sleeps on, oblivious, and I hope that her dreams are at least more peaceful than mine.

Even though every movement makes my body ache, I climb off my own bedroll and move next to hers so I can see her face in the flickering candlelight. Asleep, she is almost unrecognizable, her expression slack and peaceful. I don't know that *peaceful* is a word I could ever imagine using to describe Artemisia—no fight, no fury, no ferocity. Peaceful doesn't suit her at all.

I take hold of her hand, but it is limp in mine.

"I'm so sorry, Art. Please wake up," I whisper. But Artemisia has never been one for orders, so I'm not entirely surprised that she pays me no mind.

There's a rustling as the tent opens and a blade of light cuts in. I wipe away the tears that have formed in my eyes, before turning to see who it is.

Søren stands awkwardly at the entrance of the tent, eyes darting between Art and me.

"You're awake," he says when I don't speak, and I realize I once again put him in the position of thinking I was going to die.

I nod, biting my lip. "I am," I say. "Which is more than so many others can say."

He steps toward me, his expression torn. "Don't do that, Theo," he says. He drops down beside me so that we are eye to eye. "That's a dangerous path to let your mind travel down, and there is nothing at the end of it. Trust me. I've been there."

"It's not a path I think my mind has any control over," I point out.

"She won this battle," he says slowly. "She took far more than we did this time. There is nothing you can do to change that now. All you can do is ensure that you win the war. You can't do that if you're so wrapped up in guilt that you can't see straight. I can't tell you how to untangle yourself from it—I don't know if it's possible to, entirely—but don't lose sight of what you've accomplished. Don't lose sight of the fact that Cress did this to incapacitate you, and if you let her do that, then she's won."

I nod, looking down at Artemisia. "She'll wake up, won't she?"

At that, Søren laughs, but it sounds forced. "Art?" he says. "She didn't survive everything she's been through just to die at the hands of a socialite with gaudy taste in clothes."

I can't help but snort, mostly because I know he's right. Art will survive if for no other reason than to spite everyone who doubted she would. "How did you know about Dag-mær?" I asked.

He looks away. "We found her body in the ruins. Almost unidentifiable, but she was wearing a Fire Gem choker and it had her name inscribed on the back."

"A gift from Cress," I guess.

He nods. "There were two others," he adds. "A Maeve and a Freya. The names didn't register for me, but it's easy enough to assume who they were."

"Part of Cress's army of wraiths," I say. "They were all dead?" I remember seeing their blackened bodies before I lost consciousness, but still I need to hear him say it.

"All dead," he confirms before hesitating. "Did you . . ."

He can't finish the sentence, but he doesn't need to.

"I killed them all," I say. "I . . . I didn't just hold fire or push it in one direction or another. Søren, it was like the fire was a part of me, like I was a part of it. It was like I reached out with my own arm and grabbed each one of them. Like I felt the life leaving them beneath my own touch."

He doesn't say anything for a moment. Instead he puts a hand on the back of my neck and presses his forehead to mine. His eyes close and he exhales softly. I feel his breath against my lips, sweet from the coffee he must have had this morning.

"You saved a lot of lives," he murmurs. "I know that doesn't feel like enough right now, but it's something. And you survived. That's something, too."

I let out my own breath, feeling myself sag against him. I want to stay like this for another moment or hour or day, even, but at the sound of familiar voices outside the tent, we pull away from one another just as Blaise, Heron, Erik, and Maile enter in quick succession.

Each set of eyes goes to Artemisia first before moving to me.

"No change," I tell Heron, reluctantly letting go of her hand and turning my attention to them. "Well? What do we do next?"

Only days ago, we had this same conversation and everyone had a different idea, a different plot ready, complete with the potential upsides and downsides. Days ago, no one could agree on any one path because there were so many we could take.

Now, though, no one has any plans at all to offer up. No ideas. No suggestions. Instead the tent is only filled with a heavy, impenetrable silence.

"Blaise," I say, breaking it. "You're heading to the Earth Mine, aren't you?"

He hesitates a beat before nodding. "There's no way the Kaiserin could have known for sure we were heading to the Air Mine. It makes sense that she would have sent her people to both mines, just in case."

"But if that's the case, they would have already gotten there," Maile says, shaking her head. "There will be nothing left but ashes."

My stomach sours at the thought of all of those new deaths to add to our tally. Thousands more lives lost.

"Not necessarily," Blaise says, his brow furrowed.

"What do you mean?" I ask Blaise.

Blaise licks his lips. "The mine," he says. "If I were in the camp, and a fire broke out, and the guards abandoned us to die . . . I would go into the mine. We found it to be the case here as well. There were a few hundred slaves in the Air Mine, but they wouldn't come out until they knew it was safe. The slaves at the Earth Mine don't know that it's safe. They're hiding out there, with no idea what's happening. I intend to go in to get them."

"You can't go into the mine, Blaise," I say, surprised.

He shrugs. "Actually, I'm the only one who should," he says, his voice coming out level, though I can see the nervousness in his eyes. "I know the layout, I know the paths. Anyone else would get lost down there."

I want to protest, to tell him he's being reckless and I thought we were past his martyr phase, but I hold my tongue. Though I don't want to admit it, even to myself, I understand the logic in his words. It makes sense, but that doesn't mean I like it. There has to be another way.

Before I can reply, Maile interjects.

"All of us can't go to the Earth Mine," she says. "If the Kalovaxian scouts see our whole army heading there, their army will be ready to meet us. And it won't end well."

"I know," I say.

"We can go west," Erik says. "Meet Dragonsbane's ships like we're meant to, but instead of just giving her our injured, we'll all leave. Take a few months to gather our wits and our resources before we strike again."

Søren shakes his head. "If we flee now, we lose everything we've worked for, everything we've won. They'll take over the Fire and Water Mines again, and the Ovelgan estate.

Everything we've lost to get to where we are now will have been a waste."

Though he doesn't say Artemisia's name, his eyes still flick to her when he speaks. *She's not lost,* I want to say, but I understand what he means.

"We can't run," I agree. "Not even with the intent of coming back. We have to strike now or else we'll never get another chance. If we run, we'll no longer be the attackers, we'll be the attacked, and Cre—the Kaiserin won't stop until she's destroyed us all."

I think of Cress in my dreams, wandering through her palace, giving orders and sending others out to do her work for her, never putting herself in danger, never risking her own life. There is no chink in her armor, but strip it away, and she is nothing.

"Theo," Søren says, eyeing me warily. "You have that look in your eyes. Either you have a plan or you're about to do something foolish."

"I have . . . the beginnings of a plan," I admit. "We're going to meet with Dragonsbane, as we said we would. And then we're going to attack the palace, from the land and from the sea."

"That's a death strike," Erik says. "We don't have the numbers; we don't have the weapons. It will be like throwing pebbles at a giant."

I smile, but it's only a tight, grim line. "Not if we can make it past the capital wall, into the heart of the palace before they know what's happening."

Blaise understands first, his eyes growing bright. "You want to use the tunnels," he says.

I nod. "We know there's one from the sea that leads to the throne room and the dungeon," I say. "Are there any others you remember with an external entrance?"

Blaise frowns, thinking. "A couple, but they might be closed off by now. I never tried them."

Heron digs through his knapsack, draws out a rolled-up map, and unfurls it. "Where?" he asks, passing Blaise a stick of charcoal.

Blaise examines it with a furrowed brow before using the stick of charcoal to draw two $x$'s, followed by lines leading into the palace.

"This one lets out in the kitchen cellar," he says. "It's the one I used to get into the palace in the first place, so it was active as of a few months ago. This one, however, I'm less certain of. In theory, it lets out in the wine cellar, but I haven't tested it. I only know about it thirdhand. But they're all narrow paths. You can't send an entire army through them. The Kalovaxians will realize and slaughter us one by one as we emerge."

"I have no intention of doing that," I say, before laying out exactly what I have in mind.

When I finish, the room is silent, everyone turning my words over.

"It's a mad plan," Maile says, breaking the silence.

"Do you have a better one?" I ask her.

Maile shakes her head. "I said it was a mad plan," she says. "I never said it was a bad one. If it works, it'll be a miracle, but it could work."

Søren nods. "I'll start organizing the troops, figuring out who will go where," he says.

"And I'll get word to Dragonsbane," Heron says.

I nod, glancing at Artemisia. "Don't tell her what happened. Not via message. Some things need to be explained in person," I say.

Though I know it's the right call, I'm still dreading having to tell my aunt about Art face to face. Heron and Søren were both kind enough to insist it wasn't my fault, but I don't doubt that Dragonsbane will see things very differently. She's already lost one child. I can't let her lose another.


When everyone disperses, I follow Blaise. He doesn't look particularly surprised when I fall into step beside him.

"Come to say goodbye?" he asks, looking sideways at me.

"I'm assuming there's no cause for me to tell you to be careful," I say. "So I suppose yes, I've come to say goodbye."

That gives him a second of pause. "I meant what I said to you, Theo," he says. "I don't want to die. I intend to do everything in my power to meet you at the palace, preferably with more warriors behind me."

"Then do it," I tell him.

He hesitates again, turning his words over in his mind. "Do you remember when we met in the kitchen cellar?" he asks. "I asked you to run, to leave all of this behind in order to live."

I can see where he's going and it makes me uneasy, but I have no choice but to nod. "I remember," I say. "I was tempted to go with you, more tempted than I'm proud to admit."

"But you didn't," he says. "You didn't want to die, but you also didn't want to live in a world where you didn't do everything in your power to help the people who needed you."

He takes hold of my hand as we walk, squeezes it tight in his.

"I don't want to die," he says again. "But I can't live with myself if I stand by while others suffer. I think you understand that."

I swallow down a protest and nod. "I do," I say. "But if you go into that mine, Blaise, you're going to be surrounded by Earth Gems. That kind of eruption of power wouldn't kill only you."

"I know," he says quickly, looking away from me. "I won't let it happen."

He says it so easily that I almost believe it would be that simple. But we both know it won't be.

"I trust you," I tell him. "I trust your judgment."

He nods. "And I trust yours," he says, stopping and turning to face me, struggling for the right words. "I know I've said it before, but I love you, Theo—"

"Blaise—" I interrupt, but he continues, undaunted.

"Not the way I did before. Not the way I think I would have if we'd grown up in a world without the Kalovaxians, but it's still love. It still means something. And I want you to hear it, to know it, if I never get a chance to tell you later."

I want to protest, to tell him not to say goodbye like this, as if we'll never see one another again. *We're not going to die,* I want to tell him. *We're going to make it through this, alive and together. And one day soon, we will walk through the palace again and it will once more feel like home.*

But then I think of Artemisia, lying unconscious in the tent, with Heron watching over her. I think of Erik, who had his eye pried from its socket with burning fingers. We aren't safe. We aren't untouchable. And maybe it's better to acknowledge that, to say what needs to be said while we can.

"I love you, too," I tell him, bringing my free hand up to rest on his cheek. His skin is as hot as ever, almost too hot to touch. This close to him, I'm reminded of what it felt like to kiss him, how it felt to lose myself in his arms. How safe he always made me feel. The memories are fond, yes, but it feels like they belong to a different person, a different version of me that no longer quite exists. Still, shadows of her linger. I press a kiss to his lips, quick and soft.

"Be brave," I tell him. "Be true. I'll see you soon, with an army at your back."

I don't tell him to be safe, and he doesn't say it to me, either. We left safety behind a long time ago, and in a strange way, it is freeing to be able to admit that.

He presses his lips to my forehead before releasing me and walking away without another word.

# MERCY

———◆•◆———

THAT NIGHT, AFTER BLAISE AND his legion are gone and the others have fallen asleep, I lie awake in bed, turning over the vial of dreamless-sleep potion that Heron gave me to take. I told him I would, but now that the time has come, I can't bring myself to drink it.

Cress can hurt me in my dreams—she already stabbed me. She certainly meant me harm in my last dream as well. With Dagmær and the two other girls' deaths on her mind, I don't doubt she will try to do it again. But this time I will be ready. This time, I have a plan. I have questions. I have a way out.

I turn over on my bedroll, tucking the potion under my pillow. It takes some time for sleep to claim me, but when it does, I am ready for it, my own dagger clutched tightly in my hand.

I manage to surprise Cress for once. She's slouched down in my mother's throne, wearing my mother's crown and a black gown covered in rubies and Fire Gems, and this time she's alone, without her entourage of wraiths. She looks smaller, somehow, more vulnerable, dwarfed by the size of the room and the throne itself. When she sees me, she frowns, sitting up a little straighter.

"You came back," she says, as if she doesn't really believe it.

I step toward her, twirling my dagger between my fingers like Art taught me. After everything Cress has done, everyone she's hurt, I should be able to plunge it through her heart without an ounce of guilt. She didn't seem to have any trouble hurting me, so why should I? But I do.

"I came back," I say.

She regains some of her coldness, but there is a shakiness to her smile as she leans back, regarding me thoughtfully. "Did you enjoy my surprise, then?" she asks me.

I think about the fire, the smell of burning flesh in the air, the screams that will haunt my nightmares for years to come. I think of Artemisia, who might never wake up. I tighten my grip on the dagger in my hand, but I force myself to return her smile.

"I used to tell myself you were nothing like your father," I tell her. "But I was wrong on that count. He would be very proud of your ruthlessness."

It isn't a compliment, and despite the love I know she bears for her father, she doesn't seem to take it as one.

"I did what was necessary, Thora," she says. "And I will do it again and again until you understand."

"I do," I tell her. "Understand, that is."

That makes her sit up straight. "You do?" she asks warily, as if I'm playing a trick. "Have you come to ask for mercy, then? It won't be easy to give, but perhaps if you beg—"

"I don't want mercy from you," I tell her. "I doubt you're even capable of it. No, I meant that I understand you: who you are, what you want. I understand that you are a monster, and that there is no saving you. I understand that the only way to end this is to watch you burn."

"Perhaps for you," she says, her eyes glinting. "But my mother has showed me another way to end things, once and for all. Would you like to see?"

My throat goes dry. "Your mother," I say slowly.

Cress's smile widens and she gets to her feet, brushes past me on her way out the door. I hasten to follow as she leads me down the winding palace hallways.

"She said she told you about it, the weapon she and her lover created. Velastra. A pretty name, isn't it, for a weapon like that?"

My stomach twists. I saw what she did to Erik and Søren— I can only imagine what Cress did to Brigitta. What she must have done to Laius as well.

"She's your mother," I say.

"Yes," Cress says, glancing at me over her shoulder. "I wonder if I'll make that same pathetic face when I die. I like to think not, though I'm afraid we do have quite similar features."

"Where are you taking me, Cress?" I ask her, but I'm fairly sure I know. After all of these months, these halls are still burned in my memory. I remember my last night here, being dragged down this same path when the guards brought me to the dungeon.

"Her memory was faulty, after so many years, and it was difficult to replicate the exact tools she had on hand then.

And, of course, my mother doesn't have quite the same alchemical talents as her lover. It took longer than I'd hoped, but we had a bit of a breakthrough in creating velastra," Cress says. "I thought you'd like to see for yourself."

My body feels weighed heavy, each step a chore, but I follow her down the darkened steps, clutching the dagger so tightly in my hand that I feel the filigreed hilt digging into the pads of my fingers.

When we reach the guards on duty, she simply nods at each of them and passes, rounding another corner, then another, before coming to a stop in front of a cell occupied by a single figure, cowering against the back wall, his hands bound with heavy iron shackles.

He looks up when he hears Cress approach, and I stumble backward a step.

Laius

He came here to die, and so it was easier to think of him as dead the moment he left us at the Water Mine, his sacrifice noble and heroic. The best I'd hoped for him was a quick death, but I knew in the deepest part of my heart that Cress is not that merciful.

Still, it is another thing entirely to see him face to face, his gaunt cheeks and wide dark brown eyes, the three fingers missing from his hands and the bandages covering his arms and legs, where I imagine more flesh has been hacked away.

"I confess, Theo, I was a bit cross to discover your deception, sending a boy in the place of an alchemist, but it turns out you sent me more of a gift than you realized."

"Laius," I say, because it's the only word I can form. He can't see me, can't hear me, but I say it all the same.

"Is that his name?" Cress asks before shrugging. "It turns out that velastra is a combination of alchemy and Spiritgems. At least, that was what my mother said, and I doubt she could have thought up a decent lie in the state of pain she was in. But still, we couldn't get it quite right, couldn't make it last longer than a few minutes, even when we found the formula in her blood. But that was what gave me the idea—blood. It's the secret to life, isn't it? It's where my power is, so why shouldn't it be where his is kept as well? Blood, a thousand times stronger than any gem could be."

"What do you mean?" I ask, though I don't take my eyes off Laius.

He must be alarmed at this, Cress before him, talking to herself. But I remember what Søren said—perhaps this is normal for him. The thought makes me feel sick.

"It still isn't a permanent solution, unfortunately, but it does last so much longer now. Hours in most—days in some. But it's easier to show you than tell you, I think," she says, before stepping toward the bars. She reaches into her pocket to pull out an empty vial. No, not empty. The air within it glints in the dim candlelight, almost opalescent.

"Laius," she says, her voice cloyingly sweet. He flinches from it but slowly drags his eyes up to meet hers. "Tell me, what would your Queen say if she could see you now? Low and fractured, a weak and pathetic creature?" she asks, tilting her head to one side.

He cringes at that.

"No," I say, the word strong, though I know he can't hear it. He is not weak and pathetic. He is brave and sure, and I'm the one who has failed him, not the other way around.

Laius looks away for a moment before meeting her eyes again, and despite his pain, his bloody face, and missing fingers and flesh, his eyes are bright with anger. His gaze doesn't waver.

"I imagine she'd remind you of what happened when you thought her low and fractured and weak. I'd imagine my Queen would then show you in no uncertain terms that broken things are the most dangerous of all."

Cress's mouth twists into a grimace, and with a feral cry, she throws the glass vial into the cell at Laius's feet.

For a moment, nothing happens, the air around Laius barely shimmering. Then, all at once, it takes hold of him and his eyes go glazed and distant, his expression slack.

"Laius," she says again, a cruel smile tugging at her lips. "You should show some respect for your Kaiserin. On your feet."

As if he's moving through quicksand, he stands.

"Bow to me," she says.

He bends at the hip, an awkward bow but a bow all the same. A bow he doesn't want to give. I can see it in his expression, the flicker of hate behind those dead eyes—so quiet and far away that I wouldn't see it if I weren't looking. So weak that it doesn't make a difference. He does as he's told because he has no choice.

"It doesn't have as great a radius as I would like," Cress tells me, turning her attention to me. "A person has to be close to the gas when it's released before it dissipates into the air and weakens. And as I said, it doesn't last. In a couple of hours, he will return to himself. This isn't the first time we've tried it on him, you know. He makes an excellent test subject—so defiant, so rebellious, right until the second he inhales the velastra."

She sounds so gleeful that I want nothing more than to strike her. To drive my dagger into her chest where her heart must be, though I'm not so sure she has one. Before, I wondered if I could do it. I didn't think I had it in me. And maybe that was true a few moments ago, but now, seeing Laius with his dead eyes and his will taken away from him, I know without a doubt that I could. That I could take Cress's life in my hands and shatter it. I know that death would be too good for her.

Before I can speak, she continues.

"I do think his usefulness has come to an end, though," she says, turning back to Laius. Before I can make sense of the words, she reaches into the pocket of her gown and extracts her own dagger. My hands tighten around mine, ready for a fight, but she doesn't turn its point to me. Instead pushes it through the bars, hilt first.

"Take it, Laius," she tells him.

"No," the word escapes me in a whisper, and I find myself frozen in place as Laius's hand reaches out to take the dagger. "Cress, no. Don't do it."

She doesn't seem to hear me, her placid eyes lingering on Laius. Though he holds the dagger firmly, his hands shake, and I know that somewhere, beneath the film the velastra has left on his mind, he knows what is happening; he is fighting it with everything he has. I know that it will not be enough.

"Now, Laius," Cress says, her voice turning soft and syrupy. "You're going to slit your own throat."

I can't form words. Can't move. Can't do anything but

watch Laius do as he's commanded, the silver blade leaving a red gash in his throat. Just as the Theyn's knife cut my mother's throat so long ago now. My fingers reach up to grab the iron bars of the cell, as if I can pull them apart and reach him, as if I can save him.

But I can't. All I can do is watch as he falls to his knees, then to the ground, utterly still.

The next thing I know, I have Cress against the hallway wall, my dagger at her charred and flaking throat. I press it hard enough that blood bubbles to the surface, crimson red.

The action doesn't seem to faze her. She eyes me, tilting her head to one side. "Are you going to kill me, then?" she asks, each word dripping in mockery.

I should. I *want to*. But that is not how this ends. If I kill Cress now, like this, it won't solve anything. Someone else will take her place, someone worse, perhaps.

Who could possibly be worse? I think I might even take the Kaiser over her.

But I know Cress, I understand her, and we are too close now to change the rules of the game.

"No," I tell her, the word wrenched from my chest. "Not here. Not like this. No, but I am coming for you. With all my might and my fury and my hate. I am coming for you with everything I have. And I want you to know that when the moment comes, when you realize that I've won—when you beg me for mercy—your pleas will fall on deaf ears.

"And when you are dead, when your people are defeated and Astrea is under my rule, no one will speak your name again. There will be no record of you, no stories to pass on to future generations, no songs played in your honor. History will forget you, Cress. And when I'm dead, no one will re-member you at all. You will be nothing but a fistful of ashes scattered in the wind. Lost. Erased. Forgotten."

Cress holds my gaze, and I'm pleased to see that she looks a little shaken.

"We were friends once, Cress. You were my heart's sister, and my heart will always mourn you in a way. But the next time we meet, I will ensure that you pay for your crimes—each and every awful one of them. Including this."

"Is this the part where I surrender?" Cress asks with a mocking smile.

I shake my head. "No. This is the part where you make peace with your gods and pray that they show you mercy. Be-cause I won't."

Cress only stares at me, but I don't need her to say any-thing more. I'm done here.

I take the tip of my dagger and press it to the pad of my thumb, using the sharp pain to draw me out of sleep and re-turn me to the relative safety of my bed.


The scratch of the threadbare quilt is welcome, as is the sound of Heron's baritone snores. I sit up slowly, rubbing the sleep from my eyes. The pastel light of the rising sun is just begin-ning to pierce through the cloth of the tent, and already I can hear people outside, talking in low, tired voices as they begin to pack up the camp.

I could sleep for another half hour—even that little bit of extra sleep will be of value in the face of the busy day ahead, but I know I won't be able to close my eyes without seeing

Laius's face, without hearing his voice echoing in my mind, without being haunted by the empty look in his eyes in the instant the velastra took hold of him.

A breakthrough, she called it, but still too weak, too contained to do the damage she wanted it to. But what damage it did. Enough to destroy a person, to take their will away from them, to trap their very soul in a cage.

I bury my face in my hands, taking deep breaths and trying to focus, trying to keep my mind from circling around the horror of it, around the possibility of what kind of nightmare Cress hopes to unleash if she does manage to make the velastra stronger.

We won't stand a chance against it—I know that as surely as I know my own name, and that knowledge burrows deep under my skin and lingers.

A sound pierces through all the spiraling thoughts that threaten to drown me, no stronger than the mewl of a newborn kitten.

"Theo?" Artemisia says.

# PREPARED

—————◆•◆—————

AWAKE AS SHE MIGHT BE, Artemisia isn't quite back to being herself. As the sun rises, we walk through the camp together, her leaning heavily on me because her legs are still too weak to hold her up on her own. We both pretend not to notice.

*She's awake,* I tell myself. *That's enough.*

Everyone in the camp has a job to do, a task to complete, to get us moving as quickly as possible—everyone except Art and me, that is. Heron advised her to stay in bed altogether, but she couldn't bear to sit still and insisted on a walk while I catch her up on what she missed and my latest—and last, I think—dream about Cress.

Her jaw remains tightly clenched with each step she takes, and though I don't suppose I'll ever know for certain, I think she's struggling to keep from crying out in pain. I distract her by going over our plan with her, telling her about the passageways and how we're going to use them.

When I finish, she remains quiet, her brow furrowed deeply, though whether it's in pain or worry, I can't tell.

"It's the best plan we could come up with," I say. "We formulated it before my dream, before Laius . . ." I trail off, my stomach twisting, though I force myself forward. "But it's still the most sound plan. It will get us to the palace, and that's more pressing than ever now. Your mother already wrote back—she'll be waiting for us on the river with a group of boats to shuttle about half of our troops to the harbor."

"And the other half?"

"Will continue on foot and horseback from here to the entrances of the two passageways. I have scouts heading there now to ensure both tunnels are functional."

"I suppose you know that you can't fit many warriors into a kitchen cellar or wine cellar without someone noticing? Yes, anyone coming and going will likely be Astrean but . . ." She trails off, but she doesn't have to finish the thought.

I remember Gazzi's betrayal and how it cost Elpis her life. I remember Ion turning his back on his gods and using his gift to help his enemies and hurt me. I remember my old maid Felicie, betraying me to the Kaiser when I was only seven years old.

Just because someone is Astrean doesn't mean they can be trusted. I can't even blame them for it, really. They have been beaten down for so long that they might be content with safety over the risk in fighting for freedom.

"We have a few Air Guardians recovering after the fire," I remind her. "A couple will go with each group, there to turn our warriors invisible anytime someone wanders into those rooms. And it will only be a day, maybe two, of waiting before we strike as one."

"A lot can happen in a day, maybe two," she points out.

"I know," I say, my stomach uneasy. "But it's the best plan we have."

"I'm not saying it's a bad one," she says quickly. "But

when so much is left up to chance, it helps to be prepared for everything."

She looks down, her trouser legs rolled up above the knee to show thick bandages covering every inch of skin. I caught a glimpse of the burns when Heron reapplied ointment and fresh gauze this morning—angry red ropes of raw skin, twisted and gnarled. I can't believe she's standing now, let alone walking and talking, but then Artemisia has always been stronger than I could ever imagine being.

"I'm sorry," I tell her.

She follows my gaze to her legs and frowns, shrugging. "You don't run into a raging fire expecting to make it out unharmed," she tells me. "I don't have to tell you that. And besides, you saved my life."

"After I put it in danger," I point out. "After I'd decided to push on to the Air Mine against advice. After I ran back into that fire one more time and led us both into a trap."

"And here I thought you were apologizing to me," Artemisia says.

"I am," I say.

"And I already forgave you," she says. "I'm telling you that if I had been in your position, I'm not sure I would have done anything differently. And besides, if you hadn't decided we should go to the Air Mine, what would have changed? She still would have sent her wraiths. Only we wouldn't have been able to save as many people as we did. So it sounds like you don't need me to forgive you—you need to forgive yourself."

I open my mouth and close it again. "I could have killed you," I point out.

She snorts. "The Kaiserin's wraiths could have killed me,"

she corrects. "You saved me. I'd like to think that after the times *I've* saved *you,* we could just let things be even, but I suppose I have to say it out loud: Thank you, Theo. Thank you for saving me. My legs will heal. I'll get my strength back. And that is because of you. So kindly be quiet and let me recover in peace, will you?"

I hold my tongue and we walk in silence for a few minutes more, the quiet of the olive trees around us, the air still carrying the smell of smoke.

"It's a bit of a reversal, isn't it?" I say after a while. "It's almost like I'm your guard now instead of you being mine."

"You are absolutely *not* my guard," Artemisia snaps, giving me a shove even though she stumbles in the process. "I don't need a guard, and if I *did,* I would ensure they could at least hold a sword without their arm shaking."

I laugh. "I'm just glad you woke up before we met Dragonsbane," I say. "Queen or not, I think she might have killed me."

"Maybe," she says, but there's a crease in her brow.

"Are you worried about seeing her again, like this?" I ask her tentatively. Artemisia very rarely wants to talk about anything personal, and even in her current state, I'm a bit afraid of her. But instead of snapping at me, she only sighs.

"I'm worried about seeing her again at all," she admits, though the words are so heavy, it sounds like they are being dragged from her lips syllable by syllable. "We left things well. Seeing her again is a chance to ruin that. And this . . . no, it doesn't help things," she says, gesturing to her legs. "My mother has never really known how to tolerate weakness."

"It's not weakness," I say. "And I can't imagine she will disagree with that."

Artemisia nods, but she doesn't look entirely convinced. I hope that I'm right, but I think that Dragonsbane's thoughts will always be a mystery to me and maybe it's foolish to try to guess at them at all.

When the camp is loaded up and the horses are ready to go, Søren helps me onto his steed and climbs up in front of me because I can't ride with Artemisia this time. Instead she's riding behind Maile, and I don't know who is more annoyed—Art, at having to be someone's passenger, or Maile herself—but her expression is etched into a permanent glower.

I focus ahead, my gaze over Søren's shoulder and my arms locked around his waist as we gallop across the wide-open expanse of Astrea's midlands. My heart thunders in time to the horse's hooves beating against the ground, and I wonder if Søren can feel it against his back, if his own heart is beating as erratically.

The last choice I made was a bad one. It cost thousands of lives, injured hundreds more. No matter what anyone says, I feel the guilt of that lodged in my heart. But the others were right as well—that choice was made and now it's behind us. The only thing that matters is what we do next, where we go, how we strike.

*"I am coming for you,"* I told Cress in my dream. And I hope that this time, my choice is the right one. But I suppose there is no way to know for sure until it is too late, one way or another.

# DRAGONSBANE

———•———

I T TAKES ONLY A DAY and a half to reach the Savria River
with half our troops, though *river* isn't the right word for
it. It's more of an inlet, leading inland from the Calodean Sea
in a long and serpentine path that cuts almost all the way to
the Dalzia Mountains. I suppose *the Savria Inlet* doesn't have
the same ring to it, though, because most maps I've seen call
it a river. Whatever it might be, it's the fastest way to convene
with Dragonsbane and her ships.

The journey passes in a daze. When our army stops to
make camp for the night, I all but fall out of the saddle and
onto my bedroll, barely taking the time to swallow down a
few pieces of hardtack and dried meat, my whole body singing
with exhaustion and sore muscles from the day of riding. With
the help of Heron's dreamless sleep potion, I sleep in peace.

Søren's mostly quiet while we ride at the head of the troops
as well, but every so often he'll turn his head to make a wry
joke or to mention a detail of our plan I hadn't thought of,
and I know that his mind is far from idle.

"A distraction," he says to me on the second day, when I
can just make out the blue sliver of the river on the horizon.

"Hmmm?" I say, my mind mostly a fog.

"You told Cress we were coming, though I'm sure she suspected as much before then. That means they'll be expecting us. There will be a great deal of warriors on duty, but they'll be waiting for an invasion to come through the front gates, right? What if we gave them one? It could buy us more time coming in through the tunnels if we can keep them occupied there."

I smile against his shoulder. "A distraction," I murmur. "I think I know some Fire Guardians who could manage that."

He doesn't speak, only nods his head. "We haven't talked about where you'll be in this battle," he says, his voice tentative.

"I have to face Cress myself," I tell him. "After everything she's done—everything she *can* do—I'm the only one who can."

I wait for him to tell me that it's too dangerous, that I need to stay safe, but he doesn't. Instead he nods.

"I never thought I'd pity Cress," he says, and I can practically feel him smile. "I mean I still don't, after everything, but under different circumstances I might."

Heron is closest to us, with Erik on his other side, but even they are far enough that they don't see when I kiss the place on the back of Søren's neck, just where his skin meets the collar of his shirt. A shiver runs down his spine and I smile and kiss him there again.

"What's that for?" he asks, glancing back at me with an amused expression.

I shrug. "For not trying to talk me out of it," I say.

"Would it have worked if I had?" he asks.

I laugh, but don't bother replying. He knows the answer anyway.

Dragonsbane is already waiting when we get to the river, standing on the shore with a handful of men, three ships in the water behind her—small enough to fit in the river without trouble but large enough to hold the warriors we've brought with us.

Søren dismounts and helps hand me down, and I'm aware of her gaze on me, measuring me. As always, I can't help but feel that I'm found wanting, but when she closes the distance between us, a smile graces her lip. She might have my mother's face, but it's not my mother's smile. Still, it brings me comfort.

She settles a hand on my shoulder and squeezes—which I think is Dragonsbane's equivalent of a warm embrace.

"You're alive," she says, and I can't help but laugh.

"Try not to sound so surprised," I say.

"It's war, Theo," she says, shaking her head. "The key of it is to expect everyone to die. Then you're only pleasantly surprised to be proven wrong."

Her eyes dart to Søren behind me, and she gives him a curt nod.

"And the *prinkiti* as well, I see," she says. "I thought for sure he was dead."

"So did I," Søren replies, though he still stumbles a bit over the Astrean words, making her laugh.

"Your Astrean has improved," she notes, raising an eyebrow.

He shrugs. "I'm a quick study," he says in Astrean, before switching back to Kalovaxian. "And there wasn't much of a choice—it seemed cruel to force people to speak the language of their oppressors for my benefit."

She nods, but I can tell she's distracted. She combs her gaze across the troops gathered behind me, searching out one person in particular.

"Artemisia is alive," I tell her, drawing her eyes back to me. She frowns.

"Why isn't she with you?" she asks me. "She's your guard, isn't she?"

I hesitate. "She was hurt," I explain. "She's all right, and she's healing well, but there are burns on her legs, and riding is painful, so they're going slower, bringing up the rear."

Dragonsbane's eyes narrow and I prepare myself for her wrath—I deserve it—but after a pause, she gives a single nod.

"She's alive?"

"She's alive."

"She'll heal?"

"She'll heal."

Relief floods through her and her shoulders sag. She might have expected everyone to die, but I don't doubt that she wasn't ready to face the reality of losing her daughter.

"Then there's no need to fuss," she says, back to business. "Let's get the refugees boarded before we're seen."

"Oh, I hope we're seen," I say, following Dragonsbane toward the ramp leading up to the largest ship. "Let them tell the Kaiscrin we're fleeing. Let her believe she's won. She'll never see our attack coming."

Dragonsbane glances sideways at me like I'm a stranger to her, but one she might actually like. She nods.

"I won't be able to get the refugees to Doraz this time. We'll stay off the coast while you and your troops are in the capital. If you have need of me, you can send word, but . . ."

"But try not to have need of you?" I supply before shaking my head. "If we find ourselves in that much trouble, I can't imagine there will be anything you can do with a fleet of ships filled with people so badly hurt they can't fight. If you get word that we're in trouble, you'll leave us behind and find somewhere safe for the people in your charge."

She raises her eyebrows before nodding. "Yes, Your Majesty."

"I didn't think you would be meeting us yourself," I tell her. "At least not without a decoy to hide your identity."

Dragonsbane lets out a sound that is half sigh and half hiss. "Yes, well, it turned out my identity was a lot harder to keep hidden once our ranks were swelled almost tenfold with refugees. People talk, whether they mean to or not, and I've decided the best course of action is to embrace it. Let them tell stories of a woman pirate—as long as they make me sound fearsome, they can say whatever they like."

I smile slightly but I know it bothers her more than she lets on, to be so exposed. "I'm sorry," I tell her. "I know you valued your privacy."

She shrugs. "These are unprecedented times, Theo," she says. "If one does not adapt and move with them, all one can do is drown."

That I can't disagree with, but when Søren and I move to follow Dragonsbane up the ramp, she stops us.

"Oh, you aren't coming on my ship," she says, lifting her hand to point to a boat far behind the others, a small Kalovaxian boat dwarfed by her ships.

"*Wås,*" Søren says, unable to hide his surprise.

"I figured you would have an easier time sneaking into a Kalovaxian harbor in a Kalovaxian ship," she says. "And I understand you are already familiar with how to handle her, *Prinkiti.*"

Søren's too stunned to do more than nod, his gaze focused on his boat like it's an old friend.

"Thank you," he says after a minute, his eyes finding their way back to Dragonsbane.

The emotion in his voice seems to make her uncomfortable, and she shrugs off his gratitude. "It's only a boat," she says. "And not even a big one."

Hoofbeats approach and I turn to see Maile riding toward us, Artemisia in the saddle behind her, riding with both legs off to one side, like a Kalovaxian debutante. I know it drives her mad, but it was that or be pulled behind a horse in a cart, and Art refused that. At least this way, her legs are mostly protected, padded heavily with gauze and cotton by Heron.

Beside me, Dragonsbane goes stiff, watching her daughter dismount. When her legs make impact with the ground, Artemisia winces in pain and Dragonsbane winces as well, as if she, too, can feel it. But when Artemisia approaches, her footsteps slow and labored, Dragonsbane holds herself still, her expression calm and level.

"Are you all right?" she asks when Artemisia is close enough. It's the same way she would ask anyone on her crew: concerned, but not overly invested.

Artemisia nods. "I'm fine, Captain," she says.

"Good," Dragonsbane says. "Then you'll join me on my ship."

It's an order, not a question, but Art shakes her head.

"I'm going with Theo," she says.

At that, Dragonsbane's composure breaks and she scowls. "You're injured, Artemisia," she says, each syllable sharp. "I won't have you running into the front lines of battle in your condition. Would you send an injured soldier into a battle like this? Your own safety aside, you're a weakness."

Artemisia flinches at the last word but holds her ground. "Heron says that my legs will be better in a couple of days. By the time we reach the port, I'll be fine. I intend to finish this war just as I started it, at the Queen's side."

Dragonsbane's eyes dart to me, brow creased. Despite her insistence that Art's safety isn't her main concern, I see the fear lurking in her expression. "Well, Your Majesty?" she snaps at me. "You've already maimed my daughter. Are you going to do it again or will you send her with me?"

"Capt—" Art starts before changing gears. "*Mother.* Theo is the reason I wasn't hurt worse. As long as she'll have me, I'll be fighting at her side."

It is, without a doubt, the most sentimental thing Artemisia has ever said to me.

"As long as I have a side, you're welcome on it," I tell her.

Dragonsbane clenches her jaw, looking between the two

of us with seething eyes, but after a moment, she swallows her fury. She steps toward us, reaching a hand out to rest on Artemisia's cheek.

"You are going to come back from this battle whole and healthy, Artemisia," she says, another order with no room for negotiation. "And when you do, you and I are going to have a long overdue talk," she adds, her voice quiet and fearsome.

When she turns and starts back up the ramp to her ship, I let out a breath of relief. From behind us, Maile clears her throat.

"That woman is terrifying," she says, awestruck and a little enamored.

Artemisia shrugs her shoulders, but a small smile is playing on her lips. "Well?" she asks, looking back at Maile. "She is my mother. Where did you think I got it from?"

# WÅS

---•---

WÅS WAS ONLY MEANT TO sleep two, at most, in the cabin bed. Pressed, two more can make room on the floor. Six, however, is pushing her limits. There was no argument that Art should sleep in the bed. With her legs still healing, she needs the comfort of a soft mattress. The rest of us picked numbers to determine who would share it with her, and, begrudgingly, Art admitted that Maile had picked the number she'd chosen.

"You had better not kick," Art grumbled, rolling over to make room.

"Not like you can kick back if I do," Maile replied, getting under the covers, her eyes closing as soon as her head hit the pillow.

For an instant, Art looked like she wanted to hit her, but then she surprised everyone by laughing.

After that was settled, Heron and Erik made up space on the floor with spare pillows and blankets, and both of them fell asleep quickly as well.

It's been a busy few days since we left the Air Mine and I've spent most of it exhausted, but now that I actually have the chance to get a full night's rest, there is a steady energy buzzing through me and suddenly I'm not tired at all. Instead of trying to force myself to sleep, I get to my feet and pull the blanket around my shoulders to ward off the chill of the sea air before heading to the deck above.

Stars spill out over the sky like crystals of spilled sugar on black velvet, glittering and plentiful, but there is no moon to be found tonight. I forgot what it is like to be at sea, the steady rock of a ship, the way the air smells of salt and something else unnameable, the way the wind combs through your hair like fingers.

"Is Heron snoring?" Søren asks me from his spot at the helm.

He looks better at sea, too. Not to say he looked bad on land, but out here he's more alive, more relaxed. He seems wholly himself.

"Not yet," I say, making my way across the deck toward him. "But give him time—I'm sure he'll start any minute."

He smiles. "It's a bit like the last time we were here, isn't it?" he asks.

I laugh. "The last time we were on this boat together, Søren, I betrayed you and had you imprisoned."

"Ah, right," he says, wincing. "I think I blocked *that* journey from my memory. The time before that, I meant. When it was just you and me."

That was another night altogether, a whole other kind of excitement in the air, an energy between us that was nothing but possibility.

"We were very different people then," I tell him. "We didn't even know each other."

But as I say it, I remember the press of his lips against mine, the taste of him, the way he held me. I remember feeling like there was no one in the world who knew me better. It was a lie then—he didn't even know my real name. Still, I can't help but feel like no matter who we have been, no matter who we will be, there is a part of his soul that understands mine in its entirety.

Søren lets go of the helm for a second, crouching down to the base of its stand. When he rises again, he's holding a bottle of wine.

"I hoped this was still here," he says. "But I didn't want to have to share it with the others. We would have only gotten a sip each if I had."

"I suppose you still don't have glasses?" I ask him.

"You are a queen now," he says with a dramatic sigh, raising his eyebrows. "I suppose going without glasses is too barbaric for you?"

"I'll make an exception for you," I joke.

He laughs and pulls a lever on the side of the ship's helm, locking it into place, then takes my hand and guides me to the bow of the ship. Together, we lay out my blanket and sit down. When I shiver without it, Søren pulls me toward him so that I'm sitting between his legs, back against his chest, and his arms around my shoulders, keeping me warm while he tries to open the wine.

It takes a moment for him to work the cork out of the bottle with his dagger, but it finally comes free and he sets the knife aside, cork still wedged onto the tip. For a few moments, we sit in silence, passing the bottle back and forth and listening to the waves crash against the hull.

When the bottle is half-empty, Søren speaks, his breath warm against my ear.

"Sometimes, I think about what would have happened if we'd actually left that night," he says, his voice low. It sends a shiver down my spine.

"If we'd gone to Brakka and feasted on *intu nakara*?" I tease.

He laughs and takes another swig. "Sometimes, it's nice to imagine an easy life for a moment," he says. "Just you and me, on some foreign shore where no one knows us, where we have no responsibilities."

I lean my head back into the crook of his neck. "It's a nice fantasy," I admit.

"Yes, but that's all it is—a fantasy. It's tempting on the surface, but it's not deep enough to sustain either of us. We wouldn't have been happy somewhere else."

I consider that for a moment. "I wouldn't be me somewhere else," I say finally. "Technically, I became Queen when my mother died, but I think the moment when I truly felt it was when I faced your father, when I stood up for myself and Astrea. And I don't think you were really you then, either. You defined yourself in relation to your father, but you didn't know who you were on your own yet."

I take the bottle and drink another sip before continuing.

"Maybe we could have been happy somewhere else, with a simpler, easier life together," I say. "But we wouldn't have been us. And I would take this, here, with you—as we are now—over anything else."

He doesn't reply. Instead he draws my hair aside and drops a lingering kiss on my shoulder, where the strap of my shift meets my skin. Then, again, farther up my neck. And again. And again.

A shiver runs through me and he feels it, his mouth smiling against my throat. His hands move down, over my rib cage, over the curve of my waist, pausing at my hips. Through the thin material of my dress, I can feel the callouses on his fingers.

With shaking hands, I set the bottle out of the way and lift myself up onto my knees, turning around so that we are face to face and I can see my own nerves reflected back at me in his clear blue eyes.

"Theo," he says, his voice barely more than breath. Just one word, just my name, but it floods my body with warmth, turning me into light.

There is so much I want to say to him, so many words that I know will never be enough to encapsulate how I feel. So I don't try to tell him at all—I show him. I kiss him, slow and bruising, dragging a hand through his short blond hair. My fingers slide down his back, feeling the bones of his spine through his shirt. He lets out a soft moan against my lips, and a thrill runs through me.

I did that to him, and I wonder what else I can do.

"Theodosia," he says, breathing the name into my mouth like it's something dangerous and holy. His hands trace down my hips to my knees, where they find the hem of my shift, fingers dancing ever so slightly underneath, unsure.

I reach around the front of his shirt and undo the lowest button, then the next, then the next. When they're all loose, I push his shirt off his shoulders and look down at his bare chest, marked with scars and ugly words that will never heal completely. Seeing them breaks my heart, but I remind myself that they also mean that he survived. I remind myself that in some ways, they match mine.

Words race through me but I don't trust myself to speak, afraid of how my voice will give away how everything in me is breaking apart at his touch. Instead I kiss him again, longer and slower, and let my hands trace over his chest, over the scars and the words, because they are something beautiful and sacred.

His hands shake when he lifts my shift, and I break away from him, unable to hold back a laugh.

"What?" he asks, breathless, releasing the hem of my dress so that it falls back down. "What's funny?"

There's worry in his face, and I try to kiss it away.

"Nothing's funny," I tell him, unable to stop smiling. "I just never thought I would see you afraid—and here you are, afraid of me."

He swallows, trying to smile back. His eyes are dark and wide open, locked onto mine with such intensity that I want to look away, but at the same time, I wouldn't dare.

"Of course," he says. "You're a terrifying creature."

I smile wider and kiss him again, quickly. Before I can think too much about it, I pull off my shift myself so that there is nothing on my skin at all except for the chill of the sea air.

Søren lets out a sound that doesn't seem entirely human, a sound that raises goose bumps on my skin. His arms come around me once more, laying me back on the blanket and kissing me, kissing the corner of my mouth, kissing my jaw, all while his hands are everywhere else, exploring. When one makes its way between my thighs, I gasp, digging my nails into his back.

Søren pulls back, his face looming over mine. "Are you sure about this?" he whispers—as if there's anyone close enough to hear but me.

There aren't many things I'm sure of in this world. I'm not sure what tomorrow will bring, or the day after. I'm not sure if either of us will live long enough to find out. I'm not sure what will happen to Astrea or Kalovaxia or if peace is something we will ever find. But I am sure about him, I am sure about us, I am sure about this.

"*Yana Crebesti,*" I whisper before twining my arms around his neck and pulling him down into another kiss.

# HOME

─────── ◆ ───────

IN THE MORNING, I AVOID Søren as much as I can on such a small boat, worried that if he looks at me for too long, I will somehow combust entirely. My gift has become easier to control since I went into the mine, and even easier after I started training with Blaise, but every time our eyes meet over our meager breakfast on the deck with the others, it feels like too much—everything we did last night laid out for everyone to see. I finish my coffee in two large gulps before standing up.

"Do you still feel up to pulling the tides?" I ask Artemisia.

Art frowns at me, confused for a second, before she shrugs and crams the last corner of her share of stale bread into her mouth.

"Let's go," she says, pushing herself up to her feet. She winces in pain, but she manages to stay standing without any help.

"Are you all right?" Heron asks her.

"Fine," she says through gritted teeth. She swallows down her discomfort and takes one step toward the bow of the ship, then another. Pleased with herself, she smiles.

"See?" she shoots back at us. "I told you I'd be better. By

the time we reach the capital tomorrow night, I'll be as good as new."

Maile's brow creases. "You can't be serious about that," she says. "You're in pain. You'll only slow us down."

"Not by tomorrow night I won't," Artemisia insists, her dark eyes hard. "Tell her, Heron."

Heron shrinks a bit under Artemisia's gaze, but after a second, he nods. "She's healing fast," he admits, though he sounds like he'd rather not say anything. "At the rate she's going, she'll be just about at her normal capacity by tomorrow."

Just about at her normal capacity is still better than most warriors are in their prime. I know this, and the others must as well, because no one protests.

"If you die," I tell her, linking my arm through hers so she has some support, "your mother will kill me. And then I'll find you in the After and I'll kill you again."

Artemisia smiles and elbows me in the ribs. "Deal," she says.

We sit at the bow of the boat, at the very front where the figurehead juts out from the wood, the head of a drakkon carved from iron.

"You're acting strange," Artemisia tells me, settling herself on the deck, stretching both of her legs out in front of her. They're still bandaged up, but more lightly than they were even yesterday.

"How am I supposed to act?" I ask her, with a laugh I hope she doesn't see through. "Tomorrow night, we're laying siege on the palace—on *my* palace. Tonight, I'll sleep again on this ship, but the next night? I could be in my own bed."

"Or," Artemisia says, lifting her arms and beginning her complicated pattern of movements, "you'll be dead."

There's something admirable in her laying it out so simply, a mere fact.

Artemisia glances at me, and I could swear that her eyes see all of my secrets. "Remember when I told you we weren't the kind of friends who gossip and talk about kisses and whatnot?" she asks, and my heart just about stutters out of my chest.

"Yes," I say carefully. "You said you weren't Cress—the Kaiserin. And you're not. We don't have to be that kind of friends."

The fluidity of Art's movements doesn't show the slightest hiccup, even when she lets out a heavy, dramatic sigh.

"You have one minute," she tells me. "One minute of that sort of talk. Take your mind off what's coming tomorrow—just for a minute."

I look at her, surprised. "Are you serious?" I ask.

She frowns. "You're wasting your minute."

I shake my head, then force myself to say the words before I can stop myself. "Søren and I slept together."

Artemisia snorts. "I know *that*. You weren't subtle about it—you weren't in the cabin this morning, and he was never as subtle about sneaking into your bed as he seemed to think he was—" She breaks off, turning to look at me fully, her arms going still in the air. "Oh," she says, her voice dropping. "You mean . . ."

Suddenly I can't look at her. Instead I look at the sea ahead, the low waves beating against the hull of the ship.

"Have . . . Have you ever . . . ?" I ask, unable to even form the question.

"No," Artemisia admits, before pausing. "Well, what happened with the guard. In the camp." She's struggling for words, too, and I force myself to look at her.

"That doesn't count," I tell her, my voice firm.

For an instant, I think she might protest, but she only nods. "It doesn't count," she repeats.

She considers this for a second, looking back out at the sea and continuing her ministrations.

"I kissed Maile," she tells me after a moment, her voice neutral and offhanded.

"You what?" I yelp, loud enough to draw the attention of the others on the back of the boat, still drinking coffee and eating breakfast, who stare at us in alarm. I give them a weak wave to assure them that we're all right, before turning back to Artemisia. "When? How? *Why?*"

Art only shrugs. "I don't know," she says, but even she sounds a bit annoyed with herself. "It was when we were riding to meet my mother. We had to stop to change the bandages on my legs, and she said something obnoxious, and then we started fighting, and then . . . we were kissing."

"Did you . . . want to?" I ask her uncertainly.

That question only seems to confuse her more, but she finally nods. "I don't know. I told you before that I didn't feel that way about anyone. I'm still not sure I do. I'm not sure if it's just not men or if it's just her. I'm not sure if it was a fluke. I'm not sure of anything, really."

"Huh," I say. It's the only thing I *can* say. At first glance, it makes no sense at all—I don't think I've heard them say a word to one another that wasn't barbed. But at the same time, it makes perfect sense. "Well, if we live through tomorrow, you'll have plenty of time to figure it out, I suppose."

Artemisia snorts, shaking her head. "Minute's up. Are you still scared about tomorrow?"

I frown, looking out at the horizon where the east coast of Astrea is just visible in the morning light.

"No," I say. "I'm not scared at all, actually. I know I should be. I know what's at stake, and every time I close my eyes, I see Laius, I see Cress using the velastra on him. I see her using it on you, on the others, on me—taking away our wills until we're nothing but her puppets. That terrifies me more than I can say, more than death itself, and I won't pretend it doesn't. I know all of the things that could go wrong, I know it's all very scary. But no, I'm not afraid of what tomorrow will bring. Not even a little bit. I'm just ready. I just want to go home."

Artemisia's mouth pulls into a thin smile, her eyes focused on the horizon as well. She nods once.

"Well then," she says, her arm movements becoming faster, hands slicing through the air with a frantic energy. "Let's get you home."

I smile before a thought occurs to me. "And where is your home, Art?" I ask. I don't think she's ever referred to Astrea, or even the ship she grew up on, as home.

She frowns. "Our minute of talking about our feelings is over," she points out.

"I'm asking anyway," I tell her.

"As my Queen?" Her voice is mocking, but that's how I know I've hit at a chink in her armor.

"As your friend," I say. "And your cousin. And you know, in some cultures, the children of twins are considered siblings—"

"I am my own home," she says—mostly, I think, so that I'll stop talking.

"That sounds lonely," I tell her.

She shrugs. "You might find it lonely," she says. "But how can I be lonely when I enjoy my own company as much as I do?"

"Be that as it may," I say, "you'll always have a room at the palace, when you want it."

She's quiet for a moment. "I could use a place to rest, perhaps," she says. "On occasion."

We both fall into silence, our gazes focused on the expanse of ocean ahead, the pure blue waves cresting in an unmeasurable rhythm.

"Let's go home, Your Majesty," Art amends, her voice only mildly mocking this time. "Let's break those chains and get you on that throne and bring ruin to every Kalovaxian who ever crossed any of us."

I nod, my gaze still focused on the horizon. "Yes," I say. "Let's."

# READY

THE DAY TRUDGES BY LIKE sand trickling through a clogged-up hourglass. The boat seems to grow smaller with each moment, constricting around us so that there is no sanctuary, no peace from the others. As much as I care for them, there is nothing I wouldn't give for a moment alone. Though I know that each mile we travel brings us closer to war and inevitable carnage, I begin to yearn for it, for anything to get off this godsforsaken boat.

The others seem to feel the same way. Where everyone was abuzz with conversation when we first came on board, now it's mostly only silence, heavy and ominous. Søren and I don't even talk that night when we lie together on the deck. Instead we just hold one another until we drift off to sleep.

I should not dream of Cress, but I do, even with Heron's potion.

She sits in the shadowy embrace of the throne, tendrils of black winding their way over her limbs, stark against her bone-white skin—the monster I imagined as a child, holding her there in its grasp. The swath of charred skin at her throat is displayed proudly over the neckline of her silver gown, like a battle scar. My mother's black-gold crown circles her head, resting just above her brow.

I should not see her—I know I should not see her—but I do, and it takes me a second to realize why, to notice more than Cress, more than the throne holding her tightly. The throne is not in the throne room, not in the palace. It is in the mine. I am back in the mine.

It is not a dream, though. The realization settles over me—it is a memory, like my mother in the garden or the dead clawing at me until I set them free from my guilt. This has already happened, has already been resolved. I've already passed this test. But the way Cress looks at me is like she sees me through time and space, and it doesn't feel like a memory at all. It feels like I never actually left the mine, like I've been here all this time, lost in its depths and wandering in and out of consciousness.

Only now I'm not alone.

For an eternity of a moment, Cress and I only stare at one another. Silence stretches out between us, an un-crossable chasm.

"Was it worth it?" The words don't feel like mine. I don't mean to say them, don't choose to say them. I simply do. Like they are lines in a play that I know by heart. "You have your throne, your crown. Was marrying him worth it?"

Her hands tighten their grip on the throne's arms. "I have everything and you have nothing—you are nothing. What does it matter how I won? I did."

"You won," I echo. "Is that what this was?"

"It's war," she says, lifting a shoulder in a shrug. "You struck first; I struck best. Do you want an apology?"

If she offered one, I wouldn't accept it anyway.

"I want that throne," I tell her instead.

"No one gives you anything," Cress sneers. "You take it. My father taught me that, and he taught you as well."

I see the Theyn before me, cutting my mother's throat, taking her from me, and I swallow back bitter words.

Cress tries to lift her arms, but the tendrils of smoke anchor her to the throne, binding her there. Her black lips purse.

"We were friends once, weren't we?" she asks.

"Heart's sisters," I say. The words threaten to choke me.

She laughs, the sound jarring. "Such a ridiculous term, isn't it? How can our hearts be sisters? We've always been destined to stand on opposite sides of a war."

"Maybe," I allow, taking a wary step toward her. "But if you'd asked me before all of this, I would have said that I couldn't imagine a future without you at my side. Sometimes I still can't."

"That is your weakness," she says, but something flickers behind her eyes.

"Maybe," I say. "But it isn't only mine, is it?"

I call to the fire in me, and this time it comes readily, flames leaping to my fingertips like they are an extension of me.

Cress sees this and her eyes widen. "Don't do it, Thora," she says, her voice shaking. "Please."

I take a step toward her, then another. "My name isn't *Thora*. I am Theodosia Eirene Houzzara, and I am the Queen of Astrea," I say before letting my fire loose.

It hits her squarely in the chest, and just like the dead spirits, she disappears as soon as it touches her, leaving an empty throne.

I need to take it. I know that as surely as I know my own name, and yet I can't force my feet to move. The throne looms before me, large and dark and ominous. If I sit down upon it, I will not be the same. I will never be able to stand again without its shadows clinging to me.

"Someone needs to sit there." My mother appears at my shoulder. She's the mother from my purest memories, unscarred by time or the horrors of the Kalovaxians.

I swallow down tears. "But what if I can't do it?" I ask her, my voice barely louder than a whisper.

"Oh, my dear heart," she says, her hand coming to rest on my shoulder. And just like that it doesn't feel like a dream or a memory or anything else because *I feel her*. As if she were standing right beside me. As if she never left. "It is a difficult path the gods have sent you down, but they would never give you more than you could handle."

She says it with such conviction, but the words rouse nothing in me.

"Do you still believe in the gods?" I ask her. It feels like a dangerous question to even entertain, in the Fire Mine of all places, but I don't know when I'll get another chance to ask her. "After everything they've allowed to happen to us?"

She considers this a moment. "I don't believe the gods exist to solve our problems," she says. "But I do think they give us the tools we need to triumph. I think they gave us you, forged in fire."

It isn't an answer, but I suppose there isn't one. Some questions are too complex to ever be resolved, but maybe that's all right.

My mother holds my hand and we walk toward the throne together. Fear still gnaws at me, but with her at my side my steps are sure. When we reach the dais, I kiss her cheek. "I love you," I tell her. "And I will try to make you proud."

And then I climb the golden steps and lower myself down into the obsidian throne.


When I wake up, the sun is peeking over the horizon on one side of the ship, and on the other side, I can just make out the northeastern edge of Astrea. I pull myself to my feet and lean against the wall of the boat, staring at the shore—the cliffs that jut up, the cluster of ships in the harbor so far away that their sails are mere specks of red. And there, if I squint very carefully, I can just make out the golden domes of the palace, the white towers, the Kalovaxian flag flying from the highest one.

My breath catches at the sight, and I feel my mother's hand on my shoulder, a ghost of the memory, the dream, whatever it might have been. I imagine her beside me, going home with me, ready to take back what was stolen from us.

In spite of everything, I wish that Blaise were here beside me as well. It's our home, the place where we were born, the place where we were raised. I wish he could see it with me, like this. I wish we were sailing toward it together, ready to take back what is ours, side by side.

*I'll see him again soon,* I tell myself, hoping that if I say it enough times, I'll come to actually believe it.

"There it is," Søren says from behind me, sitting up on the blanket, sleep still clinging to his eyes.

"There it is," I echo. "By this time tomorrow, it will be ours."

"By this time tomorrow, it will be yours," he corrects.

I understand why he says it, but part of me wishes he wouldn't. It is a heavy burden to bear on my shoulders alone. I haven't thought about that much, about what ruling Astrea would actually look like once the war is behind us. In an ideal world, my mother would have been there, to guide me, to prepare me. But she isn't, and so I can't help feeling I will never be prepared for it.

Her words from the mine come back to me.

*"It is a difficult path the gods have sent you down, but they would never give you more than you could handle."*

I hope to all the gods that she's right, but there is only one way to know for sure.

"Are you ready?" I ask him, leaning back against the hull wall to survey him. In the light of the rising sun, he looks like he's been carved from pale gold. The scars that cover his bare chest are softer like this; they don't stand out as sharply. It's almost as if they are a part of him, as vital as his lungs or his heart—after all, in some ways, they've made him.

He smiles and shakes his head, oblivious to my thoughts. "I've been in a lot of battles, Theo. Many more than I can count. But I don't think I've ever felt ready for one of them. I don't think it's possible, to be ready to charge headfirst into possible—*probable*—death. I don't think that's the kind of thing you can ever prepare yourself for."

His words pool in the pit of my stomach like tar, sticky and dark. I shrug and try to look unbothered and confident. "Well then," I say, forcing my voice to sound breezy, "I guess we'll just have to not die."

He laughs and holds out a hand to me. I take it, lacing my fingers with his and letting him pull me back down onto the blanket and into his arms. We kiss softly in the warm dawn light, and when he pulls back, he keeps our foreheads pressed together, his eyes closed, long blond eyelashes fanned out over his cheeks.

"That sounds easy," he breathes. "Not dying. Why haven't I tried that before?"

"It doesn't matter," I tell him. "Try it now."

He must hear the worry leaking into my voice, because he opens his eyes, staring deep into mine.

"After all of this, Theo, I intend to see you on that throne," he says, his voice quiet and serious. "Not in spirit, not from the After or whatever lies beyond this life—I intend to see it with my own eyes, and I pity the god who tries to take me before I do."

I kiss him until the sun has fully risen in the sky, until we are bathed in sunlight, until the others start to stir belowdecks. I kiss him until it is time to start preparing for our last battle.

When the sun sets, the *Wås* approaches the Astrean shore. This close to the harbor, with this many Kalovaxian boats docked nearby, no one pays much mind to one as small as ours. They likely think it's manned by a fisherman, bringing in his daily catch to sell at market in the morning.

Still, when we disappear into the shadows of the rocks, hidden from view and close enough to the cave that we can wade there, I let out a breath of relief.

"Depending on the tides, you may have trouble getting out," Søren tells Erik, the only one of us staying on the boat.

Apparently it was always a joke between the two of them that Erik could sail a boat half-blind, but after a few test runs earlier in the day, it seems there was some truth to it.

"The tides won't be a problem," Artemisia says, passing me a bundle of wrapped Spiritgems. Even through the thick burlap, I can feel the thrum of the gems working through my blood—Fire and Water and Air Gems from the mines, all jumbled together, along with the Earth Gems we pried from the armor and weapons of the Kalovaxians we've fought thus far. I should be used to the feeling after more than a month of wearing Ampelio's Fire Gem close to my heart, but holding so many feels wrong still.

At least I won't be holding them for long.

Søren steps off the boat onto the small raft, holding on to the rail to keep from floating away. Heron hops down next, and he helps Artemisia and me down. She doesn't flinch when the water hits her legs anymore, just as she no longer flinches when she walks. She says she's healed, and there's no reason for me to disbelieve her, but it's hard not to worry, and it's easier to worry about her than everything else.

Søren tries to help Maile down as well, but she only glowers at him before jumping down on her own.

"Stay here for as long as you can," Heron shouts up to

Erik, pushing our raft away from the railing and toward the yawning mouth of the cave.

Erik nods. "Try to make it quick," he replies, his voice wry. "I'm looking forward to a meal of something other than hardtack, served in the banquet hall, with a jeweled goblet full of wine."

Flippant as it might be, it brings a smile to my lips, and for that, I'm grateful.

"When we pull this off," I promise, "there will be a ten-course feast to celebrate."

# CAVE

———•———

THE LAST TIME I WAS in this cave was with Søren, after we made our way through the tunnel, holding hands and shivering in the dark. It was after he'd lost my trust in the Vecturian battle, just before I'd lost his on board the *Wås*. And yet, here we are, side by side on our way back into the palace, and there are few people I trust more. And this time, we're not alone.

"Theo, if you don't mind," Heron says to me from behind my right shoulder, Artemisia beside him and Maile behind them. Even at low tide, the water in the cave comes up to our knees.

I bring a ball of fire to the palm of my hand, just big enough to illuminate the back of the cave and the small tunnel hidden in the recesses of the rocks. I enter first, and the others follow behind, single file, led by my light.

The tunnel is shorter than I remember it being, but that might be because I'm less miserable than I was the first time. I'm not exhausted from running, hungry from a night spent alone in a cell, cold from the evening chill in the air. Instead of dragging on, it feels like only a few moments pass before I come to the fork in the tunnel.

One path leads to the throne room, where Cress might be sitting right at this very moment. Tempting as it is to go there first, I force myself to take the other path, the one that leads to the dungeon.

The thought of that place never fails to raise goose bumps on my skin. I remember the last time I was there, how I found those three Guardians who had sworn themselves to my mother. I remember what had been done to them, blood drained, fingers cut off, kept underground for years and years as experiments for the Kaiser's mad plans.

But if the Kaiser was mad, what does that make Crescentia? After all, what she did to Laius is just the same. Not to mention how she used her own blood to poison those she called friends. Who will she be keeping in the dungeon? I'll know for sure soon, but my imagination is horrible enough all on its own.

"Your hand is shaking," Artemisia says, approaching my left shoulder.

I look and realize she's right—my hand is shaking and the flame with it, throwing wobbly shadows onto the wet stone walls.

"It's cold," I say, which is true enough. The tunnel is cold, but holding the fire, I don't feel its bite. Still, Artemisia takes the excuse in stride.

"Now isn't the time to lose your nerve," she says, and though her voice is soft, I can hear the warning underneath. *You don't get to fall apart. Not now.*

It's a warning I don't need, but I'm grateful for it all the same. I take a deep steadying breath and force my hand to still.

"There it is," Søren says, his steps sloshing in the water as he comes up on my other side. Then he walks past me to the expanse of stone wall ahead.

At first, it appears to be a dead end, but when I examine it closely, I can just make out the seam in the wall, the outline of a door. Søren rests a hand on it and turns back to look at us, his expression taut but his eyes wild in the firelight.

"Ready?" he asks.

*No,* I think suddenly. *No, I'm not ready at all.* But I think about what Søren said—you're never ready to charge into battle, but you do it anyway.

"Ready," I reply.

Søren nods and shoves the door with his shoulder, hard. With a groan, it opens just wide enough for him to slip through.

The rest of us linger behind, listening.

Heavy footsteps. Voices, low and harsh-edged as they speak in Kalovaxian. Then, the sound of a fist colliding with bone, a crack that echoes, a scuffle. Then, nothing at all for a few moments.

I hold my breath as footsteps start again, coming toward us.

Søren peeks into the opening, blood spattered over his face but a grim smile on his lips.

"It's done," he says, ushering us out into the dungeon. He's holding a Kalovaxian man by the arm—a guard, I assume, though he's been stripped of his uniform—and when we're out of the tunnel, Søren drags him into it, pushing him gracelessly to the side.

He steps into my aura of firelight again, and I take him in.

No worse for wear, but now he's wearing the guard's uniform over his shirt and trousers. In the dim lighting, he'll pass for one of them.

"Did you get the keys?" I ask.

He holds up a brass ring with three keys—two for the gates that separate the dungeon from the rest of the palace, one for all of the cells, I remember.

We start at the deepest part of the dungeon, unlocking cells and checking on those inside. Many, I realize, aren't Guardians, they aren't dangerous. They're only Astrean people, starved and hurt and barely alive.

"I only stole a heel of bread," one woman says, clinging to me with bloody fingers, her eyes wild and her hair matted. "My master had thrown it away, and I hadn't eaten in days."

My heart hurts to listen to them, but I force myself to. I stay by their side while Heron heals the ones who can't walk on their own, one by one. Then Artemisia, Maile, and I walk them back to the tunnel with directions: Find Erik. Find the boat. Climb as high as you can on the rocks around the cave and wait for rescue.

Søren pretends to patrol the next block of cells, but really he's looking for another guard and another set of keys so that we can move through these cells faster.

We need to get all of the prisoners out before we make our move.

After about twenty minutes, Søren jogs back toward us, out of breath and holding two new rings of keys. He passes one to me and one to Maile.

"Hurry," he tells me. "There are more guards down here than I expected. These two didn't recognize me, but the next ones might."

I nod, finding the key that looks the same as the one Heron's been using.

"Get the ones who can walk to safety," Heron says to us, without looking up from the face of a woman with a broken leg. "Leave in their cells any who can't move, and I'll come to them as soon as I can."

I don't bother replying. Instead Maile and I head in different directions, keys in hand.

When I unlock the first cell, I find five Guardians, though the space is cramped even for a single occupant. I don't know how I know they're Guardians, but I sense it as soon as I step inside.

"Can you all walk all right?" I ask, my voice hushed.

One man looks up at me with dark eyes protruding from a gaunt face.

"Who wants to know?" he asks, his voice rough and hoarse. When he speaks, I see that he's missing several teeth.

Unlike the last time someone asked me a similar question in these cells, I don't hesitate. "Queen Theodosia Eirene Houzzara," I say.

The man sits up a little straighter, and a couple of the others murmur to themselves, their voices too quiet for me to make out any words.

"Is that so?" the man asks, looking at me with thoughtful eyes.

"I'm happy to give you a rundown of my family history at

some later date, but just now I need you to come with me, to safety."

"Safety," a woman says with a scoff. "In case you haven't noticed, child, this is not a safe world."

"I really don't have time to convince you to escape if you don't want to," I say, looking down at the long row of cells I still have to get to. "There's a tunnel open down that hall," I say, pointing. "If you can't get out there yourself, I have an Air Guardian friend who can help."

"Do you now?" the man asks. "I don't suppose you could use another?"

I dig into the burlap sack I brought and pull out an Air Gem, and toss it to the man, who catches it deftly.

"Anyone else?" I ask.

After that, there is a clamor for gems—another air, two waters, and an earth. I pass them out and give fresh orders to help the others who have already gone, and to guide those who will be coming. "Get everyone to high ground or onto the *Wås* as quickly as possible."

"Yes, my Queen," the man says, clutching his gem in his hands.

I smile briefly before hurrying from the cell to the next one, then the one after, and the one after that.

By the time I reach the end of my row, I have no more gems in my bag and all of the cells are empty. The Air Guardians I found wasted no time jumping in to help heal those who were hurt; the Earth Guardians carried others. What might have taken an hour is done in half the time.

"Everyone's in the tunnel?" I ask, returning to the group.

Heron nods. "Any sign of more guards?"

"Not that I've seen," Søren says. "They'll be posted nearer to the entrance, or at the mess hall just outside of it."

"Well," I say, "we'll give the prisoners another few minutes to clear the tunnel. Then you can sound the alarm to summon them."

# BREAK

— ◆ • ◆ —

IT TAKES HERON, MAILE, AND me working together to push
the door of the tunnel open as wide as possible, while Artemisia checks to make sure the escaped prisoners have gotten
out safely. When she returns, her eyes are glowing.

"All clear," she says.

"Are you sure you're feeling up to it?" Heron asks her, but
she waves away his concerns.

"I'm fine," she insists. "Better than, even. After two days
at sea, my gift is begging to be used."

"Then let's not deny it anymore," I say, nodding toward
Søren, who doesn't hesitate. He takes off at a run down the
corridor, shouting in Kalovaxian.

"Prisoners escaping! Riot! They're all out!" He keeps going
once he's out of earshot, luring the guards away from their
posts on the edge of the dungeon and drawing them inside.

I hurry toward the cell farthest back and usher the others
inside. We huddle together tightly, some part of Heron's skin
touching some part of ours.

"Ready?" I ask.

They nod, but I feel their fear. This was something we

couldn't practice ahead of time. This is a theory—a sound theory, but a theory all the same. And if it doesn't work . . . I stop that thought in its tracks. It has to work, and that is all there is to it.

"Close the cell," Maile says, but I shake my head.

"Not until Søren's back," I say.

Kalovaxian shouts make their way to us, still far enough away to be mostly unintelligible, but I hold firm, one hand on the cell door, eyes glued to the dark corner of the corridor, willing Søren to come into view.

"He might have been recognized," Maile says. "He might not be coming. Do you really want to risk everything for a Kalov—"

"Oh, shut up," Artemisia snaps. "We can spare another minute."

But there's worry in her voice as well. I never thought I'd hear Artemisia worry about Søren, but I'm too worried myself to tease her about it.

*What happens if Søren doesn't come back in time?* It's a question I haven't wanted to ask myself. It's a question I don't know how to answer—no, that's not exactly true. I know the answer. I know that I will do what I have to do—close the cell door and give the order for Artemisia to strike, no matter what the cost of that is.

"*You are always fighting for Astrea, above all else,*" Blaise told me once, and he was right. I will always put Astrea above everything and everyone else, even when I hate myself for it.

The shouts grow louder, taking shape into words.

"The cells are empty," one guard yells. "All of them!"

"They can't have gone far," another one replies, but there's an edge to his voice, and I wonder if he was one of the guards who thought the same of me when I slipped out from between their fingers.

"Theo," Heron says, his voice uncertain. "They're getting close."

"Just another minute," I say, keeping my gaze on the corner. "Come on, Søren," I murmur under my breath.

"You're going to ruin everything," Maile snaps. "All for one boy."

"Hush," Artemisia says again before softening her voice. "Theo, Søren would tell you to make the call."

"He would," I say through clenched teeth. "But if our places were switched, he would never make it himself. One more minute. At the first sight of the guards, I'll shut it. I promise."

"No hesitation," Artemisia says.

"No hesitation," I echo.

The shouts grow louder still, and the pounding of footsteps echoes in the beat of my heart. My fingers tighten on the door and I imagine closing it, locking out any hope of Søren surviving. I know I can do it. I know that if I have to, I won't hesitate. But I don't want to and I won't do it any sooner than absolutely necessary.

A shadowed figure rounds the corner, and my heart leaps into my chest. All I can see is blond hair and a guard's uniform.

"Close it," he shouts, and I let out a breath of relief before I understand his words. "Close it now!" he says again, just as a mob appears at his heels. They're close—too close. There's no time for Søren to reach us, to reach safety. If he gets to us, they do as well, and then all is lost.

"Close it, Theo," he says again. "Strike now."

I let my body act, turning off my brain before I do something foolish. I start to close the door without thinking about what I'm doing, what it will cost me. I start to close the door because I will always choose my country over anyone—my friends, Søren, even myself.

A hand grabs the door above mine, and the owner pulls it open with a harsh curse under her breath. Before I can process what's happening, Maile takes a few hurried steps down the corridor, reaching behind her for the bow on her back. She doesn't hesitate before firing three arrows in rapid succession, striking down the three guards closest to Søren and causing the others to hesitate. It only buys a couple of seconds, but that's all it takes for Søren to get close enough for Maile to grab him and pull him into the cell, slamming the door closed behind her.

I take hold of Søren's hand, press it to Heron's bare arm so that all of us have some kind of contact with Heron's skin.

With a deep breath, Artemisia raises her arms, and brings them down in one fluid motion, emitting an ear-piercing scream that I feel in my bones. She ushers in the tide.

Water rushes through the open tunnel door, a flood of it that pushes down the hall, knocking the guards off their feet and dragging them beneath its surface.

It reaches us as well, spilling between the bars of the cell until it covers my feet, my knees, my waist. It floods higher and higher until my head is under as well, but I'm ready for that—we all are. We know to hold on to Heron no matter what. Even when water pushes its way into my lungs, even when the tides try to drag me away, I hold on with everything I have. Just when my lungs begin to burn unbearably, when I think I can't hold on anymore, the space just around us drains of water—or rather, Heron uses his gift to fill it with a bubble of air.

I can breathe again, and no breath has ever tasted so sweet. When I recover, I look around, taking in our surroundings.

Outside of our bubble, the dungeon is entirely full of water as far as I can see, reaching up to the ceiling. In the dark, murky water, I can make out a couple of bodies floating through it, unmoving, uniforms billowing around their limp forms.

Artemisia's eyes are closed, her expression drawn in concentration. Her hands, outstretched, tremble with the power of what they're doing, what they're holding.

It can take up to five minutes for a person to drown to death, depending on a few factors. Artemisia explained this with a frightening number of graphic details back on the *Wås*. Though many of the guards are unconscious now, and many will have snapped their necks or hit their heads in the initial rush of the tide, if we want to be safe, she has to hold this for five full minutes, which means that Heron has to hold his bubble of air just as long.

His hand is on Artemisia's shoulder, his other one on mine, while Søren and Maile each have a hold on his arms.

"How long has it been?" Maile asks in a whisper.

"A minute, barely," I say. "Let her concentrate."

Outside of our bubble, I catch sight of a guard who is still conscious, swimming and searching for air. He makes it to our cell, almost to the bubble Heron is holding, but even though he can't get in, he's close enough for me to see the desperation in his eyes, how they bulge from his face, wild and afraid.

"Drowning is a horrible way to die," Artemisia warned when we were formulating the plan.

"It's no more than they deserve," I replied, and no one disagreed with that.

But still, it's a different thing entirely to see it, to watch his face turn blue, to see him overcome with a frenzy I've never seen before, to watch him claw at the bars separating us until his fingers bleed, without doing anything to help. To watch his face go slack when unconsciousness finally takes a hold of him, his fingers going loose around the bars as the tide pulls him away, into the darkness of the water.

Next to me, I feel Søren shudder, and when I think how close he came to sharing that fate, I do the same.

After what feels like eons, Artemisia opens her eyes and drops her arms, sagging against Heron with a groan, and the water around us floods back out into the tunnel, dragging the bodies of the guards along with it.

"You did it," Heron says to Art, keeping a firm hold on her shoulder even as he releases me and shrugs the others off. Though he must be exhausted as well, the air around us is charged as he uses his gift to replenish her energy and ensure that all of the activity didn't worsen her legs.

Artemisia nods tightly, but even she manages a small, proud smile.

Heron reaches into the pocket of his trousers, pulls out a diminished lump of *molo varu*. Before we left Dragonsbane,

I melted the full thing and separated it into four parts—one for us, one for Blaise, one for the group in the wine cellar, and one for the group in the kitchen cellar.

He tosses it to me and I use my gift to heat it. Quartered, it's too small to write words on, but I can at least heat it so the others feel it. It's the signal they've been waiting for, telling them it's time to storm the palace.

# FIGHT

——◆——◆——

WHEN WE EMERGE FROM THE dungeon and climb the stairs to the first floor of the palace—passing several waterlogged corpses on the way—the siege has already begun. It is pandemonium, a cacophony of swords clanging, shouts in too many languages to count, and pained screams. The five of us move as one down the hall, Artemisia and Søren with their swords drawn, Maile with an arrow knocked, Heron and me with our hands raised, ready to draw on our gifts.

A group of six Kalovaxian guards rounds a corner toward us, in full armor with their Earth Gem–studded iron swords held high in the air.

I strike first when they're ten feet off, hitting them with a steady stream of fire. It might not reach them through their armor, but it does turn the metal unbearably hot. Their battle cries turn to agonized screams, their swords hitting the floor with a clatter. Their helmets follow seconds later.

After that, Artemisia and Søren fall upon them without mercy, dispensing killing strikes to their bared throats.

"Easy enough," Maile says. "Only have to do it a few dozen more times."

"Maybe you can even help with the next one," Artemisia grumbles, but there's no real bite in her voice. She's come alive, the way I've only seen her when she has a sword in her hand and the smell of blood is thick in the air.

We fight past two more groups of guards just as easily as the first, but I can't dislodge the feeling of dread pooling in the pit of my stomach. Maile was right—it is easy. And in all of my fantasies about this battle, I never imagined it would be. The Kalovaxians don't make things easy. Cress doesn't make things easy.

"Where are the servants?" I ask as Maile fires an arrow into the throat of a guard at Artemisia's feet. She had her sword up, ready to slice his throat, but now it falls to her side, limp, and she shoots Maile a glare.

"What?" Maile asks with a grin. "You said I wasn't helping."

"The servants," I say again. "And the nobles, for that matter. If we're catching them by surprise, there should be more people—not just guards."

"It's supper time," Søren says, wiping a spot of blood from his cheek with the back of his hand. "Maybe there was a banquet. Maybe they're all there."

"Maybe," I say, but something about that doesn't sit right.

"We're catching them by surprise," Heron says. "Making quick work of them. That's a good thing, Theo."

I nod, trying to push my unease down. "Let's keep going and find the other groups."

The halls we run down are familiar to me, from one of my lives or another, so I lead the way, winding past the chapel, past the stained-glass window of a shining sun the size of my head, past the stairway that leads down to the bathing pools.

Maybe there are Kalovaxians in there, hiding. Maybe servants as well—I hope they are—but they're not our concern at the moment. First, we need to subdue anyone who could put up a fight. It's a tactic taken from the Kalovaxians themselves, one they used on us more than a decade ago.

The sounds of battle get louder when we round a corner, heading toward the banquet hall that lies at the center of the palace, just north of the gray garden.

As soon as I turn the corner, though, an arm pulls me against a wall, the bite of cold iron against my throat.

"Theo!" Artemisia cries out, stepping toward me before she stops short, eyeing the blade at my throat.

"Drop your weapons," the man holding me says, but I can't be the only one who hears his voice shaking.

"Do it," Heron says, a note of authority in his voice that I don't think I've heard before. He meets my gaze, a reassurance there.

*Trust me,* his eyes say.

Søren and Artemisia put their swords down, and with a little more hesitation, Maile puts her bow down as well.

The man holding me makes a move to pull me with him backward, toward a door, but Heron doesn't let him get more than a step before he hits him with a gust of wind that moves like a hand, prying the sword away from my neck and out of his grasp, flinging it so that it hits the stone with a clang that echoes down the hall.

"What—" the man starts, but he doesn't get a chance to

finish. With another gust of wind, Heron snaps the man's neck, and he crumples to the ground at my feet. As the others hasten to pick up their weapons again, Heron comes to my side.

"Are you all right?" he asks.

I rub my throat. There's a nick in the skin, but it isn't deep.

"Fine. Are you?" I ask. Heron doesn't like violence, and likes killing even less.

He nods, his brow furrowed as he looks down at the man's body. "It's war," he says. "I think the gods will understand."

I place a hand on his arm, pull him with me down the hall and around another corner, only to stop in my tracks at the scene awaiting in the corridor ahead.

It's a bloodbath so crazed that I can barely tell who is fighting on what side—all I can see are swords flashing in candlelight, blood gushing over skin, and eyes wide with fury and fear. Fifty warriors altogether. Maybe even more.

One man starts toward me, and it's only when he's a few feet away that I see the Kalovaxian red of his uniform, peeking out from where his helmet meets his breastplate. Without thinking, I aim a ball of fire there, and watch as the uniform catches flame. In his haste to pat the fire out, he doesn't even see Maile's arrow until it is embedded in his chest, the steel tip having broken through the chain mail and found flesh.

And just like that, we are as deep in the battle as the others, though the five of us stay close and the other four take pains to surround me at all times. Maile and I find a rhythm, her knocking arrows and me using my gift to set them on fire. It saves some time and works out decently, though I suspect a part of it is born from her desire to keep me safe and out of the way.

I hear the sword slicing into flesh before I see it, and for a moment, everything around me moves like a dream, slow and liquid. Then, I hear Heron's cry of pain, and the scene sharpens once more. I see the blood, the sword's hilt protruding from Heron's stomach, hear the scream in the air that I realize too late is my own.

"No!" I scream, and again, the world goes still. But this time I am not frozen in place. I am not frozen at all; I am fire from my head to my toes. I don't even see the face of the warrior who stabbed Heron. I don't see any of their faces. In some ways, I think I leave my body altogether—I'm back in the inferno at the Air Mine, and all I feel is fury, burning though me, desperate and hot and insatiable.

I push past Heron and Artemisia, touch the warrior who stabbed Heron, and though my fingers barely graze him, he bursts into flame, screaming, but I don't linger long enough to watch him die. I move through the crowd, touching every piece of Kalovaxian armor I see, savoring the sight of each one of them bursting into flame. When I reach the other side of the corridor and touch the last Kalovaxian, a shocked cheer goes up from the crowd, but I barely hear them. I barely see anything.

I make it back to Heron on unsteady legs. Søren is supporting him on one side, Artemisia on the other, and the sword is still in his gut. His eyes are tightly closed, his expression pained as they help him sit down against the wall.

"Don't take it out," he says, his voice calm despite everything, his teeth clenched.

After Artemisia sits, she turns to the crowd of rebels watching behind us. "Is anyone here an Air Guardian?" she asks, desperation coloring her voice. No one replies. "A doctor? A healer?" she presses, her voice growing high and thin, but still there is no answer. There is no one here who can help.

"Can he heal himself?" Maile asks.

It's a question I haven't ever had to consider. Every time someone has been injured, Heron has been there, ready to lessen their pain at least. I never let myself think about what would happen if he was the one who was hurt.

"I've never tried it," Heron says, wincing as his hand finds the blade. "I think it missed the important bits, but if we take the sword out, there will be too much blood loss. I'll pass out, and then there will be no chance of me healing it."

He sounds so calm, as held together as he ever does. He opens his eyes and looks at me, eyes heavy.

"Theo," he says. "You can cauterize the wound."

"Cauterize the . . ." I trail off, the words nonsensical to me.

"Søren, you're going to pull the sword out. Slowly and evenly," Heron says, and Søren nods. "As he pulls it out, Theo, I need you to use your gift to burn the flesh around it, to keep it from bleeding."

Nausea makes my vision swim. "I . . . I can't do that," I say.

"Theo," Heron says again, drawing my eyes to his. "I need you to."

*If you don't, I'll die.* He doesn't say the words, but they hang in the air between us all the same. I nod, pressing my lips together in a thin line and lifting my hands to hover just above his wound, flames leaping to my fingertips.

"Ready when you are," I say to Søren.

Søren doesn't reply, his brow furrowed in concentration

as he slowly starts to pull the sword from Heron's flesh. As soon as he does, I lower the flames at my fingers so they touch Heron's skin.

He cries out in pain, gripping Artemisia's hand so tightly in his that I see his knuckles turn white in my peripheral vision, but I keep my focus on the wound, on Søren slowly pulling the sword out inch by inch. The smell of burning flesh permeates the air, making me dizzy and nauseous, but I keep my hands still, my flames steady, until the tip of the sword pulls out of Heron's stomach and I burn the skin closed behind it.

I drop my hands and sway on my feet, but Søren's hand comes down on my shoulder to steady me.

Heron's eyes slit open and he looks down at the burnt skin where his wound used to be. He nods once, a thin sheen of sweat covering his face. His breathing is ragged as he brings a hand to rest over it. A few seconds pass in tense, still silence before Heron's body sags in exhaustion, his hand falling away from his stomach. Where there was a circle of burned flesh a moment ago, there is now only a pale scar.

His breath turns steady again and he looks up at me. "Thank you," he says.

I nod, unable to speak. The world is still spinning around me, blurry at the edges.

"She's overexerted herself," Artemisia says.

"I'm fine," I say, but it doesn't sound convincing even to my own ears.

Artemisia opens her mouth to protest, but she's interrupted by an uproar of shouting down the hallway. She turns to the other warriors. "Go," she tells them. "We'll be along soon."

As they rush to follow her order, Heron hauls himself to his feet, barely wincing. "What's behind that door?" he asks, nodding down the dimly lit hall.

I follow his gaze, though it's hard to make out anything in particular. I struggle to remember where we are, where this hall leads, what's behind that door.

When I realize, a laugh bubbles up in my throat, uncontrollable and unhinged.

"Theo?" Heron asks, voice wary.

"It's my room," I say between laughs. "It's my old room. See? The shadow room doors?"

Artemisia exhales. "She's right," she says before shaking her head. "It's as good a place as any for the two of you to rest."

"I don't need rest," Heron says. "Honestly. Good as new."

"Me too," I add, though even as I say it, I'm not sure I'll be able to remain standing if Søren takes his hand off my shoulder.

"Just for a few minutes," Artemisia says. "We're going to clear the rest of this wing, and then we'll come back for you. Heron, get a fire started for her—it'll help her get her strength back."

Heron looks like he wants to argue, but before he can, Artemisia continues.

"She can't stay alone," she points out.

At that, Heron nods, putting an arm around my waist to support me.

"Hurry back," he says, his voice grave. He doesn't say to be safe or to stay alive, and for that, I'm grateful.

# SETTLE

———◆—•—◆———

MY ROOM IS EXACTLY THE same as it was the night I left. Even the bed is still rumpled and unmade. The towel I used to clean my face is still draped over the basin, smeared with the red lip lacquer and tan powder I wore to the banquet earlier in the evening. I know, even without opening the wardrobe, that my dresses still hang inside—the gaudy ones from the Kaiser and the prettier ones Cress gave me.

It's my room, my home for ten years, and yet as I stand here again, it feels so much smaller.

Heron helps me into my old bed, propping me up with pillows, before going to the fireplace and getting to work starting a fire with the tinder and flint.

"What happened, before you helped heal me," Heron says, without looking at me. "Are we going to talk about that? How you turned those warriors to ash with just a touch."

"Yes, we are," I say, tilting my head back and closing my eyes. "But not right now."

"What else are we going to do? Worry helplessly?" he asks, which I have to admit is a fair point.

I sigh. "I don't know what it was, what came over me. It

just happened. I saw that you were hurt, and instinct took over. My blood felt like it was literally boiling."

"Could you do it again?" he asks, more curious than conniving.

"I don't know," I admit. "But no, I don't think so. I wouldn't know where to even begin."

"And besides," Heron says, "if you're left incapacitated after you wield that kind of power, it might be more trouble than it's worth."

"I'm not incapacitated," I tell him, though again I can feel the lie as clearly as I can feel the instant he strikes the flint and a small flame sparks to life in the fireplace. It sings through my body like I'm slipping into a hot bath. Without meaning to, I let out a sigh of relief.

"There's no shame in reaching your limits, Theo," he says, using a small gust of air to invigorate the weak fire into a full blaze. "It means you've given something your all."

I snort. "That's easy for you to say," I point out. "When you need to replenish your gifts, you only have to *breathe*."

He laughs softly but doesn't deny it.

"I can't believe you were *stabbed*," I say.

"I can," he says. "Mostly because I can still feel it."

I prop myself up on my elbows to look at him. "You said you were fine," I point out.

He shrugs. "So did you," he replies.

I can't argue with that, so I lie back down and let the energy of the fire wash over me. I want to ask him if he's all right. If he's in pain. If he needs to rest. But we both know there's no time for rest, no time for him to be anything less than fine. So I don't say anything at all and we fall into a heavy silence as we both try to recover as much as possible, as quickly as we can.

My eyes close and I let my mind wander—not to what's happening outside my door, but to what tomorrow might bring. And the day after that. And the day after that. I remind myself what we're fighting for, what our future holds if we just push through the pain and grab it.

A hot hand comes to rest on my shoulder, and I bolt upright, eyes flying open.

I'm not asleep—I know I'm not—but Cress is standing before me all the same, dressed in a silver chiton with an ornate gold-and-Fire-Gem pin securing it in place at her shoulder. A collar necklace of Fire Gems rests against her clavicles, glinting in the firelight.

"Theo?" Heron asks, looking at me with alarm. "Are you all right?"

He doesn't see her, even though she's as real as I am.

Cress lifts a black-tipped finger to her lips.

"Fine," I manage with a smile. "I just dozed off for a second," I lie.

He nods and turns away from me again, focusing on the fire and his own thoughts.

I shouldn't be able to see Cress—I'm not asleep, after all—but here she is. Perhaps the power I used earlier drained me even more than I expected, leaving my mind open and vulnerable. Perhaps it's the fact that Cress and I are so close now, the lack of distance blurring the edges of our minds. Perhaps whatever this connection is, it's deepening.

But the *why* doesn't matter. Not now, at least. What matters is that she's in the room with me, as clearly as Heron is, but he can't see her.

"This battle is boring me, Thora," she says with a sigh. "Meet me in the throne room. Let's see if we can't settle this like ladies instead of barbarians, shall we? No warriors, no guards, just us."

The air around us fizzles and I see her in the throne room, sitting proudly on my mother's throne, eyes closed. Her pale hand rests lazily on the shoulder of a young Astrean girl with hair such a dark shade of brown, it's nearly black. Her eyes are locked on Cress, wide and frightened. She can't be more than eight years old. Cress opens her eyes and looks at the guards stationed around her throne.

"Go, join the fight," she tells them, her voice ringing with authority.

The girl whimpers, flinching away from Cress.

"Your Highness," one guard says, but she doesn't let him get further than that.

"It's an order," she says. "I won't have a single guard in this room, or in the hall outside. It is a waste when there are Astrean rebels storming my palace. Am I understood?"

The guards nod and disappear. When the door closes behind them, Cress looks at me once more. She lifts her other hand and there, twirling idly between her fingers, is the same kind of vial she used to drug Laius—full, I imagine, of the same gas that made a puppet of him.

"I'm bored," she tells me, bringing the vial close to the young girl's face. The girl eyes it with wide, fearful eyes, trying to pull away, but Cress holds her firm at the collar of her homespun dress. "Don't make me find other ways of entertaining myself."

Before I can answer, she's gone, fading into the air like smoke. I let out a breath, thinking only for a second before climbing out of bed.

"What are you doing?" Heron asks.

"Cress is in the throne room," I tell him. "She wants a meeting."

Heron's brow creases as he watches me slip my shoes back on.

"And?" he says. "You can't honestly be considering going. Do you remember what happened the last time she requested a meeting?"

"Of course I do," I say. "She tried to kill me. I can't imagine this time will be any different."

"But you still think it's a good idea to go?" he asks.

"She has a hostage," I say. "A girl, eight years old maybe. Frightened."

That gives Heron pause, but after a second he shakes his head. "You know, though, that if you do show up there, she'll still kill her. She'll kill the both of you, and your choice will have been for nothing. What reason does she have not to?"

I know he's right, but he's wrong as well.

I sigh, trying to put my thoughts into words. "This ends one way," I say. "With one of us dead. I think she's dangling this bait expecting me to come to talk, under the guise of a truce. I think she expects to ambush me. But there's a flaw in her plan."

"Which is?" he asks.

I tie my second boot and stand up, looking at him.

"I'm stronger than she thinks I am, and I'm not going in blind. I'm going in ready for whatever she has, ready to meet her in kind. She means to spring a trap for me, but this time we're going to be one step ahead of her."

"We," Heron echoes.

I raise my eyebrows. "Unless you don't want to come."

"Of course I'm going with you," he says, clambering to his feet. "But we should wait for the others."

I wave the idea away. "They're occupied," I say. "If they haven't come back yet, they're in the thick of battle. I'm not pulling them out so they can be my bodyguards. Besides, the girl can't wait."

Heron shakes his head. "You think the two of us, alone, are going to somehow make it from here to the throne room? We don't have to worry about Cress killing you—that trip alone will be enough."

"Lucky, then, that you can make us both invisible," I say.

"That won't make us incorporeal. It won't do any good if we get impaled by a sword meant for someone else," he points out.

"There are three ways we can get to the throne room from here," I say, before ticking them off on my fingers. "The clearest path, which you're right, will likely be clogged with warriors. Then there's a web of smaller hallways, usually used by servants. Less likely to be full, but you never know."

"And the third?" Heron asks, though he sounds like he already regrets asking.

"Back through the dungeon, down the passageway we came in through. It forks—one direction leading straight into the throne room, which also prevents us from being seen by any guards Cress might have posted *outside* the room."

Heron considers this a moment, eyeing me like he thinks I might have gone entirely insane. Finally, he sighs. "I don't suppose you can be talked out of this?"

"It's the only way to end this," I say. "Before more people get hurt."

Heron insists on leaving a note behind to tell the others where I've gone, which I know is a good idea, though I can't help but imagine Artemisia's scowl as she reads it.

*They had one job—to stay put,* she'll snap.

But at least she'll know we haven't been captured or killed.

With that done, Heron takes my hand in his and lets his invisibility inch over our skin until we are both invisible.

"Can you hold this until we get to the dungeon?" I ask him as we slip through the door and into the empty hallway, careful to step over the dead bodies and piles of ash as we go.

"Easily enough," he admits. "As you said, I only need air to reinvigorate my gift. As for my injury, as long as I don't have to do any lunging or heavy lifting, I should be just fine. But it isn't as though fighting is my strong suit anyway."

We wind through the halls in silence, though they're deserted. There's no sign of life—only the bodies of the Kalovaxian warriors we left in our wake when we came through the first time.

It isn't until we reach the door to the stairwell that descends to the dungeon that we hear voices, muffled and indecipherable, coming from inside.

Heron squeezes my hand, I squeeze his back, and we press against the wall, waiting to see how many warriors we're going to have to face or if it will be best to just let them pass.

The voices grow louder, underscored by approaching footsteps coming up the stairs, and I let out a sigh of relief. They're speaking Astrean.

"We don't know what we'll find," a familiar voice says, making my heart leap in my chest. "But we'll split up and disperse throughout the palace, stepping in wherever they need us."

As soon as the leader steps into the hall, I let go of Heron's hand and throw my arms around his neck, knocking him off balance.

For an instant, Blaise goes tense, but then I fade into view once more and he sighs, hugging me back.

"Thank the gods," he murmurs into my hair before pulling back and looking me over. "Queen Theodosia," he says to the group of warriors behind him, so many that I can't see all of them. They crowd the stairwell, stretching out back as far as I can see.

"What's happening? Where are the others?" Blaise continues.

I look back at Heron for help explaining, but he shakes his head. "Oh no, this isn't my plan. You're going to tell him."

I shake my head and quickly tell Blaise about everything that's happened since we entered the palace, skimming over the details of Heron's injury and my own bout of weakness. When I tell him about Cress's message and the girl, though, he frowns.

"You can't be serious."

"That's exactly what I said," Heron tells him. "But it turns out she is."

Blaise sighs but he doesn't look entirely surprised. Instead he turns to the warriors behind him.

"Gerard," he says to one of the men at the front, broad-shouldered and fierce with a face that's been badly burned. "You're in charge now. Find the others. Start at the edge of the palace and work into the center. Kill anyone who fights; imprison anyone who doesn't."

Gerard nods but doesn't speak.

"You don't have to come with us," I tell Blaise.

Before I finish speaking, he's already shaking his head. "Of course I do," he says, but doesn't elaborate. He doesn't need to say any more, I suppose—he belongs at my side, and I am happy to have him there.

Blaise, Heron, and I stand aside so that the warriors can file past. I try to keep a count of them as they go, but there are too many.

"A little over two hundred," Blaise says to me before I can ask. "The fire at the Earth Mine wasn't as bad as the one at the Air Mine. The Guardians there were able to put it out quicker, working together to create a storm of dirt that smothered the flames."

I nod, barely trusting myself to speak. When the last of them leaves, Blaise, Heron, and I make our way down the stairs into the flooded and deserted dungeon.

"I'm glad you're here, Blaise," I say to him. "I'm glad you're alive. I'm glad you're coming with me."

His hand comes down on my shoulder and he squeezes it. "Me too, Theo."

We hurry down the dungeon corridor in silence until we arrive at the tunnel entrance once more. I try to ignore the bloated corpses of the guards as we pass. When Heron pushes the door to the tunnel open, Blaise and I follow him through it. The water gets higher the closer to the ocean we get, until it's up to my hips. Finally, we come to the fork in the path. The way we came heads deeper into the sea outside now that the tide has come in, but the other tine of the fork goes uphill, careening toward the throne room. It isn't a path I've taken before, but Blaise seems to know it and he leads the way. The walk lasts only about fifteen minutes before we reach what at first appears to be a dead end.

"It's that stone, there," Blaise says, pointing to a rock in the bottom corner of the wall, barely bigger than a pebble.

"Cress needs to think I'm alone," I tell them. "You two stay behind me, invisible, until I attack."

Blaise nods, offering his arm to Heron, who takes hold of it. I wait until the invisibility fades them from view completely before I crouch down by the rock Blaise pointed to and press it.

It gives easily enough, and when it does, a doorway opens up in the wall.

I only hesitate for a second before stepping through.

# GAME

---•---

T HE THRONE ROOM IS ABLAZE with candles, casting it in a
light that is almost blinding, even though the glass dome
roof shows the stars and moon shining down from above. On
the throne at the center of the room, Cress sits with her legs
primly crossed, in the same silver chiton I saw her wearing
earlier, her eyes fixed on me. The girl I saw earlier is still at her
side, sitting on the dais with her knees pulled up to her chest.

Cress isn't surprised at my entrance through the wall. She
isn't angry to see me. She doesn't even look pleased that I accepted her invitation. Instead her expression is unreadable.

The door closes behind me, and though I can't see Heron
or Blaise, I still feel their presence.

For a moment, Cress and I only stare at one another across
the room, silent.

Then, slowly, she pushes herself up to stand and steps
down from the dais, lifting the skirt of her gown gingerly to
avoid tripping. She snaps her fingers, the sharp sound echoing in the quiet space, and in an instant the girl is on her feet,
hurrying to keep up with Cress even as tears stream down
her face.

"I knew you'd come, Thora," Cress says to me, her gaze unwavering and unsettling as she steps toward me, the heels of her slippers tapping against the tile floor, followed by the scuffle of the girl's. "It's good to see you, you know. Here. In the flesh. I thought you were dead for so long—I don't know that I really believed you weren't until this moment."

The way she's looking at me, gray eyes glassy and faraway, seeing everything and nothing, is disconcerting. I'm suddenly not entirely sure I'm not a ghost, haunting her into madness.

Before I can speak, she continues, her voice even and conversational. "You said once that I would go as mad as the Kaiserin. Do you remember?" she asks, stopping a few feet from me.

"Yes," I say, finding my voice. "But Kaiserin Anke had no choice in her fate. The Kaiser forced it on her at every turn. Maybe I could have found pity for you before, when you first became Kaiserin, but after the Fire Mine, after everything you've done since . . . you chose this, Cress. If you're looking for pity from me, you won't find it."

She laughs, but the sound is weak. "I don't want pity, Thora." She pauses, tilting her head to one side. "You haven't come here for a truce, no matter what we pretend. No. You've come here to kill me, haven't you?"

I don't deny it.

She laughs, a sound that I think will haunt my nightmares.

"You're wasting your time," she says.

I square my shoulders and draw fire to my palms, but she only watches, curious yet unbothered. She grabs the girl's arm and pulls her in front of herself, eliciting a cry of pain.

"Yes, yes," Cress says, waving a dismissive hand. "Very

impressive, I assure you. And, of course, I felt what you did to Dagmær and my other girls."

"You wanted to finish this like ladies, you said," I tell her. "I don't imagine you mean to offer a truce."

She smiles. "No, of course not," she says. "You should know better than anyone that Kalovaxians don't deal in truces."

"Then why bring me here at all?" I ask her.

Her smile fades at that. "I told you," she says. "Because you're wasting your time. Now put those fires out."

"Why? So you can attack me?" I ask her. "That's why you brought me here, isn't it?"

She rolls her eyes but doesn't deny it. "Because there's no point in killing me," she says. "This . . . gift or whatever you'd like to call it—it's already doing that."

My hands droop to my sides without me meaning to, and the flames stutter out, but she makes no move against me. I feel a whisper of movement at my back—though whether it's Blaise or Heron I can't be sure. I struggle to make sense of Cress's words.

"Are you saying you're mine-mad?" I ask her. It shouldn't be possible. Cress has never set foot in a mine. But I remember Mina's explanation, how full pots boil over. And Cress's power has always been strong—stronger than mine, maybe even stronger than Blaise's. And unlike the two of us, she has never exercised caution in using it.

Yet those who are mine-mad don't sleep, and Cress does— I've seen her in dreams. You can't dream if you're awake. Except . . . except those dreams always took place in or near the palace, always somewhere she could have really been.

Only different, twisted. But if Cress is mine-mad, her mind may be fractured enough to distort her reality.

"How long have you been hallucinating?" I ask her quietly.

She holds my gaze, blinking languidly. "Since you gave me the poison," she says. "Sometimes I think it's a dream. Or a nightmare. But it can't be."

"Because you don't sleep," I surmise.

"No," she says. "Ironic, isn't it? You've come here, prepared to kill me, but the truth is you killed me a long time ago. It's just taking its time, eating away at me slowly. Painfully. I didn't know you had that kind of cruelty in you, Thora."

"Theodosia," I say, the name forcing its way from my lips even though I can't make sense of anything else she's saying. This much, at least, I know. "My name is *Theodosia*."

She must know that by now; she must have heard it, in whispers and shouts in the streets. Hearing it from me, though, she smiles.

"It's pretty," she says. "But it doesn't suit you. You'll always be Thora to me."

I can't bring myself to be surprised by her words, but they hurt all the same. I think I would have liked to hear her call me by my name just once.

With a heavy heart, I draw flames to my hands once more, and Cress stares at them, lips pursed. Finally, she turns her attention back to my face, a wry smile on her lips.

"Come now," Cress says, bringing both hands onto the girl's shoulders and holding her tightly. "You'll do what you feel you must, but surely you don't want the girl to see that. She reminds me of you, you know. Her name is Adilia."

I let my gaze drop and meet the girl's frightened eyes. I

know my own strength, know my precision. I remember how, in the middle of the fire at the Air Mine, I could control the flames as easily as I could move my fingers. If I tried, I'm fairly sure I could kill Cress without hurting Adilia. But fairly sure doesn't seem sure enough.

"Why don't we send her off to her family first?" Cress suggests. "They're not far. And I'm certain they would love to see their Queen, too—they spoke of you often enough, you know. Sowing rebellion here in my city, making nasty little plots."

Her voice takes on a dangerous edge that prickles over my skin. I feel Blaise and Heron move closer, preparing for something, but none of us seems to understand what it is.

A chill creeps down my spine. "Where are they?" I ask.

Instead of answering, she holds out a hand, beckoning me. "Come," she says, before turning around and walking toward one of the doorways out of the throne room, dragging a crying Adilia with her. I know that pathway—it's the one that leads to a balcony overlooking the gray garden.

When she senses I'm not following, she turns to look at me over her shoulder, a disconcerting smile on her lips.

"Come," she says again, a demand and not a request. "You and I are going to play a little game."

"And if I don't want to play?" I ask, barely trusting my voice.

She lifts a shoulder in a shrug. "Then I'll kill them all," she says, pushing open the door.

I feel like my feet are made of iron as I follow her toward the door, fearful of what awaits me on the other side, but I force myself forward. It's a comfort to know that Heron and Blaise are behind me, a comfort to know I'm not in this alone, but when I reach the doorway, I realize that, alone or not, it doesn't matter. It doesn't matter at all.

Because when I step out onto the balcony and follow her to the railing, I see below that the garden is so full of Astrean palace slaves that I can't begin to count them. Many are weeping, their cries filling the air. Some are barely old enough to walk, held aloft in their parents' arms.

And standing around us, at each window that overlooks the garden, is one of Cress's wraiths, ten in all, dressed in black, each with a glass ball in hands held out over the crowd, the inside of the balls glittering with the unmistakable opalescent shimmer of velastra.

# CHOICE

—————•————

A LL I CAN DO IS stare at the thousands of people gathered below, at the threat hanging over their heads. Directly below each window, a single Astrean stands alone, a gleaming dagger in their hands. Each of their ten faces is terrified and confused—they have no idea what they've been chosen for. Maybe they even thought that being given a weapon was a lucky thing, but I see them for what Cress has truly made them: human weapons, puppets awaiting strings.

How delicate those balls of glass are, held above their heads—once they are dropped and they break, the gas will disperse and the velastra will take hold. It's more poison than she gave Laius, more than I thought she could make, but here it is. Cress said that the poison couldn't spread the way she wanted it to yet, but even if each ball only has enough velastra to take hold of the one person with the dagger, I can't let myself find out what kind of havoc those ten people can wreak. All of those thousands of others trapped in the garden, unarmed and untrained. They are lambs awaiting slaughter, and they haven't the slightest idea.

"Just imagine all the orders I could give," Cress says, idly trailing her blackened fingertips over the railing. "All the things I could command them to do with those daggers before they take their own lives, like Laius did. It will be a massacre, if you don't do exactly as I say."

Though I know Blaise and Heron are behind me, I don't hear anything from them at all—I'm not even sure they're breathing. I understand it. No matter what I think Cress is capable of, she somehow always manages to surprise me.

"What do you want?" I ask her, surprised my voice comes out as evenly as it does. Inside I am a trembling mess.

Cress turns her attention from the garden to look at me, eyes cold and glittering like silver under the light of a full moon.

"What would you want, if you were me?" she asks curiously, tilting her head to one side.

"Surrender," I say.

Cress smiles, but it is a cruel and bitter thing. "After you charge into my palace? After you destroy two of my mines, leaving me to burn the others before you could reach them?" she asks. "After you lost me my Sta'Criveran allies? After you stole my prisoners? After you killed my friends? You really think surrender would be a worthy fate for you? Try again."

I swallow. "You want me dead," I say. It's nothing I didn't expect. We've been here before, after all, the same choice, more or less, laid before me. I know what I chose then, and I know I'll do it again now. And this time, death will actually stick.

Cress shakes her head. "Oh no," she says. "That's still too

easy, still too good after everything you've done. No, I intend to see you live a long life, full of all manner of torments. Some I can't even imagine yet—but I will. We'll have such a long time, after all. Especially once I have a steady supply of velastra to give you."

I swallow the bile rising in my throat. I will be made her puppet, my body held very much alive but my mind gone from me, given over to her. It is a fate worse than death, worse than I ever imagined. But I force myself to nod.

"What else?" I ask, because I know that can't be all. "What about my armies?"

"I'm not unreasonable," she says with a sigh. "If they surrender, they'll be spared and sent to the mines, to rebuild them and work them, dosed with velastra—once we've figured out how to make it in bulk. Anyone who resists will be executed. I'm done with rebellions, Thora. They bore me."

For a moment, I don't say anything, searching the garden and the windows overlooking it, searching for any possibility of saving them, of all of us making it out of this unscathed. But there is none. Only the reality of thousands of my people, facing certain death unless I sacrifice thousands of others.

It is an impossible choice.

"Why didn't you give me that dose of velastra as soon as I set foot in the throne room?" I ask her.

Her smile turns brittle. "Because it would have been too good for you," she says. "And I want to hear you beg for mercy—not because I command it of you, but because you want to. Because you need to."

"You're afraid," I say, hoping to buy time. Time for what, I don't know. Time for a miracle, time for another option, time left in a world where I am not plagued by guilt. "You think we might actually win."

Cress's eyes narrow. "I think you've exceeded all expectations," she admits. "But this was never a fight you were going to win."

"Then why make a deal at all?" I ask her. "If you truly believed you could win fairly, you wouldn't have dragged me over here. I know you enjoy a good spectacle, Cress, but your father would be so disappointed in you, for placing that above logic."

That hits a nerve, but she doesn't reply. Instead she looks out over the railing and gestures. Before I realize what's happening, one wraith drops her ball of velastra. It hits the ground, shattering at the feet of the Astrean woman below, with the dagger clutched in her hand.

I see the moment the velastra takes effect, the way her eyes glaze over and her shoulders go slack, the same way Laius's did.

"You will kill anyone you see before you," the wraith calls to her, her voice high and bright and almost giddy. "And you will not stop until I stop you."

The reaction is immediate. The woman's hand tightens around the hilt of the dagger, and without hesitation, she lunges forward, plunging the dagger into a man's stomach. She is already moving on to the next person before his body hits the ground. With the people packed as tightly as they are, it's easy for her to move from person to person and in a mere handful of seconds, a dozen bodies fall, and dozens more screams pierce the air. But she is only one woman, and as frightened as the people around her are, there are some fighters among them still, and soon they have her wrestled to the ground, the dagger pried from her fingers.

It is over quicker than I thought, and though there are still so many dead bodies piled around her now, the damage was at least contained. Yet as soon as I look at Cress, I realize that this is only part of her plan.

"Do you know why I picked her?" she asks me. "Why I picked all of them to be my weapons?"

Without waiting for an answer, she motions to the wraith again, who drops something else into the madness below—a Spiritgem, I realize, a glittering deep-blue Water Gem.

"No," I whisper, but it's too late. I know what will happen a mere second before it does, before the woman pinned to the ground begins to twitch, a high scream prying itself from her throat.

"Let go," the wraith calls down at her. "And kill as many people as you can."

No sooner are the words out of the wraith's mouth than the woman sparks, just like the girl I saw on the battlefield at the Fire Mine. One moment she is a woman; the next there is a typhoon tearing through her skin and the hundred or so people around her are drowning in air, spitting up water, choking on it until they fall to their knees as waterlogged corpses, bloated and blue.

The screams die when she does, and those Astreans outside her radius are shocked to a silence that echoes in my bones. I feel sick to my stomach, but the wraiths only smile, watching the pandemonium unfold, the other nine still holding their own orbs of velastra, ready to do it all over again.

"No!" I shout, my hands gripping the railing. I swallow, lowering my voice. "Stop it, Cress."

"You agree to my terms?" she asks me, raising her eyebrows.

I can't answer that. My mind spins. There are more warriors fighting in the palace now than there are slaves in the courtyard—the logical part of me knows that I shouldn't surrender. If the people below die, Astrea can still triumph. We will win our country back and rebuild it. But we will rebuild it on the bones of innocents, and what kind of country would that be?

A free one. A country with a future.

*"You are always fighting for Astrea, above all else,"* Blaise told me once. And he was right.

It's a difficult choice, yes, but not an impossible one.

I swallow and take a step back, reaching behind me to find Heron or Blaise, to find some source of comfort before I give the order that will doom thousands of people, but there is nothing behind me except air. I listen closely and detect no sounds at all, no breathing, no stirring.

"What are you doing?" Cress asks, nose wrinkled.

"Thinking," I say, which isn't a lie. My mind is a whirl of possibilities, of where Heron and Blaise could be, what they're planning. Part of me worries that whatever they're up to, it might be dangerous for them, might make things worse for everyone. But they've followed me this far, they've trusted me. Now I have to trust them, and that means buying more time.

"What is there to think about?" Cress scoffs. "I think I'm being awfully generous, all things considered. You've killed me, Theo—or as good as. And I'm not even going to return the favor. If that isn't a kindness, I don't know what is."

"I need more information before I decide anything," I say, scanning the windows overlooking the garden, the wraiths behind each one. If I were Blaise or Heron, that's where I would start, but they can only eliminate—at most—two at a time, and there are nine wraiths still with orbs. As soon as something happens to two of them, the other seven will throw their own orbs of velastra.

"What about the Vecturians?" I ask Cress. "What will happen to them?"

Cress shrugs, disinterested. "I've heard that one of the Chief's daughters is fighting alongside you, leading the Vecturians in your army. I suppose the Chief might be interested in a trade, though I've heard he has so many children that I can't imagine one will be of much worth to him."

"And Søren?" I ask her, leaning over the railing, trying to see more of the garden below without looking suspicious. The five entrances to the garden are all closed, unsurprisingly. I'd wager they are locked as well, guarded on the other side. Cress wouldn't be one to take chances.

"I was too kind to him before," Cress muses. "A traitor deserves a traitor's death. Drawn and quartered, head on a pike."

I hear her, but I'm not really listening. Out of the corner of my eye, I spot something glint in the moonlight—just a faint shimmer that I wouldn't see if I weren't looking for it. There—at another balcony high above the garden. Too high to be of any threat.

I frown, trying to suss out what Heron is doing.

"Well?" Cress asks, forcing my attention back to her. "What will it be, Thora? Time is up."

The air around me stirs, nudging me forward, but the branches of the tree at the center of the garden stay still. With a thudding heart and eyes fixed on that high balcony, I step toward the railing, bracing my hands on the railing on either side of my body.

"Thora?" Cress presses, her voice sharp.

The wind presses harder at my back and I swallow, understanding what Heron wants me to do. A leap of faith in the most literal sense.

I look over my shoulder at Crescentia. "Freedom," I tell her. "That's what I choose. Freedom for myself and every other Astrean."

Before she can reply, I lift myself over the railing and jump.

For an instant, I am in free fall, plummeting down into a crowd of screaming Astreans, but then a gust of wind catches me, lifting me up and into the branches of the lone skeletal tree. I scrabble at the branches, then hold on tightly and find a decent footing on one of the thicker branches, near to the trunk.

"Attack!" Cress screams, her voice an earsplitting screech.

Her wraiths waste no time, throwing the orbs of velastra in what looks like a single synchronized movement into the crowd below, but the globes don't hit the stones of the courtyard. They don't break. Instead they hover in the air for a moment before sailing high above, even higher than the highest towers of the palace, where they break, too far away to hurt anyone.

Cress lets out a frustrated shriek that rings in my ears. "Fire!" she screams at the wraiths. "Burn them all!"

The wraiths are quick to obey, and fire begins to rain down from above, one ball of flame after another, never ending, but those don't hit, either. They extinguish just above the heads of the people. Heron's wind, I realize.

"Keep going," Cress cries out. "It can't hold forever."

My stomach sinks as I realize that she's right—even Heron has his limits, and it is much harder to hold a shield of wind over the entire garden than to throw fireballs. I summon my own flame, aiming it at Cress, only to realize that the shield has to work both ways—I can't break it any easier than the wraiths can.

Something flickers in the air beside me, and the branch I'm clinging to dips with more weight before Blaise fades into view, his eyes alight and his mouth drawn into a tight line.

"He can't hold it," I say.

Blaise doesn't deny it, but his eyes dart away. "No," he says. "Get to the ground and stay there. Keep everyone calm, no matter what."

I shake my head, struggling to make sense of his words, what he has planned.

"What are you—"

He doesn't answer. Instead he opens his clenched hand to reveal a single Earth Gem the size of his palm, already glowing and pulsing with life.

Understanding dawns on me, not entire, but enough.

"Blaise, no," I say, my voice rising.

He smiles at me then, a sad but determined smile that doesn't reach his eyes.

"I'll see you in the After one day, Theo. Don't let it be for a long time yet."

I'm frozen in place as he kisses my cheek, his mouth hot against my skin, and then he leaves me, dropping down to the ground below, feet landing on the roots of this tree that has been dead for almost a decade.

I find my body again, moving automatically and without any thought but one: *I have to follow him.*

It's harder for me to scale down the tree branches, but a moment later, my feet hit the ground, a shock going up through my legs, but I barely feel it. People press in closely all around, panicked and shouting and crying, but all I'm really aware of is Blaise and the glowing gem clutched tightly in his white-knuckled grip.

"Blaise," I say, grabbing his arm and wrenching it off the tree trunk. "Stop. There has to be another way."

Calmly, Blaise places his other hand on the tree, looking at me with resolute eyes. "There isn't," he says. "Go—keep the crowd calm. I don't want you to see it."

I shake my head, squeezing his hand tighter. "If you're going to sacrifice yourself, you aren't going to do it alone," I tell him, my voice cracking. "I won't let you die alone."

For an instant, he looks like he wants to argue, but I know he doesn't want that, either. He nods once, his eyes glancing away. He passes me his sword, closing my hands over the hilt. "When it starts—when I've done all I can and I've lost control of it—stop me before I start hurting our own people. Before I hurt you."

Numb, I shake my head. "I can't do that."

"Of course you can," Blaise says with a bitter smile. "For Astrea."

*"You are always fighting for Astrea, above all else."*

Suddenly I hate him for those words, for the brutality of them, the absoluteness, the cold ignoble truth. I hate him for understanding what that sentiment meant, long before I understood myself.

"For Astrea," I reply, but the voice doesn't feel like mine.

"Blaise!" Heron shouts from the balcony above. "I can't hold it much longer!"

"It's time," Blaise says. He releases my hands and places his on the trunk of the dead tree, taking a deep breath.

I throw my arms around him and hold him as tight as I can. I feel the thrum of power reverberate through his body, turning his skin scorching hot, too hot, but I don't let go. I hold him tighter, as if by holding him I can somehow protect him, like he has so often protected me.

The dead tree responds to his touch, stretching its branches, waking up. With my cheek pressed against his chest, listening to the erratic beat of his heart, I look up, watching in wonder as the branches don't just grow larger—they sprout leaves. They unfurl quickly, spreading wider and wider until the whole of the garden is underneath the canopy.

It's terrible and beautiful and I can't look away.

The first fireball hits the leaves with a sizzle, but it doesn't break through. Blaise's power holds the canopy, firm and un-yielding. His brow is furrowed in concentration, but he isn't losing control. He's all right.

For one beautiful moment, I think he'll survive this in one piece. All he has to do is hold one tree in place—he can do that. But then he opens his eyes and looks at me, and I realize there's more left to do. It isn't enough to protect the garden; he needs to extinguish the threat above—Cress and her wraiths.

The ground quakes beneath my feet, and screams go up from the slaves around us. They clutch one another and I clutch Blaise.

The wall of the palace, visible over his shoulder, splits, a crack running up the side of it, toward the window where I know one of the wraiths stands. There's a crack, the unmistakable sound of stone crumbling, before a scream pierces the air. It's the kind of scream that can only precede death.

"What are you doing?" I ask Blaise, unable to see anything above the thick branches.

Another tremor goes through the ground, another part of the palace crumbling, another scream.

"Earthquakes," Blaise says between gritted teeth. "Contained, but strong enough to bring the wraiths down, to drag them into the earth and close it over them again."

I imagine it, each wraith falling into rubble, being buried by more of it. None of it falls into the garden itself, which I imagine is more of Blaise's gift, or maybe Heron's.

A gust of wind whips through the garden and beyond, in tandem with another earthquake, the combined forces spreading the destruction. More screams, more deaths.

"I'm scared, Theo," Blaise tells me, his eyes finding mine. His voice cracks, and suddenly he sounds so young again, like the child I grew up with.

"It's okay," I tell him. "You've done enough. You can stop now."

But the rain of fire hasn't stopped. There are wraiths still out there, and if he stops, innocent people will be hurt. He knows this as well as I do, his eyes determined and intense and also unmistakably afraid. He shakes his head. "It's time."

I can't talk him out of this. I can't tell him to hold back. So I don't try to—not now, at the end of it. Instead I place the tip of the sword where his heart is, ready for when the time comes.

"Do it," I say, hating myself for the words even as they leave my lips, though at least they seem to bring him peace. He nods once and closes his eyes again.

The tremor that goes through the earth this time is so strong, it almost knocks me off my feet, but I hold on tightly to Blaise, to the sword in my hand. All around us, I hear the walls of the palace crumble, I feel the slaves push in toward me, getting away from the edges of the garden, where they fear wreckage will fall. Instead the rooms around the garden implode, careening to the edges in heaps of rubble, the sound of destruction and screams echoing throughout the air.

One of the screams, I know, is Cress's, but I can't think about that right now. All I can think about is Blaise in my arms, burning up from the inside out, his body trembling as fiercely as the earth beneath our feet. He forces his eyes open, and in them I see him doing battle with himself, fighting to maintain control. But it is a battle he is losing.

"Now," he says, his voice strained, forcing its way out between clenched teeth. "Theo, please."

The sword falters in my hand, but I force myself to hold it tight, to keep it pressed against his heart. I close my eyes, standing on my tiptoes and pulling him down so I can rest my head against his.

"Thank you," I tell him, and then in a single motion, I force the sword upward, into his flesh.

Blaise gives one last gasp of air, eyes flying open, seeing everything and nothing at once. For a moment, the world goes still around us. Then, he crumples to the ground, lifeless.

# DAZE

———•——

FTER THE CENTER OF THE palace collapses, the battle
yawns to a close, though I only know that because of the
sounds, how the cacophony of war fades to a quiet din, then
shouts of celebration, a clatter of swords being thrown to the
ground.

The shouts of celebration are in Astrean, and a rush of
triumph pierces through my daze. *We've won,* I think. Despite
everything. But the feeling is quickly replaced by a pang of
guilt. Because we've won and Blaise will never be able to see
it. He will never see Astrea free, even though it couldn't have
happened without his sacrifice.

I'm hazily aware of the doorway to the garden opening,
of Heron and Artemisia slipping through, making their way
to where I sit, frozen, next to Blaise's body. The hostages who
were corralled in the garden are gone, taken somewhere to
eat and clean up, so it's only us, surrounded by rubble, with
Blaise's body cold on the ground.

All of that time I spent worrying about how hot his skin
was, I never paused to think about how it would feel once it
went cold.

No one speaks. Heron must have told Art about Blaise, because she isn't surprised to see him, but still, she's shaken, her eyes stuck on his body, cold and lifeless. I suppose it's a different thing altogether to see it firsthand.

"It's over?" I ask, barely looking at them.

Heron nods, his eyes downcast.

I imagined this moment so many times, how triumphant I would feel, how happy. In my imagination, all of us cheered and laughed and celebrated. In my imagination, Blaise was always there, cheering with us.

"He died a hero," Artemisia says finally, her voice soft.

A laugh tears its way through me, harsh and ugly. "What difference does that make? A dead hero is still dead."

"He knew what he was doing," Heron says after a moment.

"He wanted to die, you mean," I say, my voice coming out raw. "Yes, I know. He told me so often enough."

Heron shakes his head, brow creasing. "He didn't want to die," he says, searching for the right words. "He wanted Astrea to live. He just knew that both of those things couldn't happen, so he made a choice. The same one any of us here would have made, if we'd been given it. The same one you made with the Kaiserin when she offered you the Encatrio."

I know there is truth to his words, but they bring me no comfort, not now. "Did she die in the earthquake?" I ask, looking up at Heron. "Cress? Was her body found?"

Heron and Artemisia exchange looks, and for a moment, I think Art might correct me about calling Cress by her first name again. If she does, I honestly think I might hit her.

"No," she says instead, before hesitating. "I mean yes, her body was found, but no she didn't die in the earthquake. We found her in the rubble by the throne room, unconscious, but alive. She's in the dungeon now, stripped of all Fire Gems. Last I heard, she was still unconscious."

I nod, the news not surprising me. Of course an earthquake wouldn't kill Cress. Suddenly I feel foolish for expecting it would have, for expecting that the gods would give her such an easy death or allow me to have no hand in it. No. I've always known this can only end one way.

"She's mine-mad," I tell them. "Even without gems, she could be dangerous. Post Water Guardians on her at all times and set her execution for dawn."

Artemisia nods, not looking surprised by either proclamation. I suppose I'm not the only one in a daze.

"You have to get up," she tells me, her voice firm. "Astrea is free, her people are celebrating—*your* people. They'll want to hear from their Queen."

I swallow. The idea of standing before thousands of cheering people, celebrating, makes me feel sick.

"He would want you to," Heron adds. "And your people need you to. Many of them were children before the siege, many were slaves this morning. Now they're unsure of what to do with the freedom you've given them. They need a leader right now; they need an example."

I don't feel like a leader. I certainly don't feel like a queen. But I know he's right. I look at Blaise again and reach out to touch his hand, limp and cold at his side.

"Have his body cleaned," I say. "Prepare it for burning— a hero's ceremony."

Artemisia nods. "There are a lot of dead heroes today, Theo," she tells me, her voice gentle but with a hard edge.

*You aren't the only one who's lost someone today.* Harsh as it is, she's right.

"Tomorrow night, we'll have a ceremony for all of them at once," I tell her. "And we'll honor the anniversary of it every year forward."

It doesn't seem like enough, but I don't think anything will ever seem like enough.

Heron holds a hand out to me and I take it, releasing Blaise as I do. Artemisia wraps an arm around my waist, Heron's arm going around my shoulders.

"We won," Art tells me, tasting the words tentatively. "Astrea is free."

"We won," I agree, hoping that if I say the words enough times, they will begin to feel real.

As we walk out of the garden, I don't look back over my shoulder, worried that if I do, that is how I will remember him—cold and dead and lifeless. Instead I think of him laughing, his eyes bright, mouth soft. I think of him in the heat of battle with an expression drawn tight and fierce. I remember him singing to me, his voice wobbly and off-key. I remember how it felt when he kissed me.

I etch him into my memory just like that. That is the Blaise I want to remember for the rest of my days.

Artemisia helps me into a clean gown, a deep violet silk chiton with a gold pin at my shoulder that is shaped like a cluster of flames. We end up back in my old room, though I know that now the royal wing is mine. I'm not ready for it yet, not ready to sleep in the same bed the Kaiser did, the same bed Cress did. Until we can get new furniture, this room will suit me fine.

When I'm dressed and my face is clean, Art brings me a red velvet box, not unlike the one the Kaiser used to use to send me my ash crown.

I know without asking that the crown lying inside this time isn't made from ash. Still, when she presents it to me, I touch it to be sure. The black gold is cold beneath my fingertips, the rubies winking in the candlelight. My throat feels tight as I remember seeing my mother wear it, how beautiful she looked, her head held high, the gems glittering like flames themselves. I remember how she used to set it on my head sometimes, her fingers delicate and cool, how it was always too big, how it fell down around my neck.

I remember Hoa, too. How time and time again she would lift that ash crown from its box as delicately as she could. I wish that both of them could be here now, to see this moment.

But it's Artemisia who lifts the crown from the box and sets it on top of my head, the circlet coming down over my brow, the metal cool against my skin.

It isn't too big anymore. It fits me perfectly.


Søren, Sandrin, and Dragonsbane are waiting outside the room when Art and I emerge, the three of them slouched against the far wall, as quiet as the dead. But they aren't dead—they're alive, and the sight of them forces all the breath from my lungs, a relief so sharp, it makes me want to weep, though I don't think I have any tears left.

As soon as they see me, all three push away from the wall. Sandrin and Søren both drop into bows, and after a second, Dragonsbane does the same.

"Your Majesty," Søren says, straightening once more.

He's changed as well, out of his bloodied clothes and into a simple white cotton shirt and black trousers. He doesn't look like a prinz, but I suppose he isn't really one anymore, and that seems to suit him fine.

I look among the three of them. I can't imagine many things that would bring them together to my hallway, but there is one reason that comes to mind immediately.

"I assume you three want to discuss the Kalovaxian prisoners?" I ask.

It was too much to hope for a reprieve, I suppose, but they're right. The sooner the question is answered, the better.

"It can wait," Artemisia says. "There's a banquet in your honor that I'm sure you want to get to."

I consider it for a second before shaking my head. "Not yet," I say. "I was planning to stop by the dungeon first. Will you three walk with me, and we can discuss it on the way?"

Dragonsbane's eyebrows lift a fraction of an inch, and she nods. "Of course."

I turn to Artemisia. "I'll meet you at the banquet," I tell her, glancing down at her own attire. It's the same thing she was wearing this morning, plus a few bloodstains. "That way you have a chance to change, too."

Artemisia looks down at her outfit, shrugging. "No point in that," she says. "Don't take too long. Apparently it's impolite to begin drinking before toasts can be made, and given that you are to be the subject of most of the toasts . . ." She trails off.

"I'll be there soon," I promise.

When Artemisia disappears around a corner, I step into Søren's arms, wrapping my own around his neck. Dragonsbane lets out an annoyed sigh, and even Sandrin clears his throat awkwardly, but I ignore them both. For a moment, we stay like that, neither of us moving. The only sound is our hearts beating together, in tandem.

"We made it," I tell him.

He nods against my shoulder. "I'm sorry about Blaise," he says.

"I am, too," I say. Talking about him feels like rubbing at a raw wound, but I don't know how to stop. Some wounds you don't want to heal all the way. Some wounds, you want to leave a scar.

I pull back and start down the hall to the dungeon, letting the three of them fall in around me.

"I'm sure you want to discuss what will be done with the Kalovaxians," I say, before any of them can get there first.

Sandrin hesitates a second and then nods. "I'm sure it's not something you want to think on now. You want to celebrate, and you should, but—"

"But there are thousands of people being held in the capital now, not to mention tens of thousands more who will be arrested when I send troops out in the morning," I say with a sigh. "And besides, I've been thinking on it. Quite a lot, as a matter of fact. Where are the Kalovaxian prisoners now?"

"Any warriors who survived are in the dungeon," Søren

says. "But the others—nobility, yes, but also children who are innocent of their parents' wrongdoings—they're being kept under house arrest until it's decided what's to be done. I know that you have to make harsh judgments, but I also know you to be fair."

"Fair," Dragonsbane echoes, her voice sharp. "But not stupid. They are our enemies, Theo. And children grow up."

"The real question is how they will grow up," Sandrin says softly.

Dragonsbane cuts a sharp look at him. "This is no place for sentimentality," she says.

"No, it isn't. But it isn't the place for decisions made from anger, either," I say, turning the problem over in my mind. It isn't a new one to me—when I haven't been thinking about how to get here these last months, I've been wondering what happens if I succeed. They're right—it's a complicated decision.

"I don't want another war in another generation," I say, looking at the three of them. "I want to end this for good. But justice must be done. And Astrea is going to be a country recovering from war for a long time to come. We'll barely be able to support ourselves and the refugees from the other countries whom I promised a home to." I pause, looking at Søren. "How many countries has Kalovaxia seized over the last century?"

He has to think about it. "Nine," he says finally.

"Countries you left in ruin, no?" I ask.

"Yes," he admits. He doesn't try to push blame off himself, though he easily could. He knows that he has reaped the benefits of those sieges even if he had no hand in them himself.

"The Kalovaxians are criminals—varying degrees of criminals, yes, but criminals all the same." I look at Sandrin. "What did my foremothers do with criminals?"

He considers this. "Trials," he says. "The criminals heard the crimes they were accused of and responded to them, either to defend their actions or to plead forgiveness and mercy. Committees were put together to hear their statements, to weigh the crimes and mete out appropriate punishments."

"Then I propose trials," I say.

Dragonsbane snorts. "You don't actually believe any of them innocent?"

"Not innocent, no," I say, shaking my head. "But as I said, there were varying degrees of bad acts. It doesn't seem fair to me to treat rapists, murderers, and slavers the same way as the farmers or the shipmasters or the seamstresses—the people who benefited from the bad acts, yes, who went along with them, but didn't actively commit crimes. I propose that the worst offenders—the warriors, the slavers, the mine guards—they may be put to death, depending on their testimony and the verdict of a committee made up of those from all countries the Kalovaxians have hurt."

Sandrin considers this and for a moment, he doesn't say anything. I wait, though, because I find I care what he thinks of my plan. He is a noble sort, after all—with a fair mind and a survivor's spirit.

"I believe that might be the cleanest way forward," he says after a moment.

"The cleanest way would be to leave no survivors, to raze the Kalovaxians to the ground the same way they've done to other countries, other families," Dragonsbane says.

"Yes, but we aren't the Kalovaxians, Aunt," I say, my voice firm. "I will not kill children, and I will not be the catalyst that turns them into revenge-hungry monsters in their own right in a decade's time. I want peace and I want that peace to last. I want trials and accountability, yes, but also redemption and mercy where it can be given. I want to plant seeds of a future that will outlast my reign."

Søren considers this, nodding. "That's fairer than I might have expected," he admits. "And I know there will be a good many executions that come of this, but what of the others? The nobility, the farmers, the people you mentioned who didn't commit any crimes—"

"But were complicit," I finish, before pausing. "There is no Kalovaxia to send them back to any longer, but there are nine destroyed countries that need rebuilding. What if we were to separate them into nine groups, send them to each country the Kalovaxians have brought to ruin? Their children will go with them, becoming citizens of whatever country it is, treated as fairly as any other. Sent to schools, taught trades, made members of society."

"And the parents?" Søren asks. "Slaves?"

I shake my head, pursing my lips. "Indentured servants," I say. "Tasked with rebuilding the country however is required. Their trial committees can determine the length of their sentences, and then they will be free, citizens of that country as well. They can't go back to Kalovaxia, so they must go somewhere."

For a moment, no one says anything, and I worry they will protest, that Sandrin will think the decision too harsh, that Dragonsbane will think it too light, that Søren will find some logical flaw that I missed. But after what feels like an eternity, Dragonsbane nods.

"I'll send my ships out to Doraz, and my crew and I will begin preparing to return the refugees to their fallen countries, to take stock of what must be done to reestablish them."

"And I will begin putting together committees from those assembled here," Sandrin says. "We can begin the trials as soon as next week, after the dead have been mourned and buried and everything has settled."

Relief courses through me and I nod. "Please do that. Thank you both."

Sandrin and Dragonsbane nod before starting back down the hall, leaving Søren and me alone in front of the entrance of the dungeon.

"And what about me?" he asks after a second.

I watch him for a moment. It's hard to look at him and see the same boy I met months ago, a boy who felt so inextricably tied to his monstrous father that I couldn't see him properly. But here he is now, his own man, with nothing of the Kaiser in him.

"I meant what I said before," I tell him. "Your penance has been served threefold, Søren. You are free to go or do whatever you like now."

"And if I choose to stay with you?" he asks quietly.

Warmth spreads over my skin, and I have to force myself not to reach for him. I bite my lip to keep from telling him how badly I want that. "Queens don't marry," I tell him instead. "It's not a tradition I intend to break."

He laughs at that. "I can assure you, I have no desire to be king or a Kaiser or anything of that nature."

"Then what do you want to be?" I ask.

He doesn't hesitate. "An ambassador," he says. "At court here half the year, the other half spent sailing to those other eight countries, ensuring the well-being of my people and quelling any hints of rebellion that might crop up in them as peacefully as possible."

"Your people," I echo. "I thought you had no desire to be Kaiser."

"I don't," he says. "But you should understand better than anyone else that it isn't always a choice. I don't want a crown, I don't want a reign—but they are my people still, and it's my duty to see to their well-being."

I do understand. "Very well," I say. "Is that all you want?"

At that, he reaches for me, and pulls me toward him so that we're standing face to face. "Well, I want you, but I didn't think I had to say that," he says. "In whatever capacity I can have you, for however long you want me, I'm yours."

I smile, rolling onto the balls of my feet to kiss him softly.

"*Yana Crebesti*," I murmur against his lips. "No matter what comes."

# DIGNITY

I LEAVE SØREN AT THE EDGE of Cress's cell block. He seems to
understand without me explaining—some things I need to
do on my own. The dungeon is dark and I bring a ball of flame
to my hand to light my way. The ground is still wet beneath my
feet after the flood, but that is the only sign of it. Already the
cells are full again, with Kalovaxian warriors this time. Each
cell block is guarded by an Astrean who bows as I pass.

When I reach Cress's cell, all I see is her body curled up
in a corner, her silver gown traded for a homespun shift, her
white-blond hair glowing in the low light. For an instant, I
think she's still asleep, but then she shifts, a soft groan coming
from her lips.

Her eyes open, focusing on me, and for a moment, she says
nothing.

I'm suddenly reminded of a very different night, when she
visited me in a cell here and stared at me from this side of the
bars with fury in her eyes, promising me my execution in only
a few hours' time.

Though I've come with similar sentiments, I don't feel any
fury in me. What anger I felt for her has been buried like the

garden after the earthquake. Now, all I feel when I look at her is sadness and exhaustion.

How did we get here? But I know the answer to that. We were always here, on separate sides of a war we didn't even know we were fighting. Maybe, in another world, it could have gone a different way. Maybe, in another world, I would have told her about the rebellion I was planning and she would have stood beside me. Maybe, in another world, I wouldn't have given Elpis the poison to use against her.

But that is not the world we live in.

"Come to gloat?" Cress asks me, sitting up, her back against the stone wall.

"No," I say, and I mean it. "I told you that when this moment came, I would offer you no mercy."

She grimaces. "Yes, I remember quite well," she says. "So why are you here? If not to gloat? If not to offer mercy?"

I reach beneath the skirt of my gown, to the holster at my thigh that holds my dagger.

"Maybe it is an act of mercy after all," I tell her, fingering the fine filigreed hilt, the sharp edge of the blade. "In the morning, you will be publicly executed in the square, in front of thousands of people cheering for your death. It will be a violent spectacle without any semblance of dignity."

She winces, but it's slight. "And?" she asks, eyes still on the dagger in my hand. "Are you here to tell me you'll keep my head?"

It's an echo of what she said to me so long ago. I drop down and fit the dagger through the bars of the cell, sliding it toward her across the ground. Then I step backward, out of arm's reach before she can do something ill-advised.

"I'm here to give you the opportunity to die in private, away from the eyes of strangers who hate you," I say. "Away from the crowds and the cheers. You can do it with your own hand. End it quickly."

Cress stares at the dagger on the ground before her, hesitating. She looks up at me.

"Why?" she asks finally.

I don't have an answer to that. The truth is, I don't know why I'm here, why I'm offering her a gift that she never would have extended to me if our positions were switched. Still, I try to put it into words as best I can.

"Because you were kind to me, once," I say. "You were kind to me when you didn't have to be. And your kindness might have come with thorns, but it was enough for me, then. Consider this exactly that—a kindness with thorns."

Cress purses her lips, reaching for the dagger and turning it over in her hands. Without saying anything, she nods, tears welling up in her eyes.

I turn to go, but her voice stops me.

"Will you . . ." She trails off before trying again. "Will you stay with me? I don't want to die alone."

She sounds so afraid that my heart twists in my chest despite everything. *You deserve to die alone,* I want to tell her, thinking about Blaise, about that garden full of frightened slaves, of the mines she burned with thousands of people inside. But I don't. I turn back around, careful to keep a distance from the bars in case she gets ideas about doing other things with that dagger.

I nod, once, not speaking.

She places the dagger's point at her stomach, her hands

shaking as she looks at me. "If there is an After like you believe," she tells me, "I hope that one day I'll see you there."

It doesn't sound like a threat but like a genuine wish. Maybe yesterday it would have moved me, but today I feel nothing.

"If there is an After," I tell her, "you won't be allowed in."

She closes her eyes, tears leaking down onto her cheeks. With one final, quivering breath, she plunges the dagger into her stomach.

# TRIUMPH

——— • ———

WHEN I STAND ON THE dais of the banquet hall, packed tightly with a crowd of people—my people, many of them still in their uniforms, wearing the rips and burns and bloodstains like badges of honor—I feel like I am not quite in my body. In some ways, I'm not. In some ways, I am still in the dungeon, watching the life leave Cress's eyes, or in the garden, holding Blaise's cold body.

I shouldn't be here, celebrating, when today has been a day shadowed by death as much as by triumph. But I am the Queen of Astrea, I remind myself. My name is Theodosia Eirene Houzzara, the Ember Queen, and there is no one left who would call me any different.

Behind me, Artemisia clears her throat from her place between Maile and Heron, with Søren and Erik on Heron's other side. When I glance at her, she gives me a meaningful look, urging me to speak.

But what is there to say? Standing before so many expectant people, I wish I'd planned something, because now nothing seems appropriate, nothing seems like enough.

I take a deep, steadying breath.

"Today marks the end of the reign of darkness that the Kalovaxians brought upon this country more than a decade ago," I say. "But it marks something else as well—a beginning. From this day forward, Astrea is free once more. So are Rajinka and Tiava and Lyria and Kota and Manadol and Yoxi and Goraki. We are all of us free once more, and we will never be chained again."

At that, cheers go up, deafening and thundering enough to make the dais beneath my feet quiver. I wait for them to quiet before speaking again. As I do, I scan the faces, finding some familiar ones looking back at me. Sandrin is there, toward the front, his eyes level on me, with Mina beside him. And in the far corner, leaning against a post at the back of the room, I can see Dragonsbane, in her usual black-heeled boots, arms crossed and eyes appraising, not quite a part of the crowd.

"There are many people who should be here tonight to celebrate our freedom, people who fought for it, who gave their lives so that we could stand here today," I continue, thinking of my mother, of Ampelio and Elpis. Of Hoa. Of Laius. Of Blaise. Of so many others whose names I never knew. "I believe they are watching us from the After now with pride."

My voice cracks over the last word, and my face begins to burn as I realize how I must look, standing here before them. A queen so weak that she would cry in public.

But as soon as I think it, I remember how my mother had no shame in crying when it was necessary. She never saw it as a weakness; rather, she believed it a strength to bear one's soul. It was only the Kalovaxians who believed there was shame in it, and they don't have the power to shame me anymore.

Looking out at the crowd, I realize that I am not the

only one on the edge of tears, not the only one who has lost someone, not the only one to find tonight bittersweet. To pretend otherwise would be to do a disservice to both the dead and the ones they've left behind.

So I raise my glass high in the air and wait for the crowd to do the same.

"To Astrea," I say, and this time my voice comes out clear and true, heavy with tears, but still strong. "To our land, our gods, and our people, both living and dead, who will never—*never*—wear chains again."

"To Astrea," the crowd echoes back and, as one, we drink.

# EPILOGUE

HE THRONE ROOM IS AS silent as a crypt, empty of everyone
except me. I'm sure that if I stepped outside this room, I
would hear the sounds of celebratory reveling still pouring in
from the banquet hall even now that the sun is rising and a
new day has been born, but with the door closed, there is no
sound at all except for the quiet rustling of my dress as I cross
the wide expanse toward the throne, each step cautious.

The wine from the toasts has made my mind fuzzy at the
edges, but I feel everything. Triumph, yes, but also grief, for
Blaise and the others we've lost, and even for Cress, if I'm to
be truly honest.

But I'm home, I remind myself.

This is not the throne room I grew up in. Though Blaise's
earthquakes were small and targeted enough to leave most of
the room intact, it still appears worse for wear. After more
than a decade with the Kalovaxians, the tile floors no longer
glimmer in the early-morning sunlight streaming through the
stained-glass windows. The floors are cracked and dirty, and
every surface here looks in need of a good clean. The chandelier is too dusty to provide much light. The walls are dingy

and stained. Even the throne itself looks worse for wear, the obsidian dull and waxy.

The Kalovaxians have always been good at taking things they wanted, less good at caring for things they had.

The wall that borders the garden balcony has been hastily repaired by a group of Earth Guardians to keep the whole palace from crumbling, but the cracks are still visible. The ground is still strewn with small bits of rubble. Maybe I'll have them leave it like this, cracks and all, so that we never forget what happened here.

In the pale light of the morning sun, the throne room is golden and soft. Like something out of a dream. Even now, I'm not entirely sure this isn't just that. Maybe in a moment, I'll wake up in a tent outside the capital, or on a ship, or in Sta'Crivero, or maybe even in my old room in this palace, surrounded by Shadows, a prisoner in my own home. But if this is a dream, I intend to savor it for as long as I can.

When I was a child, I hated my mother's throne. I imagined it wrapping black tendrils around her, holding her in place and turning her into someone I didn't know. No longer my mother, but the Queen. I resented it and I feared it and I always gave it a wide berth.

Now, though, I walk toward it. I imagine my mother sitting upon it, as she did before the siege. I see her comfortable, legs crossed, hands twined in her lap. I see her with the same black-gold crown I wear now, with her head held high as she listened to the people who came to see her, to ask for her help. I don't think I'll ever know for sure, but I like to believe she was happy on that throne, was happy as Queen.

The obsidian arm of the throne is cold beneath my

fingertips as I trace the design of flames etched into it. Countless generations of my ancestors have sat upon this throne. I would have learned their names one day, but anyone who would have known them, any record of their existence, has likely been lost to the Kalovaxians. The thought of that makes my heart ache.

Though I don't want to think about her, I can't help but imagine Cress on this throne. Did she find it comfortable? Or did it frighten her as much as it used to frighten me? I wonder if she will always haunt me. Part of me hopes she will, that I'll hold on to a sliver of her, no matter how terrible that sliver may be.

Part of me doesn't quite know yet how to live in this world without her.

I circle the dais, letting my hand trail over the throne's hard, curving edges. When I reach the front again, I take a slow, shaking breath before lowering myself into the seat. Then I place my arms on the armrests and sit up as straight as I can.

This is not my mother's throne anymore, I realize with a jolt that I feel down to my bones. It is not the Kaiser's or Cress's or any of my nameless ancestors.

This throne is mine, and mine alone, and I am no longer afraid of it.

# ACKNOWLEDGMENTS

It's hard to believe we're at the end of Theo's story but, like Theo, I couldn't have gotten here without a team of brilliant, insightful, and kind people by my side.

My editor, Krista Marino, who helped me coordinate battle strategies and map out character arcs. Thank you for understanding Theo from the very first pages of *Ash Princess*, and for your patience and enthusiasm throughout her journey. Astrea would have been a worse (and far more confusing) place without you.

My agents. Laura Biagi for first falling in love with *Ash Princess* and championing it as hard as you did, and Jennifer Weltz and John Cusick for your invaluable support and advice over the course of this exciting, frustrating, and sometimes befuddling adventure.

When I first decided I wanted to be a writer as a teenager, I looked at my favorite books and noticed that many of them were published by Delacorte Press, and since then, it was a quiet little dream of mine to have my books published by Delacorte Press as well. Now, here we are, three books in, and it is beyond a dream come true. I can't imagine having a better group of people supporting my books. Beverly Horowitz,

Monica Jean, and everyone else at Delacorte Press, I'm so grateful to all of you.

Thank you to everyone at Random House Children's Books and all the hardworking people there who have helped to make my book the best it can be and also help it find its readership. My publicist, Jillian Vandall Miao, one of the loveliest, smartest, most dedicated people I've ever met. I'm in awe of your genius. And to Elizabeth Ward, Kate Keating, Cayla Rasi, Mallory Matney, Janine Perez, Kelly McGauley, Colleen Fellingham, Tamar Schwartz, and Stephanie Moss for all of your enthusiasm and hard work.

They say not to judge a book by its cover, but with covers as gorgeous as the ones I've been blessed with, judge away. I am eternally grateful for Billelis and Alison Impey for creating such beautiful covers that so perfectly capture the spirit of the story. And to Isaac Stewart for bringing my very poorly drawn maps to life and making them works of art in their own right.

Thank you to my dad, my stepmom, and my brother, Jerry, for listening to my stressed-out and/or giddy phone calls and for being there every step of the way to celebrate with me. I would not be the woman I am or the author I am without your unconditional love and support. And to Jef Pollock, Deb Brown, and their children, Jesse and Eden, who became my NYC family and have been my biggest cheerleaders and staunchest advocates over the last six years.

Thank you to my friends, who have kept me sane and both pushed me to be my most productive and also pulled me away from the computer screen when they've had to. Cara Schaeffer, Lexi Wangler, Sara Holland, Arvin Ahmadi, Patrice

Caldwell, Jeremy West, Jeffrey West, Lauryn Chamberlain, Zoraida Cordova, Kamilla Benko, Lauren Spieller, Mark Oshiro, Dhonielle Clayton, Emily X.R. Pan, Cristina Arreola, MJ Franklin, Adam Silvera, Madison Levine, Jake Levine, Claribel Ortega, Kat Cho, Farrah Penn, Jessica Cluess, Tara Sim, Kiersten White, E. K. Johnston, Karen McManus, Melissa Albert, Amanda Quain, Julie Daly, Tara Sonin, Samira Ahmed, Shveta Thakrar, and Katy Rose Pool. I'm sure I've forgotten someone here, so if it's you, I'm sorry and I owe you a drink.

Last, but never least, thank you to the readers who have followed Theo throughout her journey from *Ash Princess* to *Ember Queen*. You are the best readers I could have asked for, and sad as I am to be leaving this series behind, I can't wait for you to see what's next.

# ABOUT THE AUTHOR

LAURA SEBASTIAN grew up in South Florida and attended Savannah College of Art and Design. She now lives and writes in New York City. Laura is the *New York Times* bestselling author of *Ash Princess, Lady Smoke,* and *Ember Queen.* To learn more about Laura and her books, go to laurasebastianwrites.com and follow @sebastian_lk on Twitter.